C000108360

# THE AMERICAN WAY

# THE AMERICAN WAY

## Stories of Invasion

Edited by Ra Page &
Orsola Casagrande

*It never happened. Nothing ever happened.*
*Even while it was happening it wasn't happening.*
– Harold Pinter

First published in Great Britain in 2021 by Comma Press.
www.commapress.co.uk

Copyright © remains with the authors, consultants and Comma Press, 2021.
All rights reserved.

The moral rights of the contributors to be identified as the authors of this Work have been asserted in accordance with the Copyright Designs and Patents Act 1988.

The stories in this anthology (excluding the 'afterwords') are entirely works of fiction. The names, characters and incidents portrayed in them are entirely the work of the authors' imagination. Any resemblance to actual persons, living or dead, events, organisations or localities, is entirely coincidental. Any characters that appear, or claim to be based on real ones, are intended to be entirely fictional. The opinions of the authors and the consultants are not those of the publisher.

A CIP catalogue record of this book is available from the British Library.

ISBN: 1912697394
ISBN-13: 978-1-91269-739-7

The publisher gratefully acknowledges assistance from Arts Council England.

Supported using public funding by
ARTS COUNCIL ENGLAND

Printed and bound in England by Clays Ltd, Elcograf S.p.A

MIX
Paper from responsible sources
FSC® C018072

# Contents

CONTENTS

# Introduction

## *No, Superman*

In May 1990, the British playwright Harold Pinter presented a brief, blistering essay on Channel 4, titled 'Oh Superman', in which he raged against the US's crimes in Central America over the previous decade and lamented the way public discourse had swallowed the US government's lies about them wholesale. The essay took its title from a recent article in *The Economist* which congratulated the US on emerging victorious from the Cold War as the world's only true superpower, and ended with the flourish: 'Over to you, Superman.'

Dismayed at the barefaced lies the US seemed to have gotten away with – depicting the Sandinista government in Nicaragua as undemocratic, when it wasn't,[1] framing the war against Central American communism as a war against atheism, when in reality US-armed assassins were murdering priests in El Salvador, while the Nicaraguan government were giving them top ministerial posts – Pinter seemed to place the blame for this distortion not on the parroting media, but on language itself. There is a 'disease at the very centre of language,' he wrote, 'language becomes a permanent masquerade; a tapestry of lies.'[2] We tell ourselves we are free, and that others need freeing. We tell ourselves, we are right, and that others need correcting. 'For the last 40 years, our thought has been trapped in hollow structures of language, a stale, dead, but immensely successful rhetoric', that represents 'a defeat of the intelligence and of the will.'[3]

By commissioning a series of short stories and essays on the history of US interventionism, this book hopes, in some small way, to redress this corruption of language. To begin with, it rejects the assumption that we live in a post-colonial age; the centres of empire have merely shifted, not gone away. It also asserts that to truly understand any empire (we chose the American empire, but we might have chosen any other), and to genuinely inoculate against the disease of language that infects those who benefit from empire, we have to turn our ears solely to those on the wrong end of it; the colonised. 'The colonial world is a world cut in two', the philosopher Frantz Fanon wrote in *The Wretched of the Earth* (1961). 'The dividing line, the frontiers are shown by barracks and police stations.'[4] It is our duty then to step over this great line, which is why the stories in this book have been commissioned exclusively from authors from the countries being trespassed upon.

The stories commissioned here cover twenty examples of US intervention – ranging from 'stay-behind' networks, assistance in the removal of opposition figures, torture programmes, all the way through to US-funded coups, civil wars and invasions. Of course, it barely scratches the surface of this history. Merely listing the many interventions omitted in this project would take up this entire introduction.[5] However long the list, we needed to start somewhere, and the beginning of the post-war, 'Pax Americana' era seemed an obvious place, given the formation of the CIA and the formulation of the Truman Doctrine (both in 1947). However, if this was when act one of the American Empire began, it had a long prologue.

The US's strategy of intervention (regarding Latin America, at least) dates all the way back to the 'Monroe Doctrine' of 1823, when President James Monroe declared America's right to 'protect' Latin America (ostensibly against European interference), with the idea being extended in 1904 with a corollary by Theodore Roosevelt to allow the US to intervene to also protect legitimate European interests south of its border. Come the early twentieth century, the US had begun exercising this imperial prerogative across the entire region with invasions of Cuba, Panama, Honduras, Mexico, Haiti, the Dominican Republic and Nicaragua – the so-called 'Banana Wars' between 1898 and 1934 – from which the military even compiled a *Small Wars Manual* (1940) – a set of strategic lessons that remained required reading for Marine Corps troops until as recently as the Iraq War of 2003.

But invasion strategies were always part of a wider, two-stage approach: stage one was US boots on the ground; stage two, the installation of special 'local' forces to protect American interests through a puppet 'strong man'. In Nicaragua, for example, US marines occupied the country from 1912 to 1933 (with only a short, one-year break in 1925-26) and only left after creating, training and equipping a constabulary army – the National Guard – to prop up the Somoza dynasty.

The political atmosphere back home wouldn't always be conducive to all-out invasions, however. So other, subtler methods for reaching stage two had to be developed; these ran the gamut from black and grey propaganda, to economic sanctions, aid embargoes, to the manipulation of emerging religious groups. In most cases, the end goal was a US-backed, locally-sourced coup. And if there were a 'Small Coup Manual', the first chapter would no doubt be dedicated to the 1893 Hawaiian coup, in which a cadre of American businessmen and agents conspired to overthrow Queen Lili'uokalani under the guise of republicanism, but with the sole aim of annexing Hawaii to the US, which they achieved in 1898.

Maintaining domestic support for such an ambitious foreign policy, going into the Cold War, required as much ingenuity as the interventions themselves. Central to the US's domestic PR strategy was the weaponisation of 'values' in the cause of empire – Pinter's 'disease of the language' writ large.

A simple slogan from the other side of the divide perhaps best sums this process up: 'Beware Americans bearing human rights.' The spreading of 'democracy', at the evident cost of human life, is typically Washington's number one priority in any mission, according to its press statements, even if the reality of its adherence to democratic values is very different.

But how is this domestic doublespeak, this mendacity back home, allowed to take root? A primary vector for Pinter's 'disease of language' must surely be simple ignorance. Many of the interventions featured in this book remain relatively unheard of, even in the countries where they took place, let alone back in the States. With some interventions, like the Gladio 'stay-behind' network, the entire Italian population remained unaware of it for decades. Only in 1990, when Prime Minister Giulio Andreotti finally acknowledged its existence, did Italians begin to learn of this paramilitary network which had, in cahoots with the CIA and neo-fascist militias, planted bombs and assisted assassination attempts through the 60s and 70s (see Gianfranco Bettin's story). Sometimes ignorance is a semi-voluntary condition, and again even local populations participated in it (not just American voters 'back home'). As Lina Meruane explores in her story, a fake history about 1973 continues to keep whole swathes of the Chilean middle class in a state of blissful, comforting self-delusion.

Writing in 1990, shortly after the end of the Cold War, Pinter seemed to predict a pivot in the offing: 'The United States was really turned on by the idea of Soviet aggression. It justified everything. It was there with the cornflakes every morning. It was part of the American way of life. You had an enemy and you loved him [...] you needed him. You were talking about death. All your references were to do with death. But you were happy. It was a good time. You could go all over the world and help your friends torture and kill other people – journalists, teachers, students, peasants, etc. – because these people, you said, were part of *them*.'[6]

Now, with the collapse of the Soviet threat, the American Empire needed a second act, and a new arch-enemy to replace the Lex Luthor of communism. Step forward... Islamic terrorism and anything that could be remotely associated with it, or appear similar to it, among America's less-than-perfectly-educated electorate. Although interests in Latin America continued to be protected, through strategies like Plan Colombia, much of the Empire's aggression transferred in 1990 to the Middle East and the so-called Muslim world, where new bogeymen needed to be found. Fortunately, Ayatollah Khomeini had set the stage for a succession of such villains: Saddam Hussein, Hezbollah, Al-Qaeda, the Taliban, Hamas, Muammar Gaddafi, Isis, and so on.

The newspeak around values also continued into this second act. In the name of securing *our* freedom, new restrictions on freedom were introduced domestically, through anti-terror legislation. In the name of bringing human rights abusers abroad to justice, anyone suspected of being 'part of *them*' could be detained indefinitely without charge or legal representation in Guantanamo Bay, or worse 'renditioned' to 'black sites' around the world for the purpose of torture. All in the name of human rights.

Once again, language was made to 'stand on its head' to use Pinter's phrase. For those in the West who had grown up in the shadow of hydrogen bombs and the threat of all-out nuclear annihilation, the light weaponry our new bogeymen supposedly carried didn't sound so threatening. A rebrand was therefore needed in the public consciousness and, right on cue, the Western media adopted a new phrase and repeated it endlessly, again and again, until eventually the vague threat of it stuck: 'weapons of mass destruction'. Even the word 'new' could be added to Pinter's vocab list of newspeak; just as the Guatemalan dictator Efraín Ríos Montt had decided to rechristen his country 'Nueve Guatemala', where 'new' here really meant the opposite – 'reactionary', 'conservative' and 'backward-facing' – so Tony Blair was now rebranding his own political vehicle 'New Labour'.

At his most despondent, Pinter asked: 'Is it that we are obliged to use language only in order to obscure and distort reality – to distort what *is*, to distort what *happens* – because we fear it? We are encouraged to be cowards.'[7]

This sense of being betrayed by language is something only a person crossing from the coloniser's side to the colonised side of the great divide might feel. For Frantz Fanon, who had grown up in the French colony of Martinique and always been on the colonised side, there was no illusion to be disburdened of, no trust in the language of empire to be betrayed by. From his perspective, 'values' are the weapons of empire from the get-go. Values are the means by which a departing coloniser hands over a set of keys to the country they are vacating to a specially selected (and by now *culturally* colonised) local 'elite' – keeping a spare set for themselves, should they ever need to move back in. 'During the period of liberation,' Fanon writes, 'the colonialist bourgeoisie looks feverishly for contacts with the [local] elite and it is with these elite that the familiar dialogue concerning values is carried on. The colonialist bourgeoisie, when it realises that it is impossible for it to maintain its domination over the colonial countries, decides to carry out a rearguard action with regard to culture, values, techniques, and so on.'[8]

This point about values cuts straight to our current moment. Consider the way that the media has reported the US's recent chaotic withdrawal from Afghanistan; women's rights have been continually referred to in the news coverage – at one stage even animal welfare (in the case of Pen Farthing) was wheeled out as a 'value' that would be abandoned by a complete withdrawal – as if any of these values had the slightest thing to do with the reasons the US invaded and occupied the country in the first place.

Fanon may have been critiquing the hollowness of specifically *European* values – whether pre- or post-enlightenment – but his argument applies to American values just as well. When judged by the people these colonisers have occupied, both sets of values are empty. 'All that the native has seen in his country is that [the colonisers] can freely arrest him, beat him, starve him: and no professor of ethics, no priest has ever come to be beaten in his place, nor to share their bread with him.'[9]

Whether we can now, in late 2021, begin to speak of a new, third act in the American Empire is still unclear. Perhaps a third act is already under way in the form of a 'privatised forever war' (to combine Neil Faulkner and Ian Shaw's two arguments here), where US interests abroad are protected by a combination of un-newsworthy drone strikes and unaccountable security contractors. Or perhaps we are transitioning into a largely virtual clash of empires where privately-owned data firms and troll farms can manipulate elections around the world for a fee. It's even tempting to ask whether the American Empire will have a third act at all; perhaps it is already in its death throes. President Biden's determined, if bungled, withdrawal from Afghanistan in the face of enormous media and moral outrage, combined with America's weakened international standing (after four years of Trump), could mark the end of the US's self-appointed role as world policeman altogether.

But we should reserve judgment. Many of the tactics covered in this book have a habit of popping back up, decades later, often accompanied by the personnel who first championed them. Thirty years after Donald Rumsfeld served as Counsellor to the President, under Nixon, during the Vietnam War, he was serving George W. Bush in the Iraq War. Thirty years after Elliot Abrams helped Reagan fight his dirty wars in Central America, he was back in the White House helping Trump interfere with Venezuela. Biden may talk about not wanting to perpetuate 'forever wars', but he has also, in his first few months of office, extended and deepened the US blockade on Cuba and proposed an increase in military spending from $705 billion to $715 billion a year (with Congress pushing for more). That amount of infrastructure – or rather that amount of *business* – isn't going away anytime soon. The only thing we can be sure will change is the language that's used to justify it. That has to keep moving, keep hoodwinking us. New, serious-sounding constructions will replace old ones: 'Low-intensity conflict' has already been replaced by 'full-spectrum dominance'. 'Kill lists' by 'suspect patterns of life'; and more bewildering buzzwords should be expected, with each new iteration reinforcing the same impression: that war is 'surgical' and that those conducting it have a clue about what they're really doing.

*Ra Page & Orsola Casagrande*
*September, 2021*

## Notes

1. The Nicaraguan general election of November 1984, in which the Sandinistas won 67 per cent of the vote, was declared a free and democratic election by observers from all over the world, including by an all-party delegation from the British parliament (led by Baron Pratap Chitnis). And yet, this fact didn't stop PM Thatcher from insinuating to the same British parliament just three months later, in February 1985, that Nicaragua was still undemocratic, or Reagan from calling the election a 'Soviet-style sham'.
2. Originally broadcast on Channel 4, 31 May 1990. Harold Pinter, *Various Voices: Prose, Poetry, Politics 1948-1998* (London, Faber, 1998), p213.
3. 'Eroding the Language of Freedom', *Sanity*, March 1989. Reprinted in *Various Voices*, p202.
4. Frantz Fanon, *The Wretched of the Earth*, tr. Constance Farrington (New York, Grove, 1962), p38.
5. Some notable omissions might include: Project 4.1 – the US military's covert research programme on the effects of Atom bomb radiation on Marshall Island evacuees; the backing of regional rebels in Indonesia against the central government lead by anti-colonialist Sukarno in 1958 (as well as support for the blood-thirsty Suharto's climb to power through the massacres of 1965); the invasion of the Dominican Republic in 1965 to block a democratic revolution attempting to reinstate its first democratically elected president, Juan Bosch (who'd been recently ousted by the military); support for the Greek junta from 1967 to 1974; the covert delivery of US-made Skyhawk and Phantom fighter jets, via Israel, to the Indonesian government in 1979 to complete its genocide in East Timor (against the instructions of Congress); the CIA's support for Manuel Noriega's atrocities in Panama, followed by the US invasion to remove him killing an alleged 3000 people in the process; Clinton's bombing of the Al-Shifa pharmaceutical plant in Sudan (which produced life-saving medicines), just to draw attention away from the Monica Lewinsky scandal in August 1998, etc., etc.
6. Harold Pinter, *ibid*, p212.
7. Harold Pinter, *ibid*, p213.
8. Frantz Fanon, *ibid*, p43.
9. Frantz Fanon, *ibid*, p43.

IRAN

# Runner in White

## Payam Nasser

Translated from the Persian by Sara Khalili

PARSAVA AMINI WAS BORN at midnight on August 8, 1939, in Shushtar – a small, ancient town on the slopes of the Zagros mountains where Rouzbeh Amini was in exile. At the time of her birth, Parsava weighed less than four pounds, had difficulty breathing, and her skin was ashen. The midwife who brought her into the world said, 'The child may not last until morning.' But it wasn't the child that died that night but the mother, the gentle, taciturn Mehrangiz Azar, whose last words were, 'It is white everywhere!'

Parsava spent the first three years of her life at the Salassel gendarmerie outpost. There were no other options; she had no mother and no maternal or paternal aunts. Like her father, she lived in exile. Her room was the butler's pantry at the outpost, and when Rouzbeh Amini had to travel to Ahvaz to sign papers attesting to his presence in exile, the soldiers took turns taking care of her. In addition to rifle practice and four guard duty shifts a week, the soldiers had to learn how to prepare the infant's milk and how to hold her correctly. Indeed, there was always one soldier posted beside the baby's cot to wave away the black flies that the outpost swarmed with in summertime.

Although Parsava had no mother and no aunts, she had two maternal uncles. It was her older uncle, Manouchehr Azar, who chose her name. The story was that years earlier, he had fallen in love with a girl named Parsava Bestami who played the piano at certain social functions. Back then, women didn't play musical instruments, especially not the piano. When Manouchehr asked Parsava's father for her hand, the man asked, 'Do you have any talents?' And it became apparent that the father would only give his daughter to a musician. Manouchehr set out to learn to play an instrument, but realised that he had no aptitude for it. Destiny would have him become a singer. But by the time he gained fame, to the extent that his songs were broadcast on national radio, the lady pianist had married someone else. But the memory of that doomed love and the name 'Parsava' had never faded from Manouchehr's thoughts. When Parsava was restless, her older uncle would sing to her, perhaps imagining he was singing to that other Parsava. Either way, his songs were cheerful and calmed the child.

The younger uncle, Mehrab, was chief of the Salassel gendarmerie outpost, though he himself believed that, given his education and years of service, he ought to be commander of the regional headquarters by this point. Mehrab was a supporter of the former foreign minister and member of the parliament Mohammad Mosaddegh, however, and among the officers who had been demoted in the aftermath of the conflicts between Mosaddegh and the Shah. Mehrab wasn't that cheerful a man, but after Parsava's birth, his mood and disposition changed and he started doing things that seemed quite out of character. For instance, during his breaks at the outpost, he would carefully fashion pieces of fabric, cotton balls and yarn to make smiling dolls for his niece, and when no one was around, he put on puppet shows for her, making faces that had the child giggling uncontrollably. Parsava was the only souvenir of his lost sister, and even though she was no more than a few months old, with every day that passed she looked more and more like her mother. Soon, her skin that had appeared so dark at birth due to a lack of oxygen regained its natural colour, and her weight increased to fourteen pounds.

The reason why Parsava was born in exile is a story that trails back to the talents and temperaments of her father and grandfather. Rouzbeh, her father, had been born to a wealthy and cultured family. His father, Emadoldin, had been a teacher at the Royal Court. Rouzbeh learned to read and write at the age of four and had an unusual memory. A library with thousands of volumes of books was at his disposal and by the time he was seven, he had memorised hundreds of verses of poetry and was comfortable reading adult books. He finished secondary school in four years instead of six and received his diploma at the age of sixteen. Rouzbeh's wish had been to study literature at the newly-founded university in Tehran and become a writer. But by then the family could no longer afford university tuition and expenses. In no more than a decade, they had been reduced to poverty. Emadoldin Amini had lost his wealth during World War I. In those years of economic depression, he set up offices that extended loans to bankrupt farmers, most of whom were unable to repay the funds. Emadoldin's benevolence, and of course carelessness, meant that by the time he left this world, nothing was left for his inheritors. As a result, Rouzbeh enrolled in the Officers Academy instead of university. The advantage of the academy was that it offered students accommodation and three meals a day at no additional cost. What's more, its entrance exam was free.

Because of his fine penmanship and literary talents, Rouzbeh was designated to serve as secretary to the director of the academy. In the course of reviewing office correspondence, he came to realise that the ranking officers were involved in financial fraud and were pilfering a large portion of the academy's annual budget through long-term, interest-free loans to themselves. Bank executives were complicit in the scheme and a network of corruption was at work. Rouzbeh wrote a report on his discovery and submitted it to the judiciary division of the Joint Army Board. This he did ignoring the chain of command and without seeking the permission of his senior officer. His punishment was dismissal from his post. Yet, he maintained his objections and distributed fliers throughout the academy outlining the corruption of the senior officers. This time, he was placed under arrest, court-martialed in July 1937, and sent into exile in Shushtar.

Mehrab Azar took a liking to Rouzbeh because of the actions that had landed him in exile. At the time, Mosaddegh was in a semi-forced retirement from politics at his house in Ahmadabad, and Mehrab was writing to him once a month, encouraging him not to give up hope and reminding him of his many followers and others who shared his sentiments and desired political change. Soon, he had Rouzbeh write these letters for him, being able to bring some literary flair to them. His writing was laced with proverbs and verses of poetry, it flowed smoothly and had a certain music to it. All of which led Mehrab to conclude that this young writer could be a suitable husband for his sister.

Mehrangiz was eighteen when Rouzbeh first met her. A quiet girl with a delicate figure whose favourite pastime was to craft snowy sceneries with pieces of wood, cardboard, cotton balls, and eggshells. Small-scale maquettes that often featured a hut, a couple of trees, and snow-capped mountains. There was often a little girl in these scenes running, playing, or making a snowman. Mehrangiz loved snow and wrote poems and stories about it, but it never fell in Shushtar.

Rouzbeh and Mehrangiz married in May 1938, and Rouzbeh promised his wife that after his term of exile, he would take her to Ardabil, where it snowed all year round. But Mehrangiz left this world before his exile ended.

*

In the summer of 1942, when Parsava was three years old, exile ended. Reza Shah, under pressure from the United Kingdom, had passed his crown and throne to his son, and the political environment in the country had opened up. Rouzbeh, after signing various pledges and promises, was permitted to return to the Officers Academy in Tehran and resume his studies. He was twenty-four, and to make up for lost time, he needed to spend longer hours at the academy. An Armenian nurse was hired to take care of Parsava and run the household. Marina came every morning and left when Rouzbeh returned home. It was the first time Parsava was experiencing the presence of a woman in her life. At first she sulked and pined for her father, but she quickly grew accustomed to Marina who was single and had no children of her own.

For hours, Marina would sit Parsava on her lap and sing Armenian songs to her. Some she repeated, and at night Parsava would hum them as she lulled herself to sleep. Marina had studied at the midwifery school, but she was also well versed in the art of cooking and baking. She prepared Armenian dishes that both father and daughter loved. The aroma of basterma and cinnamon-flavoured gatas often filled the house.

After a while, Marina no longer left at night.

⋆

Parsava started school in the autumn of 1946. Rouzbeh's studies had ended and he was working as a riflery and military ops instructor at the academy. He now spent fewer hours there and paid greater attention to his daughter and her studies. Parsava, rather than attending to her schoolwork, pursued the daily reading assignments her father determined. The home exercises were more advanced than the school curriculum. Academically, Parsava was always several months ahead of her class and had so much free time at school that formal education seemed silly to her.

With cardboard and coloured paper, Rouzbeh made his daughter books and wrote children's stories specially for her. He illustrated them, too. There were several volumes in the collection, each addressing a question about animals. They had titles such as *Why Do Giraffes Have Long Necks? Why Do*

*Elephants Have Tusks? Why Do Eagles Have Wings?* And Parsava loved them because her father had made them for her.

'Why don't humans have wings?' she asked him once.

Her father replied that if he had wings he would build a home on a mountaintop and they would eat their lunch sitting in a tree. Parsava said if she had wings, instead of climbing the stairs to her classroom at school, she would fly in through the window. And they concluded that if humans had wings, stairs would have never been invented.

'Not all creatures that have wings actually fly,' Rouzbeh added. 'For instance, hens.' And he explained to his seven-year-old daughter that hens don't fly because they don't need to. People feed them and in return the hens lay eggs for them, otherwise they get their heads cut off. He said when we don't put our talents into practice, we will forget and lose them. He said most people are never allowed to fly, are never allowed to show their abilities. Most people are like hens that only lay eggs for those who wield power, and if they refuse, they get their heads cut off.

Back then, Parsava didn't understand any of this. She didn't know that her father was a member of the communist Tudeh Party, which supported Mosaddegh's cause even though he was not a communist sympathiser. She didn't know that her uncles and a number of senior officers had also joined their ranks. She didn't know that Marina was a supporter of the cause and was taking care of her so that her father could tend to his missions and responsibilities. She didn't know that they were secretly mobilising for an armed revolt. At the time, all Parsava knew was that she was frightened, and she didn't know why. She only sensed that the story about the hens was more than a children's story to her father.

Parsava wondered about the unusual events taking place around her. There were now weekly meetings at their home. Several men and women would come, talk, take notes, and occasionally exchange books or bags. She couldn't figure out what they were doing, but she became anxious every time her father stressed that she should not talk about what she sees and hears at home to anyone at school. Parsava had no difficulties with her lessons and was the top of her class, but now she was becoming absent-minded and had started to lose things. Not a day went by without Parsava leaving behind a textbook or something else on the school bus. She had two other problems as well. To begin with, she was incapable of making friends and keeping them. When a classmate became Parsava's friend, she had to give all her attention to Parsava and was not allowed to socialise or play with anyone else. Of course, hardly anyone agreed to such constraints. Also, for the first time in her life, Parsava started having nightmares. Recurring dreams of being lost inside some ruins and unable to find her way out. Having been told her whole life that she should be brave and strong, she kept these troubles to herself.

⋆

Towards the end of January 1948, it snowed for three consecutive days. On Thursday, Parsava and her father went outside to play. Together, they made three large snowballs and stacked them on top of each other to make a snowman. Then Parsava went looking for something to use for its eyes and nose. Her father walked a bit farther to bring twigs to use for the snowman's arms. Parsava carefully chose three pine cones. Two small ones for the eyes and a large one for the nose. Walking back, she saw her father with two men. They were both tall, had moustaches, and were wearing long, wool overcoats. They were asking him questions, and one of them grabbed the twigs he was holding and threw them aside. Just then, Rouzbeh Amini broke into a run. He raced away and the two men chased after him. Parsava thought they looked like three boys playing Catch Me If You Can. She stood frozen for a few seconds, unable to understand what was happening. Then she realised this was not a game and reflexively took off after them. As she ran, one by one the pine cones dropped to the ground like ripe fruits from a tree.

The three men disappeared around a corner and by the time Parsava got there, she no longer saw them. She looked around. There was snow and nothing but snow. Her feet were freezing, but she realised she was suddenly sweating in an unusual way. She felt a burning inside her chest. The world stood still and her heart stopped beating.

*

Parsava fell face-up on the ground. Her eyes half open, she could see the sky and the large snowflakes settling on her face. Then everything went black, and then all white. But this white was not the whiteness of snow. She felt her body floating in the air like a dandelion in a breeze. She felt light, swaying on an invisible wave. She was neither cold nor did she feel the burning in her chest. She tried to gather her senses and after a while was able to focus. Her entire being filled with awareness. What she was experiencing dated back to antiquity, an ancient, forgotten reverie. Parsava was drowned in wonder. She looked around. She saw nothing but white. The ground was white, but not with snow. It was warm and its texture was like ceramic-smooth, uniform ceramic, with no seams, no edges. It was as though she were standing on a gigantic egg. She jumped in excitement. She lay down, rolled around, got up, and screamed a few times. Such boundless white was outside the realm of imagination.

Hours passed and her excitement ebbed. She walked for a long time in every direction, but it seemed she was still right where she had been before. There were no guides or markers and no points of destination. As such, going from one place to another seemed meaningless. Not a living creature in sight, not a tree, not a shadow, and not a spot of colour anywhere. The horizon was one with the sky in every direction. And the sky was not as she knew it. It was the white beneath her feet that joined with the white above her head. The earth and sky were one. *Perhaps I'm inside a crystal ball and a bright light is shining on it*, she thought.

Parsava couldn't remember how she had arrived there. She had no recollection of the past, and she was not making any effort to remember. She learned that it is edges and shadows that define objects, dimensions and distances, and without them, direction and destination are meaningless. When all points are uniform and identical, east and west make no difference, near and far are not distinct. Contrary to what she had imagined, a spotless world was not one without flaws. It was neutral.

She discovered things that gave her pleasure. She could run with her eyes closed. When there are no obstacles, there is no need to see. She raced around blindly and felt free, unrestrained in an infinity. Fear of collision was meaningless. Direction had no significance, colours had no substance. Pure white was the same as pure black, and she could sleep while running with her eyes shut. She could dream and all the while her legs remained awake and did their bidding. She could change the world in her dreams. She built a road, trees and animals nearby, she created days and shadows and towns. She imagined what she would see when she opened her eyes. Would she see the same scene as before? That same boundless white?

But something new happened. A sound echoed in her mind, she hit an obstacle and was thrown to the ground. She opened her eyes and saw a blinding light shining on her face. She saw a man and three women pounding on her chest to get her heart beating again. She knew she couldn't resist against this return. It was like waking up after a long, deep sleep. She couldn't will herself to go back, not when four people were violently shaking her to wake up.

★

Parsava had an atrial septal defect of the heart that affects the blood flow to the lungs. Her mother had no doubt suffered from the same but, of course, without detection. It is said that stronger genes more acutely transfer adverse attributes, and Parsava's heart was extraordinarily identical to her mother's heart.

The second time eight-year-old Parsava opened her eyes, she saw her uncles. She had been unconscious for forty-eight hours, and in that time, Mehrab and Manouchehr had rushed to her side from Shushtar. A short time later, Marina arrived and the men left. During the ten days that she was in the intensive care unit, the three of them took turns visiting her. Manouchehr would sing those cheerful songs of her childhood. Although several years had passed since Parsava had heard them, she could still remember every verse. Mehrab, honouring their old traditions, put on a puppet show for his niece. Though too old and sick to find them funny any more, Parsava still forced a laugh and pretended to still be that three-year-old girl in whose giggles her uncle had rediscovered happiness.

When Parsava was released from the hospital, she had to change her way of life. The doctors insisted that she keep an eye on her weight and her diet. She needed to refrain from eating spicy foods. She also had to avoid stressful situations. Most important of all, exercise and physical exertion of any kind were off limits. Anything that increased her heart rate could kill her.

Throughout her convalescence, her father had not been there beside her. Rouzbeh had been arresteSd because of a series of magazine articles he had written under an assumed name. Marina found out that the military court had sentenced Rouzbeh to three years in prison. Not long after, the court of appeals took into consideration his service at the Officers Academy and reduced his sentence to one year. Parsava could visit her father only once a month. Political prisoners were not allowed more than a monthly visit from relatives.

In the spring of 1948, Rouzbeh was released from prison, but he couldn't return to the Officers Academy. He was dismissed from his position and was now spending his days at home. Even though the Tudeh Party meetings were no longer being held at the house, Parsava noticed that her father was writing more fervently than ever before. He would lie down on his bed and write for hours while leaning on his left side.

He couldn't sit at his desk because of a constant back ache that was a souvenir of his arrest. Several of the discs in his spine had been injured in the course of his interrogations. Stretched out, he would sip tea, smoke cigarettes and write and write. Seeing her father like that, made Parsava cold with fear. It would not take long, she felt, for prison, separation and loneliness to enter their life again from among those notes and articles. But Rouzbeh told his daughter not to worry. He told her that he was only writing satirical stories with no political nuances for popular magazines. He promised he would not do anything that would separate them again.

Writing satire was not considered a crime, but on February 4, 1949, there was an attempt on the Shah's life in front of Tehran University and the secret service set out to detain everyone whose name was on the government blacklist. Of course, Rouzbeh was accused of something more than having a criminal record. One of his satires was an adaptation of King Midas's story, titled *The Midas Syndrome*. The storyline was that one day King Midas decides to go on a hunt. He rides to a forest and hunts a deer, grills its meat and eats it. When he returns to his palace he notices something strange. Everything he touches turns into faeces. To rid himself of that horrid curse, Midas turns to his ministers and counsellors for help and they recommend a sorcerer to reverse the spell. The sorcerer tells the king that to be cured, he has to hunt ten deer in ten days and consume their meat. The trouble was that each time Midas touched his hunted deer, it turned into faeces and he had to eat it.

The prosecutor read the story out loud in court, pointed his finger at Rouzbeh Amini, and shouted, 'This man has attributed faeces-eating to the Shah.'

As a result of this inference, Rouzbeh Amini was again sentenced to three years in prison. What made matters worse was that he had written the story under the pseudonym Rouzpars. It was simply a combination of his and his daughter's names, but the prosecutor construed it as the writer's claim that insulting the Shah will bring the light of *rouz* (day) to *Pars* (the ancient name of Persia).

★

A year went by and in August, Parsava only had Marina with her to celebrate her tenth birthday. Marina baked a cake and decorated it with icing and fruits. Parsava's gift was a bubble maker. A bottle of soapy liquid and a stick with a loop at its end that made bubbles fly in the air. It was a simple toy that Parsava loved. She had never seen anything like it, and she immediately filled the room with bubbles.

As they ate their slices of cake with tea, Marina shared a memory of her own tenth birthday. Her father had bought a toy machine-gun for her. It was made of wood and when you pulled the trigger, a cork would shoot out of its muzzle. Her mother didn't appreciate her father's choice and argued that things such as dolls and dresses were more appropriate for a girl than a machine-gun. The two had gotten into a big fight. Marina went into great detail about her parents' quarrel, and there were so many comical asides in it that they both fell about laughing. 'We laugh now,' Marina said, 'but that day, I was terribly upset.' And she explained that as the years go by, sometimes unpleasant events turn into funny or sweet memories.

'But bubble makers aren't just for girls or just for boys,' Parsava said, and she assured Marina that she loved her birthday gift. Marina remained quiet for a while and then told Parsava that she was old enough and smart enough to understand the things she tells her. Parsava stopped eating. She sensed that Marina was about to tell her something important. Marina said she had learned through her friends that the secret service was searching for her. And that she might have to leave Tehran for a while and that she would not be able to take Parsava with her.

'Did you write political articles for magazines, too?' Parsava asked.

'No, what I've done is worse,' Marina replied, but she didn't explain that her crime had been stashing a pair of sidearms in a safe house for a year. The house, in the Sepah neighbourhood, was where a group of Tudeh party members printed fliers and banned books and stored weapons stolen from police stations. Word had spread that the secret service was investigating the house, and the party leaders had ordered those affiliated with it to leave the city for the time being.

Marina told Parsava that a woman named Farangiss would come and take care of her three days a week. She added that Parsava shouldn't worry about being lonely, because her uncles had promised to visit her twice a month. 'I will be back as soon as it's safe again,' Marina said.

★

That night Marina slept in Parsava's room. Near dawn, when Parsava jolted awake, Marina was not there. She called out to her several times, but Marina had gone. Late morning, an elderly woman arrived carrying a canvas bag that looked like a rice sack with a shoulder strap. She took out plenty of different foods from it. *This is a magic bag*, Parsava thought to herself. When Farangiss finally spoke and asked, 'Where are your pots and pans?' Parsava froze. The woman's voice sounded like a shriek.

The plan was that Farangiss would come to the house every other day to prepare Parsava's meals and clean the house. It didn't take long for Parsava to learn that she was a kind woman who rarely spoke and was an awful cook. She never complained, and before leaving, she always squalled, 'Let me know if you ever need anything.'

★

In October that year, Mohammad Mosaddegh founded the National Front, and three months later, entered the $16^{th}$

parliament as representative for Tehran. Mosaddegh was gaining more power by the day and gathering his supporters around him from every corner of the country. Mehrab, who was among his followers, traveled to Tehran from Shushtar twice a month to meet with him and members of the National Front, so Parsava was able to spend time with him. Mehrab never forgot one of his visits to Parsava. Every other Thursday, their set routine began with a movie together. They would stroll along Lalehzar Avenue, from one cinema to another, and choose one that was screening a film appropriate for Parsava's age. Afterwards, they would go to Orient Cafe, which served cream puffs as large as a coconut. Walking into the cafe, the chime above the door would ring, and from wherever he was, the owner would call out a welcome in Armenian, *'Bari galust!'*

The niece and uncle would have a cup of brewed coffee and a cream puff, and then go for a walk along Roosevelt Avenue. They would talk about Parsava's lessons and homework, about Farangiss and how her cooking always lacked salt. Parsava would tell her uncle about things she had learned to cook for herself – rice and three kinds of stew. They would talk about Marina who was running a small café in Armenia by this point, and Manouchehr who had recently moved to Isfahan to study the old melodic figures of traditional Persian music under the tutelage of Master Jalal Taj Esfahani. Now and then, they also talked about politics. Mehrab predicted that under Mosaddegh's leadership, in less than a year parliament would pass legislation to nationalise the country's oil industry. And he was convinced that Mosaddegh would become the next prime minister.

In April 1951, Mosaddegh formed his government. Despite the Senate's lack of enthusiasm, widespread public support and pressure from various parties resulted in the Shah ordering Parliament to issue a vote of confidence. Subsequently, Mehrab was invited to Tehran as one of the commanders of Mosaddegh's security detail. Parsava was happy that she could now see her uncle more often. But things didn't turn out the way she had assumed. After moving to Tehran, Mehrab became so involved in the prime minister's security concerns that he could only see his niece once a month. Parsava realised that sometimes being closer means being further apart. But she didn't remain alone for too long. That July her father was released from prison. There were still eight months left till the end of his sentence, but with the formation of the new government, the political atmosphere had opened up and most of the prisoners whose crimes were considered 'cultural' in nature were released. Rouzbeh was even permitted to return to the Officers Academy as an instructor. Marina, too, returned from Armenia, and life for Parsava became like a replay of a perfect scene from an old movie.

In March 1952, Mehrab, Rouzbeh, Marina and Parsava celebrated the Persian new year together. That evening, Manouchehr travelled to Tehran and joined them. He performed the musical techniques he had learned, and announced that he would soon become engaged to a young lady named Parinaz Neekpay, who was an accomplished violinist. They all celebrated and sang until dawn. All Parsava wanted was to watch them. Seeing those four people altogether in a single frame brought her more joy than she could imagine.

Four months later, Mosaddegh's government was dissolved. He wanted the Ministry of War, the Shah would not concede and in response had said, 'Then command that I pack my bags and leave the country!'

Mosaddegh resigned, packed his bags, and went to his house in Ahmadabad, a village west of Tehran. The Shah appointed Qavam as the new prime minister. Mosaddegh's indignation lasted five days. During those five days, Rouzbeh published five impassioned articles in the *Bakhtar-e Emrooz* and *Seday-e Mardom* newspapers. Manouchehr traveled from Isfahan to Tehran and sang an ode to Mosaddegh that was broadcast on the streets rousing people to rise and revolt. Mehrab meanwhile organised pro-Mosaddegh groups among the bazaar merchants of southern Tehran to protest. The army occupied critical areas of the city, the bazaar closed, thousands of people poured onto the streets, and dozens of people died. On July 21, Qavam resigned and Mosaddegh returned. This time, he not only became prime minister, he also gained the Ministry of War. People celebrated on the streets.

All of this was unfolding before the eyes of thirteen-year-old Parsava. She was now a teenage girl who clearly saw how circumstances in the world are as unreliable as a soap bubble floating through the air. She sensed that great joys are as anxiety-provoking as great wraths. And it didn't take long for her nightmares to come true. Every day, Mosaddegh pulled a new rabbit out of his hat. He dismissed the monarchists from the cabinet, cut the military's budget, expropriated Reza Shah's properties, cut off the royal court's budget, prohibited the Shah's contact with foreign diplomats and once again allowed anti-Shah political parties to publish their newspapers. In August 1953, he called a referendum for the dissolution of parliament. Rouzbeh wrote an article under an assumed name for *Mardomsalari* newspaper portending that half the members of parliament had been paid off by the US and Britain, and that such a parliament had no legitimacy. After publication of the article, Rouzbeh was named head of security for polling stations. Soon after, he and his brother-in-law Mehrab, were put in charge of security for the office of the prime minister. Rouzbeh Amini was shining like a firework launched into the air.

This meteoric ascent lasted just three days. In the late-night hours of August 15, the Shah agreed to the CIA's Operation Ajax and an order for Mosaddegh's arrest was issued. That night a colonel and a small squad of soldiers arrived at Mosaddegh's residence in Tehran claiming to have a royal decree, announcing his dismissal as Prime Minister. Rouzbeh was in charge of Mosaddegh's personal safety that night and, having received earlier intelligence about the plan, his team were well prepared for it: clearly outnumbering them, they arrested the colonel and all his men on the spot.

Mehrab meanwhile was leading Mosaddegh's forces in the surrounding streets, who launched into action, setting up road blocks, and arresting officers known to be loyal to General Zahedi, the former minister and now figurehead of the CIA's coup attempt. Mosaddegh's security teams had triumphed. Rouzbeh and Mehrab felt as though they had defeated the Shah himself. Indeed, this sentiment was not far from reality. At noon the following day, the Shah fled the country. People poured onto the streets and celebrated his departure. Mosaddegh returned to power, but remained at his residence for three days with hundreds of armed forces protecting him.

For those three days, Parsava was home alone. Marina had given her a telephone number with which she might be able to contact her father. 'There's been an attack on the prime minister's house,' Marina had said. 'Only call after eleven at night.' And then she had taken a few notebooks from under the drawers of a dresser and left.

Parsava managed to speak with her father only once, and for no more than twenty seconds. The call was at 11 o'clock on the night of August 18. 'When all of this is over,' Parsava said to her father, 'let's go to Shushtar, to visit Mom's grave.' At the other end of the line, Rouzbeh was taken aback. They had never spoken about this before. 'I will definitely come home tomorrow night,' he replied, certain that he would be with his daughter the next day. The Shah had escaped and Rouzbeh felt triumphant.

At eight the next morning, a crowd of thousands chanting the names of the Shah and General Zahedi stormed the office of the prime minister. Mosaddegh ordered that the agitators be stopped, but the police and gendarmerie forces did not intercept them. The clergy did not object to the incursion either. Money was spent by the CIA. The military as well as hordes of thugs and vagrants bused in from south Tehran had also received a good sum of money from the British Intelligence Service to be out on the streets and of one voice. Along their route, these dissenters set fire to dozens of properties – newspaper offices, headquarters of different political parties and so on. At noon, they arrived at Mosaddegh's residence and attacked it like hungry wolves. Twenty minutes later, they faced defeat. At four in the afternoon, they lay siege to the house for the second time. Now, the army was supporting them. Thousands of bullets were fired and scores of people were killed, but Mosaddegh's security teams triumphed again. The third attack took place at six in the afternoon. This time, it seemed as though the entire country was storming Mosaddegh's home. Six Sherman tanks opened fire on the house and at this point it began to collapse. In those very moments, the Shah and his wife were in Rome, according to rumours, furniture shopping for a new house there. Meanwhile, General Zahedi seized the national radio headquarters and broadcast news of Mosaddegh's arrest and the imminent return of the Shah to the open arms of the people, declaring himself the new prime minister.

The city fell silent. Parsava was standing at the window waiting her father's return. It was mid-August and the night was so long it felt like she must wait for an eternity.

*

Two days later, on Friday afternoon, a young woman rang the house doorbell. She had short hair and a childlike face, and looked as though she had not slept in a long time. She introduced herself as Parinaz Neekpay. The young woman who was to marry Uncle Manouchehr. Parinaz had come from Isfahan to tell Parsava that Mehrab had been killed in the coup d'état. But she had little news of her father. She said she had heard that he had escaped and was in hiding somewhere. Marina and Manouchehr, along with a hundred other members of the Tudeh Party, had been arrested. Parinaz gave the girl some money and told her she would let her know as soon as she heard anything.

'What should we do now?' Parsava asked.

'I write letters to Manouchehr every night,' Parinaz said.

Of course, no one could correspond with political prisoners. Parinaz explained that she writes these letters and will keep them for the day Manouchehr is released. Then she took out a bowler hat from her bag and said, 'This is the only thing I have of him. It's always with me, it goes everywhere I go.' It was a brown hat in a plastic bag that she had tightly knotted, as if to make sure the hat didn't escape.

*

From then on, Parsava wrote to her father every night. On sheets of paper torn from her notebook, she described the events of the day and confided her thoughts and feelings. She didn't keep the letters, however. With no address and no envelope, she simply dropped them in a mailbox at the end of her street.

This went on for four months, until one night in late December 1953. It snowed heavily that night and Parsava fell asleep next to the letter she had written. At dawn she jolted awake feeling terribly dizzy, as if she were seasick in her own room. She was short of breath, like a goldfish fallen out of its bowl. What was choking her was a profound sense of loneliness. She sat up and was horrified at the sight she saw. Her pajama pants and the bedsheet were wet with blood. She jerked her arms and legs to her chest so fast that the bed groaned under her. She pulled away from the bloodstain on the sheet, checked her body, and gasped, *I'm sick*!

Parsava bathed and got dressed. Then she stuffed the bloody sheet into a black garbage bag, took it outside, and plodded through the ankle-deep snow over to the trash bin and threw the bag in. The cold felt like a creature creeping up her ankles to her knees. She went back inside and slept for a long time. When she woke up, the same scene had repeated itself. Her pajama pants were bloodstained. *I must be dying!* she thought, bursting into sobs. When the simmering well of her tears dried, she sat crouched down on the floor for fifteen minutes. The solution she came up with was to use swaths of her old clothes. She cut a shirt into four pieces and tucked one inside her panties. Then she struggled and turned her mattress over so the stain wouldn't show.

The next day, she had to cut up two frayed pillowcases and an old shirt that was a bit tight on her. As she used the pieces of fabric, she put them in a plastic bag or wrapped them in a sheet of newspaper and examined them to see if the bleeding had reduced or not. She decided to tell someone what was happening before all her clothes turned into rags or she died from a lack of blood. She had Farangiss and Parinaz's telephone numbers. Several times she decided to call her uncle's fiancée, but each time, she changed her mind. Finally, she convinced herself to call Farangiss. When she told her about the strange illness, Farangiss screamed and shrieked, 'Congratulations, my dear!' and among her explanations and advice, she suggested Parsava use a hot water bottle whenever she had stomach cramps.

Parsava had been so terrified by the bleeding that she had completely forgotten she had also had stomach aches. She searched the closets and dressers looking for the hot water bottle. Finally, she remembered that her father had used it for his back pain, and she went to his wardrobe. The moment she opened its door, she froze. She felt a new sense of excitement, a connection to existence that she had not known before. Her father's scent lingering among his clothes drove shivers through her sensory receptors. Thousands of fragrances cascaded through her new-found feminine awareness. Her newly come of age sense of smell, like that of a she-wolf, could distinguish different scents. She gathered her hair in her hand and buried her face among the shirts. Alice had entered Wonderland. Millions of olfactory nerves had woken from a thirteen-year sleep and were telling her that this sharp, acidic smell is her father's soap, this other one is his aftershave cologne, and this one is from the bits of tobacco left in his pockets. Parsava shook the clothes to waken their sleeping melodies. Every odour spoke to her and revealed a secret. From the sharpness of the smell of sweat she could tell whether each item's owner had been anxious or passed the hours quietly when he wore it. With complete certainty, she could calculate how many cigarettes he had smoked or what food he had eaten. It was a moment of revelation, and in the universe of Parsava's senses, every smell had turned into a clue. There was a new awareness and sense of womanhood in her soul. It was as if in a dark and dense forest, she had climbed a towering tree and from there could observe her surroundings clearly. Now she could understand the obsessiveness with which Parinaz cared for her beloved's hat. She was safeguarding his scent, preserving the invisible particles left in the hat, the imperceptible vestiges of her lover's body.

She opened the window and breathed in the smell of fresh snow. The smell of the snowmen she should have made. The window, like expectant eyes, was open to the street. Seconds passed and the air in the room grew so cold that Parsava's breaths turned into dense steam. Through the window, she could smell someone's arrival, the scent of freedom and that of trees dressed in white.

She went outside and rolled up three large snowballs, stacking them on top of each other before finding three pine cones and a pair of twigs. When she was finished, she stood next to the snowman and waited until she saw a shadow in the distance. It was someone trudging through the snow. Parsava began running towards the shadow. Faster and faster, she ran until she was racing with all her being, with all her heart, all her mother's heart, all her childhood songs, her unanswered letters, her nights of waiting, her days of loneliness playing with cloth dolls, all those scents lingering among the shirts. She had to run until that cold sweat once again settled on her brow, run until that sacred burning pressed against her chest. She wanted to run until she was beyond the frontier of wandering, beyond the sphere of fear and waiting, run until she could say to herself, *This eternal white, it is white everywhere, it is white, white...*

# Afterword: Black Gold, Red Fear

## Olmo Gölz

University of Freiburg

THE COUP D'ÉTAT of August 19, 1953, represents a crucial turning point in Iranian history in the twentieth century. It overthrew the popular Prime Minister Mohammad Mosaddegh and ensured the safe return to his throne of Mohammad Reza Shah Pahlavi, who had previously fled abroad. Moreover, the coup, orchestrated largely by the CIA and the British SIS, transformed Iran into a client state of the United States, and the Islamic Revolution of 1979, which was directed largely against the Shah and the perceived foreign domination by the United States, would have been inconceivable without the coup. As an immediate consequence for Iranian politics, the coup brought all democratic dreams of secular Iranian nationalists to an end and led to the crushing of the hitherto strong communist movement in Iran. Ironically, as a result of the coup, the British side *lost* almost all of its previously strong influence in Iran – the very influence that was based primarily on unrestricted access to Iran's rich oil fields in the Persian Gulf region. As early as 1901, the then Shah granted a concession to the British entrepreneur William Knox D'Arcy for the exploration of Iranian oil reserves. When rich oil deposits were actually discovered in Iran a few years later, the Anglo-Persian Oil Company (APOC) was founded, renamed the Anglo-Iranian Oil Company (AIOC) in 1935 and known today as the British Petrol (BP). The AIOC was never ready to share its oil revenues fairly with the Iranians and the British did not recognise the mood of the time, in a world that no longer functioned according to the colonial habits of its imperial past, even as British influence in the region after WWII continued to shrink.

As a reaction, a secular nationalist movement emerged on Iranian soil, whose main demand was the nationalisation of the Iranian oil reserves and the popular politician Mohammad Mosaddegh appeared as its frontman. The issue of nationalisation had such unifying power that even the Communist Tudeh party, particularly strong among the oil workers and intellectuals, supported Mosaddegh and his pro-democratic, multi-faceted 'National Front' alliance in pushing through his agenda. At the end, the young Mohammad Reza Shah had little choice but to support the new Prime Minister Mosaddegh, who came into office by democratic elections in 1951, campaigning for the nationalisation of oil resources. The story of the 1953 coup d'état, however, is a multiply entangled one, involving Iranian actors with different political agendas, the rise and suppression of nationalist and democratic movements in the Middle East, the global Cold War order, and the decline of the influence of Great Britain in favour of US influence in the region.

Initially, however, the events that led to the coup were triggered both by the lack of British willingness to accept what would have been an economically disastrous loss of the oil reserves in Iran and by the injured pride of a former empire that was prolonging its last breath. Hence, the British administration started as early as April 1951, the month of Mohammad Mosaddegh's inauguration, on plans to overthrow him, but repeatedly failed in its attempts over the course of the next two years. After the discovery of a British planned coup to be conducted by Iranian General Fazlollah Zahedi, the Iranian government broke off all diplomatic relations with Great Britain and expelled her citizens from the country. Due to the deteriorating strategic conditions, the British side turned to the United States, which had sympathy for the British plans, albeit out of a concern for the red threat, more than an avarice for black gold: From the US perspective, the main fear was a strengthening of communist and thus Soviet influence in Iran. From this perspective, securing the oil reserves was only of secondary importance, as the US's partnership with Arab countries were providing more than sufficient supplies at the time. Be this as it may, the former and new superpowers in the region conspired with a shared goal.

The initial discussions eventually led – thus far there is no dispute – to an attempted coup d'état planned by the American CIA and the British SIS, which failed on the night of August 15-16, 1953. On May 13, 1953, the architects of the plot met in Nicosia, Cyprus, to develop a joint Anglo-American strategy that would lead to the overthrow of the government of Prime Minister Mohammad Mosaddegh and was code-named 'TPAJAX' (now often referred to as 'Operation AJAX'). The strategists worked together to draw up the operational plan that formed the decisive basis for the attempted coup in which Mosaddegh was to be replaced by General Zahedi. With no boots on the ground in Iran, the British secret service provided the CIA with intelligence information and access to the vast net of allies and informants they had built up in Iran over the last few decades. On Iranian soil, the grandson of former US President Theodore Roosevelt, CIA officer Kermit Roosevelt, who had been sent there especially for this purpose, was to put the plot into action.

On the evening of August 15, the troops of the Shah's praetorian 'Gard-e Shahanshahi' (referred to in Western literature as the 'Imperial Guards') marched out and placed the deputy commander-in-chief of the army and the foreign minister under arrest. At the same time, the commander of the Gard-e Shahanshahi Nematollah Nasiri (who would later become chief of the notorious brutal secret service SAVAK), accompanied only by a few soldiers, went to Mohammad Mosaddegh's residence to confront him with a 'royal decree' signed by the Shah ordering the dismissal of the Prime Minister, and then to arrest him. However, with the help of the effective military network of the communist Tudeh party, Mosaddegh had been warned, so that loyal units in turn awaited the appearance of the Gard-e Shahanshahi. Nasiri and his guardsmen did not show any resistance and were arrested on the spot. No blood was spilled and the entire praetorian guard was subsequently disarmed and placed collectively under arrest in a barracks. Incomprehensibly, however, the Guard was allowed to remain in a barracks in downtown Tehran near the political power centres and the residence of Prime Minister Mosaddegh. A circumstance that was to have ready significant consequences for the outcome of events three days later. For the time being, however, the planned coup in the night of August 15/16 failed to get off the drawing board.

As an immediate reaction to these events, the Shah, who had already toyed with the idea of going abroad in February – 'to take a cure,' as he announced at the time – fled to Rome via Baghdad and was probably coming to terms with the realisation he would never again be allowed to sit on his throne. From his perspective, the only question that might have arisen was whether his country would be ruled by the increasingly authoritarian but still popular Mohammad Mosaddegh, or if it would fall completely into the hands of those communists of the Tudeh party who, in their white shirts, had dominated the Tehran streets since at least the summer of 1952. However, the failed coup is only the beginning of the entangled story of the CIA-orchestrated conspiracy, the largely provoked escalation of violence, the questionable role of paid bullies, alleged fatwas by leading clerics, and the ultimately successful overthrow in favour of the Shah.

On August 17, Kermit Roosevelt received a message from CIA headquarters recommending him to also leave the country. However, he resisted the recommendation and, after a conversation with General Zahedi who was hiding in the US embassy, believed he could still bring about a coup. As a first step, they instigated a highly anti-royalist propaganda campaign as a 'false flag' operation – distributing grey or black propaganda

– to ultimately discredit Mosaddegh. The CIA conspirators and their Iranian partners were helped in this by the fact that the winners of the failed-coup conflict themselves created a heated atmosphere. In particular Hossein Fatemi, the foreign minister arrested by the Gard-e Shahanshahi on the night of the planned coup, was conspicuous by his sometimes extreme radio statements, in which he denounced in drastic words the Shah as responsible for the events and openly advocated the abolition of the monarchy. At the same time the communists believed that they could paint themselves as the heroes of the hour, and likewise attracted attention with radical slogans. Statues of the Shah were thrown down, communist slogans made the rounds, radical political demands were chanted, bazaar business shops were smashed. However, this did not exclusively happen as a result of an organised campaign by the communist movement. Some of these iconoclastic and violent actions were the work of agent provocateurs of the British and American intelligence networks, in order to deliberately fire anti-communist sensibilities as well as hurt religious, monarchist or secularist-nationalist political feelings. As a result, on the one hand, the impression manifested itself that a raging anti-royalist mob had taken control of the streets, while on the other hand, public opinion became increasingly convinced that CIA-fired rumours were true that the events of August 16 were actually a communist-motivated coup in order to prevent a legal transfer of power from Mosaddegh to Zahedi.

These events exerted pressure upon the Prime Minister. The American ambassador Loy W. Henderson (1892-1986), according to Kermit Roosevelt's statement, let himself be instrumentalised by the latter and threatened Mosaddegh with withdrawing all American citizens from Iran if the government did not ensure their safety. Mosaddegh meanwhile had to counteract the impression the Tudeh party had gained the upper hand over both the street and public opinion and that the government had lost control of the situation. Mosaddegh, caught in a dilemma, chose the path of raison d'état over that of trying to surf on the wave of populism. Although the populist wave could undoubtedly have drowned him, in retrospect the path he took also turned out to be a fatal mistake. Mosaddegh ordered the military and police to act against his own supporters on the street, which those days meant first and foremost the communists. On August 18, military units had brutally put down the demonstrations organised by the communists, easily to be identified by their white shirts and their radical slogans. Although the question of the troops' loyalty to either the Shah or his antagonist Mosaddegh had never been on the table before, a paradoxical constellation suddenly occurred, in which the gatherings were crushed on the order of Mosaddegh, by soldiers who shouted pro-Shah slogans as they did so. As a reaction Tudeh party officials ordered their supporters to clear the streets and to no longer support the Prime Minister.

On the morning of August 19, Mosaddegh stood alone, without remaining allies inside the political elite and without the support of the street. After Mosaddegh had already lost his former coalition partners in the National Front due to both his increasingly authoritarian style of government and his flirtation with the communist supporters of his radical politics regarding the nationalisation of the Iranian oil, these new events also deprived him of the support of the Tudeh party – the still enormously strong and only remaining consistent political faction that was able to mobilise en masse.

When the streets were finally free of communists as well as National Front sympathisers, an alternative, conservative public was formed, again fired by the conspirators in the American embassy who made sure that the rumour of Mosaddegh's supposedly legal removal gained momentum. On the morning of August 19, 1953, several daily newspapers issued a copy of the Shah's decree from the week before, which ordered the removal of the Prime Minister. Soon afterwards, groups recruited from the lower echelons of Tehran's population marched towards the city centre around Maydan-e Baharestan, the seat of Parliament. This royalist demonstration was backed up by club-wielding bullies who had been mobilised by mob leaders. The various questions surrounding these mob leaders – had they been bribed by the CIA? did they act on behalf of some influential Ayatollahs? had those Ayatollahs in turn been bribed? or did they act in their own interest following their own conservative and royalist agenda? – are the inexhaustible source of all disputes about the coup d'état inside and outside Iran to this day. The respective answers to these questions change the interpretation of the event dramatically, so it can either be seen as a spontaneous (anti-communist, pro-royalist) popular uprising; or as a thoroughly planned and executed SIS-CIA intrigue to the detriment of Iran (regardless of the outcome); or even as an early manifestation of an Islamic political movement that expressed its political will at the behest of more decisive Ayatollahs.

However, while there is an ongoing dispute about the reasons for the appearance of these thugs in the streets, their effect is clear: they provided the tune for the day. Swiftly and indiscriminately attacking passers-by, they shouted the same slogan that the military had used when they put down communists the day before: 'Long live the Shah!'

With the pro-royalist sound of the street behind them as well as a lot of very recently learned lessons, including the actual or supposed communist, anti-royalist excesses of the past two days, parts of the army again intervened in the events – this time in favour of the Shah. Compared to the night of August 15, this, however, was now happening with differing preconditions in terms of the balance of power; this time the Tudeh military network was not able or willing to take part in the events. To compound this, a large part of the units loyal to Mosaddegh were apparently unwilling to risk intervening independently, due to the fact that the events were now taking place in broad daylight with the public mood playing a much more decisive role.

Starting at 10am, the insurgent mob was protected and encouraged by the military as a whole. Units loyal to the Shah occupied the central squares of Tehran with tanks and troop carriers, but instead of taking action against the crowd, they visibly allied themselves with it. The dynamics thus created a predominance of pro-Shah forces on the streets, which in turn attracted other police units. Additionally, the Gard-e Shahanshahi freed itself amidst these chaotic conditions and took action immediately. By noon, forces loyal to the Shah had gained control of the events in the capital and were henceforth able to strategically order the initially uncoordinated actions. As a result, symbolically and strategically crucial places were attacked and taken. These attacks involved police stations, army barracks, ministries, squares, and, most significantly, the radio station. Eventually, in a radio broadcast, the Shah's royal decree, the centre piece of the SIS-CIA conspiracy that simulated a legal transfer of power to General Zahedi, was read out in public.

In some places in Tehran, the fighting continued for the time being, with the bloodiest battles over the Prime Minister's residence which was defended by troops loyal to Mosaddegh, who had three tanks at their disposal. The Gard-e Shahanshahi, laying siege to the property with six tanks of their own and the support of many civilian actors from the subaltern milieu, finally overran the defenders, with some 200 soldiers losing their lives – twice as many as in all the other clashes in the capital combined. Mosaddegh himself was able to escape in time at first, but was arrested the following day. By storming the residence, the success of the coup was effectively sealed. In addition, General Zahedi gave a short speech on the radio in the late afternoon, in which he announced that a telegram with the following content had been sent to Rome: 'King of all kings, now that the people have conquered the capital, we eagerly await your return.'

CONGO

# The Lumumba Business

## Fiston Mwanza Mujila

### Translated from the French by J. Bret Maney

THE MINERS EMPTIED OUT without warning like a theatrical troupe that goes offstage without a word at the end of an exhausting rehearsal. Dressed haphazardly in threadbare dungarees, sleeveless shirts, torn trousers, dented helmets, fur coats, and assorted charms to shield themselves from the cold or tropical rain, they trudged barefoot or shod in wellies, sandals, or hand-me-down shoes. Dozens, hundreds of them filed out mechanically, their bodies worn thin by fatigue and a chronic lack of sleep.

After the other miners had left, I stepped out of the boss's sheet-metal office with a guy who went by the name of Rambo III. It was inside the office the boss liked to do his dirty work. After the recent events, he was intent on making sure the dismissals took place under what he called 'optimal conditions'. Nicknamed 'Patriarch', the boss was known for his greed, his unvaryingly foul mood, and his libido. A thousand and one stories swirled around the fellow: they said he never ate breakfast and gorged himself daily on pizzas to save his pennies; they said he and his three kids squatted in a tiny apartment; they said he could stay in bed for days on end; they said he wore the same underwear from the 1st to the 30th of the month; they said he never laughed, not even with his wife – despite their being together for almost thirty years – or his children.

We walked towards my truck, which I'd parked at the entrance to the mine. Rambo III was furious. His face, usually so cheerful, was distorted by anger. Rambo III stalked ahead of me, Rambo III spat on the ground in protest, Rambo III (yep, still him) called me every name in the book, as if I was the one who had just shown him the door. I did my best to reason with him:

'Take a deep breath, you'll get things sorted.'

'You traitor!'

'Simmer down, mate.'

'Don't use that tone with me!'

'C'mon, mate.'

'I'm not your mate!'

But the guy just wouldn't calm down. I darted around him to open the door of the truck. He gave me a withering look and climbed in.

'Is this how you did the others?'

'Listen, brother...'

'You arsehole!'

'What did you just sa–'

'Fuck you!'

I almost hit him but stopped myself at the last second. I had chauffeured dozens of people in my beat-up truck, but I was still struggling to get used to the new role Patriarch had saddled me with: escorting home every miner the company fired. For the last few months, copper had been in free fall and the company was taking a hit. To stop the bleeding, Patriarch had begun, in his characteristically lovely way, to can the workers. Like an army general, he would stamp across the pit, stop before a miner whose appearance he didn't like, and order him to pack up his stuff – his boots, cigarettes, hard hat – and get the hell out. All of us workers had the same meagre status as day labourers, and nobody had the gumption to stand up to

Patriarch, whose arrogance was legendary. In the beginning, the company was easily getting rid of ten workers a week. When Patriarch went on his rounds, the guys didn't even dare look at him, lest they get the dreaded order to clear out. Then, one morning in September, we were all shocked to find Ezekiel's lifeless body in front of the company gates. The day before Patriarch had ordered him never again to set foot on the job site.

'You, I don't like your looks. Today's your last day.'

'Patriarch, you can't just throw me out of a job like I'm some thief. I've always shown you respect, haven't I?'

'Copper's in free fall. What do you want me to do?'

'But Patriarch...'

'I'm going to count to ten. When I'm done, you better be gone.'

Everybody in the company knew Ezekiel as an easy-going young man who savoured life to the fullest. He never failed to show up at work with his transistor radio. He was passionate about Zairean rumba, football and designer clothing – he could talk about it all day long even if his own wardrobe was made up of nothing but secondhand duds.

Knowing that Patriarch never changed his mind once he'd made a decision, Ezekiel picked up his radio and left. That evening, when the mine was deserted, he came back with a knife and opened his veins.

Ezekiel's death cast a gloom over the entire company. Patriarch wasn't seen for two days. But when he finally showed his face again, he dismissed three miners on the spot, making use of the same, feeble excuse: copper was in free fall and there was nothing he could do about it. Alas, Ezekiel's bravura was still fresh on everyone's mind. The fired miners returned to the mine during the night and killed themselves.

Patriarch was livid. 'Do you think my business is a public graveyard?' he raged. 'Whether you like it or not, I'm going to keep kicking you to the kerb. It's not my fault if copper prices are out of whack, and that's all there is to it!'

A week later, two more miners topped themselves. Following Ezekiel's lead, they returned to the company gates at night and – still following Ezekiel's lead – slit their wrists. Finding the bodies, Patriarch went ballistic:

'What is this bullshit! You get fired, and instead of looking for another job, you come to my workplace and slash your own wrists. This behaviour is unacceptable!'

Several days later, another miner killed himself the day after he was dismissed.

Several days later, another miner killed himself the day after he was kicked to the kerb.

Several days later, another miner killed himself the day after he was dismissed.

Several days later, another miner killed himself the day after...

For a month, Patriarch didn't fire anybody else. But if you thought that was the end of it, then you didn't know the man. The guy knew every trick in the book and always had a plan b. He developed what he proudly termed his 'caring companion programme'. When he fired a bloke, he would call me. 'Driver, over here! Take him with you. Drop him off with his wife and kids and order them to keep an eye on him, because if he kills himself, it's not my fault. He can still blast out his brains but not at my place, not in front of my business!'

I raced across town with Rambo III, flooring the truck the whole way. I wanted to be rid of my passenger, who had kept up his steady barrage of insults, as quickly as possible. To lower the tension, I turned on the radio. A Zairean musician sang acidly:

*Na welaki kitoko nayo na bomengo eh*
*Lelo na lembi na ngai oh*
*Lelo na lingi, na ngai liberte*
*Okoki ko somba ata avion*
*Nako zonga te oh, nakei libela*[1]

After half an hour, we arrived in the Southern district of the city where Rambo III lived with his wife, a former history teacher redeployed as a banana seller and part-time hair stylist. As soon as she saw the company car pull up, she rushed towards us. She knew, it appeared, how Patriarch handled his dismissed workers:

'Fired?'

'Without the least warning!'

'Good afternoon,' I said, hesitantly.

Rambo III's wife gave me a dirty look. She was probably also aware of my role in escorting home the potential suicide candidates and negotiating on Patriarch's behalf.

'Good day, Madam,' I repeated.

'What do you want from us?'

'Patriarch gave me a message for you.'

I followed them inside. The house was stuffed with unrelated bric-a-brac: petrol cans, an automobile rim, a massive cupboard, a scuffed television set that had seen better days... On a wall gleamed a gigantic photograph of Lumumba. Rambo III's wife motioned for me to sit down. I noticed that there were no chairs in the room.

'Sit your ass down wherever,' snapped Rambo III.

I lowered my backside onto a petrol can. The wife and husband sat on the floor. I started fishing about for the right words, the appropriate phrases. There was no question of repeating what Patriarch had said.

'You know, Madam, copper is in free fall, and we're in Katanga province. So, as the ores go, we go. Since copper isn't doing so well, since copper has been running, let's say, a little fever, the company has had a slowdown and, um, as a result, the boss has had to trim the fat...'

'What are you trying to say? At your age, don't you know how to express yourself?'

'Patriarch has decided to sack everyone,' I blurted out, 'because if he doesn't the company will go under...'

'And what are we supposed to do to survive with our six kids and the youngest with only a few years on his clock?'

'I don't know, Madam. But Patriarch requests that you keep a good eye on your husband so he doesn't kill himself in front of the business like seventeen others have done before him.'

While I was speaking with his wife, Rambo III had been staring at the photograph of Lumumba tacked to the wall. It was one of the more popular shots of the Congolese hero: Patrice Émery Lumumba shown sitting on what looked to be either the bed of a pickup truck or perhaps a jeep's jump seat; without his glasses, his suits, his neckties and bowties, just wearing a white, short-sleeved shirt. In his eyes, you could see the sun, the moon, and the flood. What could he have been thinking about? His children? His wife? The Congo? The Russians? The Belgians? His Congolese foes? A group of soldiers bustled about him. They were binding his arms and yanking his hair…

Rambo III continued studying Lumumba's face, wiped away his tears, or perhaps it was sweat, and muttered to himself like a marabout in the middle of a ceremony. He appeared to be trying to conjure Lumumba or enter into direct communication with him. All of a sudden, he started to shout with glee, to cry out at the top of his lungs: 'WE'RE RICH! WE'RE RICH! NO MORE POVERTY! FOR US, FROM NOW ON, ONLY FINE CARS!'

He's completely lost it, I thought. By what miracle has he become a man of means when he and his lady were just snivelling they didn't have enough to get through to the end of the month, what with their six mouths to feed and school fees and rent and the electric bill to pay, as well as the nappies for the little one.

'Stop acting like an idiot,' his wife hissed after a stunned pause.

'I'm telling you we're rich. As of tomorrow, we're made of money.'

He said this with so much conviction that his wife and I perked up our ears.

'Explain yourself, Rambo.'

'I'll hire you tomorrow if you want!'

He was on his feet, his hands in his pockets, looking just as haughty as Patriarch did when he stamped across the mine searching for miners to give the boot.

'We're going to knock down these two walls and expand the house. But what am I saying, we're going to demolish the whole house and build a new one several storeys high. The children will have their own rooms on the first and second floors.'

His wife stood up. I did the same. I had no idea what was going on in his head. Either he had lost his marbles or we had.

'And where are you going to find the money to do all that building?' asked his wife.

He answered, with unexampled arrogance, by pointing at the photograph of LUMUMBA, our Congolese hero. 'The money will come from Lumumba. He will provide.'

'But he's been dead since 1961,' I interrupted.

'Rubbed out by the Americans,' added his old lady.

'No, the Belgians! They're the ones who colonised us, and they're the ones who eliminated Lumumba,' he spat back at her defiantly.

'Rambo,' said his wife, intending to correct the record. 'That's a load of bollocks. It was the Yanks, the CIA, who took out Patrice Lumumba... He was uncontrollable, a real will-o'-the-wisp. He was getting cosy with the Russians, and you know the Americans and the Russians weren't about to walk down the aisle together!'

'My darling, the Belgians were the ones who had it in for Lumumba. He'd already driven them into a corner with his speech. Before he left the podium, he stared at King Baudouin and told him, 'From this day on, Belgium will be a Congolese province!''

'Liar! We've all seen the ceremony. The images speak for themselves.'

'Images edited to look that way!'

Rambo III was no longer listening to his wife. He had begun to pace the room with the air of a conqueror. Thousands of thoughts pinged in his brain as if he was some conquistador yearning for uncontacted tribes to discover, rivers and territories to map, railways to build for transporting copper ore, forests and savannas to devirginate, houses and hospitals to erect, vaccines to inject into African kids with swollen bellies, and masks, bracelets and figurines to haul away. He sighed deeply before making the following confession:

'In this country Lumumba is honoured everywhere. Even people who don't know where or *who* murdered him still worship him as a hero.'

'It wasn't Mobutu; it was the Yankees who...'

Rambo III's wife was, by this point, overwrought, even hysterical – just like her husband. Still intent upon winning the argument, she began monopolising the conversation. To strengthen her position, she burst into tears, yelled, insulted everyone and his brother, waved her arms, and tore at her hair and skirts when she lacked for arguments or if the spotlight wasn't on her, with the ultimate aim of causing chaos – a general riot with maybe a couple of wounded knocked senseless by beer bottles and carried to the nearby health centre – and thereby to put an end to the debate. Nearly all of this she accomplished in the next minute:

'Lumumba, Lumumba, ah, Lumumba, Lumumba, Lumumba, Lumumba, Lumumba, Lumumba... The Americans had the perfect alibi for tossing him out the window. It was after the Second World War, and they and the Russians were busy going at it, even in Africa, through their stand-ins. Lumumba, Lumumba, Lumumba... When Katanga province declared its independence, Lumumba went to the UN so the blue helmets stationed in the Congo could put down the secession. But the Americans and the UN – it's six of one, half a dozen of the other. The United Nations stayed out of it... Patrice went to the Soviets next... Ah, the Yanks didn't like that. They became very angry. They telephoned Mobutu on the spot.'

The Americans: Hello!
Mobutu: Yes, the Colonel here, who's speaking?
The Americans: It's us!
Mobutu: Oh! But what do you want from me?
The Americans: You want to be President?
Mobutu: Excuse me?
The Americans: President?
Mobutu: Of a football club? V. Club, for example? Or Imana?
The Americans: No, Mr Mobutu! President of your country... Doesn't that interest you?
Mobutu: Me, President of the Congo?
The Americans: Yes, you. We'll give you some ideas.

Rambo III responded with a vigorous counter-attack. 'False and doubly false! It was the Belgians who contacted Colonel Mobutu.'

The Belgians: Monsieur Mobutu?
Mobutu: At your service.
The Belgians: Would you like to rise to the highest office in the land?
Mobutu: Excuse me?
The Belgians: Would you like to become President?
Mobutu: Of what country? France?

I started to laugh at the way these two clowns acted out the history of their country. It was as if Mobutu wasn't a big enough boy to decide for himself how to oust Lumumba, and as if Lumumba couldn't demand independence and write his famous speech without some nutcase or other whispering in his ear.

Rambo III took a deep breath. And went on:

'If we create a bar and name it after Lumumba, people will come by the thousands. Lumumba is desirable. Lumumba is sexy. Lumumba is illuminating. Lumumba draws the crowds. Lumumba creates passion and excitement. Lumumba is addictive.

You get me? In this country, anyone who wants to be taken seriously, the politicians, the idiots, the pimps, the two-timed husbands, the unemployed, all claim to be followers of Lumumba. Even his executioners have become certified *Lumumbistes*! They all crow that they went to Lumumba's school, that they hold his values near and dear.... Beers with Lumumba's name on it, people will drink them down! Underwear with Lumumba's name on it, people will snap them up! Lumumba means money!'

He ran out of the room. Returned a few seconds later with beer and cigarettes. I sipped my beer, a little jealous. Like him, I also kept a picture of Lumumba in my flat, but I'd never imagined you could make money off him. How come it had never occurred to me, I asked myself, that Patrice is really a business venture? I bade goodbye to Rambo, who assured me he no longer had any intention of committing suicide.

Two months later, stretched out on my makeshift mattress, I could no longer get to sleep. Rambo III or maybe it was Lumumba was haunting me. I got in my car and sped off. I parked a few blocks from the man's house and started walking over. When I saw it, my jaw almost hit the ground. His house had been replaced by an unrecognisable structure. I knew the bloke for his extravagant taste in clothes; I was unaware he also had a gift for architecture. The new house was shaped like a turtle. On its facade, a sign ten metres high: LUMUMBA'S BAR. I inched closer. A swarm of people inside. People were getting down, drinking beer, laughing their heads off, talking. They arrived from everywhere and were of every sort: dishevelled, in suit and tie, stricken with smallpox, spoiled rich kids, teachers of French as a foreign language, traders, politicians on the campaign trail (with their grating laughter, furiously doling out dollars and Congolese francs in small denominations), uninspired poets, mack daddies disguised as Father Christmas, prophets from the Pentecostal revival churches, bongo players, recent divorcés, professional wrestlers, ophthalmologists, miners, and acrobats. Yet all this beau monde, after having hardly gulped down two or three beers, sought some connection with Lumumba:

'My father saw him with his own eyes.'

'My mother used to visit with his aunts.'

'We're from the same village.'

'One of his uncles courted my grandmother!'

Behind the bar, as haughty as ever, a little stoned, hair styled à la Lumumba, besuited, an enormous bow tie around his neck, Rambo III mimed Patrice's body language amid the cerebral cacophony of clinking glasses, cries, and dancing feet.

## Note

1. I chased after your beauty and wealth
   Today, I am tired
   Today, I want freedom
   Even if you bought an airplane
   I wouldn't come back, I'm gone for good

# Afterword: Air is his Grave

## Emmanuel Gerard

ON 13 FEBRUARY 1961, Godefroid Munongo, Interior minister in the secessionist government of Katanga, announced the death of the Congolese Prime Minister Patrice Lumumba at a press conference in Elisabethville (today Lubumbashi). Almost a month earlier, on 17 January, Lumumba and two of his political companions had been transferred from a military camp near Leopoldville (today Kinshasa), under the custody of Colonel Joseph Mobutu, to the capital of the secessionist province. The press had covered the arrival of the heavily beaten Lumumba at the airport of Luano, but for a month, no news of Lumumba's fate had been conveyed to the outside world. Indeed for decades, the circumstances of Lumumba's death have been hidden. Munungo had claimed at the time that the three prisoners had simply escaped custody, and then been caught and killed by commoners in a village, whose name he did not reveal. From the start, however, fingers pointed in the direction of the Belgians and the Americans. Their role and that of the Katangese in Lumumba's end is now well documented.

On 30 June 1960, Belgium accorded independence to its vast colony in the centre of Africa without any solid preparation.[1] Brussels had ignored the 'winds of change'. The decision had been taken only a few months before, at a round table conference in January, gathering the Belgian government and Congolese representatives. In hastily giving way to the pressure of the Congolese demands, Brussels' hope was to maintain its influence. However, in the May elections, Patrice Lumumba, a proud nationalist and leader of the *Mouvement National Congolais*, was victorious and became Prime Minister. Brussels worried, as leading industrialists dubbed him a communist, and took measures to protect Belgian business interests. On the eve of independence, Belgium imposed a Treaty of Friendship and Cooperation putting its officers and civil servants in key positions in the Congolese administration.

In a famous speech, Prime Minister Lumumba, on the very day of independence and in the presence of the Belgian King Baudouin, denounced 80 years of colonialism as a form of slavery. The mistrust between Belgium and the new Congo republic deepened. Shortly after, the mutiny of the Congolese army, still under European command, started a dramatic episode that would lead the new republic into chaos and almost destruction. Violence against Europeans provoked their exodus and gave Belgium an excuse to send in some 10,000 paratroopers without consulting the Congolese government. Brussels justified the operation as humanitarian. However, in Katanga, the southeastern corner of the country, the Belgian military supported the secession of the region proclaimed by its leader Moïse Tshombe to shield the Anglo-Belgium mining company Union Minière from Lumumba's interference. Behind closed doors, the Belgian government expressed an intention to bring down the Lumumba government, which it regarded as ineffective and even illegitimate.

Lumumba made an appeal to the UN to end the aggression. The Americans saw Congo as an important piece in their domino theory and considered any chaos there as a likely breeding ground for communism. Keeping the Cold War out of the Congo would become the American mantra. The Soviets should not be given any pretext to intrude in Congolese politics. For that reason, US President Eisenhower supported a substantial UN intervention to prevent bilateral help from any corner. The Swedish UN Secretary General Dag Hammarskjöld saw Lumumba's demand as a window of opportunity to put his organisation into the foreground. Decolonisation was changing the world and the UN could steer it in a new direction. Thus the Congo crisis, which held the attention of the entire world, was born.

Lumumba expected the UN to help him oust the Belgian military and to end the secession. The UN deployed an impressive force of 20,000 'blue helmets' to the Congo. However, the cooperation between Lumumba and Hammarskjöld broke down when the UN Secretary General, facing the complexities of international diplomacy, refused to use UN troops to smash the secession, arguing that this was an internal problem. Consequently, Lumumba wanted the UN operation terminated. This rupture between Lumumba and Hammarskjöld altered the geopolitics.

Eisenhower faced a difficult situation. His support for the UN operation and his stand against Belgian policy in the Congo created tensions in the NATO alliance, crucial to his Cold War with Russia. The civilian head of NATO, the Belgian politician Paul-Henri Spaak, threatened to resign. Eisenhower was also apprehensive that the end of the UN intervention in the Congo might invite the Soviets in, so he decided that the Congolese Prime Minister should be eliminated. From the end of August, the CIA set up a number of covert operations with the express objective of killing the prime minister. These plans were unearthed in 1975 when, in the aftermath of the Watergate scandal, the American Congress forced the CIA to hand over documents pertaining to its covert operations.[2]

Since the UN refused to use force to put Tshombe down, Lumumba decided to end the secession in the South-Kasaï and Katanga regions with his own troops, the Armée Nationale Congolaise (ANC). For this operation, he got logistical support from the Soviets who put planes and trucks at his disposal. Eisenhower, but also Hammarskjöld, found in the Soviet support and the civil casualties in South-Kasai fresh arguments to get Lumumba out of the way. The Americans, the UN and

Belgium found themselves in an awkward coalition to oust Lumumba and also found an ally in Lumumba's sometime associate Joseph Kasa-Vubu, president of the Congo.

On 5 September, in a speech on Leopoldville radio, Kasa-Vubu dismissed Lumumba as prime minister. At the president's demand, the UN closed the airports to prevent Lumumba from bringing in military support. However, Lumumba did not give way, and in another radio speech, he dismissed the president. A few days later, Lumumba got the support of a parliamentary majority. The chaos deepened and on 14 September, Joseph Mobutu, chief of staff of the ANC, seized power. Lumumba did not yield. Americans and Belgians now coalesced in actions to put him down. They advised and put pressure on Mobutu to arrest Lumumba. However, they met with UN resistance. Hammarskjöld altered course after heavy criticism from Soviet leader Nikita Khrushchev. In a stormy General Assembly session of the UN, Khrushchev demanded Hammerskjöld's resignation for his role in the Congo crisis. UN troops now protected Lumumba in his Leopoldville residence.

This stalemate lasted until the end of November. A major event then changed the equation. The UN General Assembly recognised Kasa-Vubu and not Lumumba as the legitimate representative of the new member state. Seeing no future in Leopoldville, Lumumba fled his residence and started the long journey to Stanleyville (today Kisangani), where his deputy Prime Minister Antoine Gizenga had reassembled his followers and a part of the military. Lumumba's escape provoked panic in Leopoldville, but on 2 December Lumumba was seized by Mobutu's troops. When he arrived as a prisoner at Leopoldville airport, journalists and photographers were able to take pictures of the mishandled Prime Minister. These were the last images taken of Lumumba – indeed one of them stands at the heart of Fiston's story.

A civil war was in the making. In December and January, Gizenga's troops conquered the Kivu province, made an incursion into Katanga and started an offensive to the west.

Lumumba became a nuisance and a danger for Leopoldville. If he were liberated, he would become the leader of a mighty and militarily victorious coalition. There was also uncertainty about what policy towards Congo the incoming American president J.F. Kennedy, whose inauguration would take place on 20 January 1961, would follow. Therefore, the Leopoldville leadership decided to get rid of Lumumba quickly. They chose Katanga as the scene for the crime. The transfer was prepared by Belgian advisers and got the approval of the Belgian government. To make it happen, the CIA representative in Leopoldville withheld information from Washington about the imminent transfer.

Victor Nendaka, head of the Congolese intelligence agency, was in charge of the operation, assisted by his Belgian adviser. On Tuesday 17 January in the early morning, he took Lumumba and two of his companions, Maurice Mpolo and Joseph Okito, out of prison. The journey took them by car and by plane. They arrived at 5pm in Elisabethville. That same evening, the three prisoners were executed in the bush in the presence of Tshombe and his ministers. A Belgian police officer and three Belgian officers of the Katangese Gendarmerie were present at the scene. The next day, Munongo ordered the corpses to be reburied and finally again unearthed and destroyed. The Belgian police officer who destroyed the corpses kept two teeth of Lumumba's body. In 1999, facing questions of the media, he revealed his role in this final episode.

All those involved denied their participation in it. US ambassador Adlai Stevenson, at a tumultuous session of the Security Council of the UN on February 13, when the news of Lumumba's death became public, demanded without any sense of irony the free and untrammeled exercise of democracy for the Congolese people.

Lumumba's death altered the course of the Congo's history. For the people of Africa and Asia, Lumumba became the icon of their emancipation struggles.

## Notes

1. Belgium's colonial empire consisted of the Belgian Congo, so named in 1908 after the transfer of the former Congo Free State created by King Leopold II in 1885 to Belgium, and additionally Ruanda-Urundi, two provinces conquered from Germany in World War I and administered as trust territories for the United Nations (formerly the League of Nations). Ruanda-Urundi became the independent states of Rwanda and Burundi on 1 July 1962.
2. Following the revelation that two of the Watergate burglars had formerly worked for the CIA, and had been given assistance by the agency following the break-in, the CIA undertook an internal review (known informally as the 'family jewels') in late 1974. This review became the source material for journalist Seymour Hersh's bombshell article in the *New York Times* (22 Dec 1974) that revealed the existence of a long-running CIA intelligence program targeting US citizens, a direct violation of its charter. In response, on 27 Jan 1975, Congress established a special eleven-member investigative body to look into abuses of power by the nation's intelligence agencies, to be chaired by Democratic Senator Frank Church, subsequently known as the Church Committee. The committee's interim report is titled: Alleged assassination plots involving foreign leaders.

CUBA

# Goodbye, Moskvitch

## Ahmel Echevarría Peré

Translated from the Spanish by Adam Feinstein

*To José Antonio Echevarría, my father.*

We called it *The Old Lady* and it was a '67 Moskvitch. Blue. They sold it to my father, José Miguel, in the mid-1980s. Or they assigned it to him. The sale passed from the hands of an Interior Ministry unit to those of a State Security officer who remained in service until 2003. That officer was my father, and he was still a Captain.

At the end of the 1980s, he got round to repairing and painting it. It was a thing of true beauty.

*The Old Lady*: that's the name my sister gave to the car. Aleida is seven years older than me: she's the same age as the Moskvitch. And my mother, using a yellow woollen thread and half an eggshell, made a little decoration to hang from the rear-view mirror. It was a tiny chick which dangled there, almost timelessly, like an innocent hanged man.

'I've sold it,' my father said, walking in. He removed his cap. It was blue, the visor soiled with sweat and salt. Lying there on the sofa, the cap looked like a metaphor. A bad metaphor: it was inscribed with the 'I' for *Industriales* in white. That was the name of his baseball team, the team capable of dealing a death blow to any fan's hopes with a single disappointing result mid-season.

'Did it really go all that badly?' I asked.

Aleida gestured to me. Leave him alone, the gesture said.

I had to wait. But how long would I have to hold out before I found out whether he'd been paid much less than the asking price? My father was a terrible businessman. Then I watched as he made his way over to the fridge, tall, obese, stubborn. He'd retired with the rank of Major and a degree in Arts and Letters.

The retired official wiped the sweat from his face with a handkerchief. With his back to me, he undid his shirt buttons. The shirt was blue and sweaty, *just like his cap*, I thought, as I stood at the window in the morning watching my father and sister leave the house together. I couldn't go with them, because I'd been ordered to rest after an operation on my wisdom tooth. I crossed my fingers after they closed the garden gate...

Before he even had time to open the fridge door, he had to wipe the sweat from his face again with the hankie. After gulping down half a litre of water, he shut himself in his room.

'Don't ask, I don't know what's wrong with him,' said Aleida. But she went on to spare us none of the details of the conversation between our father and the buyers. Or *the* buyer: a man five years older than my Dad.

'Bring me a glass of water,' she said.

My sister had sat down on the sofa. His money belt was lying next to the cap. Although the cap was out of style, my old man kept wearing it. Blue. After downing half her glass, my sister picked up the money belt. The cash was inside.

Aleida looked at me. 'And how are *you* feeling? Is your cheek a little swollen?' I nodded. 'Of course, Papa had asked for 1000 CUC more than they'd agreed,' she said. 'I wasn't expecting that. I think the buyer could tell.'

My sister said the man had stared at my father for a while, then smiled. Aleida said she thought she'd detected something more than just an ironic smile on his face, but she couldn't say exactly what. Because the buyer said to our father: 'Josemi, that price is pretty steep.'

Aleida noticed my look of surprise. The buyer, whose right cheek was marked by the scar from an old wound and who also had a piece of ear missing on the same side of the face, looked at our father. Neither man said a word. The psychological sense of time must have passed more slowly than the clock on the wall indicated. It was an old clock, made of beautiful wood. Just as it struck the top of the hour, a woman appeared. Black. Wearing a dark blue uniform and a white cap and apron. She muttered an apology, left the coffee cups and the water and asked to be excused. She returned to the kitchen.

The man said: 'My daughter likes the car. I don't understand it myself. But she says it's a classic car.' My father looked at him but didn't reply. 'Anyway, she likes it,' said the buyer. 'The mechanic says it's in good condition.'

The final stages of the sale can be condensed into a single, extended stretch of time. In it, two daughters and two fathers are positioned at opposite ends of an exchange. Suddenly, the Moskvitch slowly meandered through my memory. Excursions, trips to the hospital and the cemetery with my mother's illness, then death. The little chick dangling from the rear-view mirror and *The Old Lady* gradually lost their lustre under the unforgiving sun. By the time 2012 arrived, the Moskvitch was spending more time in the garage than out on the road. The roof over the garage and, for that matter, the rest of the house had borne the buffering of time with less decorum than *The Old Lady.* Just like the Moskvitch, the house was given a makeover in the 1980s. It was an enormous building from the 1950s, on the outskirts of Havana. But once again, time had caught up with the roof and it was with a view to saving it that my father had decided to sell the car.

The girl, who was married with a child, heard through a neighbour that the *The Old Lady* was up for sale. She contacted us. The girl, Thelma, spoke to my father. After making sure it would be a good investment, she asked my old man to wait for a month until the money came through.

'I'm off home,' said Aleida. I accompanied her to the door and she told me to get some rest. As we were saying goodbye to one another, I heard a noise: my father had emerged from his room.

'I'll call you later to see how he's doing,' said Aleida. 'I don't really understand why he's feeling bad. They didn't bargain him down, after all.'

'Aleida, did Papa mention where he knew the buyer from?'

'No. And I didn't ask him, either. It didn't feel like the right moment.'

I nodded. But Aleida said: 'No idea why I'm pissing around here when I've got so many things to do.'

The next noise I heard was the bathroom door. My old man, after coming out of the bedroom, would be taking a shower and then, instead of eating lunch, he'd take a nap for a few hours. When he woke up, he'd have an omelette with toast and juice. On his own. That was José Miguel, the former officer Ariel, or Josemi, as Thelma's father called him.

Josemi. Very few people called him that: friends from his childhood or his teenage years, or one or two old acquaintances.

'I brought your medicine,' I said, as I handed him a double Havana Club rum on the rocks. I was drinking mango juice myself.

'What do you want to know?' he asked. 'Does it hurt? Let's drink to the sale of the car,' he added. We clinked glasses. He took a swig. 'I hardly recognise you,' he said. And he almost smiled.

'Aleida told me what happened,' I said. And I watched him take a gulp of rum. A long one. He handed me the glass. 'Bring me another. As a reward, I'll you what you want to know.'

When I returned, I said straight off: 'How do you know that man?'

My father half closed his eyes and lowered his head. Then he said: 'His name is Ismael. We first came across each other at Playa Girón. I never saw him again – until today.' My father took another swig of rum and stood up. Looked like he was going for more ice and the bottle.

The only memory of my father's role in those days of the Playa Girón landing was a piece of cloth. I found it in a drawer when I was a little boy. It was a section of parachute. My father and a battle – encapsulated in a piece of cloth and a photograph taken by Tirso Martínez. In black and white. In the photo, Fidel is about to leap out of a T-34, although my old man isn't among those with him in the tank. The other moment I remember that involved my father and Playa Girón was Fidel firing shots from an SAU-100, sinking the *Houston*, one of the boats from the 2506 Brigade. Why had I never asked him about things he'd seen and lived through there?

'We met at a well,' he said, when he got back. 'The well wasn't far off. A few of us had been given the order to look for water. They picked me,' he said. And then he started telling me all sorts of details. And the photo began to acquire a new shape, and new meaning. It was a hot morning and the landscape was severe, with the sea stubbornly battering the reef, spraying salt everywhere. It would not have been exactly my father there in that landscape, as I knew him: it would have been a young police officer assigned to Station 9, just turned 21 at the start of that month. As we chat there in the room, I could feel a gumboil building up in my mouth. I was 38 and I'd never asked him why he decided to become a police officer. 'On April 18, my squadron was on reserve duty in the Unit,' he said. 'We took part in the meeting where they selected five volunteers for the Police Combat Battalion…' While he was speaking, I tried to imagine the building, the rhythm of work, the cells and the prisoners, the patrols in the parking lot. The meeting takes place in a small square. The head of the Unit is also there. A Captain. He calmly looks the other members of the squadron up and down.

Darkness has fallen on the square and my father is in full uniform. The young man's ID number is 3076 and he's the youngest member of the squadron.

On the square, the Captain transmits the order which has reached them from the Station by telephone. When he gets to the part about calling for volunteers for the National Revolutionary Police Battalion and says: 'Those who are willing to volunteer, raise your hand', only one hand goes up. Francisco's. He's older than my father, twice his age, what's more he's black and was raised in the Sierra Maestra with Fidel's troops. After volunteering, he has to leave the ranks and wait for the other volunteers to join him. My father has still not met the doctor who will give birth to me. He remains in the ranks looking around him. I shouldn't even call him 'Father', but Infantryman 3076. The Captain is still speaking and the squadron is completely silent. Then Infantryman 3076 raises his hand, but the Captain ignores him.

The Captain's face goes bright red. 'For fuck's sake,' he yells, gesturing at the Infantryman. 'Aren't you ashamed of yourselves? He's just a kid and *he's* volunteering.' What could they say? What would I have said, at 38, standing in that square if I had chosen to be a police officer? And the Captain says: 'Echemendía, leave the ranks and stand next to your comrade.'

'Josemi, do you have any idea what you're letting yourself in for?' Francisco whispers. '*I* do.' Infantryman 3076 looks at him. 'Yes, I think so.'

'In that case, what more can I say?' and Francisco slaps him on the back.

Not long afterwards, more hands go up to the right of the Station Leader. Following the Captain's orders, the reserve squadron stands at ease and disperses from the square. 'They gave us each a Czech rifle,' my father said. An R-2 with a bayonet and three ammunition magazines. After inspecting the weapons and the magazines, the volunteers climb into jeeps. They are expected in the parking lot.

In the Cuba y Chacón Unit, the police top brass are

preparing the PNR Battalion. They begin distributing the men among various companies. The Infantryman is relieved to find they will not be separating him from Francisco. 'I didn't know anyone else,' my father explained. 'They swapped my rifle for a Czech machine-gun with four magazines; we also got a Colt 38 and a backpack containing all the necessary provisions.'

'They allocated us to the 4th Column, the Back-up Squadron,' he said. His is the 45th squadron. There's a leap in time in his account. Yes, he does have a certain talent for this. You can listen to him for hours without getting bored. 'We got into closed trucks and left for Girón,' he explained. 'The sun was just coming up. Even though it was so early in the day, the road was not deserted.' The way he tells it, Infantryman 3076 is travelling in a closed truck. But my father said that there is a lot of movement of military lorries, artillery and tanks transported on trucks. They reach Jagüey Grande as it is getting dark. They stop off and many of them decide to get out of their vehicles. The Infantryman buys cigarettes. He smokes black cigarettes. And he also buys himself a fizzy lemonade. Two of them, actually.

He is drinking the second of these when a man comes up to him and greets him. 'Let's hope they wipe them out,' he says, without mincing his words. 'It was criminal.'

'What are you talking about?' the Infantryman asks.

'They bombed the section where the buses run. They were full of military personnel. They just turned into balls of candle wax. Some of them tumbled out of the bus with their clothes on fire.' Infantryman 3076 leaves his lemonade half-finished. His heart pounds. 'They killed a lot,' the man says. 'It's a terrible way to die, being burnt alive.' The man stops talking for a moment, then adds: 'So you're heading for Girón? Have you got your Copper Virgin on you?'[1] The Infantryman nods before putting the bottle down on the counter.

After an interruption to his account, the brief stop-off in Jagüey Grande comes to an end and the police officers are ordered back on to the trucks. The convoy continues on its way.

They are travelling in a closed transport vehicle and yet, according to my father, he can see the buses from inside his truck. They are in flames. 'It was like something out of Dante,' he said. The convoy slows down as it passes the buses and then picks up speed again once it has overtaken them. Then there's another leap in time and place and the convoy comes to a halt. It's getting dark again and they are in Soplillar. 'We got out of the trucks and we settle down nearby, or as best as we are able, without moving far from the vehicle,' my father explained. 'I can't say I managed to sleep. Maybe fatigue won me over and I got a little kip. I was nervous but I still felt pretty much in control.' They stay there until sunrise.

At around 5am, the battalion is woken up. Infantryman 3076's heart must be racing, pounding like it was earlier. The officers line up and have their backpacks and shovels taken away. In return, they're handed boxes of ammunition. My father's eyebrows arched as he took another sip from his glass. The sun is already baking hot in Soplillar. What felt like fine sand in the early morning now seems like pure dust on an embankment with no asphalt covering. These are dry days. Whitish dust. A long embankment. At midday, the sunlight can bounce straight off the road. The glare is unsettling. 'They divided the battalion up into two columns, one on each side of the road,' recalled my father. 'In the middle lay the embankment.'

My old man made a gesture of apology: he had to go to the bathroom. While I waited, I thought once again about the photo of Fidel preparing to jump out of the T-34. For the tank to reach the beach, it probably had to drive along the embankment where the Police Battalion was positioned. The embankment can't be seen in the photo, but what did that matter? In the scenario that I had recreated in my mind, you could already hear the sound of artillery. 'There were two anti-aircraft cannons either side of the embankment, 37mm, I think,' said my father. And the pom-pom guns. The Infantryman must see the artillery units as the two columns advance along the embankment. He walks along, sweating, drinks from his flask.

Small sips of warm water. The artillerymen are little more than kids. None of them can be older than 18, the Infantryman no doubt thinks to himself. It's as if they're playing games. 'After a while, I saw a plane,' he said. 'It was flying over the zone where the 2506 Brigade must have been stationed.' Sun, breeze, saltpetre, fine dust; throats bone dry, lips as dry as their throats and the morning light gleaming off the embankment.

In the scenario that I am recreating, which is framed by a sort of rectangle like a photograph, there's a section of cloudless sky and, in the distance, the sea is breaking against the reef. The vegetation is sparse and the landscape is extremely severe. A plane swoops in a diagonal descent towards the extreme right-hand side of the scene. The aircraft turns away towards the sea; before it reaches the coast, parachutes start raining down over the territory occupied by the Brigade preparing to take the beachhead. 'I couldn't make out whether the parachutes were carrying men or supplies, or both,' said my father. Then the kids receive the order, according to Infantryman 3076. 'The firing from the pom-poms came in continuous bursts, whereas the 37mm cannon fired intermittently,' my father explained, taking another swig from his glass.

I thought I could make out an intensity in my father's eyes. You couldn't call it euphoria; no, it was a chaotic mixture of alarm, fear, incredulity, anxiety, uncertainty. Plus a dose of conformity or resignation? I imagine it was the same intensity with which the officers barked out their commands. Orders, curses, encouragement; all designed to rouse the Battalion to action. The accounts in the textbooks, films, TV series, novels, all gloss over this part. And yet, what my father described was not fiction at all. Even if my mind embellished or magnified all the events taking place in and around a beach which was preparing to be taken and, at the same time, defended, it could not avoid the cliché of squadron leaders and officers cheering the Commander-in-Chief, the Nation, and then the repeated calls to choose between the Fatherland and Death. Perhaps that is because binary ideas are the ones that people understand most clearly. The PNR Battalion pushes onwards. It advances along the ditches. 'We had still not entered into combat,' my father admitted. 'But you could already hear explosions and we were ordered to lie close to the roadside.' The sound of mortar rounds. At this point in the story, a rush of adrenaline prompts Infantryman 3076 to stick his head over the top of the parapet. To the right and towards the back of the scene that I am mentally reconstructing is the sea, with the reef a little closer; and the mortar batteries must be hidden over to the left. The embankment virtually divides the scene I'm recreating in two. No one is warning the Infantryman, so there he is up above, watching the explosions. The first ones are in the sea, then against the reef. Then in an area where the coastal vegetation looks like a sparse, severe carpet. According to one observer positioned on top of a water tank, the mortar battery seems very measured at first. Then they let loose and it's trial and error, with the sound not only heightening the fear but making it all the more appalling by seeming to close in all the time. Then someone lying next to him grabs the Infantryman's shirt. 'And they pulled me back down,' my father said. 'What the fuck, Josemi, get down!' they scream at him. And the man who would be my father thirteen years later curls up into a ball.

'It's all down to luck,' he told me. 'Pure luck.' But that's not what I tell him, because he's only 21 years old and he's lying at the bottom of a ditch like a terrified animal. It is now the early hours of the morning. After every explosion, stones rain down and the dust hangs in the air. 'If you stayed in one place, a missile could kill you,' my father recalled. 'If you pushed ahead, it might still kill you, but your chances of surviving were higher.' Then they give the order.

Was my father telling me an epic story or a tragic one? In his account, the Battalion advances; a few police officers are killed on the spot or wounded by shrapnel. The aircraft have still not traced and eliminated the person giving the instructions as to where to fire the mortar rounds. The two ranks of soldiers on either side of the embankment are gaining yards. The route ahead is fairly straight but further on, the embankment twists to one side. The vanguard drags itself forwards in silence. As they reach the bend, they run into an ambush. They suffer further losses. 'Many,' my father said. Meanwhile, the bursts of mortar fire intensify on both sides. For my father, the sound of the war takes on the mood or tone of a solemn melody or a humming swarm. 'A really loud noise,' he said. 'The only defence against the mortars was to drive forwards,' he added, before taking another sip from his glass. 'Francisco said to me: "We have to go on and risk it, there's no other way."' When the angle is very acute, a huge bomb blast hits the battery. *Go, get up*. They run. Stumbling. Explosions. Then they hurl themselves down onto the roadside again. A rainstorm of stones, and the dust mingling with the saltpetre and the gunpowder, leaving the nose and the throat parched. You can breathe more easily if you hold a damp handkerchief to your nose. A little more easily, anyway. And then stand up after taking a couple of breaths. They advance slowly. 'They killed many of us,' he reflected. In the next scene, a missile will fall on the roadside, not too close by. The shards will kill several policemen; they had been travelling in the same truck as Infantryman 3076. They were at the front of the column, just over ten yards ahead. Standing up, the Infantryman can now make out the gap in the line of men. 'Josemi, don't just stand there like a dummy!' Francisco yells at him, and so once again he quickens his pace. The dead bodies lie ahead. Dust, blood, wounded bodies, disfigured faces, lots of blood on Quintana's uniform. He is pale, bald, and those eyes of his, so bright. 'He was wounded in the forehead and there were two more wounds to his torso,' my father said. 'When I came up next to him, I could tell for sure that he wasn't dead, although he looked it. Blood was pouring from his forehead. Mortar shards had ripped his shirt and embedded themselves in his chest.' 'Ambulance, bring the ambulance,' screams the man behind Infantryman 3076. The yelling gets louder all along the roadside in the opposite direction from the sea: a chain of screams moving backwards towards the rearguard of the Battalion. The medics dash across the embankment, throwing themselves against the nearer roadside when the bombing intensifies, then climbing back up onto the embankment and making their way towards the wounded man, or a soldier or a dead officer. They come and go. A frenetic rhythm matched each time by a scream of alarm or a cry for the ambulances to help transfer the wounded. But this time the medics are held up and the Infantryman and another police officer try to stem the wounded man's haemorrhage. 'There was not much we could do for him,' my father confessed. 'When Quintana died, the light went out of his eyes, they lost their glow, as if a membrane were suddenly clouding his vision. His was the first corpse I ever saw.'

Around mid-morning, a new sound mingles with the solemn symphony of machine-gun, cannon and pom-pom fire. A rasping sound. Dominating the whole embankment. The tanks approach from the rearguard. 'There was a high cloud of dust behind us. There were three of them, T-34s,' said my father. 'They ordered me and a group of comrades to advance behind the tanks.' So they leave the roadside ditch, crouching, under fire. The mortars start to strike the iron of my tank. 'Josemi!,' someone screams. 'Get out of there, you'll be killed!' Infantryman 3076 hesitates, then looks round to see who was doing the yelling. It's Francisco. Then he turns back towards those who are walking beside him. 'Yes, they had to get back to the side of the road,' my father explained. 'But only a few of them decided to follow me.' Just feet from the ditch where he had been lying, the intensity of the firing ratchets up still more. 'They began to aim 75mm cannon at us,' he added.

As my old man was speaking, a couple of questions pounded in my head. Why did they send a battalion of men, simple Infantrymen, with so few high-calibre weapons, into battle against an enemy brigade that was so well equipped? And why delay the entry of the tanks and the Armed Forces? Was I listening to an epic tale or a tragedy in which my father was not even playing the grimmest role? The cloud of dust stirred up by the tanks as they advance over the embankment thins and almost immediately turns into a column of smoke and flames as the 75mm cannon fire strikes the three tanks one after another. My father referred to a humming sound. Seconds later, the blast hits the first T-34 leaving several policemen dead, then more humming and a second explosion. The third tank moves forwards a few yards. One of its crew climbs out. 'He had burns to his face and some of his skin was peeling off,' he said. 'I gave him my flask and he poured water over his face in a stream. He was a young mulato.'

The sun scorches the metal of the flasks and what little water they still contain. Then the Infantryman hears the voice of the Chief of the Back-up Squadron. 'Get a few men together, three per squadron,' he shouts to the chiefs under his command. 'We need water. Each of you take a couple of backpacks and fill as many flasks as you can.'

Infantryman 3076 is among the group sent to the well. My father said his heart skipped a beat, knowing they had to separate from the battalion and walk 150 or 200 yards. He takes the medallion of the Virgin from his pocket, and clenches it in his fist before leaving the roadside trench. Now, above the embankment, he can see that pure, sparse carpet again, that severe, wide expanse, a clearing of parched land and rocks. It extends for a number of yards and yes, it hasn't occurred to him, but it can help them considerably in their dash to the well. Having left the ditch under a hail of shrapnel, the Infantryman trips and almost falls just as the vegetation gets a little taller. They start running. The backpacks are an uncomfortable burden. The grass is not too long or thick. He stumbles on stones hidden among the weeds which have grown high enough to resemble a hillock less than 30 yards away. But they still have to crouch down as they run. Explosions. Bursts of fire. From time to time, they throw themselves to the ground, wait for a few moments, and then stand up again. There's little difference between the embankment and the 150 or 200 yards of waste ground. Because under the rain of mortar fire, the ditch offers them hardly any protection. They walk separated from one another, taking care to maintain their distance. As he stands up, the Infantryman notices that they are only a few yards from the hillock. All they need to do is start running, making sure not to lose their balance, despite the two backpacks swinging behind them and the stones scattered all over the ground. They are in the shade of the bushes now. They've all made it. On edge. Parched throats. There's shade, a tad cooler, although it provides limited relief because it is so humid, the swamp is nearby – you can tell from the constant lash of the mosquitoes. But what does an insect bite matter, he thought. Ramón, who is commanding the squadron, orders them to split up into groups of three. Those advancing on the extreme left take very little time to alert the others. Some stones around the pit, forming a kind of parapet, an old bucket, a rope. Narrow hole, deep, a small dark mirror of water, a few leaves floating in it. He imagined it differently. Then they decide to organise the filling of the flasks. Three of them will stand guard; the Infantryman, together with two others, will open the flasks and hand them to those assigned to fill them up. They will also be responsible for closing the flasks and putting them back in the backpacks. After he completes his part of the operation, the Infantryman decides to replace the water from his own flask. Fresh water down his throat and on his face. My father couldn't remember if it had any aftertaste; it almost drenches his shirt. The sun will soon dry it out. They hear a noise. Branches snapping. They all look at one another.

What happens on that hillock will take place slowly and deliberately. That's not just because of the psychological time which my father imposed on this part of his account. Because the backpacks are heavy, Ramón gives a signal ordering them to leave the packs on the ground. Slowly. And to crouch down. He gives other signals to indicate that the police officers have to split into groups. They walk slowly, bent double, careful not to make a sound. They try to establish what might have caused the rustling in the branches. It can't have been one of the many crabs heading down to the coast. They're confused and think they hear thunder instead of cannon fire. The Infantryman leaves his flask on the ground. What they heard was not exactly a murmur or even the brief, almost muffled sound emerging from a mound where the singing of the birds and cicadas took them by surprise, or the breeze tangled in the foliage. The sound of mortar fire, artillery bursts and machine-gun fire continues. And then the psychological time changes gear because one of the police officers signals to Ramón that he thinks he's seen a bulge mixed up in the dead foliage, the vegetation, the rays of the sun filtering through the leaves. Their eyes all dart to the place where something seems to be moving. Is it a razorback, an iguana fleeing from the coast? Suddenly, some branches crunch not far from one another. Two swellings. Too big to be a boar. There's no time to shout 'hold your fire'. Of the six closest to the moving object, three open fire: of those three, two shoot in the same direction, while Infantryman 3076 fires in the opposite direction. Playa Girón meant several 'firsts' for my father: his first battle, his first corpse, his first well, his first shots fired outside of training exercises. And also his first wounded enemy soldier, as well as his first superficial wound – to his own arm. 'Actually, it was just a warm graze,' he insisted. 'Here, on my left arm.' Then the Infantryman remembers the medallion of the Copper Virgin, and he feels around in his pocket.

The Infantryman's heart is beating very fast. Euphoria. Nervous tension. His hands are still trembling. When he sees the bulky object draped in camouflage fatigues fall to the ground, he stops shooting. A scream, groans. Ramón orders them to cease firing and for the three of them to check whether he's dead. So, with his weapon pointing at the wounded man, he heads towards him. Two other police officers go with him. They aim their rifles at the body lying among the leaves. White, tall, thin. A wound in one cheek and an ear half torn to shreds. Blood is running down his neck. 'Someone see how Echemendía's doing,' Ramón orders, after disarming the wounded man. 'I don't think it's serious,' the Infantryman says, and one of the police officers takes a bayonet and rips open his shirt. 'Don't move: I'm going to splash some water over you and tie a tourniquet and then we'll get the medic to examine you.' Don't let it dry, they tell him. And it turns out they don't need to secure his arm.

'Here, you left this on the ground.' They hand the Infantryman his flask. As he puts it back in its case, he feels the bites stinging on his neck. He's forgotten all about the mosquitoes. But the infestation matters less than the fact that he's still alive at 1.30pm. And the screams of a policeman pointing his rifle at the wounded man bring him back to that instant where he first witnessed an exchange of fire close up. 'Eladio wanted to make the gringo pay for my wound, as well as all those we'd lost in the bombing,' my father explained. 'I was confused,' he added, taking another swig of water. What would I have done, what would I have said? Would I have survived, like he did? Would I have even gone to Playa Girón in the first place? And I thought about my father's Copper Virgin medallion, about his superficial wound after the exchange of fire, and also about their decision not to take shelter behind the tank. Yes, reality is far stranger than fiction, I thought, while I was listening to my father.

Eladio wants to execute the wounded man, so the Infantryman, his hands still trembling slightly, approaches the group. 'That guy would have killed you, Echemendía,' Eladio says. 'He would have gouged your chest open!' And the leader of the group, Francisco, stands up beside the Infantryman, in front of Eladio. 'But he *didn't* kill him,' he says. 'Josemi's got a minor wound in his arm, and unfortunately, this guy's still alive,' he says, pointing to the wounded man. 'It's wrong to kill someone in cold blood. I would have pulled him off a horse, like I did to the other one, but not like this.'

'And why the fuck not?' screams Eladio.

'Ask Echemendía…' The Infantryman looks at Eladio, then at Francisco and Ramón.

'There'll be no asking anyone anything,' says Francisco. 'I

don't fucking want him killed in cold blood and that's the end of the matter. Pick him up. Chuck some water over his face, and let's go. There are a whole lot of people waiting for us and they're dying of thirst.' Infantryman 3076 simply nods. In his silence, a number of questions will detonate in his head when everything else calms down. What were those two chaps doing there, so far from the beach? Did they know the place, were they local to the area? Were they planning to poison the well? Escape? Hide? Too many questions for the nervous, frenzied Infantryman to think about. Too many questions for me. In any case, the man's wounds aren't serious. He'll survive, the Infantryman thought. They'll hand him over to the Chief of Squadron, at gunpoint, under fire and half crouching, after a bit more dashing and hurling themselves to the ground.

'Thanks, Josemi,' the wounded man says to the Infantryman. And he looks at him: at his cheek, at the ear. Then he remembers the burning sensation in his arm. 'Why thanks?' The wounded man shrugs. Then he says: 'I probably wouldn't have done the same, I don't know. But thanks.'

When they are virtually at the edge of the wood, Ramón orders them to halt. An aircraft. It bursts into the frame recreated in my mind from the right-hand side. The plane is much larger than I imagined. The noise mingles with the sound of the bombing and the salvos of mortar fire. It loses height as it approaches. It's almost grazing the ground when it reaches the embankment. 'I didn't know whether it belonged to the Cuban Air Force or the Brigades,' my father confessed, finishing the glass of water. 'It didn't open fire. And I couldn't see it firing over the beach or dropping parachutists, either.' I wanted to ask him whether it was a fighter plane or a bomber, but there was no point.

My father was not one for philosophising or going off on tangents. I am, though. But after he'd finished his glass, he looked over at me, clenched his lips and said: 'It's difficult to bear so much pressure, so much stress, for hours at a stretch. Some of them were really scared. Yes, any one of us could have died there.

I was afraid at first. But it was a controlled fear, and I pushed ahead along with all the others. When I shot my first round, I felt rather relieved, but the real relief came when I got back to the ditch. It was as if someone had opened a valve and all the fear, or whatever it was, hissed out like a torrent of steam.'

They hand over the backpacks with the flasks and the prisoner. Only then does he feel he is beginning to recover. 'It was also a kind of physical relief,' my father added. 'I didn't say a word for quite a while. Any of us could have died there and I nearly died myself twice.'

Then I noticed a smile come over my father's face. 'I felt much safer once I'd fired my first shot and after having survived for the second time. The whole time, I was suffering from normal fear, if normal fear exists, like most of the others there.'

'I don't understand what you mean by normal fear,' I said. 'Couldn't it be something else, with another name?' He shrugged. 'I don't think so,' he said. 'But it's not resignation.'

'The prostate,' he said, and smiled. While I waited for him to return from the bathroom, I remembered the photo of Fidel leaping out of the tank. It's now no longer the image that encapsulates the battle and my father. But what image can conjure up this new landscape? Of the Infantryman crouching as he fills the flask? Or my father behind a burning tank after it's been struck by cannon fire? There is no account of any battle that doesn't include the story of the surrender. The battle was not a long one. Less than 72 hours, according to the textbooks. Eighteen hours of heavy fire, according to my old man. When he got back, he settled down to tell the story of what they call the *dénouement* in schools. That's when he brought up Captain Sandino, his role in the Battalion and in the start of the fighting after encountering an ambush on the first bend in the embankment. 'For a time, Captain Sandino was the Chief of my Unit,' my father began again. 'Of Station Nine. From November 1965, Captain José Q. Sandino would be Chief of Staff of the

Production Aid Military Units.' But I decided not to ask my father what he thought of the forced labour camps.

The evening begins to wane over the harsh landscape, and the rumours of surrender begin to reach the Battalion. 'Headquarters gave the order to advance,' my father said. 'The Air Force would give us back-up.' Several planes are now flying over that same frame with the embankment, that landscape recreated a number of times in my mind. Approaching the coast, they set their sights on the beach. And they swoop down in a nosedive. Firing. Time and time again. My father heads for the coast in the company of a section of the Squadron. From the reef, they can see the Brigade vessels. To the Infantryman, it seems as though the boats are advancing towards the beach and he tells the rest of the group: 'This is not over yet.'

The Air Force and the artillery then launch an assault to prevent the Brigade re-embarking. The solemn symphony starts up again. 'A humming sound,' he said. And the boats retreat in the face of heavy fire. On their return from the coast, they regroup as a column. The sun is no longer a problem, but the heat is, the dust, the saltpetre, the gunpowder. They increase their speed and join forces with the squadron so they can make their way together to Brigade Command Headquarters. 'Hugs, greetings, laughter,' my father recalls. 'It was quite a sight…' He is happy not just because he has survived but because he has fought with people who'd fought in the Sierra, in the Underground… That's when I looked over at my father. Yes, there is no way of fully sharing the joy he had described, the euphoria. I tried. But it was simply too difficult from the safety of my house, as I suddenly remembered the reason for *The Old Lady* no longer being around. I needed to put myself in his shoes, as a 21-year-old, to understand why he decided to become a police officer and then to volunteer for the Battle. But all I can manage is a very poor imitation of the state he was in, similar to that of all the other members of the Battalion, exhausted, hungry. Many of them, still affected by the sustained stress and fear, have now spread out around Command Headquarters. The Chiefs of Battalion order a review at Headquarters. They need a general report from everyone. In return, food boxes are handed out. 'They were distributed among the troops on the night of the 19th and at mealtimes on the 20th,' my father recalled. They sleep there and the next day they are ordered to encircle the area of the embankment facing the hillock with the well in it. A little circle of besiegement with its back to the sea. My father couldn't remember whether the circle was in place for one or possibly two days. 'But what I do know is that, on the 20th, in mid-morning, Fidel came by in a jeep,' he said. 'He was heading for Command Headquarters. The green beret, the black-framed glasses, his beard totally white from the dust of the embankment.' The Fidel described by my father is the same Fidel, aboard the T-34, caught on camera by Tirso Martínez but the one in my memory is wearing a spotless combat uniform unblemished by grimy grease spots and sweat marks, and wearing gleaming boots. There is no smell in the photo, either. I was never bothered by what that particular Fidel smelled of, nor the one who gave those speeches in the square. My father smells of violet cologne in the mornings after he's shaved and I've never asked him whether he used the same cologne before he met my mother: Violets… Perhaps he used it for the first time after my grandmother gave him some as a present.

She will be waiting for him at the Cuban y Chacón Unit, along with the relatives of the other members of the Battalion. My father said that Grandma was crying. 'When she saw me, she didn't hug me,' he said. 'She stroked my face and my hair, she looked at me and cried.' My grandmother's hands grasp his arms. 'I thought I'd never see you again. In your Unit, they said you'd been killed,' Grandma says. They looked for him in all the funeral homes. Yes, it was a misunderstanding. Before he left for Girón, he'd handed a wallet over to Station Nine Headquarters. It contained money, a gold bracelet and a picture card of the Copper Virgin. 'I asked them to contact my family and hand the wallet over to them,' he said. 'But the days went by and they heard no news of me. They called the Unit and they were told to come and collect Infantryman 3076's belongings, and they couldn't provide any further information because they had no communication with the Police Battalion.' My grandmother had rented a car. She sits in the back and when the Infantryman says: 'Mima, I can't fit in there. If you don't move over, there won't be room for me.' She takes him by his arm and sits him on her lap. She spends the whole journey weeping. She kisses him. 'You're filthy,' she says. 'You look like a beggar.' 'My uniform was torn and I was wearing a bandage,' my father explained. 'I hadn't had a bath or a shave for days.' On the evening of the 20th, they would be making the journey back to Havana, but it was mid-morning and Infantryman 3076 was still posted on the embankment. Battalion Headquarters have not yet disbanded the circle. A little after an hour later, the Infantryman sees the jeep which earlier that day had been taking Fidel to Brigade Command Headquarters. It's now on its way back, with a column of dust in its wake. The Commander-in-Chief is sitting in the back. Fidel is chatting to those sat next to him. He's sweating and dirty, his beard still white from the dust thrown up on the embankment, maybe reeking as heavily as Infantryman 3076.

'Shortly after midday, we saw an American car,' my father said. 'We ordered it to stop. The driver said: "I'm not armed." He was a civilian. He asked for permission to get out. He was bringing us food. There are more cars coming behind, the driver explained. He looked nervous but happy, at the same time. The Infantryman was not that close to the car, but he could see what was going on from where he stood. Francisco was one of those who had ordered the car to stop,' my father went on. '"Josemi!" Francisco smiles. A tremendous smell emerges from the driver's window. The back windows are closed to prevent dust getting at the food. "Give them a hand taking the stuff out," Francisco tells the driver. Stuffed wrasse.

Half chickens, fried. There is more food in the car boot.' Then Francisco summons Infantryman 3076.

'I don't remember whether they only sent my Squadron to the siege circle,' said my father. 'But all of us who were there began to share out the food among us.'

'A little while later, the other cars arrived,' my father recalled. 'I saw the smile on the face of the plump young man. He was hungry, ravenous. I took two pieces,' he said. 'Two chicken halves, a whole chicken. Fried, still hot, a real feast. I sat down in the shade of some bushes and ate.'

## Note

1. Our Lady of Charity, also known as the Copper Virgin (La Virgen de la Caridad del Cobre) is the patron saint of Cuba, representing hope and salvation in the face of misfortune, and thought to protect soldiers in battle. According to religious legend, in 1612 two Native American brothers, Rodrigo and Juan de Hoyos, and an African slave child, Juan Moreno, were sailing in small wooden boat off the Cuban coast when a violent storm struck. Juan, the child, was wearing a medallion with the image of the Virgin Mary, and when the three began praying to it, the storm cleared instantly. The men were taking salt to a slaughter house which supplied the inhabitants of a small mining town in Santiago del Prado, now known as El Cobre.

# Afterword: Playa Girón


## Félix Julio Alfonso López

Translated from the Spanish by Julio Barrios


*...After Girón all the people of the Americas were a little more free.*

– Fidel Castro

On April 15, 1961, the US news agency AP published a cable that falsely stated: 'Pilots of Prime Minister Fidel Castro's Air Force rebelled against his regime today and attacked three key air bases with bombs and rockets.' The story was absurd, *fake news*, intended to confound public opinion and justify the events that would immediately follow. In reality, that day, eight B-26 planes of the US Air Force, coming from Puerto Cabezas on the Atlantic coast of Nicaragua, disguised by false insignia, machine-gunned the airports of Santiago de Cuba, San Antonio de los Baños and Ciudad Libertad, with the intention of destroying the precarious revolutionary aviation on the ground. The attack occurred around dawn on the 15th, and was resisted by the country's anti-aircraft batteries which managed to shoot down one of the falsely marked planes and damage two others.

Among the victims of the attack was a young militiaman, Eduardo García Delgado, who, just before he died, wrote the name 'Fidel' in his own blood on the door of his second-floor office in the Revolutionary Armed Forces (FAR) base in Ciudad Libertad, just outside Havana.[1] It was, no doubt, the prelude to an invasion.

How had the relations between the young Cuban revolution and the government of the United States reached such a point? Hostilities had in fact been unfolding since the very triumph of the Revolutionary Army commanded by Fidel Castro on January 1, 1959. The flight of the dictator Fulgencio Batista and other figureheads meant the end, not only of an undemocratic and criminal government, but of a system of domination that the United States had installed over Cuba since the beginning of the twentieth century, and through which it had exercised various degrees of economic, political and diplomatic control over the island. The taking of Santiago de Cuba by the rebels, in January 1959, the final act of the revolution, began a profound and radical process of transformation of the old regime which directly undermined the power held by the Cuban bourgeoisie and large American corporations. Early revolutionary legislation, such as the Urban Reform Law, the reduction of telephone and electricity prices, the closing of mafia-controlled casinos, and the Agrarian Reform Law, in May 1959, immediately triggered into opposition the domestic bourgeoisie and the vested corporate interests of the United States. It was in this context that, in an unofficial capacity, Prime Minister Fidel Castro visited Washington in April, invited by the Association of Newspaper Publishers. He was received with a cold and impolite demeanour by the authorities, despite the fact that Castro had declared, to the Senate's Committee on Foreign Relations, that his government's objective was to maintain good relations with their northern neighbour, always on the basis of full equality and reciprocity.

With the Agrarian Reform Law promising to redistribute land ownership in a country where 75 per cent of the arable land was in foreign hands, of which more than two million hectares belonged to just five American sugar companies, the young revolutionaries had gone one step too far; they had crossed the Rubicon. Just two days after the law came into effect, on June 5, Florida Democratic Senator George Smathers proposed reducing the sugar import quota assigned to Cuba (reducing the amount of sugar that could be imported from Cuba into the US). In January 1960, all the lands owned by the United Fruit Company in Oriente Province were expropriated. The United Fruit Company was a branch of the same monopoly that had been decisive in overthrowing Colonel Jacabo Árbenz in Guatemala in 1954, and among its shareholders and directors were Secretary of State John Foster Dulles (director of the CIA), Allen Dulles, and the ambassador to the UN Henry Cabot Lodge. Immediately aerial bombardments began that set fire to sugar cane fields throughout the island and pressures within the US to suppress Cuba's sugar quota intensified.[2]

The escalation of aggressions reached a point of extreme gravity at the beginning of March 1960, when two catastrophic explosions on the French ship La Coubre in the bay of Havana killed over a hundred people. The ship had contained arms and ammunition purchased in Belgium, and the explosion was clearly an act of terrorist sabotage. At the funeral of 27 dock workers killed by the explosions, Fidel uttered for the first time his historic phrase: *Patria o muerte* (Country or death). In June 1960, the main oil refineries (owned by the British and US corporations Texaco, Esso and Shell) were nationalised after they refused to refine Soviet oil, triggering retaliation against the Cuban economy that resulted in the suppression of Cuba's sugar quota into the US and yielded the response from President Eisenhower: 'This initiates economic sanctions against Cuba. Now we must undertake further measures: economic, diplomatic and strategic.'[3]

Action had already been underway since March, when 'Operation Pluto' was approved; this was a strategy, concocted between the CIA and the Joint Chiefs of Staff of the Armed Forces, to deliver training in Guatemala to an army of Cuban exiles with the purpose of invading the island, seizing a portion of its territory and proclaiming a provisional government on that territory which would be immediately recognised by the United States and other Latin American countries. Operation Pluto was designed as an amphibious, air and land infiltration operation, in which the technical and military training of US advisers would be decisive, although crucially, at the time of landing, the US's presence would not be in evidence. 'There will be no pale faces on the beach,' stated Richard Bissell, the brains behind the operation. Simultaneously, the CIA deployed complementary initiatives to undermine and overthrow the Cuban government internally, such as psychological warfare, clandestine radio broadcasts, the incitement of internal subversion, the infiltration of commandos, and the supplying of arms and explosives to opposition guerrillas. All this intended to set the stage for a future, even bigger invasion of the whole country. The option of assassinating Fidel was not ruled out and, since August, the CIA had been making contacts with members of organised crime gangs with a view to carrying out the assassination.

The political front for the Cuban exiles participating in this destabilsing campaign was the so-called Democratic Revolutionary Front (FRD), headed by professional politicians such as the former Authentic Party leader and sometime Prime Minister (under Batista) Manuel Antonio de Varona; the former Minister of State Aureliano Sánchez Arango; representatives of the Christian Democratic Party such as Professor José Ignacio Rasco, who was highly influential in the Catholic counter-revolutionary circles; and dissident members of the '26 de Julio' military movement, such as Manuel Artime Buesa, a doctor with a strict religious background and leader of the 2506 Brigade, who had been appointed as political representative of the FRD in the territory they intended to occupy.

The concentration of military resources and equipment in Guatemala provoked Cuban Foreign Minister Raúl Roa to protest at the UN in October 1960, where he also asserted that an invasion plan against Cuba was underway. That same month, Washington called in the US ambassador in Havana, Philip Bonsal, for consultation. Meanwhile the young presidential candidate for the Democratic Party, John F. Kennedy, incorporated into his campaign the plight of the 'freedom fighters in Cuba'. In response to the increase in aggression and economic pressure, in October 1960, the Cuban government nationalised all the properties owned by US corporations that remained on the island.

Incoming President Kennedy was officially notified on November 18 of the invasion plans for Cuba, and on January 3, 1961, in one of his last acts in power, the Eisenhower administration broke off all diplomatic relations with Havana. In one of his first proclamations as president, Kennedy stated that his policy towards the island would aim to contain communism in the Western Hemisphere and thus launched his economic development program for the region known as the 'Alliance for Progress'. Meanwhile, and despite all the evidence that the majority of Cubans supported the revolution, the counter-revolutionary plans did not halt and on March 14, 1961, the CIA decided that the landing operation would take place at a point on the south-western coast of Cuba known as the Bay of Pigs, after ruling out another point further east between Casilda and Trinidad.

In March 1961, the leaders of the FRD led by Varona and the People's Revolutionary Movement (MRP), founded by former minister Manuel Ray, decided to unify the anti-Castrists in exile in what they named the Cuban Revolutionary Council, at the head of which sat the former Prime Minister of the revolutionary government José Miró Cardona, possibly only as a figurehead. The Revolutionary Council's objective would be to constitute a provisional government in the territory occupied by the invading forces. Fidel Castro's immediate response was to declare that the formation of the Revolutionary Council was the prelude to a larger effort by the United States' government to destroy the revolution. By the beginning of April, the State Department published the so-called White Book on Cuba, in which it described the government of the island as a 'betrayed revolution', a 'satellite of the Soviet Union' and a 'threat to freedom and democracy in Latin America'. As President Kennedy declared that there would be no armed action by US troops against Cuba, on April 13, the main department store in Havana, El Encanto, was set ablaze in a new terrorist attack.

Two days later, eight CIA-commissioned B26 bombers, painted with fake FAR insignia, simultaneously attacked three Cuban airfields: Ciudad Libertad (formerly named Campo Columbia), San Antonio de los Baños (both near Havana), and Antonio Maceo International Airport at Santiago de Cuba, killing seven and wounding around 50.[4] The next day, April 16, at the funeral of some of the victims, Fidel Castro proclaimed the socialist character of the revolution and called on the people to take up their rifles and resist the imminent armed incursion. At dawn on April 17, the mercenary invasion began as they approached two points on the Bay of Pigs – their code names were Red Beach (Playa Larga) and Blue Beach (Playa Girón), being remote and sparsely populated areas, sitting on the margins of a large swamp, the Ciénaga of Zapata. Cuba's largest battalion of soldiers was located more than thirty kilometres from the coast, in an area called Central Australia. Departing from Puerto Cabezas, Nicaragua, the main invasion vessels carried a company made up of more than 1,400 men, with a colossal war arsenal. This included: five Walter M-42 tanks; eleven 2.5-ton trucks equipped with 12.7mm machine-guns; 30 (81mm and 106.7mm calibre) mortars; eighteen 57mm recoilless guns, four 75mm recoilless guns; 50 bazookas; nine flamethrowers; 46 (50mm and 30mm) machine-guns; 3,000 rifles; M-1, Garand submachine-guns, Browning automatic rifles, M1 and M2 carbines, and M3 submachine-guns; eight tons of explosives; communications equipment, telephones and field boards; 38,000 gallons of fuel for vehicles, 17,000 gallons for airplanes; 150 tons of ammunition; 24,000 pounds of food; gallons of drinking water; 1.5 tons of white phosphorus; 700 air-to-ground rockets; 500 cluster bombs; 300 gallons of jet oil; 20 tons of 50mm ammunition; ten jeeps; one five-ton tanker truck; one tractor; one tractor crane and 13 trailers. As maritime support, they had five merchant ships and 36 small landing crafts with outboard motors. In addition, they brought: two infantry landing ships reconditioned as escorts but heavily armed; three multi-use landing barges; and four landing barges for disembarking soldiers and vehicles.

The 2506th Brigade was a clear reflection of the social demographic that had been usurped by the revolution. Among them were ex-military men, policemen and henchmen of the overthrown Batista regime, members of aristocratic dynasties and the great bourgeoisie of pre-revolutionary Cuba, merchants, landowners, industrialists formerly involved in sugar mills and mines, bankers, some journalists, as well as a scattering of ordinary working people. Among the most sinister characters that made up the company was Ramón Calviño, one of the most cruel torturers of the Batista regime and Emilio Soler Puig, aka 'El Muerto (The Dead)', a gangster who had previously murdered leaders of the communist labour movement. José Pérez San Román was the commander and Erneido Oliva the second-in-command.

To coincide with the landing, the US press published a press release that had been drawn up by the CIA, announcing the beginning of the 'liberation of Cuba'. A clandestine radio station on Swan Island broadcast all over the island calls for the uprising of the Cuban people. From the Operation Pluto headquarters in the Pentagon, operations were directed and supervised by Richard Bissell, CIA Deputy Director for Special Plans. Among his team were: Tracy Barnes, Bissell's deputy; CIA Deputy Director, General Charles P. Cabell; Howard Hunt and Frank Droller, who were in charge of Cuban politicians and covert operations; David A. Phillips, in charge of propaganda; Jack Esterline, in charge of the task force for the invasion of Cuba; and several dozen more officers from the CIA, US Army, Navy and Air Force.

A Cuban militiaman gave the warning, on the early morning of April 17, of the presence of lights and boats in the vicinity of Playa Larga: it was a vanguard of frogmen who had reached the shore to install signals for the landing vessels. In support of the invasion, a group of paratroopers were also deployed on the inner edge of the Ciénaga to cut off communications with the rest of the country. The 339th Battalion, commanded from Cienfuegos, was immediately mobilised, engaging in the first skirmishes against an invading brigade and restricting it to Playa Larga. Throughout the first day of battle, the revolutionary air force shot down seven B-26 aircraft and put two ships, the USS Houston and the USS Río Escondido, out of action, destroying armaments and essential supplies needed to support the ground forces. By nightfall on the 17th, the revolutionary forces had succeeded, without artillery or heavy weapons, in expelling the paratroopers to the south, thus preventing them from cutting off communications with the rest of the island, and reducing the area of beachhead that had been gained.

The following day, April 18, saw the launch of the counter-offensive, in full, of the Rebel Army that comprised of the militia battalions from Cienfuegos, Matanzas and Havana, as well as the combatants of the National School of Militias, the National Revolutionary Police, and anti-aircraft defence batteries, which used artillery acquired from the Soviet Union and Czechoslovakia. During the offensive, personally led by Fidel Castro, the mercenary troops that controlled the two access roads to Playa Girón were forced to retreat to the San Blas area. In Playa Larga, the invading troops decided to abandon their positions and go to Playa Girón to join the other half of the invasion force, thus enabling the Cuban troops to take control of Playa Larga.

The last day of fighting was April 19. That day the assailant forces retreated from San Blas to Playa Girón; those that remained were encircled and surrendered in the early hours of the morning. Captain José Ramón Fernández and Fidel Castro himself went to the Playa Girón area and participated in the last combat actions. Finally, at 5:30 in the afternoon, Playa Girón was taken, at which point the assailants tried to flee, some jumping on boats, others venturing through the swamps, most were captured. Artime Buesa himself became a fugitive for two weeks as he tried to hide in the marshes. Fidel's orders were final: 'That the tanks do not stop until they reach the very waves of the sea, because every minute that these mercenaries are on our soil constitutes an affront to our country.'

The operation had ended in complete failure, for the Americans, and the total defeat of the members of 2506th Brigade, who had suffered over a hundred deaths and with 1,197 taken prisoner. On the revolutionary side there were 176 deceased combatants and 300 wounded, 50 of them with life-altering injuries. In words of 'Gallego' Fernández, one of the leaders of the resisting forces: 'The idea, the enemy's strategic and tactical point of view, was well conceived [...] they [only] lacked a reason, the justness of the cause they were defending.' Commander Fidel Castro's announcement was undeniable: 'The invaders have been annihilated. The revolution has emerged victorious from this battle. Within 72 hours, it has destroyed an army that for many months had been organised and trained by the imperialist government of the United States [...] That day in history, Yankee imperialism suffered its first great defeat in America.'

Many analyses, blessed with the benefit of hindsight, were proffered over the following years to explain and excuse that crushing failure of the CIA, which brought such ridicule to the Kennedy administration. Even if Kennedy had inherited Operation Pluto from Eisenhower, it was his administration that ultimately bore responsibility for its failure ('Success has many friends, defeat is an orphan,' Kennedy famously said). Arthur Schlesinger, Jr., assistant to the president, would reflect, with a certain amount of truth, that: 'Historically, we have played a double role in Latin America. Sometimes we are the good neighbour, sometimes the bully of the hemisphere. [...] Dr. Jekyll promotes the long-term interests of the United States, Mr. Hyde leaves bitter anti-Yankee sentiments wherever he goes. Bay of Pigs was the work of Mr. Hyde.'

During the interrogations, one of the invaders cynically acknowledged, when asked by a prosecutor why they had allied with a foreign power to attack their own country, that: 'There are moments in politics when one has to negotiate, so to say, with the Devil himself.' On the other hand, the writer Eduardo Heras León, Ahmel Echevarría's teacher, who fought in the defence of the island and author of a memorable book about those epic days titled *La Guerra Tuvo Seis Nombres (The War Had Six Names)*, explained the reasons for the victory with extraordinary simplicity:

> Those of us who had the honour and fortune to have participated in those three days of combat did so without having a 'historical awareness' of the event. We did not go to fight thinking that we were living an important moment in history. We did not make abstractions or philosophise about the importance of the 'historical minute in which we found ourselves'. We simply went to fight the mercenaries who wanted to destroy the Revolution. And it all boiled down to those simple and clear terms: we, the revolutionaries, were going to pump lead into the invading counter-revolutionaries. They could not pass: it was simple as that.

## Notes

1. http://www.granma.cu/granmad/secciones/giron/pa07.html
2. https://www.nytimes.com/1960/01/20/archives/planes-again-raid-cuban-cane-crop-drops-fire-bombs-on-fields-havana.html
3. *Cuba and the United States: A Chronological History,* by Jane Franklin, Ocean Press, 1997
4. https://www.jfklibrary.org/learn/about-jfk/jfk-in-history/the-bay-of-pigs

SOUTH AFRICA

# Please Step Out of the Vehicle

## Lidudumalingani

THE BIG THUD ON the roof is definitive. It comes once and once only, unsettling the night and the peace that comes with it. Deep in sleep, Simon hears it as something having fallen from the sky. A planet, perhaps, one of those small ones, snapping off its thin thread, plummeting some billion miles, passing other shocked planets on its way, a glitch in the radar of a satellite, beaming signals to earth, and landing on his roof. Only a few hours earlier, Simon had folded himself into bed, later than usual, according to his meticulously worked-out schedule: going to sleep at 23:00, waking at 06:00, arriving to work at the house at 07:00, and so on. Officially, he was the politician's driver but on days when he had meetings at home, or was away on travel, Simon made himself useful as the gardener. Mr Mandela always laughed at him, called him 'the man who never rests', given how he was continually on his feet, doing something. The way Simon sees it, the gardening needed to be done, and while he had nothing else to do, it is the least he could. Simon has been driving the politician around for a while now. He jokes with his friends that if he didn't show up, Mr Mandela would refuse to be driven by anyone else; he'd just walk. They laugh at his admiration for the man, teasing him about when he was going to ask him for his hand in marriage.

It was an act of fate that landed Simon the job as Mr Mandela's driver. At least that's what he believes. One night, on his return from a community meeting, he'd given a lift to an ANC comrade who'd failed to return home before a local curfew; he needed to get out of the township quickly and quietly before the police were any the wiser. Simon offered to drive him home, in his beat-up Corolla, and took him down so many back roads and side streets, the man didn't know where he was until they pulled up outside his front gate. Word got around. If you wanted a getaway driver, Simon was your man.

Unsettled by the thud on the roof, he reaches under his bedside cabinet, retrieves a gun, and whispers to his wife to stay in bed. Before heading out, he checks on the children. The gun was smuggled in from Angola, along with other armour, explosives and military gear. Simon had become disillusioned by many of the leaders of the anti-apartheid movement, politicians that he saw at Nelson's house, or at the meetings he drove him to, and together with some activists in his township, in Soweto, he had decided to fight apartheid on his own terms. The 'Freedom Guerillas', as they decided to call themselves, were going to fight apartheid with weapons, and bring a different kind of freedom to the one planned by the ANC. Nelson and his rich friends were taking too long, living comfortably, cosying up with the enemy, and forgetting the people they were supposedly fighting for.

When Simon steps out into his modest front yard, in a T-shirt, shorts and slippers, gun unfamiliarly clutched in his right hand, his heart beats faster than it has ever done before. After the thud on the roof, the night is eerily quiet. *No good can come from this,* he thinks, then tries to shake off his fears by playing over the words of the Angolan guerilla who'd trained them in the desert, at night. He points the gun in the dark, squints his eyes to scan for any movement, then yells out:

'Come out now or I start shooting.'

Suddenly a flood of lights blinds him, he fires in the dark, but what good are bullets against light. For a short moment, as his eyes adjust to the glare, Simon hears the shuffling of feet. He's not sure if they're moving towards or away from him. He yells but nothing. Still dazed, the bright light clicks off and a black bag goes over his head, his feet come off the ground, as hands lift him from his ankles and underneath his armpits. For a minute, he tries to fight them off, but nothing comes of it. He realises his right palm is empty. Remembering the gun, he wonders for a second if he has it in his left hand, instead, even though that hand can barely hold a pen. There's a first time for everything.

Moments later, Simon sits motionless in the dark, his head still covered by the black bag, a cold zinc floor beneath his feet, and the disorientation of being in a fast-moving vehicle, unable to see. He can't tell if there is anyone in the back of the car with him. If there is, they've made no movements so far, not even shifting in their seat. In the darkness, in the quiet of the night, beyond the clunking of the vehicle, Simon hears the sound of music blasting from afar, and immediately knows where he is. He knows Soweto by heart, every street, every back road, having memory-mapped it out in his mind, in case he ever had to make a getaway. The music fades, and the car climbs up a short hill; Simon knows they are now on a long stretch of an empty road, before eventually arriving in Rosettenville. In the dark, he imagines the lights of the township slowly thinning out, reflecting off the newly-tarred road, and creeping into people's front rooms. For a few minutes, the car carries on, before taking a left and then coming to a sudden stop, in the middle of nowhere by Simon's calculations.

Simon is dragged out of the car through a door and over an uneven floor, then dropped into a chair. He can tell the chair is old, it groans as he lands in it, then settles into itself, creaking only slightly with subsequent movements. Though Simon's heart is beating faster than usual and fear creeps slowly under his skin, the moment isn't entirely terrifying. The darkness softens to a dim light, and through the cloth bag Simon can now make out a man in a suit standing in front of him with something – perhaps a file of papers – in his hand.

'We have a new mission for you,' he says in an undisguised American accent. 'We would like you to collect some information for us.'

The request is a command, not seeking an answer or any interaction. In a panic, Simon wants to protest that he's never done undercover work before, that all he's really good at is reading maps and getting people from A to B via unusual routes. He wants to protest that he's just an ordinary man and that surely these people can find someone better trained for this kind of job. He wants to protest that whatever the mission is, he's not the man for it.

The solitary suited man who travelled all this way to an abandoned building just to relay this news to him, interrupts Simon's thinking, telling him it is essential. The decision has been made for him, that he has nothing to worry about, and that all he has to do is listen carefully to the details, as they are laid out to him.

'You just need to continue with your job, just report to us, every night,' the man says.

Simon almost lets out a cry. He's tempted to think that this is some sick joke by his Freedom Guerillas comrades, but the accent throws him off. Otherwise, that would explain it. He hasn't grassed for the police in years, and only a handful of people know what he does for a living these days. He always left his house in overalls. People thought he worked in the city, tending to some white man's garden.

'My job? I just sweep up leaves and prune trees. What am I spying on?' Simon attempts to reply.

'Listen, we know you are Mandela's driver. Quit the games,' a different voice spits back. 'Your country's freedom is at stake here.'

Not once has Simon ever doubted his patriotism and has never felt that he needed to prove it. Above all else, he admires Mandela, even though, of late, he has become disillusioned with other ANC leaders and the communists they move among.

Even so, his admiration for Mandela has not yet entirely waned. And now, here he is, rousted out of bed, dragged in pyjamas to some dungeon, and told to spy on the man.

The thoughts in Simon's head take quick turns, but the question they all come back to is 'Why'. Why did he need to spy on Mandela? At last, someone pulls the bag off his head, and he sees clearly for the first time since he was in his front yard. A thought comes to his mind: now that he has seen the man standing in front of him, he can't say no, just like in the movies, once you see the face, you can't betray it, otherwise you're dead.

Simon protests. He can't do it. Mandela is a hero to the people.

The man softens his voice and tries another approach. It's for Mandela's protection, he explains. They – he doesn't explain who 'they' are – have intel that Mr Mandela is in danger, and that this is an effort to keep him safe. As if the man can hear Simon's thoughts, he then explains that they obviously cannot tell Mr Mandela about this, because it has become clear that one of his closest, most trusted associates has been colluding with foreign forces, who fear that Mr Mandela is becoming too powerful and needs taking out.

Simon hesitates for a moment. Scans the room. This isn't a new revelation to Simon. He and his Freedom Guerillas have long suspected the ANC top brass were being infiltrated by communists; that was their entire argument. But even as he thought this, he saw it as an internal matter, one that needed to be dealt with by them.

Growing impatient with Simon, a short, stocky woman marches forward from a dim-lit periphery of the room and places an open dossier on his lap. At the top, photographs of Simon and his Freedom Guerillas comrades at a secret meeting, beneath them, shots of him on rifle ranges, and loading crates of munitions onto a truck, others of him with his wife and children.

His saliva hardens into a ball of phlegm, and he can't swallow.

Unlike the man in the suit, the woman is curt. Simon either does what they're asking, she says, or the pictures will find their way to the police and a bomb will be found in his house. One identical to the bomb that was used a month ago to destroy a car belonging to a police captain. Simon can't imagine how the woman knows he is the one who placed the bomb in that car. And he isn't about to ask. Nor is he about to ask about the bomb soon to be found in his house. There is no bomb there currently, he knows that. He isn't stupid enough to bring such things into his own home. Still, he knows for sure the police will find it.

After a short time, or what feels like it to Simon, a hand snatches the dossier from his lap, and he is told that now the ball is in his court. He can go home if he wishes, to the police welcome that would be awaiting him in his front yard, or he can choose to help protect Nelson Mandela. Simon knows more powerful black men have been framed on far-less convincing charges. And with him, it would not all be lies: he *did* join an anti-communist militant group; they *did* blow up a police car outside a station where many of his comrades had been tortured and killed. And although it was clear to his group that this was not an act of terrorism but of defiance, making that argument, first to the white policemen who would happily beat him to within an inch of his life, and then to a judge, would be impossible. That is if he even saw a damn judge and didn't, as many of his comrades had, jump to his death, or hang himself in a cell first. The choice, even as Simon struggles to dispute it, seems clear.

Without saying anything, someone behind him pulls the cloth bag over Simon's head and the lights are replaced with pitch darkness. From underneath his armpit, he is hoisted into the air, his feet left trailing, scuffing the ground with the tips of his shoes. For a moment he can see the hostile police welcome waiting for him back home: his belongings tossed into the street, his furniture broken, his wife and children wailing by the roadside. He imagines arriving at the exact moment when the police captain emerges from his house, with the bomb in his hands.

'Wait,' he yells into the darkness, not knowing if the man and woman are still there. 'Okay. I'll do it.'

Nothing is said in reply. Only the sound of hurried footsteps as he's dragged backwards towards the car. As they set off, all is silent momentarily until the man's voice starts up, detailing in precision, what Simon's mission is, and how he will be reporting to them from now on. Simon is quiet, only able to nod, in between the rocking of the car. The man and woman are not seeking confirmation from him. It is not important what Simon makes of the details of the operation. He has agreed and that agreement stretches out into every last detail of the plan.

The next morning, before the sun has risen fully, Simon is standing on the lane he believes they took him to the night before. He has driven up and down the main road to Rosettenvile several times, to make sure he hasn't miscalculated where the turning was. But he must have done, because there is nothing here now. Dirt fields and scraps of bushes. But last night, he remembers the car driving for a moment after the left turn, and then stopping here in front of some old factory that didn't exist. It was as if everything that happened was a dream, or something he'd made it up: to achieve what, beyond torturing himself? Getting out of his old Corolla, he looks for the tracks of other cars in the dirt, for footprints, or even the marks of a makeshift structure. But nothing. He stands there for a long while until, in the distance, he can hear the township of Soweto slowly waking up, setting about its morning routine. There are few cars on this road, only the occasional driver who knows it as a shortcut eventually disappearing, in the distance, behind a football stadium. Further off, Simon can hear the cars going to town or joining the highway. Everything about Soweto is as he remembers it, going about its business, the complex choreography of people commuting to work by bicycle, bus, or on foot.

The instructions stated Simon was to report as usual, 7am sharp, and make sure Mandela met every appointment punctually and didn't deviate from his itinerary. No sudden changes of plan, the instructions had said. It is now almost 7am and Simon is still standing by an open road in the middle of nowhere. When he eventually realises the time, he jumps into the Corolla and speeds off, kicking up dust behind him, checking one last time in the rearview mirror that there is still nothing there.

On arriving at the house, unlike most mornings, Simon skips his ritual of coffee on the veranda with the domestic staff and falls straight into watering the plants. He can hear them snickering at him. The laugh of Nodlamini, a domestic worker who has been with Mandela since he was a teenager, was a fixture in Simon's morning routine. But somehow today feels like his first day at work.

Though there are security guards at the house, Simon's eyes instinctively scan the grounds, even beyond it, timing every car that parks on the street. His fondness for Mandela had not been feigned and even though, in his heart, he cannot now be sure that it is truly for the man's safety, he feels his own vigilance can only help the situation. It is not long before Mandela emerges from his house, immaculately dressed in his familiar navy suit with brown fading stripes. Tea in hand. As soon as Nodlamini takes the empty cup from Mandela's hand and heads back inside the house, Simon steps forward, greeting him and politely enquiring about the day's itinerary. Today, Mandela will not be travelling, but having meetings in the house. Simon suggests they have it in the garden: 'The pompon tree is looking lovely at the moment,' he says, almost swallowing his tongue.

Indeed, in the afternoon, Mandela sits with his comrades around the garden table, forming a tight circle of anti-apartheid revolutionaries. Not far off, at the edge of the lawn, where the lavender trees have grown high against prying eyes, Simon prunes at some branches. His ear turned to the table, he only catches the occasional word or a splutter of laughter. Coming closer, on the pretence of inspecting an apple tree, Simon still can't hear much more than wind in the lavender trees' branches.

In the weeks that follow, Simon keeps his eyes peeled as he drives Mandela around, making a note of every street and turn, and most importantly every building. He stays up late into the night writing up the day before, recollecting every detail, unaware of whether anyone is reading them. *No obvious threat to Mandela's safety has been observed*, Simon writes. *But then I am mostly kept at bay. The subject goes into buildings then comes out again a few hours later. I sit outside.* Every morning before work, as instructed, Simon drops his report into a postbox outside his local post office. Occasionally, he watches from the corner to see who picks it up, to no avail. Then nothing. No reply, no further instructions, no requests for more detail on this or that. It is as if he had dreamt the entire mission. That is until one night, when, in his spare time, he attends a Freedom Guerilla meeting, he notices a car following him. He manages to lose it, or at least force it to follow him less obviously.

It is a few months into 1962 when things begin to rapidly shift in South African politics. There are whispers that the Swart government is after Mandela. There is an arrest warrant. After a briefing with Mandela and other comrades, Simon maps out different routes, never taking the same one more than twice a week. Everything is much more tense. Unlike before, the chats between Simon and Mandela are shortened to only a few words, then only greetings. Simon feels distrusted and his admiration for Mandela begins to drift. The routes start changing without any notice to ones Simon has had no say in. Cars are changed without notice. Now, Simon drives Mr Mandela only to local meetings, nothing adventurous, nothing out of town, nothing at night. On some days, Simon is simply told he is not needed.

He continues to type it all up each night, deliver his report, and hear nothing, even after Mandela stops coming back to the house at all. In July, Nodlamini tells Simon a second driver has been appointed as Mandela's schedule has become unusually busy. Mandela is spending all his time, he learns from the staff gossip, at the house of an English theatre director, and one day a green Ford Fairlane is seen parked outside the house, presumably the new driver's. Tired of driving all the way to Mandela's house only to sit in the car out front, Simon starts using his gardening duties as an excuse to spend more time at the back of the house so that he can spy on the street behind – a far less conspicuous route to the house. After a few days, on one such visit to the back of the house, he catches a glimpse of the green Fairlane, picking up a passenger from the side of the road. Simon scrambles to see the face of the driver who has replaced him; lean, muscular, and determined, it is unmistakable, even in the driver's uniform and cap. Mandela's new driver is himself.

Surely the Americans would be happy with Simon for solving this mystery. Having gone to ground for the last few weeks and eluded even Simon's surveillance, they had an answer. He had been moving back and forth right under their noses. As per Simon's original instructions, if another car or driver comes into play, his job is then to follow it; make excuses to go into town and report on its routes. The task is easier than Simon expected, and the domestic staff continue to give away crucial pieces of the puzzle. There is also a rumour, though it's not clear where it's come from, that the arrest warrant has been dropped.

Hearing this, according to the staff, Mandela changes plans and decides to travel to Natal to meet with Albert Luthuli. The two are to discuss the ANC's relationship with the Pan-African Congress. Recent meetings abroad with other African leaders, need to be followed up on.

Then, one quiet Sunday morning, dressed as someone else's chauffeur, Mandela and his new friend – presumably the theatre director – drive out to a farm in Rivonia, marked 'Liliesleaf' on the gatepost. From there, they then head towards Natal. As soon as the direction is clear, Simon stops at a public call box and calls his emergency contact number. He delivers the information, but on the other line, no one speaks.

The next day, as Simon makes breakfast, the radio announces that Mandela has been arrested, in Howick, while pretending to be the driver of an Englishman called Cecil Williams. His head spins. 'That's not the agreement we had!' Simon shouts unhinged at the radio. 'Why has he been arrested if the job was to keep him safe?' Simon's wife stands in the doorway hearing everything. He quickly covers himself, saying he was referring to Williams – that he is the man whose garden he has been tending. Once again he gets away with a lie. Frantically Simon types out a letter and heads to the postbox; he demands answers. This time, he doesn't wait in his car to see who might pick it up, but instead pretends to drive home, parks several streets away and returns on foot, to spy on it from further down the street. Nobody shows. He makes up all kinds of scenarios, each of them as paranoid as the next, theories that he would never share with others. Who would believe him anyway – that his CIA handlers dug a hole underneath the post office box, and snatched his reports away unseen as they dropped?

The news of Mandela's arrest spreads quickly. Simon sits in front of his house, in his car, waiting for the next news bulletin. According to what he can piece together, Mandela and Williams must have driven for hours without issue, until they reached Cedara, outside Howick, in Kwazulu-Natal. In the news reports, Sergeant Vorster is quoted as saying it was nothing but a routine traffic stop. *There was nothing routine about it,* Simon thinks. He gave Mandela up. He is a traitor. Each news bulletin repeats, again and again, how Mandela identified himself as David Motsamayi, a chauffeur working for a theatre director who was travelling to Durban for research. Sergeant Vorster had become immediately suspicious because of how well-spoken the chauffeur was. 'The curtain has been brought down on Mr

Mandela and Mr Williams' most deceitful play,' the broadcaster signed off.

When Simon hears about the charges against Mandela he can barely breathe. Mandela is accused on two counts: inciting persons to strike illegally (during the 1961 stay-at-home protest) and leaving the country without a valid passport. The sun sets at the end of the street, and Simon continues to sit in his car, watching the world outside turn around him in a frightening swirl, hoping against hope that none of this will ever be public knowledge.

## SOUTH AFRICA, 1962

# Afterword: The Arrest of Nelson Mandela

## James Sanders

NELSON MANDELA'S ARREST ON 5 August 1962 condemned the ANC revolutionary to more than 27 years of imprisonment. This would prove to be the defining experience of Mandela's life. Before 1962, Mandela was perceived by Africans to be a glamorous 44-year-old political leader; to white South Africans and the international community he was almost invisible. By the time of his release from prison in 1990, however, Mandela had become a liberation hero, a symbol of resistance, a statesman and was fast on his way to becoming the most famous person of colour in the world. From a prejudiced white South African perspective, he had mutated from being 'the native who causes all the trouble' to 'the magical negro' (to use Hollywood cosmology). But for all his ascent into the global consciousness, the betrayal that had thrown him into jail in the first place remained barely examined for decades. The only explanation offered, was a hint in the Johannesburg *Sunday Times* immediately after that arrest that Mandela had been the victim of a struggle within the South African Communist Party (SACP). Indeed in an interview with me decades later, Winnie Mandela told me that Nelson had been a secret member of the SACP since the mid-1950s and had recruited her into the Party.[1]

The magazine *New African* (November 1962) acknowledged: 'Reports stemming from a variety of places [...] have repeatedly suggested that Nelson Mandela was 'sold out' to the Special Branch by Communists.' But there was no ANC or SACP inquiry into how the leader of Umkhonto we Sizwe (the armed wing of the ANC) had been so easily captured. It was almost as if nobody really wanted to know; including, peculiarly, Mandela himself.

The years passed by and the details of Mandela's arrest became small beer following the multiple arrests of ANC revolutionaries, most significantly at Rivonia in 1963. Whispers and rumours circulated, of course, within South Africa's journalistic, police and intelligence communities. Perhaps, the most persistent story referred to Mandela's betrayal by a member of Durban's Indian community. This story seemingly emanated from Gerard Ludi, the 'super spy' who was the prime witness against SACP leader, Bram Fischer.[2]

Twenty-four years passed before the controversy of Mandela's original arrest sprung back into life. On 14 July 1986, the (Johannesburg) *Star* carried an extraordinary story on page 11. Credited to *The Star*'s Foreign News Service, 'Mandela's arrest: a tale of betrayal' revealed that 'a retired senior police officer had told *The Star* in Paris that Mandela was 'betrayed' by an American diplomat at the US Consulate in Durban – a man who was in fact the CIA operative for that region.' The true story might never have emerged had the CIA operative not attended a party at mercenary chief Mike Hoare's flat where he had bragged 'under the influence of drink' about the role he played in Mandela's arrest. The party had been attended by a number of journalists and security officials but the story did not filter out to the South African media. *The Star*'s informant claimed that the 'highly personable' American had been 'anxious to supply his government with Pretoria's Bantustan plans[3] and the information he needed was available from Colonel Bester, then head of the Natal police. In exchange for the information, he told Colonel Bester the date, time and route Mandela would be taking.' *The Star* found a second source for the story in G. H. Calpin, author of *There Are No South Africans*, who had also attended the party.

With the benefit of hindsight, it appears likely that forces within the South African security establishment had been enraged by the fact that in June 1986, the Comprehensive Anti-Apartheid Act had begun its passage through the American House of Representatives. It is certainly possible the CIA story was leaked as a warning shot across the bows of the American government. In the United States, CBS News named the diplomat as Donald Rickard. It was also noted that Rickard had been included in Julius Mader's *Who's Who in the CIA* (1968) as 'OpA … Durban'.

Nelson Mandela was finally released from prison on 11 February 1990 and by June that year he was on the verge of his first visit to the United States. The *Atlanta Journal-Constitution* announced on its front page on 10 June that 'Ex-official tells of US 'coup' to aid S. Africa'. A former CIA officer in Pretoria (Waldo Campbell) had told the newspaper that soon after Mandela's arrest, 'Paul Eckel, then a senior CIA operative, walked into his office and said approximately these words: "We have turned Mandela over to the South African security branch. We gave them every detail, what he would be wearing, the time of day, just where he would be. They have picked him up. It is one of our greatest coups".'

The article focused its attention on general CIA interference in South African politics, claiming that by 1962, a CIA 'covert branch in Johannesburg […] devoted more money and expertise to penetrating the ANC than did the fledgling intelligence service of the South African government.' Gerard Ludi told the American reporters that 'the CIA had a highly successful "deep cover" agent in the inner circle of the ANC branch in Durban.' Paul Eckel also told Waldo Campbell that the information leading to Mandela's arrest had 'come from a paid CIA informant in South Africa, who had been taught to communicate with his CIA superiors there through an elaborate series of indirect contacts, known as "cutouts".'

When Mandela was asked about the *Atlanta Journal-Constitution* story while he was visiting Bonn, he told journalists: 'Let bygones be bygones, whether they are true or not.' His wife, Winnie, interjected: 'If it is true, then I may not want to hold that same view [...] It is a matter that has caused a lot of pain and tears over the years.' The *Washington Post* added on 11 June that Donald Rickard was 'now retired and living in Colorado, he declined to comment [in 1986] and he declined again yesterday.'

In December that year, Mandela's autobiography *Long Walk to Freedom* was published and was cautious about the arrest. Mandela recalled: 'The movement had been infiltrated with informers, and even well-intentioned people were generally not as tight-lipped as they should have been. I had also been lax.' Mandela appeared more than a little concerned that somebody very close to him could have been the source of the betrayal: 'Was it an informer in Durban? Someone from Johannesburg? Someone from the movement? Or even a friend or member of the family?'

By mid-1996 I was at the School of Oriental & African Studies in London completing a PhD on how the British and American media covered South African news in the 1970s. One of my interviewees had been Anthony Sampson, the renowned author of *Anatomy of Britain*, *Observer* reporter and former editor of *Drum* magazine. It transpired that Sampson had been commissioned by HarperCollins to write an authorised biography of Mandela, and following my interview with him, he contacted me to ask whether I wanted to be the researcher on his book. Our job as Anthony put it was 'to squeeze blood out of a stone'. *Long Walk to Freedom* had been one of the best-selling political autobiographies in history: the sort of book that is on everyone's shelf. I was tasked with discovering documents, solving historical mysteries and ascertaining whether Mandela outwitted and double-crossed other ANC politicians during his rise to power. It was an exciting research project – perhaps, the top South African research gig of the decade. With Mandela now the first black President of South Africa, I was given carte blanche to access official government papers and ask questions of anyone who would answer. In the process, perhaps my greatest research coup was to discover the whereabouts of Mandela's prison files, previously believed lost or destroyed. It was a heady time.

In our many interactions with Mandela himself, it was apparent that a number of subjects were of no interest to him. Mandela would often comment on the manuscript as a work in progress but he certainly did not express any interest in ascertaining the truth about his arrest. Having read the newspaper reports, we knew that former CIA official Donald Rickard had been reported as the likely candidate. In 1997, while in New York City, I managed to obtain a telephone number for Rickard in Pagosa Springs, Colorado. I phoned him up and laid out the nature of my research for the authorised biography. Rickard certainly played his cards close to his chest and told me that we would be 'making a mistake' if we named him 'as the man who shopped Mandela'. At the time it seemed to be a dead end. In the authorised biography, Anthony Sampson concluded that the claim was 'credible … [but] cannot be substantiated.'

Almost a decade later, in 2005, I picked up the story again – I was writing the first history of the South African intelligence services and tracking the numerous intelligence loose ends. I told the Donald Rickard story in all the detail that had been gathered up to that point. While acknowledging that Mandela had undoubtedly been 'reckless' with his own security, my conclusion laid slightly more emphasis on the CIA angle. I noted that I had been told repeatedly that 'Hendrik van den Bergh, a senior security policeman in 1962, who would later become the head of South African intelligence, privately admitted that Mandela was 'given' to the Security Police by the CIA.'

However it wasn't until after Mandela's death in 2013, that the story really caught fire. In early 2014, I was hired by a film production company to investigate the 1962 betrayal. Director John Irvin's film was to be titled 'Mandela's Gun' and would address the ANC's turn to violence. I asked for three weeks' research budget and made plans to visit both South Africa and the United States.

In South Africa I picked up faint traces of Donald Rickard's posting 50 years earlier. I spent many futile hours trying to trace his former secretary and I began to understand the peculiar CIA culture whereby so many CIA officials of the 1950s and 1960s were the children of missionaries. I was surprised that a number of South Africans appeared genuinely concerned that new research might implicate the CIA. I was also told that Hillary Clinton, who often visited South Africa, had been asked by people close to Mandela to request information from the CIA on the Mandela arrest and received the passive-aggressive response: 'You don't want to know.'

In the US, former agency officials were keen to explain that CIA knowledge of South Africa was minimal in the 1960s: 'We were sent down there to try and be nice.' Paul Eckel was described as old and working out his post, his glory days having been in the 1950s. Donald Rickard was perceived as a fantasist and a fool who had made himself the laughing stock of the agency when he submitted the manuscript of a play whose central character was a compulsive masturbator to the CIA Publications Board. Former intelligence officers appeared to believe that Rickard was not capable of engineering Mandela's arrest. One former CIA employee told me that 'there was absolutely no corroborative evidence to support the theory' of CIA involvement in Mandela's arrest: 'As they say here in the States, that dog won't hunt.'

Having concluded my research in Virginia I flew to Denver and set out on the six-hour drive over treacherous snow-clad mountains to Pagosa Springs. I had hoped to doorstep Rickard but in a semi-blizzard this proved impossible. I eventually telephoned him and he asked me to put all my questions in an email. When I called him back there was no answer. In New

York, before returning to the UK, I telephoned Rickard again. He told me that he wanted to help and offered to send clippings and documents. He then asked: 'How is Mike Hoare?' I told him that Mike Hoare was believed to be senile – he certainly had not been quoted in a South African newspaper for decades. I then zeroed in on the key question: 'Did you ever meet Nelson Mandela?' Rickard replied with a startling answer: 'No, and I didn't want to meet him. Mandela was the most dangerous communist outside of the Soviet Union.' Somewhat stunned by this answer I think I laughed which probably wasn't the correct response. A month later, I telephoned Rickard again and he told me that he wasn't willing to talk any further because I had put things into the public domain. I asked how I had done that and he replied that I had sent him an email. Exhausted and irritated by this feeble excuse, I concluded that Donald Rickard was a paranoid 1940s cold warrior.

In retrospect, I had the bulk of the story in February 2014: Rickard's obsessive anti-communism, his fascination with Mandela and his close friendship with the mercenary Mike Hoare. What I was missing was the actual confession. I reported back to John Irvin that Don Rickard could have had some foreknowledge of Mandela's arrest in 1962 but that I believed he had magnified his role.

Two years later, John Irvin and his producer, Claire Evans, rehired me; they were still editing *Mandela's Gun* and they required a 'headline' for the film and wanted to have another stab at the Donald Rickard story. I told them that there were no guarantees but if they could afford a trip to Pagosa Springs, Colorado it was conceivable that they might catch Rickard in a talkative mood. A few weeks later we drove into Pagosa Springs, now no longer in a blizzard. I had confided in Claire Evans that I was concerned that I was the problem with Rickard and that it might be an idea for Claire to visit Rickard's house, knock on the door and see what happened. This ploy worked like a dream – the first thing that Rickard said to Evans was 'You're not here with that James Sanders? I don't like him, he writes nasty things about my friends.' By suppressing my ego, I learned a crucial lesson – sometimes it is right to get off the pitch if it ensures that your team secures victory. Rickard's confession was conclusive.

The next day, Evans returned with John Irvin and recorded Rickard's memories on their phones. It was a startling story sealed in a time warp of militant anti-communism. Rickard said that '[Mandela was] completely under the control of the Soviet Union, a toy of the communists'. He believed that 'Natal was a cauldron at the time and Mandela would have welcomed a war … We were teetering on the brink here and it had to be stopped, which meant Mandela had to be stopped. And I put a stop to it.' When Rickard was questioned about Mandela's reputation as the saviour of South Africa, he replied: '[Mandela] described himself as being a democrat but he was lying, of course. He prided himself on being a communist.' Rickard had a lot more to say about Indian spies in the ANC and his great friendship with mercenary 'Mad' Mike Hoare.

A few days after we left Pagosa Springs, Donald Rickard died – he was 88 years old. Despite winning prizes in film festival competitions, *Mandela's Gun* has never received a cinema or Netflix release. I do not have a copy of the recordings of the Donald Rickard interviews. The Mandela family, understandably, protested about the behaviour of the CIA fifty-six years previously. Intriguingly, the CIA neither responded to the global story – republished or précised in literally hundreds of newspapers or broadcasts – nor acted against the writers who promoted the scoop.

Perhaps the oddest element of the story was the least known or understood: the relationship between Donald Rickard and Mike Hoare. The inscriptions and forewords in the republished Hoare books show a bond between the two that verged on 'bromance'. The dedication in Mike Hoare's *The Road To Kalamata* (republished 2008) reads: 'To my great American hero, Donald C. Rickard'. Privately, Hoare had always acknowledged his debt to Rickard. In June 1968, in London, Mike Hoare wrote in Rickard's copy of *Congo Mercenary*: 'To my good friend Don Rickard who taught me many things, including the meaning of Service with Humility.' The role, if any, that Mike Hoare played in the betrayal of Mandela remains a complete mystery.

## Notes

1. Winnie Mandela confided this in 2014 while the author was working with Barbara Jones on a proposal for a 'Winnie in her own words' autobiography. The proposal was unanimously rejected by publishers in the US and UK.
2. In brief: this unfounded rumour was that G. R. Naidoo, a famous *Drum* photographer, had been the informant. Most anti-apartheid campaigners took great offence at this suggestion, perceiving it to be a cynical attempt by the South African security police to sow division between South Africa's African and Indian communities.
3. The 'Bantustan Plans' were the South African government's secret plans to create independent homelands, and eventually independent states correlating to South Africa's many ethnic African communities. This was known as 'grand apartheid' and was designed to strip Africans of their South African citizenship.

# Conditions

## Paige Cooper

UNFORTUNATELY, HER FATHER'S INCOME could not sustain the private inpatient programme fees, and three days before Joy's fourteenth birthday he drove to the Institute and extracted her stepmother from treatment. Joy rushed home from school to greet her, but arrived into a dim, fetid silence. Her father waved her away from the back bedroom, as if from a mess he didn't want her to clear: 'She needs to recover herself. She'll perk up tomorrow.' Joy was left once more to construct their two tomato sandwiches. She made a third, but it was returned defaced. When her father retired to his desk for the evening, Joy crept to her parents' bedroom. Her stepmother's face was swollen and ancient. Her soft body rustled in its gown. She opened her eyes to glint at Joy, then closed them against her.

In class the next day, Joy turned in her seat to address her sole friend, a rashy girl with an affected accent: 'My mother is feeling much better. I'm afraid I must rescind your invitation to the Beatty lecture on Thursday. I suppose,' Joy added, as the girl's face crumpled, 'If you could get your own ticket we might still sit together.'

She said this, though they both knew that to get hold of a ticket at this point was impossible. The lecturer would be Julian

Huxley – the lesser Huxley, in Joy's estimation – speaking on 'The Possibilities of the Mind,' that is, psychosocial evolution. Months and months ago her stepmother had tapped some secret reserve of social or financial capital and procured three seats in the main auditorium. Her father had wrinkled his forehead and suggested that perhaps a dancing party with her schoolmates at a neighbourhood restaurant might be a more charming way to celebrate, but they'd ignored him.

It was late October, and snowflakes were helplessly erasing themselves in the street's black varnish of dead leaves. In the auditorium's foyer, men wore suits and women wore gloves and stoles, as if they'd come for the opera, or at least a ballet. Even the academics had polished up their hornrims. Joy wore her usual dismal twin-set, and her father his quotidian suit, but, for her stepmother, Joy had selected their favourite dress. Its red silk gleamed like a jewel in a fallen state's national museum; it seasoned her stepmother's disturbing foreignness with the salt of aristocratic tragedy; it had the authority to translate her illegible history of regimes and camps, the suspicious qualifications from a university that no longer existed in a city with four unpronounceable names, into a seductive allegory – the kind that equated beauty with intelligence and with goodness. Joy held her stepmother's plump, cool hand as they found their seats. Her former friend did not appear.

The lesser Huxley, supreme in his role as chief populariser of progressive science in the Commonwealth, spent some time explaining his preferred angle on evolution: much about rocks, rocks in space, and then the relative, subjective attractiveness, to man, of flowers pollinated by bees versus those pollinated by carrion-feeding flies. Joy was leaning so far forward off her chair that her bare knees hovered inches above the hardwood. Huxley didn't much look down at his notes; he was an agile and convincing speaker. 'One thing is certain,' he was saying in his crisp, landed way, 'the well-integrated personality is the highest product of evolution. But we are beginning to realise that even the most fortunate people are living' – his voice dropped, gravely – '*far* below capacity.'

In future years, neither Joy nor her father would recall the crux of the lecture. For her part, Joy's primary memory of the evening would be the moment when her stepmother rose from her seat and stood, solitary as an assassin, in the auditorium's field of tipped faces. There she paused, picking at her chewed-off lipstick with her chewed-off fingernails. An alarmed throat was cleared somewhere behind them. Huxley continued his oration. The ruby dress had, truthfully, become quite tight, the overtaxed zipper stymied below a pink blob of armpit. Joy had applied her eyeliner for her, her blush, her undergarments; she'd washed, brushed and set her hair. She'd buckled her stepmother's pumps, then, when the woman froze like a fawn, unbuckled them and replaced them with a pair of patent-leather flats.

'What's wrong?' Joy whispered.

'Dorota!' Joy's father hissed. 'Sit down!'

Instead, Dorota started sideways down the row, shuffling across laps, provoking sounds of outraged disgust. Joy caught the sweet, ammoniac smell. But it wasn't until Dorota reached the broad aisle – Huxley continuing on, lost to the thrill of his own ideas – that Joy saw the quick drip, the long-running rivulet under the seats, and how her stepmother's dress clung hot to the back of her, the red silk soaked black.

When Joy meets the Chief – which she must, at some point, as he has piloted the Institute since its inception two decades ago, and it is widely known he is the hands-on type – she plans to say something memorable. Joy is twenty-one and it will be necessary to distinguish herself from the many toothy young women in the place; other typists, but also nurses, occupational therapists, roaming day patients clutching their papers and purses, and, settled deep in their wards and private rooms, the inpatients.

The Institute is both smaller and more crowded than she'd imagined as a girl, when she knew it only by its façade as she waited outside for her father. She'd loiter on the portico, examining the plaited flora carved into the tall, heavy doors, or winching her head back to admire the snarling hound with the long tongue mortared into the masonry above them. Whenever they heaved open, expelling yet another man in a suit, she'd spider back into her cranny between the limestone columns and watch the man march importantly down the steep, sunny drive.

Joy still admires the hound: its viciousness is both galvanic and tranquilising. She has hopes that the hound, when it chooses, will choose her. Above it, the word that the shipping magnate who built the mansion chose as some sort of motto, maybe, or prayer: *Spero!*

'That's Latin for "better dead than red",'[2] her father had explained.

'No, it's not,' said Joy.

'No, it's not,' he agreed.

'Can I come in and see her?'

'Next time,' he said, as always. 'Look at the view.'

Joy was uninterested in the view: the city, then the river, then one or two doddering mountains rising like boils on the horizon. Instead, if her father was taking too long in his visit, she would circumnavigate east around the ivy to visit another limestone animal head, this one a horse. The bust of some calm, anonymous equine, no particular name to it, jutting over the wide stable doors. Placid as the cases who now take their treatment there, in the Behaviour Lab, tended by the Chief, his chosen acolytes, and a battalion of the proudest nurses, all of whom he calls, Joy has been told, *lassie*.

When Joy meets him, she'll start with the obvious: 'Such an honour to meet you, Doctor.' And then, to catch his interest, she'll add, 'I feel I've known you since I was a little girl.' She imagines this exchange will happen as the Chief pauses to comment on the author of her book – perhaps in the autumn warmth of the unkempt public garden behind the Behaviour Lab where she spends her lunch break perched, spine stiff, rereading *Brave New World* with the title faced prominently out.

Following the Huxley – which is, frankly, a bit transparent as far as the sexual liberation aspect is concerned – she picks through the new Burgess. The Chief's taste in science fiction is well known, as is his appetite for new cars and scientific instruments. The man has an eye for the future. It's also known that, if his professional calendar allows it, which it almost never does, he takes his lunch in this garden, alone. However, the afternoons have begun to chill and the mountain's foliage is firing up and it is inevitable that Joy will soon become sociable with the other young ladies of the typing pool.

Returning to her typewriter, she passes under the hound, as she does twice, four, eight times a day, though the Institute has many doors and none of them are ever locked – the Chief's attitude being that in a modern psychiatric facility there is no place for medievalism, every patient must be a free and fervent worker in the war for his cure and is therefore welcome to quit if matters don't suit him. The hound reminds Joy of her stepmother; she never misses a chance to be reminded.

She clips up through the vestibule and past the reception desk, up to the second floor, where the entire typing pool is stacked into half of what once might have been a child's bedroom. The shipping magnate's ghost has been stripped from the Institute's interior: plaster for plastic, hardwood for linoleum, shimmering chandeliers for fluorescents that can find any fault. Every door is unlocked but every door is a blast door, heavy and resistant as a submarine dragged up to drydock. Joy passes research psychiatrists, residents, clinicians – first-class minds from New York and Europe, Latin America and the Far East, representing every new field in psychiatry – making their advances in converted cupboards, sharing tables in any spare metre of corridor. The EEG lab is in the kitchen in the basement; the electroshock room with its hot reek was formerly a pantry. Through the servant's stairwell one can access the new wing, which has a room for each patient, a beauty parlour, a snack bar, plus a common area where the art therapists keep potted plants and parakeets. The library remains a library, though, and there is a modern little café where everyone – doctors, visitors, patients, administrators – has equal access to croissants and allongés.

Joy's contribution to the Institute is administrative correspondence. Even with her diploma, and two years typing for the cardiology department at the Royal Victoria, she must start on the bottom rung. She is the newest of six. Because the other half of the former bedroom belongs to Doctors Roper and Tan, it is not permissible to speak. If speaking must be done, it is to happen in a whisper in the corridor. Seated at her typewriter, Joy clatters through hours of sniffling, little coughs, and the intermittent cannonfire of the unlockable wrist-breaker doors. She types, edits, and posts unpaid invoices and reminders of unpaid invoices – first, second, third, twelfth – to the families of former and current patients. *Dear Mr. and Mrs. Thom Ellis; Dear Mr. and Mrs. Gerald Domanski; Dear Mr. and Mrs. Stanley Hyman.* They come from everywhere: Halifax, Winnipeg, Medicine Hat. The amounts, at first, are astonishing. No province's health insurance will provide for a stay in a mental hospital. Most of the doctors take on private patients to supplement their earnings, and Joy types those bills, as well. She resents executing work on behalf of the bookkeeper. Her skill is transcription; charts, dictation, deciphering bedside notes. She is meant to earn the loyalty of a doctor, an ambitious one like Tan, become his preferred typist, then his personal secretary – rise with him in his career. But her real fantasy, the one she lingers on, is usurping the woman who sits outside the Chief's office. The Chief's office is on the third floor, where she has never been. This fantasy is unspeakable, of course. As autumn settles itself, she eats where the other typists eat, smiles when the other typists smile. The typing pool, along with some of the lower-ranking secretaries, eat each other's baking according to an elaborate hierarchy of skill and obligation. When Joy senses her time has come, she buys jam cookies off the shelf.

When she meets the Chief – which will happen any day now, she makes all sorts of excuses to linger in corridors and stairwells – she'll skip the coyness. She'll launch in: 'My mother was a patient of yours.' Will the famous man remember? One of his innumerable dozy schizophrenics. Nervous, paranoid, hostile, withdrawn. A neurasthenic, frostbitten Slav, remarkable, perhaps, for her own training as a neurologist. He'd treated her personally. That the Chief himself treats patients in the midst of his teeming brew of administrative and professorial duties, his papers in world-class journals, his speeches in New York and London, not to mention his chairmanship of the international associations he's founded, must be evidence of something. A potent, world-changing species of genius, broad and humane in his care for all the lives he's altered. Perhaps the Chief will raise his eyebrows: 'You don't say! What a coincidence!' Or perhaps: 'Of course, the lovely lady doctor. Please convey my warmest regards.' Or perhaps his countenance will darken, he'll grimace: 'Doctor Winning. What a tragedy that one was. You must regret it terribly, what happened to her. If only I'd been allowed to finish the treatment. What a godforsaken waste.'

In accordance with his quarterly schedule, Joy's father invites her and Francis for dinner. It is a windy, trumpeting blue Friday, the last of its kind for the year, and if Joy had her way she'd walk there straight from work. But her father despises tardiness, and Francis will be waiting with his fat little heart in his eyes, and so after cinching her coat, descending the stairwell lingeringly, and sending a last glance up at the hound, she trots down the steep drive and boards a westbound bus.

It's rush hour, but the bus is empty. Even so, the man who gets on at the next stop walks half the length of the aisle towards her. Hawk nose, silvering crewcut. Broad brawler shoulders but an officer's posture. He sits down beside her, shakes out the *Gazette*, then refolds it elaborately. She flushes. His hat hangs on his outer knee. No overcoat, as if he's mistaken, as if he's not actually going anywhere. He smells clean, professionally hygienic, like 6am in early June, like the woman who launders him isn't distracted by too many other duties. Joys inhales.

The bus labours across the mountain's flank, under the ramparts of the General Hospital, up Côte-des-Neiges, and then into the still, shadowed luxe of Westmount. Joy pretends to gaze at the blood-gold leaves on the maples in the light's syrup, but she's really taking in the bare, square knuckles. The lean soldierly quadricep. He jiggles his knee as if impatient for his paper to reach its purpose. His suit is neither grey nor blue.

He's settled on the page with the columns of numbers: New York's stock prices faced up, Montreal's folded beneath, not worth reading. Joy regards, from the strained corner of her eye, the inset ad for Ogilvy's: a pair of slender wraiths in bombastic fur hats and black coats of immense volume. *THE IMPERIAL RUSSIAN LOOK: Furred and fitted and madly romantic.*

'Now, you have to wonder who would let his wife dress in that get-up,' the man says.

'Pardon me?' says Joy.

He angles the page with the ad at her. 'People like to think that's what's going on over there. Soviets reading poetry and playing chess in fur coats. Black caviar and champagne. More like they tie a rag on a foot and call it a boot.'

Joy blinks. 'They sent the first woman into space three months ago.'

He chuckles. 'Don't forget the first dog.'

'Pardon me,' Joy says, again.

'You look like a smart girl.' The man appraises her with a sparkling eye. That swampy accent; plainly an American. 'Do you believe everything you read?'

'This is my stop,' says Joy. 'Pardon me.'

He snorts, and swings himself neatly up, but not back, so that she must duck under his armpit to escape. She slinks up the lurching aisle. The driver startles when he sees her. The vehicle brakes. Over the handrail, Joy glances back at the American. He winks.

Damp, heated, furious, she clatters down to the sidewalk and blows yards by Francis, who squawks, loudly, 'Sweetheart!'

The bus pulls past with a warm sweep of air. The American must see this: her potbellied, loyal husband huffing after her. Francis and his junior-high education, his new, half-fledged business servicing suburban construction sites on the south shore.

'Oh!' Joy turns and lifts her glove to brush back her hair, as if she'd overlooked him. She's near blind with rage. She chirps, 'Look who it is.'

'I thought you'd like it if I met you.'

'I thought we said we'd meet at Daddy's.'

'I know you said that,' said Francis. 'Don't get cross at me.'

She tucks her chin so Francis can kiss the point of her nose. She takes his arm. The syrup light is dissolving, leaving the evening grim and gelid, like a failed aspic. Francis tells all about his day, then makes a few sighs of envy regarding the stateliness and quietude of the neighbourhood.

'If I lived in that one I'd wake up whistling every day,' says Francis, nodding at his favourite manse. He was raised downhill near the river, on a street in Point Saint Charles which he refers to as Scumbum Avenue. Joy hums wordlessly back. She is arranging her mind as if she is walking alone, as if she is sleep-walking.

At the grand corner house they climb the pitted steps, then descend around the shrubs to the small door of the basement apartment. 'The help's hovel,' her father called it, ever since they moved in. He greets them with his collar buttoned to the throat but cravat-less, his frame slighter than ever, his white hair wisped into a backwards-leaning pouf. He resembles – has always resembled, to his perpetual fury – a small, expensive dog.

'Well, well,' he says, pressing his cheek aridly to Joy's, shaking Francis' hand, 'Well, well, come in, dinner's on. Can you smell it?'

'Smells very fine,' says Francis, putting on his fancy elocution and patting his own tummy. Physically he is not, Joy has to admit, a dissimilar breed; short-legged, short-sighted. When she'd first brought him home, her father's interrogation had been brief. What did he read? Oh, this and that. The end.

'I had the girl make a roast,' her father announces, hovering.

Joy folds Francis' coat onto the sofa's arm; the closet is hopeless, the door won't even latch closed. 'She was quite resistant about it, it being Friday. Noodle, I was hoping you'd take over with the gravy. Apparently it's quite complicated.'

Joy steps into the slack, decrepit holes of her stepmother's old house slippers and follows her father into the kitchen. She surveys the situation – ill-kept, oily, any possibility of hygiene dissolving under the lightest glance, since the only girl her father could hire to help comes cheap and knows it – and does her best to further the cause of dinner without disturbing the kitchen's underlying sedimentary layers. She prefers to never see this place in daylight, when the zoo of disorganised thought is exposed by rogue drabs of sun. She would rather remain planted in the dining room, which is the least vexing room in the place, the rest of which she has not seen since she married Francis. It's always cold; in a few weeks the retired banker upstairs will turn off the heat and remove himself and his wife and their remaining son to the Côte d'Azur.

Joy pulls the cast iron pot out of the oven – a scalding wash – and heaves it onto the stovetop with a thud. On the shelves and in the cabinets, porcelain and glass clink warningly. Joy's father uncorks the whisky.

'How is Dorota?' Francis accepts his ration. 'I hope she's up to joining us?'

'Unlikely,' says Joy's father.

'Bad week?' says Francis.

Her father snorts. 'She hasn't spoken in days. There's no reasoning with her. It's endless. The last time it was a month without a word.'

'Are these... leeks?' Joy asks, poking at the pot's contents with a fork.

'I truly have no idea what they might be,' says her father, without looking. He tips the rim of his glass to Francis' and they remove themselves to the hearth. The two of them will be immediately drunk, then sober up over dinner as they reprise their single shared topic: radio. Francis reminiscing again about the shortwave he once rewired as a boy, her father polishing his angle on the dire cultural ramifications of the medium's corruption. Then they'll be drunk enough again that Francis will insist she call a taxi home, which will sadly diminish the store of cash she's been squirrelling away for a trip to Ogilvy's. Joy opens every cupboard in search of cornstarch. Eventually, she spots the fresh tin perched on top of the breadbox, a saving grace courtesy of the resentful *fille*.

When Joy finally achieves her place in the dining room, the various stages of the meal laid out, her father is quoting Orwell: 'Even when they're telling the truth they're lying.'

Francis nods and inserts a plug of tender beef into his mouth. 'Oh, excellent, very good.'

'– not so much a broadcast as an inculcation,' her father continues. 'Repeat something often enough and people lose the imaginative capacity to conceive of a different –' he swirls his hand '– *mode*, let alone outcome. Look at Soviet cultural education – my wife, even now, in her current condition, walks out of the room when she hears Tchaikovsky. Just try to stop her. They call it a radio, but it's a loudspeaker. Forced. *Zwangsradio* in German; in Russian I don't know the word –'

'*Tarelka*,' Joy murmurs. 'Because it looks like a plate.'

'Very fine, Noodle,' says her father. 'And I should say: what a nice gravy.'

Francis perks up, detecting a pause: 'Well, in fact, the two directions, having both, now that's the most difficult part of the wiring –'

Joy folds her napkin to show its pure side. 'Just because,' – she raises her voice and Francis hushes – 'Just because a technique has been used wrongly doesn't mean it is a wrong technique. For instance, a loudspeaker repeating the right phrase for a few months can save a person years wallowing in Freudian analysis. Of course, you have to have the training to home in on the correct words, but –'

'Ah, of course!' Her father sneers. 'The *correct* words! If only someone had –'

On the other side of the door, the kitchen convulses. The sound of a coal mine collapsing, a munitions ship catching fire and exploding, compartment by compartment, torpedo after torpedo. All three of them turn at the eruption, which is trailing after itself in smaller smashes now, even as Joy rises, and pulls open the door.

Dorota stands, barefoot, beached on a murderous reef of fallen crockery. Shattered crystal. A snake's spine of broken bowls shot in their stack across the floor. Her mane is brassy and tangled, her nightdress stained, her shins bruised and scaled. She clutches a floral teacup; the rest of the tea service has fallen to smash in the sink. The kettle rattles on its burner, building its shriek.

Dorota twists to face Joy. The ill, thin skin around her pink, lab-mouse eyes. 'Who let you in?'

'Mama,' says Joy. She shuffles forward into the shards wearing Dorota's slippers herself, her hand outstretched. 'Don't move. You'll cut your feet.'

Dorota pitches her teacup at the floor.

Shards fly and nick Joy's ankles. She is still wearing Dorota's slippers.

'What a stupid, ugly, selfish girl you are,' Dorota says. She steps carelessly forward, then back, around, and finally crunches bloodily away, back into the rank warren of the basement apartment. 'A stupid, ugly, selfish girl.'

It's long past midnight by the time Joy and Francis arrive home to their little apartment on Esplanade. Francis pours milk into a tall glass, right up to the brim. The meniscus trembles as he lifts it to his lips. He pats Joy's haunch as she peels out of her stockings. Together, they fold down the coverlets and climb each into their own side of the little bed. Joy leans over and sets the timer, the tape, flicks the switch.

'*Utro vechera mudreneya*,' says the speaker as Joy adjusts the volume.

'The morning is wiser than the evening,' Joy repeats back.

'Jesus have mercy,' says Francis. 'Can't we have one night without the sleep lady?'

'Consistency is important to the hypnopaedic process,' Joy says. Verbatim from the instruction manual.

'It didn't much help your stepmother,' says Francis.

Joy reaches under the covers to a delicate fold of belly, and pinches it with all her dactylic viciousness.

'Don't!' Francis cries.

'Don't,' Joy agrees.

The cat jumps onto the mattress and, purring, walks directly into Francis' arms. 'I just can't see the point of learning, what is it – Portuguese?' he says. 'When are you going to use it?'

'It's good stimulation for the brain fibre,' says Joy.

'Wife, if you're trying to psychologise me into taking you on holiday, I'm onto you.'

Joy shushes him, and he nuzzles pointedly into her. She allows it.

'When I leave,' she murmurs, mouth on his ear, 'I'll go alone and leave you here to cry all by yourself.'

Francis moans his encouragement. His cat leaves, disgusted.

'*Kakda byut bigi; kakda dayut biri,*' the speaker advises.

'When they beat you, run,' Joy repeats. 'When they give, take.'

In late November, word trickles down that the Chief has in mind another paper – he is already at work on one about factors in memory disturbance, and one about the Institute's successes with his de-patterning technique on schizophrenics – which will presumably be published in *Psychiatric Quarterly* or the *British Journal of Psychiatry* or *Comprehensive Psychiatry* or some other prestigious journal. Within a week, the Chief's secretary appears in the door. The typists look up, the clattering slows but doesn't stop. Joy is on her feet before the woman has so much as crooked a finger.

'No shortcuts, no mistakes,' the secretary says in the stairwell. She's not five years older than Joy, barely any taller or prettier. Neither has she offered her name. 'You have no idea how close he is to a Nobel.'

In a dry sub-basement the secretary selects archived audio tapes in accordance with a handwritten list. The Chief is in the habit of recording all of his patient sessions, all of his notes, and these tapes are catalogued, labelled, and stored with the rest of the Institute's files. There is a system of sliding steel shelves in which it is easy to imagine a person being overlooked and crushed – the secretary's hand spinning the silent wheel, gliding thousands of kilos along like a passing hull. A thriving population of cannibalistic centipedes spill between the boxes. The Chief's secretary flicks away the more hostile specimens. Joy steals glimpses of the list: written, it seems, in the Chief's own hand.

Eagerly, Joy lugs her box of tapes upstairs and commandeers one of the Institute's three dictaphone rooms. Transcription is laborious, monotonous – fifteen seconds backward for every three forward – but she sets about it with relief. The past-due notices to the families of patients have become depressing. Asking for three hundred dollars from a household a block down from Francis' mother in Point Saint Charles; one might as well ask for three million. Transcribing this box alone could take a month or three. Half-eaten centipedes fall out of the tapes as she transfers them into the playback apparatus.

The patients' voices are soft and whining. The Chief's is alert, smooth, brusque, highland frills shorn down by his transatlantic tenure. After each session, he relays his verbal notes to the tape, and Joy transcribes those, as well. She pictures him in his glasses and shirtsleeves, leaning back behind his desk, speaking into the microphone, alone in his office up on the third floor, squinting with a furrowed brow out the mullioned windows. Neither does he care about the view. Most of the patients are schizophrenics, though they don't know it at first. They think they suffer from more predictable complaints: melancholy, nerves, depression, hypertension, anxiety, phantom pains, despair, asthma, domestic stress, hostility, low libido, postpartum lassitude, a sore leg, tremors. Most of them have seen several specialists already. Most of them were considered hopeless before they arrived here.

To himself and the tape recorder, the Chief relays their course of treatment: de-patterning via thrice-daily Page-Russell electroshocks; partial sensory isolation; chemical sleep; psychic driving, negative and positive. The prescribed medications require Joy to pause, repeatedly, and look up spelling: curare, sodium pentothal, desoxyn, LSD. Largactil as required. In cases of poor response: sodium amytal, nitrous oxide, psilocybin, mescaline, PCP.

Each audio tape bears a single date, and it can take some searching on Joy's part to find the indicated session with the indicated patient, cross-referenced by bed number. Joy rolls back and forth through each day, zeroing in on her target, but also she lingers, sometimes, listening. Patients confess their secrets, describe their childhoods, weep. Sometimes, they don't believe the treatment is necessary, or helping. Sometimes they revolt with appalling immaturity and vileness. The Chief chides them gently or firmly. They apologise, they're ashamed of themselves. She ought to be so much better than she is. She is a child, an idiot child. Everyone knows that I am a stupid, ugly, selfish girl.

Joy's fingers pause on the keys. She's three weeks into the task. She halts the tape. Checks its date.

The Chief goes on, 'What did you mean when you said that, do you think?'

'I said that?'

'It's your tape. You said it to me ten days ago. I thought it was interesting. Do you think it's interesting?'

'I don't know why I would say that.'

'Perhaps you believe it, deep down.'

'I did not specialise in neurosis, I specialised in surgery. In Lvov my father was a physician. His father was a physician.'

'Do you know the date today?'

Silence.

'No? What about the president in America?'

'Is this America? I think this is Montreal.'

'How old are you?'

'I was 26 when I graduated. I would have been 25, but the war.' Then she says, quietly: 'I don't understand. Tell me what is wrong with me that you are speaking to me like this.'

A click, and then Dorota's voice, fuzzy and faint, doubly recorded, starts again: 'I am a stupid, ugly, and selfish girl. Why should I have lived? I am a stupid, ugly, and selfish girl. Why should –'

The voice repeats itself, over and over, even as Dorota protests, 'Please turn it off. Please stop.'

'Mrs Winning,' says the Chief, 'you are suffering from a completely treatable condition.' His tone is expansive, general. 'Fortunately, as you know, this is our precise area of expertise. You're sitting in one of the world's foremost psychiatric facilities. Do you remember why you came here?'

Silence.

'You came to ask me for a fellowship, based on how you described your education abroad. But it was evident to me, and the other doctors here, that what you needed was treatment.'

'Treatment for what?'

Her voice starts again, tinny and faint: 'Why should I have lived?'

Joy's hands have ceased their typing. She starts again, but forgets to roll back the tape. She continues on at what she imagines is her usual cadence. Alone in the dictaphone room, she moves her fingers appropriately over the keys, catching fewer and fewer words. She doesn't pause for spelling or punctuation. She types half-phrases, starts one word, moves on to the next without finishing it.

The tape clicks twice; the Chief's post-session notes. His tone is clipped: 'De-patterning hasn't quite reached second stage after ten days. Retains languages, but current home life is nearly erased. Sense of place and time is blurring nicely. Patient remains morbidly negative. Inappropriate affect – she laughed when I asked her whether she agreed with my diagnosis of schizophrenia – and further evidence of paranoia: she continues to tell the nurses that she did not consent to the shocks and does not want them. Intractably fixated on her ability to practice medicine. Ten additional days de-patterning at least, probably twenty, and as far as –'

Joy removes her headphones, stands, smooths her skirt. She steps out into the corridor.

At the reception desk, one of the assistants to the Chief – Rubenstein, Roper, or maybe Cleghorn, they all look the same in their suits and weekly haircuts – is hissing a venomous stream of reproaches at the receptionist on duty. His shaven throat is pink and flexing, straining up out of his Windsor knot. He's got his claws set on the desk, looks set to leap over it and dig his thumbs into her eye sockets. The receptionist's face is neutral. She gazes past him at the wall.

Joy passes with her eyes averted. At the end of the corridor there is a fire door, and then a stairwell, and another fire door. The doors to the sleep ward are painted bridal-gown ivory, though the years have left dark scratches which reveal wartime steel, the kind meant to shield a people from their enemies. Joy heaves through door after heavy door until she reaches the ward.

The humid air smells of mouths. Every bed is identical. Beside each one, a tape machine spins. Joy is the only person on her feet in the dim, warm cavern. Everyone is asleep, swimming in their cocktails. The nurse's station is deserted. There is a low hum of voices, as if a conference is taking place around a corner, in an office; expert men conferring genially.

Halfway down the aisle, Joy reaches Bed 17. The woman in it is not her stepmother. It's been seven years since her stepmother lay in this bed. Yet she looks waterlogged, slicked down, wizened like a baby rat, and she has the same sweet, mephitic fug. Bed 17 murmurs something, but when Joy leans down to listen it's clear the voice is from a speaker under the pillow. It purrs: 'People like Margaret. They like her because she is warm, friendly, and affectionate. Margaret is beginning to reach out to people with more and more confidence.' And then it repeats: 'People like Margaret. They like –'

The speaker at the neighbouring bed is murmuring: 'Walter is happy and contented. Walter thinks of things the same as his neighbours do. Walter gets along with people and is warm and friendly with them.'

Across the aisle, Bed 14: 'You are sure and confident of yourself. You are at ease with your husband.'

Bed 12: 'The thing is, nice, normal people want nothing to do with you. Once they get to know you, they just don't like you.'

And then: 'You've always put yourself before everyone else. Ever since you were a little child you've been ungrateful.'

And then: 'You killed your mother. You killed your mother. You killed your mother. You killed your mother. You killed your mother.'

The Chief's office is on the third floor. Her palm sticks on the banister's polish as she mounts the wooden steps in the shipping magnate's stairwell. The old glass warps the view, wavers the exhausted daylight. Down in the river, a cargo ship slides along behind the office towers.

The third floor is empty but not silent. Demure clattering. A whiff of hearty conversation. Dainty carved doors, gleaming hardwood. Glass tulips set into the panelling emit a feeble sepia. Every wainscoting fingerprint, every swipe of dust on the benighted portraits made obvious by the white winter sun.

To get to him, she will need to maneuver past that nameless secretary – a woman accustomed to triaging petitioners without mercy. She'll lie. A personal emergency – her husband was injured at work, they say it's very bad, they say he might die – and she'll weep, plangently, until the Chief comes out of his office. She imagines the Chief's furious secretary, and then she imagines Francis downed and comatose with a half-crushed skull, and she imagines the Chief taking her in his arms and holding her, stroking her hair, his warm, broad chest, his warm, powerful arms, and she imagines stabbing him, with a letter opener or a carving knife, she imagines it, through wool, fat, muscle, up between his ribs, to the point that matters.

At the end of the hall, the door opens.

' – pleasure,' a man is saying. Hawk face, anodyne suit.

'Of course,' an old man replies, heeling him. Crumpled. A turtle beak, spectacles, tweed. The accent is there, yet he sounds nothing like himself, no high-altitude godly chill. The Chief hesitates in his own doorway; his mouth gapes seekingly. 'You know I must ask you, one more time. Whether there's any chance. A renewal with another body, or –'

He stumbles on, wincing. It's as if she isn't there.

'Unfortunately, Doctor.' The American lifts his hands to interrupt, but doesn't finish his sentence.

The Chief watches him go. Then he glances at her, where she's standing in another doorframe. 'You're on the wrong floor,' he snaps. 'Who are you?'

Then he turns and stalks back inside.

The Chief's door bangs, the secretary murmurs. The American's footsteps run out of carpet and echo on hardwood. It is difficult for her to think. It takes almost too long.

From the top of the stairwell she calls, 'Pardon me.'

He's halfway down, and she clatters after him.

'I remember you,' she says. She reaches for his shoulder. 'You followed me onto the bus.'

'*Ty ne ponimayesh shto ty tut delayesh.*' His accent is worse than hers, the words spoken for a stifling classroom, not a ticket seller at a train station, not a hostess accepting a bouquet on the doorstep.

'I don't understand?' she says, repeating the three words she caught.

In the foyer's bad light, he has a sunken, disconsolate aspect. He evaluates her like a news column. 'I don't think you do.'

Then he is out the tall, heavy doors. He spins his coat onto his shoulders as he goes. The hound, as always, does nothing.

Joy had refused to meet her, initially. At her father's first heedless mention of his plans for a new wife, she'd pitched a fit so horrid – in the middle of the Saturday shopping, the butcher paused in his butchering to locate the source of the screaming – her father threw up his hands and walked away. She'd continued to shriek. Rigid, incoherent, wet-faced, run down under the hooves of a cavalry of nightmare fears. The bell tinkled, the door closed behind him. The butcher passed her a dime out of his till so she could take the trolley home.

She did not speak to her father for a week, and neither did he address her. She was nine, and when he began speaking to her again, she took it to mean he'd forgotten the incident, that she'd won the territory. She imagined the woman would recede and her life would continue in its hateful but familiar way.

But the lunch came – pickles, soup, crackers – where he raised the subject a second time. 'Whatever your difficulty, Noodle, you must be civilised. You are a child and it is your duty to strive to understand the world.'

She wept silently and nobly in the car that afternoon as she accompanied her father to the university; to a small, unimpressive office in a squat building.

'This is Doctor Margolin,' her father said.

A snowy eagle of a woman stood up from behind her desk. 'Good morning, Joy. I'm Dorota. Please to meet you.'

'*Pleasure*,' Joy corrected, and her father, misunderstanding, patted her shoulder approvingly.

'We'll leave you to it,' he said, and closed the door.

Dorota lifted a tray from the filing cabinet behind her and set it down in a conspicuously clear patch of her desk. Jam cookies, fresh from the package, arranged in a tidy, pathetic pinwheel. Dorota regarded the tray as if she required a translator for it.

'Should I marry your father?' she asked the cookies. 'It's true it's already agreed upon, but it is not too late. Please sit.'

Joy, who had previously sworn to remain silent no matter

what was threatened during this interrogation, said nothing.

'He is an intelligent man, but I think his intelligence is frustrated by the circumstances. Perhaps we all three have this in common. Does he treat you fairly?'

'No,' Joy muttered, despite herself.

'Hm,' said Dorota. 'Since you are also an intelligent girl, you should be careful what you read. *Ot umnova nauchischsa, ot glupova razuchishchsa.*'

Joy, quite used to ignoring what she didn't understand, selected a jam cookie and snapped it in half so that its red heart smeared bloodily apart.

'From someone clever you will learn; from a fool you will,' – Dorota paused to search – 'unlearn. Be deprived.'

'Be depraved,' said Joy.

Sparkling gems of sugar snowed onto the little girl's dress. No stranger would ever mistake them for mother and daughter – Joy was silky and dark, snub-nosed and sharp-toothed like a pine marten – but she had that same deep crease down the centre of her brow that Dorota rubbed at, futilely, whenever she caught herself in a mirror. The line of thought; the masochistic line that marks a person who thinks deeply and unceasingly. She'd heard a lot about Joy: that the girl was manipulative, truculent, ravenous, and in possession of what her father termed a mile-wide mean streak. Dorota had many things to tell such a girl: don't learn to type or they'll assume you'll do the typing, don't learn to cook or they'll expect you to cook. Don't marry early, don't marry your father, don't marry at all, unless you've found both satisfaction and affection. And one is more important than the other.

Dorota's office did not have a window. She gazed at the girl as she spoke to her: 'I know what kind of doctor I am, and I learned for two years what kind of wife, before my first husband was killed. But I do not know what kind of mother I am. So, I would like you to tell me your conditions, and I promise I will do my best to observe them.'

'What do you mean?' said Joy.

'An agreement. Terms. You understand.'

Dorota folded her hands. Her office was small and windowless because she was employed only one day a week in the department, taking the cases the others didn't want. She resented the charity. She thought frequently of the day when she would tender her resignation here in order to resume her real work, which had been interrupted by so many interminable, frightening years with no comprehension or faith in what might come next.

Joy brushed the sugar off her mouth. 'First,' she said, 'you must never leave me.'

'Very good,' said Dorota. 'And second?'

Joy sighed. As she considered, her eyes wandered over the papers and books on the woman's desk. The words on them meant nothing to her. 'Second,' she said, 'You must always remember me.'

CANADA, 1963

# Afterword: Dr Ewen Cameron, De-Patterning and MKUltra


## Professor David Harper

University of East London


THE EXPERIMENTS AT THE heart of Paige Cooper's story sound as if they are straight out of a dystopian conspiracy thriller but they really happened. They were conducted in the 1950s and early 1960s by Dr Ewen Cameron, a British-born psychiatrist and Director of the Allan Memorial Institute in Montreal (McGill University's treatment facility). Cameron sought to develop what he saw as a revolutionary new psychiatric treatment but his experiments were secretly funded by the CIA as part of what historian Alfred McCoy[1] refers to as 'a veritable Manhattan Project of the mind.' Cameron gave his procedures pseudo-scientific names like 'de-patterning' and 'psychic driving.' He varied them over time and from patient to patient but they typically involved a mix of the following:

*Drug-induced coma:* Each experimental 'treatment' for Cameron's patients (two thirds of whom were women) would usually begin with 'sleep therapy' (i.e. a coma induced by administering barbiturates).

*De-patterning:* During the drug-induced sleep, patients would be woken up for feeding, the toilet and to be given regular electroshocks (i.e. ECT) which would start after about three days of sleep. The combined sleep-electroshock 'treatment' lasted between 15-30 days, sometimes up to 65 days. So that patients did not harm themselves as a result of the epileptic seizures caused by the ECT, they were immobilised with muscle relaxant drugs like Curare. In the standard electroshock therapy of the time, doctors would give patients a single dose of 110 volts, lasting a fraction of a second, every one or two days. However, by contrast, according to John Marks, 'Cameron used a form 20 to 40 times more intense, two or three times daily, with the power turned up to 150 volts'.[2] Cameron's aim, as stated in his journal article in *Comprehensive Psychiatry* in 1962[3] was to cause disorientation and confusion via 'massive' and 'pervasive' memory disturbance. After this, according to his article, a patient might 'be unable to walk without support, to feed himself, and he [sic] may show double incontinence'.

*Psychic driving*: Patients were next subjected to negative taped messages (e.g. 'my mother hates me'). The aim was to 'get rid of unwanted behaviour' and then this would be followed by positive messages 'to condition in desired personality traits'.[4] The messages (taken from recordings of Cameron's interviews with patients) were played repetitively on a tape-loop system via loudspeakers or a football helmet contraption for 16 hours a day for several weeks. Cameron sought to intensify the effect by placing his patients in a sensory deprivation 'box' in the stables of the hospital and giving them cocktails of drugs which would immobilise them but keep them awake whilst they experienced hallucinations induced by psychedelic drugs. Val Orlikow described her experience as 'terrifying' – she received LSD between one and four times a week together with either a stimulant or depressant and was then left on her own to listen to a tape playing excerpts of her last session with Cameron. In the case of a patient named 'Mary C,' Cameron kept her in his sensory deprivation box for 35 days, gave her repeated electroshocks whilst she was in a drug-induced coma after which she endured 101 days of 'psychic driving.' At the end of her 'treatment,' according to Cameron, 'no favorable results were obtained', a result that comes as little surprise.[5]

The link with the CIA emerged only after years of dogged investigation. In 1974 the *New York Times* published an article by

Seymour Hersh about unconstitutional CIA activities based, in part, on an internal report the CIA called the 'family jewels'.[6] Hersh's article sparked investigations by President Ford's Rockefeller Commission[7] and the US Senate's Church Committee.[8] It was revealed that the CIA had used LSD on unsuspecting members of the public in the US and that, in 1953, Frank Olson (a US Army biological warfare specialist) had fallen to his death from a tenth-floor window several days after being given LSD without his knowledge or permission. However, the investigations were hampered by the fact that CIA Director Richard Helms had ordered all records to be destroyed in 1973.

But in 1977, 16,000 pages of documents relating to the CIA's financial history were found following a Freedom of Information Act request by John Marks, a former State Department employee turned author. Marks and his research team managed to identify and interview some of those involved and, in 1979, he published *The Search for the 'Manchurian Candidate': The CIA and Mind Control*. This revealed that Cameron had begun to receive money for his research from the CIA in 1957 via a front organisation called the Society for the Investigation of Human Ecology. Marks showed that Cameron's research was sub-project 68 of an extensive CIA-funded programme of research into brainwashing and 'mind control' run by Dr Sidney Gottlieb, a chemist who was the head of the CIA's Technical Services Division (TSD). The overall research programme involved many leading psychologists, psychiatrists and social scientists (some who were aware of the CIA's role and some who weren't). It was called MK-Ultra: 'MK' meant it was a TSD project and 'Ultra' was a code name. According to Marks, CIA officials would travel periodically to observe Cameron's work, something Paige Cooper alludes to in her story.

In 1980 the Canadian Broadcasting Corporation's *Fifth Estate* programme broadcast an investigation into Cameron's experiments including interviews with several of his former patients. In the subsequent decade, three books on the studies were published including Anne Collins' *In the Sleep Room* based on interviews with former patients. In 1988 the CIA finally agreed an out-of-court settlement with nine of Cameron's former patients including Mary Morrow who inspired the character of Joy's stepmother Dorota in Paige Cooper's story. Morrow, a doctor, had approached Cameron for a fellowship in psychiatry but he decided to admit her as a patient claiming she appeared 'nervous'. She underwent Cameron's 'de-patterning' regime of electroshock and barbiturates for 11 days.[9] In 1992 the Canadian government agreed to pay compensation to 77 former patients on condition that they agreed not to sue the government or the hospital but hundreds of other former patients were left without compensation.

The story of Cameron's experiments is a long and complicated one[10] but he should not be regarded as a rogue maverick. During his time as Director of the Allan Memorial Institute he was President, in turn, of the American Psychiatric Association, the Canadian Psychiatric Association, and the World Psychiatric Association. In the 1950s the numbers of people in psychiatric hospitals were at their peak and provided a captive population on which overly optimistic psychiatrists could try out experimental methods with few safeguards – these were the days, for example, when lobotomies were routinely practised. Poorly designed studies, such as Cameron's, were published openly in mainstream psychiatric journals all the time. In 1955 Canada's *Weekend* magazine even included an article on Cameron's work entitled 'Canadian psychiatrists develop beneficial brainwashing.' Patients and families deferred to the authority of psychiatrists: 'I thought he was God,' Val Orlikow said of Cameron.[11]

The CIA's research programme began in the midst of paranoia and suspicion about 'communist brainwashing' following show trials in Moscow and Eastern Europe and the coerced 'confessions' of captured US servicemen in Korea in the early 1950s. But this initially defensive purpose was transformed and the programme's results fed into manuals the CIA used themselves and in the training of interrogators in countries allied with the US during the Cold War. An important lesson is that such paranoia, combined with secrecy and a lack of oversight and accountability, can easily lead to abuses – something also seen in the UK's use of interrogation techniques in Kenya in the 1950s and Northern Ireland in the 1970s.[12] Following the attacks in New York on 11 September 2001, the Bush administration embraced 'enhanced interrogation' methods like waterboarding, abandoning well-established legal norms. Once again, some psychologists proved willing to help design psychological interrogation techniques.[13] We forgot the lessons of history then and, unless we keep retelling the stories of the past, it is likely we will forget them again in the future.

## Notes

1. McCoy, A.W., *A Question of Torture: CIA Interrogation, from the Cold War to the War on Terror.* (New York: Metropolitan Books, 2006)
2. Marks, J., *The Search for the "Manchurian Candidate": The CIA and Mind Control.* (New York: Times Books, 1979).
3. Cameron, D.E., Lohrenz, J.G., Handcock, K.A. 'The de-patterning treatment of schizophrenia'. *Comprehensive Psychiatry, 3*(2) (1962), pp65-76. https://doi.org/10.1016/S0010-440X(62)80015-7
4. Marks, J., op. cit..
5. Marks, J., op. cit..
6. CIA's 'Family jewels' report: https://nsarchive2.gwu.edu//NSAEBB/NSAEBB222/index.htm
7. Rockefeller Commission: https://www.fordlibrarymuseum.gov/library/document/0005/1561495.pdf
8. Church Committee: https://www.intelligence.senate.gov/resources/intelligence-related-commissions
9. Remnick, D. 25 Years of Nightmares. *Washington Post*, 28 July (1985). https://www.washingtonpost.com/archive/lifestyle/1985/07/28/25-years-of-nightmares/cb836420-9c72-4d3c-ae60-70a8f13c4ceb/
10. For a recent account see the five-part investigative podcast series by WBUR (Boston's NPR) released in April 2020: *Madness: The Secret Mission for Mind Control and the People Who Paid the Price* https://www.wbur.org/endlessthread/2020/04/24/madness-part-one-the-sleep-room
11. Marks, J., op. cit..
12. McCoy, A.W., op. cit.; Harper, D., 'The complicity of psychology in the security state'. In R. Roberts (ed.), *Just War: Psychology, Terrorism and Iraq* (Ross-on-Wye: PCCS books, 2007), pp15-45.
13. Harper, D., op. cit; McCoy, A.W., op. cit..

# Love & Remains

Kim Thúy

Translated from the French by J. Bret Maney

SHE WAS NINETEEN YEARS old. Her straight black hair swept down her back to her waist as if someone had placed the individual strands there one by one. Her hair was so thick, so regal, that not even the wind dared ruffle it. It remained in place while the hems on the long flaps of her Vietnamese dress swayed to the rhythm of her deceptively timid footsteps. The young woman's hair hung over shoulders that had yet to bear any real weight or burden. At the annual victory celebration of the two great women warriors who had saved Vietnam from its Chinese enemies, Hà had once been chosen by her classmates for the elephant procession. Her school had honoured her with the role of Trưng Trắc, one of these two sisters revered as national heroines. She had been their queen for a day.

Hà was the third child in a family of eight. Like most Vietnamese young women educated at the time, she decided to earn a teaching degree at university. She enrolled in a programme for teachers of English as a second language, even though she had attended a secondary school founded by the French and run by French directors. Hà was of the generation that had lived through the winding down of French colonisation in the 1950s and the beginnings of the American military involvement. She didn't have to cross a bridge to pass from one era to another. France did not have to yield to the United States because it turned out it was a relay race. That's why Hà had Lamartine's verses imprinted on the right hemisphere of her brain and the bewitching sounds of rock 'n' roll on the left. Some say Hà was lucky to live in a country where three cultures fought to hold a place in her heart. Others, meanwhile, were at that very moment fighting so that her Vietnamese culture wouldn't have to defend itself in order to occupy the entire space of her identity.

Fortunately, Hà was among those who had the privilege of taking the best from each, slipping between lines of fire, flying over traps and mines, and finding refuge in the bosom of her family to shield herself from the rain of herbicides and the thunder of the B-52s. Adored by everyone around her, she allowed herself to believe in the romantic possibilities she glimpsed in the songs of Françoise Hardy and the passionate singing of Elvis Presley. At first, she had been excited to discover the notes left by secret admirers on her desk. On her way to university, she enjoyed the smitten gazes of students who followed her from a distance without missing a single one of her footsteps. Unlike other young women, Hà was not afraid to cause a stir by flirtatiously running her hands through her long hair. When she wanted to make someone fall in love with her, she smiled at him discreetly while batting her naturally curled and tender lashes.

Hà's beauty soothed the scorching sun of Saigon's tropical climate and tempered the fiery debates between patriots and nationalists, between 'pro' and 'anti' factions, between dreamers and doers. One day, in the midst of these many voices and rumours of future unrest, a man ten years older than Hà offered her some shade by means of his own shadow. Hà instantly fell for this doctor. He treated patients with harelips or acid burns caused by jealous lovers or injuries from traffic accidents... But his preference was to be at the front, where he could save a leg riddled with bullets, sew up an ear, or amputate two arms to save one life. He wore his youth like a bulletproof jacket. He gave himself body and soul to the wounded until the very moment he met Hà, when he felt for the first time the fear of dying. For sixty-eight days in 1968, he experienced the exhilaration of love at the same time as the loss of his courage. Hà's whispered confidences accompanied the muffled voices of his patients. Who to love? How to love? These questions were answered by a shard of glass that slit his throat as he picked out a ring at a jeweller's shop next to an open-air restaurant. The explosion of a grenade injured several people and killed one instantaneously. Hà learned the news in the evening paper. A few days later, the jeweller who had been showing the doctor various diamonds confirmed that he had died in love. Hà was nineteen. It was the end of innocence.

After this grenade blew up, Hà aged so quickly that her parents married her at twenty-one to a young engineer from Saigon's prestigious Phú Thọ National Centre of Technology. Xuân spoke little. During their courtship, he harmonised with Hà's silence by sitting for hours, often alone, in the family's drawing room. On days when the birds succeeded in luring Hà into the garden, the engineer would walk beside her with a parasol in hand. Unlike his colleagues, who carried pens in their shirt pockets, he always had a clean handkerchief to wipe away Hà's sudden tears. He held it out to her without asking any questions. All these aimless turns around the courtyard led them to the altar, where they prostrated themselves before their ancestors and their new shared destiny. Without exception, everyone present took for granted they would have children and a life as calm and gentle as the natural silk of their wedding garments.

As foreseen, they had children. They went to the pictures. They travelled to Dalat. Xuân now carried a parasol in one hand and hefted Hà's bag in the other. For her part, Hà celebrated Xuân's love for her in poems she wrote as if it were her own. She embellished her love until it reached gigantic proportions with twinkling stars and a deluge of hearts accompanied by fanfare and applause. In the image of ideal love and the ideal lover, she combed Xuân's hair, smoothed down his wayward locks, cut his nails, picked out his clothes. She often told her students and friends that she and Xuân had never had a disagreement. Never a dispute or quarrel in this marriage drawn with coloured pencils in two dimensions. They lived in perfect happiness until the end of the war, on 30 April 1975. Then, overnight, their marriage broke into a thousand pieces as North Vietnam roughly took hold of the South in preparation for swallowing it whole.

Xuân was called to a meeting by the new directors of the American company for which he had been working for the past year. He left his home and family with his wallet tucked in his trouser pocket and his briefcase, containing a notebook and pens, under his arm. He told Hà he would definitely be back for lunch. However, when he arrived at the office, Xuân was loaded onto a truck with about fifty other men. Together, they set off into the unknown. Xuân's secretary ran to tell Hà what had happened. The two women traced the truck's route, following the directions of people who had seen it pass. Hà found the first camp where Xuân was detained. All the prisoners were suspected of being pro-American, unpatriotic because they had been on the losing side of the war. The civil servant, the professor, the veterinarian all served the same sentence, without distinction. All received the meagre ration of a single peanut per day, while Vietnam has, since then, become one of the fifteen largest peanut growers in the world. Fortunately for the prisoners, nature supplemented their meals with grasshoppers, ants, and the occasional rat.

Hà used to bring Xuân pork she bought on the black market, shredded fibre by fibre, seasoned with fish sauce, and dried on the coals overnight so that Xuân could garnish his rice water with a few strands of meat. Sometimes, by giving a portion to the guards, she managed to see Xuân and deliver the food to him in person. Even face to face, they said nothing to each other. No one dared to speak because every conversation was listened in on and logged, and could be used against the prisoners. To keep from crying, Hà and Xuân avoided each other's gaze. A man caught weeping had been summoned by the director of the camp and severely beaten. His offence was wallowing in emotion instead of purging himself of his capitalist ideas through study of the teachings of Lenin and their new political and spiritual leader, Uncle Hô. This prisoner was frequently punished; he was one of the soldiers who had had to strip off their uniforms and discard them in the street when the Americans had abruptly pulled out of Vietnam. The treatment of the former soldiers was, on average, more brutal. It was as if they were stand-ins for the American servicemen, the sworn enemies. Yet these South Vietnamese soldiers were hardly the only trace to be eliminated of the American presence in the country.

Today, even forty-five years after the war, millions of bombs, mines, grenades, shells, mortars and other unexploded ordnance still lurk in the rice paddies, in backyards, under the feet of schoolchildren. Every time a farmer's scream is blotted out by the detonation of a 'bombie',[1] every time an explosion forever erases a child's vision of the blue sky, the United States is heard from again. According to what they say, it will take three hundred years before demining operations clear the last bomb.

In a different way, Operation Ranch Hand, the aerial spraying of herbicides during the war, has also left its mark on Vietnam, both geographically and genetically. The so-called 'Rainbow Herbicides' killed the trees, dried up the land, and blighted humans across generations. The Vietnamese who didn't succumb to cancer gave birth to children who resemble casualties of war: kids with heads too heavy to hold up, babies with eyes turned inwards so as not to witness atrocities, babies born with holes in their hearts… The chemical legacy of twenty years of American occupation of the country is spread over 20,000 square kilometres of land and runs through the veins of more than three million people.

Had the newly victorious communist government known, in 1975, that their enemies would never withdraw from the nation's soil, collective memory, or the rhythms of everyday life, they would not have ordered the re-education camp directors to be so unflinching in rooting out ideas, silencing opposing views, and emptying their prisoners' heads of thoughts.

Unlike the former high-ranking military officers, Xuân was docile. He knew how to pass under the radar, blend in with the colour of the mud, disappear in the blinding sunlight. He filled his ears with cicadas' songs, the guard dogs' barking and the rare noise of a motor scooter's engine. Since Xuân's heart was empty, the director of the camp suspected him of wanting to flee on the road he listened for in the distance. The director had no supernatural powers to read the true meaning of Xuân's silence. But he knew that all of his prisoners had one and the same dream: to escape from his clutches.

The director transferred Xuân to another camp, which was merged with another, which in turn was moved to another corner of the jungle, elsewhere. Hà criss-crossed the country in search of Xuân, carrying her provisions on her back. The authorities' vague answers did not discourage her from climbing onto bicycles, spending the night illegally in the homes of generous and courageous hosts, walking into and out of dead-ends… going on and on until the straps of her sandals, repaired with glue, nails, and sweat, gave out. One evening, after two days of waiting in front of a barbed wire fence whose sharp edges pointed in every direction, Hà collapsed beside a bush, no longer knowing where to go. Another woman came and sat down next to her, nursing the same knot of silence in her belly. They stayed that way until the middle of the night when a whisper was heard between the trees. A man's voice, low and barely audible, uttered a single sentence: 'You, on the right, your husband is dead; you, on the left, yours has left camp. Go now! Leave!'

Was Hà on the right or the left according to the point of view of this man? Had he been looking at them from the front or the back? Was he one of the camp guards or a prisoner? Had the women really heard this voice or was it a nightmare? At dawn, the women parted without a word.

Hà travelled south on the train towards her children, towards the chance that Xuân was waiting for her in his armchair in the drawing room. As on the journey north, she had to disembark at the 17th Parallel, the old demarcation line between North and South, East and West, communism and capitalism. There had been three times as many bombings of Vietnam than during the entire Second World War, and here the bombs had mangled the rails. The train passengers had to get off and walk a few kilometres to another train to continue their journey. Having left behind all the food she was carrying to thank the good Samaritan at the camp, Hà crossed this disaster area quickly. Unlike the other passengers, she walked with a determined stride, unaware that a sinkhole nine metres deep awaited her, and that no one could save her from being swallowed up by the collapse of a tunnel, once used as a bomb shelter, that had nonetheless held up for the past six years.

Hà would never learn that Xuân was ultimately reunited with their boys. He lives today in Washington, D.C., thanks to Humanitarian Operation, the American government programme that allowed former prisoners of the re-education camps to resettle in the United States as future citizens.

After a twenty-year war followed by a forty-five-year peace, it has become impossible to separate the United States from Vietnam, and vice-versa. The US population includes more than two million Vietnamese Americans and, in Vietnam, more than 1,500 American soldiers remain missing in action. Their relatives continue to search for them in bone fragments like Hà's sons, who are still looking for their mother's body to this day.

*War lasts. Love remains.*

## Note

1. The local name given to the millions of tennis ball-sized bomblets dispersed by American cluster munitions during the war.

# Afterword: Vinh Linh, Underground

Xuân Phượng

Translated from the Vietnamese by Diep Lien Nguyen

Rather than attempt an historical outline of this war, I would offer a short glimpse from my own memories of it, as a documentary filmmaker. In 1967 I was part of a team of filmmakers that set out from Hanoi in the North to the village of Vinh Linh, the site of the 17th Parallel, the provisional military demarcation line between North and South Vietnam (1954-1975). In 1965, American crafts invaded Vinh Linh a total of 5,415 times, bombing it 666 times. In 1966, American crafts conducted 12,949 invasions and bombed it 5,245 times. In 1967, the year we made the film – *The 17th Parallel: The People's War* – US aircrafts invaded Vinh Linh 3,238 times and bombed it 1,362 times on average per month.[1]

*May 1967*

After two days of travelling – on ferries and over bombed-out roads, with our cars crawling through the night using only the faintest of lights – we arrived at Thanh Hoa.[2]

Our three Jeeps were camouflaged and well-hidden in a trench. The eleven people that made up the film crew shared a couple of bamboo mats between them, which they lay down on other, specially prepared trenches. Next to us were a number of well-enforced foxholes to shelter us in case bombing started. I was fast asleep, exhausted from the journey, when heavy explosions and the flashes of spy plane photography rudely awakened me. Binh, the best cameraman in our group, shouted: 'Bombies!' I barely managed to grab a first aid kit before diving into the nearest foxhole. Once inside I saw, the two French co-directors – the Ivens (Joris Ivens and Marceline Loridan-Ivens) – were sitting in the corner, surrounded by soldiers. The explosions intensified and every minute or so, our surroundings were lit up as bright as day. At one point Binh screamed out loud: *'I am hurt.'*

I quickly checked his neck. A widening patch of fluid. I located a surgical knife, pressed against his neck with my hand and felt a round object under the skin. Another explosion. Joris shouted out: 'Phượng, stay calm. Take care of Binh, but do it quickly.' I held the knife in one hand, and with the other hand squeezed and pinched at the metal ball, sliding it across the neck, under the skin. Eventually, with some help from the knife, the bloodstained metal ball dropped into my palm. The bleeding stopped and the wound was stitched. The bombardments from American warplanes came to a sudden halt, and everything was strangely quiet.

At dawn, we crawled out of the foxholes to find the Jeeps damaged: the radiators had been punctured, the seats thrown out. Phi Hung, the person in charge of our safety, reported back to Hanoi for instructions. Realising his intentions, Joris crawled through the trench to hand deliver a note to be wired through. It read: 'We have not covered one tenth of the distance we need to. We are still determined to go to Vinh Linh. We will not return to Hanoi. Signed Joris and Marceline.' In the afternoon, Hanoi replied: 'Replacement Jeeps are en route. Proceed with the journey. Keep the guests safe.'

From that point onwards, we sought shelter in military compounds and tunnels during the daytime, or occasionally in the shade of trees under the banks of rivers. At dusk, we hurled ourselves into cars, travelled at high speed, dodging bombs and flares, crossed pontoon bridges and roared along mountain roads. The most terrifying moments, though, were when ghostly blue flares rose into the sky or when an American warplane roared across it.

That night, after safely crossing two ferries, our three-car convoy was still heading south. There were five of us packed into the car being driven by Ngoc: the Ivens, Phi Hung, Binh and me, nauseous with fear as we travelled beneath ghostly flares, dodging bombs aimed at the road. Then came an impact. Ngoc rear-ended the truck in front of us. The Jeep bounced into the air, and fragments of glass lacerated my face. I jumped out the car with blood pouring out of me. Marceline screamed: 'My legs!' In the dark, members of Youth Volunteers, who had been fixing blast holes at the time, scrambled to help and brought us into the vaulted entrance of an air shelter (as we learnt later the shelter saved our lives). The Volunteers tried to help me, plucking fragments of the shattered glass out of my face. And when I opened my eyes, I saw with relief that Marceline was still moving in Joris's arms; her right leg was already bandaged up and tied to a splint. When we arrived at a local medical centre away from the front line, doctors attended to us individually. My face was cleaned up and amazingly, thanks to my youth, I think, the bleeding had stopped. With new pains still registering, I was ready to translate Joris's questions to the doctors. Marceline's injuries were more serious than we first thought and she would have to be admitted to the Ha Tinh Military Hospital. This temporary facility was twenty kilometres from the main road, hidden in a bamboo forest. Ivens made a decision: 'Marceline will stay for treatment. But the rest of us will depart tonight.'

### *Our First Night under Vinh Linh*

Our underground tunnel had been constructed a few days before we arrived. Its entrance, like all the others, was a discreet hole, camouflaged with green leaves. Below its door were stairs leading deep into the earth. It was hard to travel through these tunnels as your hands had to guide your every step. Newly cut roots, dripping with tree sap, stuck out from the walls at every angle, giving our hands plenty of cuts and bruises. It grew darker the deeper we walked.

'Entering hell,' Chon, the cameraman, whispered in my ears.

The Committee of Vinh Linh had arranged things for us putting out individual beds, separated by a thin wall, in a kind of underground hotel. The Ivens stayed in a larger room. (After a seven-day stay in Ha Tinh Military Hospital, Marceline had been brought back to us, in one of the three jeeps, through bombs and bullets.) The air in our bunker felt very stuffy and claustrophobic, made worse by the asthmatic breathing of Ivens, next door. Thus, in total darkness, we spent our first night underground.

*Another Night Underground*

After another long day enduring bombs and bullets, we slept deeply. Suddenly a shout rang out in the darkness: 'Is anyone here a doctor? Help me, help me please!'

Marceline woke me up, a man with a dim oil lamp said in a strong Vinh Linh accent: 'Help us! My wife has been in labour for two days. We don't think she's going to make it.' He broke down in tears. Chon, the assistant sound engineer, and I followed his footsteps in the blackness. The tunnels of Vinh Linh form a very complex underground maze with countless routes and intersections. A whimpering became audible despite the darkness surrounding us. I made contact with the source of the moans with my hands. A woman was lying down; her belly was swollen but her body temperature was cold. Behind me I realised there was a group of people quietly watching the scene. To comfort the woman, I ordered a bucket of hot water and requested everyone clear out. Then I instructed the woman: 'Hold your breath and push really hard.'

'It hurts too much!' she screamed, 'I can't do it.' She was giving birth for the first time and had no experience of this. Before long we were both screaming and I was beginning to lose it... I was sweating all over, exhausted but finally the baby's head appeared. Then came its cries, and a few minutes later, I heard the sobbing of the young father. It was a strange, but harmonic symphony in this underground, dirt tunnel. After making sure that both mother and baby were in good shape, we returned to our branch of the tunnel system. Surprisingly, Joris and Marceline were still awake waiting for us. I was very tired and told them: '*Ça va.* It's OK'. Marceline gave me a hug. But all of a sudden we start to hear my screams again, combined with the cries from the mother, and barely inaudible groans of others back in that tunnel. Then came the baby's cries, and immediately after that the father's cries. As it turned out, as I was tending to the labour with no light and no medical equipment, Chon had captured everything with his sound recorder.

Back in our tunnel, everyone was now awake and gathered round the small tape recorder. Joris put his hand on my shoulder: 'Do you know why I am so passionate about being a war correspondent?' he asked. 'It is because we have the opportunity to record the victory of life over death, even nine metres below ground.' Personally, I could not forget the way the Ivens stayed up all night long, waiting for me, concerned for this Vinh Linh baby.

Two days later, the father presented us with a few cassava tubers. He grabbed my hands: 'I can't thank you enough,' he said. 'Please have the honour to name my son.'

'I will name him Nguyen Xuân Phượng,' I replied. 'The same as me.'

Forty years later, in 2007, upon returning to Vinh Linh for another film project, I tried to find Nguyen Xuan Phuong, who by then would have been a forty-year-old man. The Committee of Vinh Linh, the Radio and Television Station of Quang Tri, the newspaper of Quang Tri all offered their assistance. But during the filming period, including a trip to Quang Binh, we failed to find that baby.

Life had gone on with that horrific war, and we simply lost track of the family.

## Notes

1. According to the General Statistics Office of Vietnam, National Archives Center III, Prime Minister's Office, file 393.
2. A city is situated on the Ma River (Sông Mã), about 93 miles (150 kilometers) south of Hanoi.

# An American Hero

## Gianfranco Bettin

Translated from the Italian by Orsola Casagrande

'He thinks he's a hero, an American hero,' the Hound told him.

'American? But he's Italian, like you and me,' Bares replied.

'Manfroi thinks that America is the new Rome, the modern Empire, and Italy a border from which to defend it.'

That's how the Hound, a great journalist and a decade-old friend, had explained it to him.

Without convincing him, though. He knew little about history, empires and politics, but he had once known an American hero, a true hero, John, years before, and he was nothing like Manfroi.

The war had been raging. He was just a kid. Around the industrial area of Venice, on the mainland, where he was born, the Germans had come en masse, in the winter of 1944. There were bombings, resistance strikes, reprisals. His father had died on the Russian front, leaving his mother to look after him, aged fifteen, and his sister Adelina, aged six.

After the war he had made a living however he could. At eighteen he joined the State Police. Inspired by that American hero, or so he had always thought.

Now, a recently retired Public Security Commissioner, Toaldo Bares, was listening to the Hound talking to him about a completely different breed of hero, Manfroi – Bruno Manfroi

– self-styled American, though Italian by citizenship. His name had emerged years earlier in old stories of conspiracies and bombs, but now here it was again, reappearing in a new dark, bloody story.

The city had been scared by crimes. Fierce, obscene crimes.

Vania Lombardi had been killed in her house. She had been tied up and gagged and then raped with a vacuum cleaner hose, before being finished off, stabbed in the abdomen and right in the heart, where the blade was found still lodged. She was 31, a secondary school music teacher, engaged but living alone.

Two weeks later Letizia De Rossi was killed in a similar way. She too had been tied up and gagged in her house, but she had been tortured for a longer time, with cigarette stubs burned on her arms and bare legs. She was raped with a broomstick, and then killed, once again with a knife directly into the heart. She was 51 years old, a railway worker, divorced, living alone.

A few days later it was the turn of Mariangela Bui, 40, a shop assistant in a mall. Again the assault took place in the victim's house. She must have been watched, because, unlike the other two victims, she lived with her husband and two children. They had gone to a football match in Milan that evening. The killer must have known, or, if he had acted randomly, he had been extremely lucky. Her husband and children found her late at night, after returning from the match. An umbrella was used to rape her. Tied up and gagged like the others, she had suffered burns on her arms and legs, and had a knife still stuck in her heart.

Mariangela was the niece of Toaldo Bares, his sister's daughter.

The killer – the investigation was inclined to think it was a single perpetrator – had found the knives and the other objects used for the violence in his victims' houses. There were no traces of struggle, as if the victims had been tied up and gagged under threat. Maybe at gunpoint. Nothing had been stolen from the apartments. The predator had other goals.

A kind of low-level mass hysteria descended after the second murder, following the waves of fear caused by the first. After the third, it turned to panic. The killer had struck just four days after the previous murder, while two weeks had passed between the first and the second. A palpable fear spread through the city of a maniac on a killing spree, a frenzy of rape and torture possibly fuelled by the attention he was getting.

The crimes had all taken place in the same tough and crowded neighbourhood close to the industrial district, on the southern outskirts of the city. Bares was born there. His mother and sister had carried on living there. And his niece, Adelina's daughter, had set up her own family there.

Bares, on the other hand, having joined the police, had moved around the country for many years. He had served in the north at the beginning of his career, before transferring to the south and the Mafia and Camorra areas. After that he has returned to Veneto, to be stationed between Verona and Belluno. The last dozen years before retiring he had worked in Venice, as Commissioner. Those were the years of the struggle against Felice Maniero's *Mafia del Brenta.*[1] Bares was among those, not many in reality, who had always suspected the syndicate of being the powerful, ruthless organisation it turned out to be. The Hound had thought the same.

Bares and the Hound hadn't seen each other for some time. The former policeman now lived in the countryside, in a quiet little town. He had been a widower for some years with no children, and had been carrying on with the owner of the one of the town's bars. It was at Mariangela's funeral that he'd seen his journalist friend again. The Hound, embracing him, had noticed, behind the dark lenses, how bloodshot his eyes were.

In the neighbourhood where the crimes had been committed – where some truly tough people lived – word on the street was that someone would soon be avenging 'those poor women' and solve the matter 'their own way'. But there was also a lot of fear, tension.

It all ended suddenly when Sante Boboli – known as Bobo – a thin and unhealthy-looking forty-year-old who lived alone in the oldest part of the neighbourhood in a dilapidated single-family house – was found hanged from a beam in his house. He was an introvert, with a history of drug dealing and theft. Three pairs of knickers were found in his house, and were later identified as belonging to the murdered women, in all likelihood the same knickers they were wearing at the time of the assault. The discovery was considered proof of Bobo's guilt, even though his DNA had not been found at the crime scenes.

In some circles, though, there were doubts about his suicide. Some suspected that the local mob – known for its links to some of the most feared elements of *Mafia del Brenta* – had identified the serial killer and, following their own moral codes as well as wanting to alleviate the recent police pressure on the territory, had indeed solved the matter in its own way.

Toaldo Bares had been very fond of his niece, Mariangela. He would have preferred to have found the torturer and murderer himself. He had scoured the neighbourhood, which he knew both from his childhood days and professionally, as a hunter. When he ordered a raid on the area, as the city's commissioner, he always found what he was looking for. To this day, he remained both feared and respected by the criminals.

It was the Hound who came looking for him a month after Bobo's suicide. He drove out of the small town where he lived, in a one-storey house near the river, with a small front garden and a vegetable garden in the back.

At Mariangela's funeral two months earlier, they had exchanged only a few words.

'Any idea?' the reporter had asked him.

'It's weird stuff.'

'Did you know the other women?'

'Only the first, Vania. She was the daughter of an old schoolmate of mine, but I hadn't seen her since she was a child.

I didn't know the other.'

'I talked to her once, De Rossi that is, about an old story. Years ago. She lived in Venice at the time.'

'Yes, she'd only lived there a few years.'

The Hound understood from this that the former commissioner hadn't been sitting on his hands; clues were being gathered, rumours collected.

Then Bares embraced him sadly and, with his relatives, accompanied his niece to the cemetery.

Now they were seated in front of an unlit fireplace, under two large windows facing the river.

'I received an anonymous call,' the Hound began.

'And?'

'And it seems that the story may be different.'

A muscle on Bares' face twitched. 'A bit weird, indeed.'

'You said it.'

'Your man, Bobo, I don't see him in the role of serial killer. Nutcase, maybe. Wanker, yes. Bus groper, sure. Porn addict, prostitute user, of course. I arrested him a couple of times. Drugs, theft. Little things. He was mean. But a serial killer?'

'That all matches with what the criminals I spoke to told me.'

'And the phone call?'

'Someone who wanted to sound foreign.'

'Did you record it?'

'He called my landline number. I'm still in the phonebook... I don't have recording devices ready to set up that quickly here.'

'What did he say?'

'That Letizia De Rossi was afraid of the old fascists.'

'The old fascists?'

'Yeah. So something came back to me.'

'The time you talked to her. In Venice.'

'A memory is like a hard drive!'

Bares grinned, with his eyes he was telling the journalist to go on.

'You know I've always been working on bombings. The fascist bombings as well as the state ones. And you know that the Venetian fascists were involved in most of those.'

'A well-connected mob,' Bares interjected. 'I knew Pasquale Juliano, the commissioner who caught them in Padua after the first attacks in '69, before he was taken off the case. There was a real policeman, unlike his traitorous bosses who stitched him up to protect the fascists.'

'Yes. If they had left him to carry out his work, there would have been no Piazza Fontana bombing, for example. Nor many others.'

'And this Letizia?'

'She was Bruno Manfroi's lover for a few years.'

'Manfroi? Wasn't he an informant?'

'He was the man who, on behalf of the CIA, helped the Venetian fascists with the bombing conspiracy. The one who authorised them to plant the bombs and who, in the early days, was preparing them himself. I've been pressing him for a while. He tells me things.'

'Didn't he repent?'

'He confessed to a few things, after they collared him for arms trafficking, but said very little about the bombings. He says that he was only a "controller" of the subversive groups on behalf of the Americans, in the Cold War years – there to stave off the communist danger, back when it was convenient to have a few squads and potential coup leaders standing by. And when it was also necessary to keep an eye on them, to prevent them from going off the rails. Or that's how he tells it. Although what he doesn't say is that not everybody in the US intelligence services agreed with this line.'

'And the bombings?'

'He distances himself from all that.'

'Does he just blame the fascists for them?'

'Yes. He says that at some point they wanted to go it alone. Fear and disorder were what they were after, to provoke a coup, like in Greece. He says that people in his position were actually defending Western democracy from both the communists and the fascists, even if they had to conspire with them sometimes to do it. He considers himself a Western hero. A kind of honorary American.'

'Bullshit! He's Italian, like you and me. What is he doing now?'

'He's not well, he's in a clinic, far from here. He had a stroke. And a tumour. I don't believe him when he says he doesn't know anything. But when I push it, he pretends to have confused ideas, he stammers, he closes down.'

'Did you get him to trust you?'

'He lets me see him at the clinic. No one else visits him. We talk. I take him books.'

'Is he under surveillance?'

'I've never seen anyone. But it was a struggle to find out where he was.'

'And could he have anything to do with these killings?'

'I was thinking of Letizia De Rossi. If she was afraid of the old fascists, as the tip said, maybe she was afraid of him too. When I spoke to her, she seemed angry at Manfroi and the other fascists. She was not only Manfroi's lover, she was also a militant of their group, although she was younger than the others and had joined after the bombings, in the last phase of their activities.'

'I was far away from there at the time. What did they do next?'

'Some escaped, others went back to living quiet ordinary lives. You always survive on the right of politics. And you generally stay in touch with each other, just in case. Especially when new inquiries about the bombings start closing in again. Then, they all collectively retreat into their shell.'

'The first thing to do,' Bares said, 'is to know the truth about Boboli. If he didn't commit suicide and if he wasn't executed by the underworld, then anything is possible. Using objects to rape the victims may not have been the dirty fantasy of someone suffering from impotence, but a way to leave no traces, and to confuse things.'

He met with the Hound a week later.

'The underground can be ruled out,' he began. 'And suicide too. At least in two of the murders they are sure that Bobo was not involved, as they also told you.'

'And how do they know?'

'They just know, and I believe them. I spoke to someone I have known since childhood. One of the real local bosses. It suits them fine for everyone to think Bobo is the killer; that way the police let up with their siege of the neighbourhood. But they are sure that Bobo wasn't involved.'

The Hound had also made his own inquiries. He had reread his notes from the interview he'd conducted with Letizia De Rossi all those years ago. Among the things he had not published were allusions to the American intelligence officer who followed Manfroi. When he collaborated, after being accused of subversion and various attacks, Manfroi defended himself by asserting his links with the US intelligence. He had even mentioned a name, then another, but it turned out they didn't exist. Letizia De Rossi had hinted that they were false names, a cover-up. She also alluded to the fact that, with a little money, things could be learned and that she could reveal more.

The journalist hadn't taken her very seriously. She came across as a confused woman looking for money. He already knew she owed money, that she used cocaine and had a drink problem. But now, after they'd found her tortured and killed, and after learning that she feared some 'old fascist', he needed to think again.

He had also been digging into the so-called 'old fascists'. As much as they hated him, a couple of them had become talkative and a bit mythomaniacal in their old age, and succumbed to his maieutic arts and talked. Maybe it was one of them who'd made that anonymous call to him, he thought. One even explained that Letizia had been blackmailing someone with those old stories or at least was trying to.

'So, someone wanted to get rid of De Rossi: would Vania and Mariangela have been killed just to throw everyone off the scent? And Bobo too?' Bares asked. 'Seems a bit elaborate.'

'It's a possibility. It suits their style. They were used to killing ordinary, innocent people, people – on trains, in banks, in the square – just to influence the political situation, to put pressure on the state.'

'Names?'

The Hound did not answer, but said he had been back to see Manfroi at the clinic.

'As soon as I mentioned Letizia De Rossi, he pretended to have one of his memory lapses; he always gets them when you get serious with him. The closer you get to the heart of darkness, the more he gets suddenly confused, or pretends to be, running away from the issue.'

As they stared at the papers on the desk in front of them, the two of them wove together what they knew, connected some dots and tried to build a bridge between the recent brutal events and the ferocious bombings that had marked Italian history and that Letizia De Rossi had ever so faintly touched upon, despite almost certainly knowing some of the more unmentionable aspects of them.

'Tomorrow I'm going back to Manfroi,' said the Hound.

That afternoon, Bares went to his niece's grave. The following evening he hardly slept. Before dawn he went to an unguarded parking lot along the Terraglio road, left his car there and stole another. With that, a light-coloured Fiat Tipo that did not attract much attention, he parked near the house of the Hound.

The journalist left at around nine, got into his dark green Alfa Romeo and drove off.

Bares followed him and eventually reached Carnia and the clinic where Manfroi was staying. He parked on the avenue in front on the clinic, just before the gate leading to the private car park inside the clinic's grounds, where the Hound had parked.

An hour and a half later he saw the Hound come out, cross the clinic car park and get into his car.

He called him on his mobile.

'You are telepathic. I just left Mr. Fubbi.'

'And who would that be?'

'Mr. Gerardo Fubbi alias Bruno Manfroi. He's registered there under that name.'

'And…?'

'He practically admitted everything, but without actually knowing he was doing it.'

'Explain yourself.'

'He is in really bad shape. Really. Sometimes he just raves constantly. He always did this. Only, before he *pretended* to be raving, to tell lies or to say nothing, while now it seems that the consequences of the stroke make him say the actual truth. A little bit of it, at least. When I mentioned Letizia, he first pretended not to know her, like last time. But then he muttered that she was a blackmailing slut and that real secrets can't be touched. And whoever touches them dies.'

'Well, that's a confession.'

'Practically yes. But unusable, you know that as much as I do. You could see that he was suffering, that he was almost delirious. At one point, a doctor and a nurse arrived and decided to sedate him. And goodbye Fubbi. O Manfroi.'

Bares was silent. Sunk in the Tipo, one hand holding the mobile and the other closed in a fist, his nails stuck in the flesh.

'Is he in intensive care?' he asked.

'In Neurology, in a single room. I left him sleeping like a little angel.'

*The little angel of death*, Bares thought.

When he saw the Alfa Romeo go away, he stuck a fake grey beard to his cheeks and chin, put on a pair of spectacles that he'd never really needed, and put a cap on with a dark visor, grey like the raincoat he was wearing. Then he got out of the car and entered the clinic. With a determined pace he stopped in front of the information banner hanging in the hall, as if looking for a doctor. Instead, he looked at the directions to the wards and walked confidently towards Neurology.

Nobody stopped him or asked who he was. The corridor where the inpatient rooms were located was deserted. Manfroi-Fubbi was in the last room. His door was half open and Bares walked over and looked inside. He was alone, asleep.

A pillow would have been enough. Found there, like the tools of torture and death found in the house and used by the torturer of Vania, Letizia and Adelina. And Bobo.

A soft pressure. A little pressure would have been enough.

He approached.

*You should look at me in the eyes though. You should understand, you should know that your time has come. I have to do it* – he thought.

*I have to do it.* So said the young American, coming out of his hiding place behind the old house where Bares lived with his mother and sister.

He had arrived secretly a month earlier, in the winter of 44/45. He had gone up the peninsula from Anzio, bypassing the German and fascist positions, entering the territory of the Italian Social Republic and reaching Venice. He had to make contact with the partisan formations and, in particular, in Porto Marghera, report by radio on the movements and positions of the Germans who were garrisoning it.

He was of Italian origin, Bares remembered that his name was Giovanni, that is, John. He never knew the surname. He was a policeman, before leaving for Europe with the army. He carried out those special, high-risk tasks, beyond the lines. He knew a little Italian, learned from his parents who had emigrated from Piedmont twenty-five years earlier. His mother had given birth to him as soon as she had landed in New York.

The Germans had understood that someone was operating clandestinely under their noses and had begun to check, search, rake the neighbourhood and its surroundings. It took a traitor, however, to capture the young man. His name was Pietro Dondi and he had seen John hiding inside a semi-abandoned house, not far from where Bares lived.

The Nazis, led by Dondi, surrounded the area, but could not find the young American. John had discovered a practically invisible hole among the brush and bushes and hid in it. In the little house they had found the radio, but not him. And so they threatened to shoot five men in the neighbourhood, in retaliation.

They put them against the school wall and an officer shouted through a megaphone in Italian and English that he would order firing if the American spy did not come out within five minutes.

Not even two had passed when John came out of his hiding. He passed by Bares' house and his mother said to him: 'My child, what are you doing?'

She had fed him a couple of times. Bares had heard him telling a little of his story: he told of his Italian origins, that he was a policeman, that he loved New York and America.

'What are you doing?' his mother repeated.

'*I have to do it.* I can't let them be executed,' he said, and walked over to the Germans.

'Here he is, it's him!' cried Pietro Dondi.

He was imprisoned and tortured. He was saved because negotiations had begun, while partisan actions intensified and the Allies were approaching Venice. At the negotiation table, the release of prisoners was requested and John was eventually let out. Bares saw him again when the Germans left and the partisans took control of the city. One day, John returned to greet his mother, and Toaldo Bares asked him what the Germans had done to him.

'Bad things, but nothing that cannot be endured and forgotten,' he replied.

'And the infamous Dondi?' asked his mother. 'I hope they hanged him.'

'I saved him,' John said.

'You?'

'Yes. They wanted to shoot him on the spot. But I convinced them to put him on trial. A free country can really have a new beginning if it pursues justice in a court. They taught me that at the police school in New York,' he said, smiling.

He bore the marks of the harsh treatment reserved for him by the Germans and the fascists. He had one arm in a sling and was limping, his face bruised. But it conveyed strength, confidence, loyalty.

Toaldo Bares never saw him again.

*I have to do it*, he repeated to himself. He looked at Manfroi asleep, perhaps slipping towards agony, or perhaps towards another recovery yet, another bit of life. A monster of history who had to meet justice and not revenge, he thought. He also thought that perhaps justice would not be done, not even this time. It wasn't done for the infamous Dondi. He got away cheaply. He just swapped one city for another, shortly after 1945.

Yes, not all the necessary justice was done, but that wasn't a good reason to give up looking for it.

He left Manfroi's room without looking at him again, entered the corridor and left. He stopped under the trees. Lime trees, he noticed, planes and poplars.

'I have to tell this story to the Hound,' he said to himself.

## Note

1. *Mafia del Brenta:* A crime organisation which started as a small gang of criminals controlling racketeering along the Riviera del Brent between Padua and Venice, but which became an international syndicate under the boss Felice Maniero during the '80s and '90s.

# Afterword: Scars and Stripes

## Maurizio Dianese

Translated from the Italian by Orsola Casagrande

On 12 December 1969, between 4.37pm and 5.16pm, a series of explosions rocked Rome and Milan. The bombs in Rome left fourteen injured at the headquarters of the Banca Nazionale del Lavoro (National Labour Bank) and three at the entrance of the Risorgimento Museum. A third, placed at the Altare della patria (Altar of the Fatherland), caused no significant damage. In Milan, the story was far more tragic. A bomb at the Banca nazionale dell'agricoltura (National Agricultural Bank), on Piazza Fontana, resulted in seventeen deaths and 88 injuries. Another planted at the headquarters of the Banca commerciale (Commercial Bank) of Milan failed to explode and was detonated by a bomb disposal squad. These five bombs and the date – 12 December 1969 – will forever be seared into Italy's modern history.

Today, 50 years on, we know everything about the Piazza Fontana bombing. That is that to say: we know that the script of the attack on the Banca nazionale dell'agricoltura was written in Washington, while the casting was organised in Rome. The main scenes of the tragedy that brought the country to the verge of a military coup, were instead shot in Veneto, between Venice, Mestre, Treviso, Padua and Verona, before the production moved to Milan.[1] It took decades for the details of this so-called 'strategy of tension' to come to light. However, 36 years' worth of trials have failed to result in adequate sentencing for either the main culprits or those responsible for misleading the investigation.[2]

Everything, however, was clear from the beginning. A few days before the Piazza Fontana bombing, on 7 December 1969, journalist Leslie Finer used the expression 'strategy of tension' for the first time in an article published in the British weekly, *The Observer,* and based on documents that MI6 had stolen from the Greek ambassador in Italy. Finer argued that the Unites States, supported by the newborn (in 1967) regime of the Greek colonels, had orchestrated a precise political-military plan. The plan was designed to put pressure on certain European governments and thus favoured, through terrorist attacks, provocation and intimidation, all forms of political shift to the right, be they moderate or authoritarian (such as the establishment of the junta in Greece in April 1967). In Italy, Finer wrote, 'a far-right group and some military officers are plotting a military coup with the encouragement and support of the Greek government and its Prime Minister Georgios Papadopoulus. The goals of this plan would be early elections, the elimination of the centre left, a return to moderate politics, a presidential-oriented constitutional reform, the total marginalisation of the left.' The piece only fell short of hinting at Italy's limited sovereignty, due to the interference of the United States.

Moreover, Finer's article outlined a strategy that was very reminiscent of Operation CHAOS implemented by the CIA between 1967 and 1974.[3] Initially conceived to counter, through infiltration and provocation, the American student and pacifist movements back home, this is how historian Aldo Giannuli describes its roll-out: '[The project] was also extended to Europe by urging local secret services to expose the foreign influences (clearly Soviet) behind those movements which had simultaneously exploded in France, USA, Argentina, Germany, England, Mexico, etc. It is in this context that the relations between the CIA and Aginter Press[4] (the group of former OAS refugees in Lisbon, capable of infiltrating leftist movements), will find fertile ground and develop. Some will argue – not without reason – that the real purpose of the plan was to destabilise the European allied countries in order to accentuate their dependence on NATO. In other words, fomenting internal destabilisation to stabilise the Alliance.'[5]

In Italy, the strategists behind this 'destabilise to stabilise' operation – as the neo-fascist Vincenzo Vinciguerra would later call it – were the SID (Italian Military Intelligence and Security Service, now SISMI) and the American secret services. After all, 'from an historical point of view, it is undeniable that the SID worked in close contact with, almost submitted to, the American services,' as Gerardo D'Ambrosio, former Deputy Prosecutor of Milan who investigated the Piazza Fontana bombing, explained in an interview for *Corriere della Sera* on 28 April 2005. In other words, the Americans required information from the Italian services, but gave none in return, as can be deduced from a 1959 note from SID, found by Police Inspector Michele Cacioppo who talked about it at the Corte di Assise di Brescia (Assize Court of Brescia), on 20 May 2010.

It is clear from this note – Cacioppo explained – that 'there was a steady collaboration because when the Americans, those of the CIC (Counter Intelligence Corps) deployed in the Verona and Vicenza offices, asked the Italian counter-intelligence for information, they asked Milan and Padua. Most of the American requests were filed to these two centres. In 1966, it was decided that all counterintelligence centres were to report to Department D (of the SID) on what type of activities and what information they had exchanged with the Americans. From the responses sent by all the centres to Department D, which in turn issued a note for the head of the service, we can see that this collaboration was in fact one-sided. The Americans asked, but never gave anything in return. Another thing then emerged: The Americans were raising their voice, as also proved by the papers of SID and SIFAR (Italian Armed Forces Secret Services). The Americans were the masters of the Italian intelligence, so to speak.'

In an interview with *La Repubblica*, dated 4 August 2000, Gianadelio Maletti, who in 1971 was the head of Department D (counterintelligence) of SID, stated: 'I had direct relations with the CIA. With Howard Stone, known as Rocky, head of the Rome station, and Mike Sednaoui, an agent of Algerian origin. Italy was, for the CIA, the most important security section in all of Western Europe. The information acquired in Italy was then contrasted with the other major centre in Europe, the German one. Germany had been a recruiting country since the end of World War II. The CIA wanted, through the revival of angry nationalism and with the contribution of the far right – Ordine Nuovo (New Order) in particular – to stop this shift towards the left. This is the basic assumption on which the strategy of tension was built.'

'How was the CIA going to achieve that?' *La Repubblica* asked. 'By letting things happen' – Maletti replied. The CIA, he continued, used Ordine Nuovo 'with its informers and collaborators in various Italian cities and in some NATO bases: Aviano, Naples [...] had liaison functions between various Italian and German far-right groups and dictated the rules of conduct. It also supplied the material [...] numerous caches of explosives brought from Germany through the Gotthard Pass directly to Friuli and Veneto [...] In 1972 the counter-espionage centre in Padua reported that caches of explosives had arrived from Germany, destined for Ordine Nuovo. I reported it to the higher levels, but nothing happened. We also reported that the explosives used in Piazza Fontana came from one of these caches.'

In this way, the American intelligence services not only 'let things happen', but played an active role in the bombing campaign carried out by Ordine Nuovo, since those explosives arriving from Germany came from an American base. Moreover, the CIA in Italy directly 'manoeuvred' Carlo Digilio, who was in charge of making the neo-fascist bombs used in the attacks.

'There is no direct evidence that the CIA was actually the instigator of Piazza Fontana,' Maletti told *La Repubblica*, 'but that's the case. It cannot be said that the CIA had an active, direct role in the bombings, but that they knew about them and knew their targets and authors is a fact. The CIA tried to do what it had done in Greece in 1967, when the military coup took out Papandreou. In Italy, the situation got out of hand. The bombing was not supposed to cause so many deaths.'

Like Frankenstein's monster, the project set up by the Americans to prevent Italy from 'shifting' leftwards and getting closer to the Soviet Union, got out of hand, even though they had complete control over key men of the project, such as Federico Umberto D'Amato.

Born in Marseille in 1919 of Italian parents, and Commissioner of Public Security, during the war, D'Amato had carried out counter-espionage activities for and in collaboration with the Anglo-American secret services, in particular with the head of the United States secret service, the Office of Strategic Services (OSS), James Angleton. Immediately after the war, D'Amato had become superintendent of the Special Secretariat of the Atlantic Pact. In practice, he was the liaison officer between Italy, the United States and NATO. In 1954, he entered the Ufficio Affari Riservati (UAR – Office for Reserved Affairs of the Italian Ministry of Interior) – the main agency responsible for misleading the investigations into the bombing of 12 December 1969 – and remained there for most of his career, formally becoming its director only in 1972 but having been its strongman since the beginning and indeed beyond 1974 (when he was officially reassigned to the border police).

D'Amato was so important that when he died, in 1996, one of the most prestigious rooms in the NATO headquarters in Brussels, was named after him, a posthumous honour, never obtained by any other member of the Italian intelligence. He was, therefore, a man with links to the very highest echelons of NATO and was also a key figure in the bombing season that began in the mid-1960s. As well as being followed every step of the way by the CIA, D'Amato was also no doubt fully informed about everything that was happening since, like Digilio, the explosives expert, and other members of Ordine Nuovo, he was on their payroll, reporting regularly to the NATO base in Verona, in Via Roma 8, home of the FTASE Command (Allied Land Forces Southern Europe).

The Venetian Carlo Digilio was easily the most important of these informants,[6] having direct contact with the Venetian cell that was implementing the 'strategy of tension' through bomb attacks, under the direction of the Italian services controlled in turn by the American services. In a meeting with his American counterpart, David Carret, in the first days of December 1969, Digilio, simultaneously a CIA informant and a weapons expert working for Ordine Nuovo, told him what was about to happen only to discover that Captain Carret already knew: 'the right [...] were preparing something big.'[7]

The meeting – the two met twice a month – took place in Piazza San Marco. Carret and Digilio sat at the Caffè Quadri to exchange information. Digilio recalled that the US Navy officer didn't flinch when he was told that the neo-fascists of Ordine Nuovo were about to deliver a 'big bang'. If, on other occasions the Carret had invited Digilio to step in and defuse or at least build less powerful bombs for the Venetian, Paduan, Treviso and Veronese fascists to use – on trains, in stations or at trade fairs – this time, however, he acted as if nothing was to be done. At the next meeting, on 7 January 1970, three weeks after the Piazza Fontana bombing, Captain Carret, who had just returned from a short holiday in the United States, further reassured Digilio, who was quite worried, to say the least, about what was happening in Italy and about the involvement of the Venice members of Ordine Nuovo, whom he knew well. After all, he lived in Sant'Elena (in Venice) and went dining at the restaurant Allo Scalinetto, near the Arsenale, where all the Venetian neo-fascists regularly met.

'Carret told me that Ordine Nuovo would not be affected by the investigation. I had the impression,' recalled Digilio 'that what was happening was a concurrence of factors already preordained and decided.'[8] By the Italian secret services in collaboration – or indeed guided – by the US services.

'I would not be surprised if one day it turned out that even segments of the secret services of allied or neutral countries, not just enemies, had an interest in maintaining the tension in Italy between the communist and anti-communist front,' said the former Italian president Francesco Cossiga in an interview in 1995.[9] And the SID counterintelligence chief, Maletti, confessed to journalist Andrea Sceresini that those days in December were governed by 'a precise American strategy: I am certain that both the head of State [President Giuseppe Saragat] and Giulio Andreotti [prime minister] were aware of it.'[10]

What we know for sure is that the Venetian branch of Ordine Nuovo, led by Carlo Maria Maggi, had been watched by the US intelligence agencies at least since 1967, thanks to the periodic information reports of Digilio, who followed in his father's footsteps when it came to collaborating with American intelligence, he even inherited his father's code name.: Herodotus.

'My father worked as an informant for the Americans, specifically for the OSS (Office of Strategic Services) after 1943,' Digilio told Judge Guido Salvini in the interrogation on 5 March 1994. 'Around 1966 my father introduced me to Captain Carret and I became part of the same structure my father was working for. Around 1974, Captain Carret was replaced by Captain Teddy Richards, who told me he was stationed at the NATO base in Vicenza, while David Carret was stationed at the base in Verona.'[11]

In the 2000s, the Milan Public Prosecutor's Office sent the FBI a request to identify both David Carret – already identified by several witnesses from the photographs taken at the time in Verona, where he was stationed – and Teddy Richards. To this day, no answer has been received.

Digilio is not the only Venetian member of Ordine Nuovo to have established a relationship with US personnel. The list is long and includes many neo-fascists, starting with Sergio

Minetto, Marcello Soffiati (certificates of the attendance of right-wing extremists to the US military base of Camp Darby in Pisa were found in his house in December 1974) and Giovanni Bandoli, a civilian attached to the American forces. All three were from Verona, but in reality, as we have seen, the US services were constantly monitoring what was happening across the whole of Italy since they also used the Italian services directly. The officers in direct contact with the Venetian members of Ordine Nuovo were more likely those of the Counter Intelligence Corps, the US military's intelligence services, even if CIA agents were present in the NATO bases and, as Digilio claimed, the CIA were paying him 'in Italian liras, a sum that was around 300,000 liras, which I received almost every month.'[12] Not an insignificant amount of money at the time.

David Carret was Digilio's 'controller' and also the person paying him. A solid relationship had been established between the two over time, to the point that Carret let his guard slip more than once, as when he confirmed to Digilio that the strategic objective of the bombing season in 1969 was to achieve a shift to the right in Italian politics. A shift not brought about through a military coup, but through a strengthening of the state. 'Later Captain Carret confirmed to me that that project, which was watched closely by the Americans, had failed due to the hesitation of some Christian Democrat politicians such as Mariano Rumor,'[13] the then prime minister, who, in the aftermath of the Piazza Fontana bombing, the neo-fascists thought would call the state of emergency, thus opening the door to the army, in a move that would have strengthened the 'Atlantic' wing within the government. It must be borne in mind, in fact, that at that time, the main governing party, the Christian Democrats, had made significant overtures to the Italian left as well as to the workers' and student movements, something which was worrying both the moderate wing of the party and the President, the Social Democrat Giuseppe Saragat, someone definitely very close to the US.

'Carret explained to me,' continued Digilio, 'that even though there had not been the hoped for shift to the right, the situation was still under control and, despite the reaction of the left, Ordine Nuovo would not be affected by the investigations. He also told me that in the days following the bombing, both Italian and American military ships had been ordered to leave the ports because, in the event of widespread demonstrations or clashes, if they were anchored in the ports it would have been easier for protestors to target them. I remember Carret telling me that Italy was on a "path of thorns".'

Indeed, the popular reaction to the Piazza Fontana bombing was immediate and left no room for doubt. Italians were ready to take to the streets to defend democracy. The huge crowd that attended the funeral of the victims in Milan on 15 December was so big as to convince the murderers and instigators not to proceed with other plans.

The investigations that had initially followed a trail towards Italian anarchists, only 'swerved' onto a trail leading to the neo-fascist thanks to the Treviso investigation led by judges Pietro Calogero and Giancarlo Stiz based on the statements of Guido Lorenzon.

Lorenzon was a teacher who had received the confidences of one of his students, Giovanni Ventura who, with the Paduan Franco Freda, was among the leaders of the Venetian neo-fascists. Lorenzon told everything he had heard, thus enabling the Treviso magistrates to arrest both Freda and Ventura. The rest of the Venetian cell of Ordine Nuovo, however, would remain 'untouched' for over twenty years.

Only in the mid-90s did judge Guido Salvini reopen the investigation, exposing in detail the subversive plots, including the involvement of Digilio and therefore of the Americans. But Salvini would then be stopped, right at the finishing line, by other magistrates who, in good or bad faith, effectively blocked his investigation.

The result is that we know everything about the strategy of tension and the bombing season of the late '60s, from a historical point of view, while nothing has been established from a judicial one and, to this day and perhaps forever, the Piazza Fontana bombing simply has no perpetrators, unless you count Freda and Ventura who can no longer be tried because they were acquitted of the charge of massacre twenty years ago.[14]

It is what Guido Lorenzon called 'the curse of Piazza Fontana', which became the title of the book written by Judge Salvini and Andrea Sceresini about the case. A book that tells in detail how a thousand times we have come only one step away from reaching the truth, in the form of a verdict, only for someone's long hand to reach back over and block it all again. And there seems to be an unwritten rule under all these legal frustrations: there must be no trace of interference from the Americans in this. The Italians did everything by themselves.

As for the US, former President Francesco Cossiga has also said that in that period the States were exercising an 'observation without repression' policy that refrained from interfering with the subversive events deemed useful to maintain the *status quo* in Italy. In short, many of the men who revolve around Piazza Fontana lead directly to the NATO base in Verona, in Via Roma 8, where the FTASE Command was located.

This long and bloody period of Italian history, that still stains us as a country, were draped in stars and stripes.

## Notes

1. Italy had seen a wave of non-fatal bombings by far-right groups earlier in 1969: in Milan, on 25 April, three bombs exploded: the first in the Fiat pavilion of the Milan Trade Fair, leaving twenty people injured, and a further two at Central Station; whilst on 8 and 9 August, eight bombs exploded on different trains – at the stations of Chiari, Grisignano, Caserta, Alviano, Pescara, Pescina and Mira, injuring twelve people – with two further bombs being found, unexploded, in Milan Central and Venice Santa Lucia stations.
2. Initially anarchists were thought to have been responsible. Giuseppe Pinelli, a railway worker and member of Milan-based anarchist association 'Ponte della Ghisolfa', was arrested and shortly after, while being illegally detained by police, died after falling from the fourth-floor police station window. Another anarchist, the dancer Pietro Valpreda was arrested and convicted, but after eighteen years in jail (including three years pre-trial) was acquitted and released in 1987. It is suspected he was mistaken by a witness for the neo-fascist Antonio Sottosanti, who apparently looked very similar to him.
3. A CIA domestic espionage project targeting the American people from 1967 to 1974, established by President. Johnson and expanded under Nixon, designed to uncover possible foreign influence on domestic race, anti-war and other protest movements. Launched under Director of Central Intelligence Richard Helms, by chief of counter-intelligence James Jesus Angleton, and headed by Richard Ober.
4. An international mercenary anti-communist organisation disguised as a pseudo-press agency and active between 1966 and 1974. Founded in Lisbon in September 1966, Aginter Press was directed by Captain Yves Guérin-Sérac, who had been involved in the foundation of the OAS (Secret Armed Organisation) in Madrid, a terrorist group known for fighting against Algerian independence towards the end of the Algerian War (1954–1962).
5. Giannulli, Aldo, *The Strategy of Tension: Secret Services, Parties, Failed Coups, Fascist Terror, and International Politics – A Definitive Balance Sheet*, (Ponte alle Grazie, 2018), pp115-116.
6. The son of a soldier and an US informant who worked for the NATO base in Veneto under the code name. 'Herodotus', Carlo Digilio (1937-2005) followed in his father's footsteps, replacing him

when he died in exactly the same informant role, even keeping the same code name. At the same time, Digilio worked as an active militant in Ordine Nuovo, and was nicknamed 'Uncle Otto' by his friends. Later he would confess to being directly involved in both the Piazza Fontana and Brescia massacres, as a gunsmith and explosives expert for the Ordine Nuovo militia headed by Carlo Maria Maggi. Under investigation in the 1980s for attempting to reconstitute the Fascist Party, he fled from Venice to Santo Domingo. Arrested in 1992, he was extradited to Italy, where a ten-year sentence for reconstituting the Fascist Party awaited him. In April 1994, he began to collaborate with the Milan judge Guido Salvini. Digilio is the only person ever convicted of the Piazza Fontana massacre, but thanks to his collaboration, the sentence was prescribed and the court ruled a 'not having to proceed' sentence in 30 June 2001. He died, by a twist of fate, on 12 December 2005, the anniversary of the Piazza Fontana massacre.

7. Testimony given on 5 March 1997.
8. *ibid.*
9. Cossiga Francesco, in an interview given to Lucio Caracciolo, *Limes.*
10. A. Sceresini N. Palma, M.E. Scandaliato, *Piazza Fontana: Noi sapevamo* (Piazza Fontana: We Knew), Aliberti 2010), p103.
11. Testimony to judge Guido Salvini, 5 March 1994.
12. Testimony, 21 February 1997.
13. *ibid.*
14. In 1973, Ventura pled guilty to his involvement in 21 bombings in total, denying only the Piazza Fontana massacre, and was found guilty of 'subversive association' in relation to the non-fatal spring-summer bombings, going on to serve 11 years in prison. Freda was found innocent and continues to be a prominent figure of the far-right.

# Petit Four

## Hüseyin Karabey

Translated from the Turkish by Mustafa Gündoğdu

He glowered at the young man standing in front of him whispering to his friend. It made him uncomfortable. Normally, in such situations, he would reach for reassurance in the form of the gun holstered under his left arm. The tram was late. To avoid a 500-metre uphill walk, around twenty people stood at the platform waiting for Europe's second-oldest metro. It was a popular spot at this time of day, more than enough people around.

They were students, he was sure of it. He didn't recognise them, but he never forgot a face. Now his friend was looking at him sideways too. Out of the corner of his eye, he could see exactly what they were doing. Slowly he edged to the front of the crowd. Like most other people living on the Asian side of Istanbul, his daily commute would start with the ferry to Karaköy then take this 100-year-old tunnel the last stretch of the way to Beyoğlu. He loved this route, it enabled him to be among all kinds of people from different walks of life – something Istanbul was always great for.

The military coup had an impact on all aspects of daily life. On 12th March that year, high-ranking soldiers had released a statement forcing the government to resign and ushering in a new, transitional regime appointed by the military. A state of emergency was declared in various provinces and widespread arrests continued. He knew all this because the coup had been his idea. This was why, that morning, he refrained from engaging with the young men staring at him on the platform. The chances of him being recognised were low and he never suspected he'd be attacked in broad daylight. Of course, he hadn't orchestrated the coup alone. He'd had a large institution behind him. But it was his devilish plan that had brought the coup to fruition, and for this reason, he felt the people around him always sensed what an important person he was. Finally, the tram arrived and everyone boarded. He glanced back at the two students. This time they weren't even trying to hide their glares, openly gesturing towards him as they talked.

Of course, it wasn't just the two men that made him nervous. Today was an important day, and he was on his way to a make-or-break meeting. First, though, he had to stop by the CIA office at the American Consulate. Yes, he was an agent. Moreover, he was the chief of the Istanbul station. To reiterate: he was a very important person.

He always knew one day he would live in Istanbul but he didn't think it would happen so early in his career. He was expecting to be assigned a post in Cyprus but at the last minute, headquarters asked him to take the helm in Istanbul instead. Little did he know the next five years in Turkey would be such a turning point in his career. Things would change for him, he knew, but he assumed this would be in regard to his personal life rather than his work.

After 90 seconds the tram had climbed 500 metres up the steep slope. Police officers standing by the door checked those leaving the tram in a hurry. It was then he noticed the students who'd been standing right behind him had disappeared. While the uniformed officers just stared into people's faces, two other plain-clothed officers, standing further back, casually crosschecked the faces in front of them against wanted photographs in their hands. Dewey noticed one of the plain-clothed officers recognised him, and tried to remember where he'd seen him before. Maybe it was at the meeting last week – a routine session with MİT, the Turkish Intelligence Service. The kind where they gave out new instructions and checked the status of previous orders.

Dewey had told himself how important he was from a very early age. It was more of a feeling than something he knew as a fact. He had grown up with three brothers and two sisters. They weren't Mormons or anything like that, but his parents had been very conservative in their beliefs and hadn't believed in birth control. When he was six years old, his grandfather sat him down and said: 'Number One! You are a very important person. A very, very important person! Never forget this!'

His grandfather never called him by his name. Although he had two older sisters, he would always refer to him as 'Number One', being his first grandson. When he asked his grandfather why he was such an important person, his grandfather said, 'You will know when the time comes.' He never asked this question again but always expected the next time he saw his grandfather he would explain more. Nowadays, he no longer needed an explanation. He knew his grandfather was right.

Two officers he valued always attended his MİT meetings. Tarık was MİT's long-standing director responsible for Istanbul. His father had been among the founders of the Turkish Republic. He was very fond of Tarık, and saw him as a friend. Once, during an operation, he had saved Dewey's life, putting his own life at risk. The incident had moved him greatly. For days he wondered if he would have found the same courage in a similar situation. In training, he'd been taught the most important duty is to save his own life first. *Stay alive – you are important*, was the mantra. But when he felt the cold breeze of death on his neck that day, he felt something different and swore, if he ever had another son, he would name him 'Tarık'. The other important MİT officer was Hiram, a new generation intelligence officer brought up in CIA schools. The agency had an international programme through which it developed long-term contacts with young talents like him. Through various channels, they would gather information on promising students in the army, police and local intelligence agencies in allied countries and then provide them with rigorous training. The CIA would also pay these assets' salaries (sometimes supplementary salaries so they could keep their day jobs). Hiram was one such asset.

Hiram was the person he was to meet on this most important of days. Even Tarık didn't know about the meeting. Officially Hiram worked for MİT, but both he and Tarık knew who their real boss was. A third person was to attend the meeting, someone they needed to convince their plans would work, namely the Deputy Consul General of Israel in Istanbul. Organising the coup had been a small detail in this much bigger plan. Perhaps they were being over-confident, but nothing would be the same again if they pulled it off. The plan was also designed to eliminate anyone who tried to prevent its own implementation. This was the moment his grandfather had told him about...

He had a lot on this plate. So many things needed his attention if this was going to work. But none of these would have been a problem if he hadn't had other things on his mind. His marriage to Maggie was over and they still hadn't talked about it properly with their children. Their fourteen-year-old daughter knew it was serious this time, but their eight-year-old son was oblivious. For all he knew, Dad was away at work. He was always away. And Maggie did what she could to distract them from his absence.

Dewey had practically grown up with Maggie. They had met in Third Grade at primary school. Within a year they were already talking about where they would get married when they were older. Before they knew it they were married and with two kids. Maggie had always arranged her life around her husband. His first post abroad was in Katmandu. This was followed by Nepal and New Delhi. They never stayed in one place for longer than two years, and all the responsibilities for finding new schools and setting up each new home fell on Maggie. Even when he was in the same city, he sometimes didn't come home for days but when he did Maggie always greeted him with a smile. Whenever he looked at her, his mother would come to mind. He was lucky, he knew it but still, something was missing. At the end of the day, he wasn't like his father or his friends from college either. Ambition and a love for the work were what drove him. He wasn't cut out for ordinary, family life.

Beyoğlu was packed with historic buildings or, to be more precise, with history. Many of the buildings were built even before their country was formed. All of them had stories, and the Karaköy tunnel was no different. That was what impressed Dewey so much. The distance from the tunnel's exit to the consulate building was about ten minutes on foot but he would savour the journey with a series of small rituals. One of them was drinking a coffee at the historic Markiz patisserie. He would never have his official meetings here. This was a private place for him in Beyoğlu where he could enjoy his coffee in peace while watching passers-by. Today, though, he had no time for coffee but, as he neared the patisserie, he was alarmed to see the two students from the tram again. They were walking towards him although they hadn't seen him yet. He reached under his arm again out of nervousness. The street was crowded so he turned into his patisserie as a precaution. His training told him that this was not an organised threat. If he was the real target his adversaries were amateurs. Even so, he had to be on guard. He always believed, when the time came, he might get attacked from behind or, worse, walk into crossfire after turning a corner. He never thought an attack would come on a busy main street from two student amateurs who'd scarpered at the sight of a couple of cops.

At college, Dewey had studied international relations and proved to be a Grade A student, later being accepted for a masters at Columbia University. His thesis, on how South Asian countries will be affected by the USSR in years to come, was found to be a good piece of work by his professors. When word of it reached the CIA, he received an invitation from the agency. No doubt he had been recommended by one of his tutors who was also on the agency's books. There was no official application procedure for the CIA. They would come and find you and then make you the offer. He often heard rumours about their recruitment at university and, if he was honest with himself, he was waiting for their invitation to arrive. He was ecstatic when it finally did, but the first thing he thought was: *How would Maggie feel about this?* As always, Maggie was supportive. Without any thought for Maggie's career, they married shortly after, in a small ceremony attended only by family, and immediately moved to Washington for Dewey to start his training.

The waiters at the Markiz recognised all their regulars, especially important ones like him. On entering they would immediately show him to his usual place: a table by the window under an Art Nouveau ceramic panel depicting autumn. Dewey took his seat, first checking behind him the way he always did. He tried to look calm. The two students could no longer be seen out on the street. There was no table behind his and, from where he sat, he had clear sight lines on the door and out into the street. His Turkish coffee had already arrived and the waiter asked if he would like anything else. 'No, thank you,' Dewey replied in Turkish. The waiters assumed he was a professor at Robert College. He never said he was but one day he bumped into a French friend there, a history teacher from the college. They caught the waiters' attention, not just because they were two foreigners speaking Turkish but because of what his friend was saying. After listing all the palaces built in Istanbul in the 1840s, his friend began talking about an ancient passage running directly underneath the Markiz patisserie. One of the four panels symbolising seasons had been broken as they were being loaded onto a ship. This was why there was no panel in there for winter. The French friend occasionally provided information to the agency but this coincidental meeting made the patisserie staff think Dewey was also a teacher. When he realised this, Duane didn't disappoint them. He was a teacher, of sorts, as it was, he thought. Usually, he wouldn't eat the complimentary piece of Turkish delight until after he'd finished his coffee, but this time he ate it first. He needed some sugar. Then he took a sip.

Perhaps he should calm down a bit, he thought. He needed to assess the situation as rationally as he could before making a move. He summarised the situation to himself: Maggie hadn't spoken to him that morning, or asked him anything during breakfast with the children. When he said he needed to speak to her in private, Maggie told the children to give their father a hug as he was leaving for work. This was her usual, polite way of kicking him out of the house. It would have been easier if Maggie just screamed and insulted him, but she would never do that. And what could he have said in reply if she had? 'Maggie I've fallen in love with a married woman, and I'd like to be with her. So I guess I don't want to be with you anymore.'

Perhaps he was just an adrenaline junkie; there was no other explanation. He didn't even speak the same language as his new lover. She was the wife of the General Manager of a German automotive company. Dewey didn't speak German and she didn't speak English. In this mesmerising city, they conducted conversations in very broken Turkish. Helga had a strange beauty. She had yet to tell her husband that she wanted a divorce. Their meetings were in secret and they constantly ran the risk of getting caught. So perhaps that was the attraction for him. He was angry with himself, but not enough to stop what he was doing. So that morning he had left the house with a huge sense of guilt. He thought walking to the consulate building would help him shake it off so he had asked his driver and guard to meet him there. He needed to clear his head before the meeting. The walk had indeed helped until the sight of those young men threw him into turmoil again.

This wasn't the only reason the two students got to him. It was more complicated than that. All those innocent-looking faces weren't just a nuisance, they were enemies of the state. But not everyone saw it this way. Even he didn't entirely see it this way, not yet at least.

It all started when he was first assigned to Istanbul in July '68. Just as had happened in Paris in May that year, similar student protests were taking place in Turkey. Paul, the former station director, invited him to his terraced house in Gümüşsuyu. It was a kind of handover meeting between them. Although the mid-July sun blazed down, the terrace itself was cool thanks to a breeze coming in from the Bosporus. The terrace boasted a spectacular view of the entire historical peninsula and the strait. On the right, stood that great symbol of the city, the 1500-year-old Galata Tower and opposite it the mighty Hagia Sophia. On the left, they could see the blue waters of the strait zigzagging up to the Black Sea complete with warships from the 6th Fleet of the American Navy. That Paul had been in the region for a long time was evident from his near-perfect Turkish. Like Dewey, he joined the agency from academia. He was an experienced agent with years of service in the field behind him. For the agency, the most important thing was speaking the local languages and establishing relationships with the local communities as much as possible. Paul had benefitted from this approach, being fluent in Russian, German, Turkish and Arabic and conversant in twelve languages in total. Dewey had taken Turkish lessons for six months after it became clear he'd be heading there, but next to Paul everyone felt a little incompetent. People coming from academia usually got more administrative roles in the agency. There weren't many out in the field. Paul had accepted the invitation to join after completing his PhD at Harvard. Maybe that's why they were looking for someone like him, Dewey thought. What he hadn't known yet was that Paul chose him personally.

Paul nodded towards the 6th Fleet anchored just in front of the Dolmabahçe Palace, saying in Turkish: 'Look, Dewey, that place will soon be bursting at the seams!'

He didn't quite understand what Paul meant. Not yet fluent in Turkish, he simply pretended to understand when he didn't. At that moment a fleet of small boats, carrying US soldiers, started to approach the Kabataş bank. All of a sudden, a crowd of students appeared from nowhere, thronging the harbourside where the soldiers were trying to dock, and chanting 'Yankees Go Home!' The crowd was growing and everyone on the terrace watched it unfold. Dewey slowly began to realise what his chief had meant. He was getting excited. Quickly things became chaotic. A brawl broke out between the youth groups and the soldiers. A couple of American soldiers got knocked into the water which only increased the crowd's excitement. More American soldiers fell, or were thrown, in. Strangely nobody else seemed to intervene. It was the first time Dewey had witnessed something like this, and what was even odder was he could nothing but watch. The few armed guards protecting the unarmed American soldiers, refrained from using their weapons. Then, abruptly Turkish riot police arrived and the place was indeed bursting at the seams. The mass of students gave up the fight and started to disperse.

Dewey turned to Paul excitedly: 'Did you know that was going to happen?'

'Not to the last detail, but it was obvious that something was going to happen.'

'How so?' Dewey asked.

'The students declared a few weeks ago that they were going to protest against the 6th Fleet. Soon after, police raided their dorms, provoking them some more. They even went a little further and threw a student out of the window of his dorm. After that, we were expecting something, though we didn't know it'd be at the dock. And we didn't want to interfere.'

'Why?'

'Why do you think, Dewey? We called you here, so you would know the answers to these questions.'

Dewey normally liked these mind games but on this occasion, he felt belittled, like he was a child being tested. Paul fully understood the situation he was dropping Dewey into and he wanted to enjoy the advantage he had on him for a moment. Yes, Dewey was an important person but Paul was even more important than him. Paul could see his young self in Dewey, so didn't tease his colleague any more.

'Look, Dewey! Do you know what the problem is? These students are very sympathetic, relatable people; they only want a better, freer and more equal life. Moreover they come from the wealthiest, most respectable families in the country. Turkish society just sees them as dreamy romantics. Now imagine what would happen if they got their hands a little dirty, if suddenly they started beating up soldiers who only came here with peaceful intentions and throwing them into the Bosphorus, and if businesses started losing money because of these actions?'

Dewey understood. Adrenalin surged through him as he finally realised that in just his first week here, he was seeing something play out he'd only studied in the abstract in his four years at Langley. He loved this feeling. He cast around, looking for something sweet urgently. He took one of the chocolates from Paul's coffee table and ate it. *This is what it is to be alive*, he thought. They needed to change the image of the students in the public eye. This was why he had come to Istanbul.

The voice of the Markiz waiter interrupted his thoughts.

'Another coffee, sir, or something else?'

Wrenched so unexpectedly from his thoughts, Dewey's hand reached automatically under his left arm again. Realising it was the waiter, he smiled and gently brought his hand back.

'Well then, I guess it's time for some of your famous petit four.'

This was the second morning ritual he couldn't resist: his sugar addiction. He needed it now more than ever. He hadn't finished his analysis of the threat yet, and his brain needed sugar. He had been trained how to analyse such situations at CIA headquarters. It was basic protocol: if you felt under threat, you analysed the wider situation, made a decision, then stuck to that decision.

After two years of basic training in Washington, he was sent to South Asia, the region his master's thesis had focused on. In the space of six years, he served in three different countries, and at each stage his talents were reported by his superiors back to head office. No one in the agency had expected him to flourish the way he had, and before long he was being invited back to Washington for future planning.

Dewey had been to the capital many times but never to visit Congress. Some of the senators who were regularly briefed by the agency wanted to hear firsthand about his successes in India. With permission from his chief, he talked with great enthusiasm to the senators about his work. At one meeting, he was presented with his first medal, although there were only ten people in the room. That day it struck him once again how that every joy, and every sadness, the job brought him must be experienced in the dark. And yet, he was very happy. He had just been decorated and summoned to headquarters for a better post. Maggie couldn't believe it and cried with happiness when he told her. It was then that he also realised how much of an effort Maggie had been making to keep the family functioning in places thousands of miles from home, even when he was barely at home. When he thought about the fact that she never once complained about it, his abiding feeling was shame.

For the first time he was being given a desk job, and they could finally enjoy a settled life with the children in America.

After six difficult years, it was a dream. They found a typical American house with a garden and white fence only 30 minutes away from the new CIA headquarters in Langley, Virginia. Maggie was happy. The children were happy. The whole family was happy, at first. But it didn't last.

His first day at Langley was great; everybody greeted him like a hero. His new supervisor explained to him why he'd been called back to the US: the government was investing in a whole new department and he was going to be part of it. From now on the CIA would not wait for a reason, let alone an invitation, to intervene in another country, it would create reasons. If the conflict in a country wasn't bad enough, the CIA would ferment it until only they could solve it. The new department would be called the Counter-Terrorism Unit. He would have to go through another long period of training if he was to accept the new departmental position, which he did without hesitation. He had joined the agency to defend his country, after all, and score new victories over communism. Academia had never been right for him. This was where he wanted to be – involved in both planning and action.

Maggie didn't ask him many questions about his new post. This was the perfect scenario for her and the children, but quickly Dewey started to feel suffocated. He missed being out in the field. Maggie sensed his impatience with the new role but didn't bring it up.

For four years his daily routine, between the office and home, bored him senseless. He felt like he was chained to his desk at Langley while the rest of the world burned. Finally, some long-awaited news arrived. For the first time he was going to be appointed chief of a station. He wasn't told where exactly but rumours suggested it would be Cyprus. Excitedly he began preparing. He would travel out first and, once he was settled, Maggie and the kids could join him. Maggie was not happy about this news but she wasn't prepared to lose her marriage over it. At the eleventh hour, there seemed to be a change of thinking and his post was moved to Istanbul. He was surprised, but happy with the decision, having grown to love the city already with the sea passing through its middle like a meandering river. This is how the city works; it welcomes you first, mesmerises you and then leaves you addicted to it. During his years in South Asia, he always arranged his flights to connect through Istanbul and found an excuse to stay there a day or two. As beautiful as the city was in the daytime, it was even more so at night. He was a night owl and loved nothing more than drinking in tiny corners of the city, and generally getting lost in it. Now, in the summer of '68, he was returning to it – a city that could hide anyone who didn't want to be found – for an official post! His job was clear; to put into practice what he had only trained to do in theory for the last four years. The CIA's main centre in Turkey was in the capital, Ankara, but the office in Istanbul was still significant both in terms of staff numbers and operational importance. Ankara was too dull. Undercover work was almost impossible in such a bureaucratic place where everyone knew, at a glance, who was who. Besides, the place was crawling with cops and security details. Istanbul was the opposite. A city of entertainment, replete with surprises and characters that were hard to find anywhere else.

This time, when the waiter brought his petit fours, Dewey neither flinched nor reached for his gun. As soon as the plate hit the table, he went for the strawberry one, always his first choice. He would leave the sugary caramel piece until the end. He concluded his analysis. There was no threat. He hadn't been followed. Now he was to concentrate on his meeting with the Deputy Consul General. He had met Aron before, though he probably wouldn't remember it. He had visited the Consul General, Ephraim Elrom, in his office two months before the kidnapping. The pretext was to brief Elrom about the itinerary of a congressman who would be travelling to Israel via Istanbul.

The Consul General had met Dewey at the door to his office just as Aron was leaving. They greeted each other but Aron knew that the meeting would be private so he didn't linger. It quickly became clear that the meeting was really about something else. It would not take an intelligence officer long to figure that out. But Dewey couldn't work out what that something was; he had some theories but when he tried to raise them, it went nowhere. For a while, they chatted about this and that until eventually, Elrom politely asked Dewey the real reason for his visit. Dewey didn't know what to say, so Elrom gently changed the subject to avoid any further embarrassment.

In reality, the Consul General wasn't a diplomat. His background was in intelligence and he had a legendary reputation. Maybe that's why Dewey had been so keen to meet the 70-year-old in person, on any pretext. He was going to be part of a big plan. Moreover, this wily old man knew that he had been followed for the last month. Mossad had been informed and they, in turn, told the Turkish police accordingly. Finally, via MİT, these reports made their way to Dewey. Frankly, whether the threat was serious or not, MİT would always bring it to his attention.The officers trained by the CIA knew what to look out for. Sometimes they would add inconsequential threats or follow-ups to the reports just to show that they'd been busy. MİT officers working for the CIA not only got their salaries from them they would also get bonuses when they brought them a case that could be regarded as serious. Before the coup, Dewey would receive tip-offs that certain diplomats or NATO personnel had been followed. Often it was idealist student groups who were slowly arming themselves. But until now, nothing serious had come to his desk about these followings. Dewey knew that the Soviets and Eastern Bloc agencies were always conducting counterintelligence activities, but their tracking methods were so easy to detect.

The information in Elrom's file was serious however. It has been disclosed that he'd been followed by several groups. Despite Mossad's warnings, Elrom had neither changed his daily routines nor increased his security personnel. It was up to the Turks to protect him, he said, while he was Consul General in their country. Clearly Elrom was the easiest of all the diplomatic targets. At the same time every day, he made his way from his flat in the Seyhan apartment block on Elmadağ Street to the Israeli Consulate in Nişantaşı just a kilometre away, with only his driver and bodyguard, David, for protection. He would return to his flat for lunch and wouldn't go back to the consulate again if he had outside meetings. He was like clockwork. The distance between his flat and the consulate was short and had no alternative route. Although he wouldn't take on extra security, Elrom always carried his trusty 7.65 calibre gun which he was allegedly pretty handy with.

Elrom was one of the fathers of Israel, a founding member of the Haganah, which laid the foundations for Mossad. The Haganah had been formed to protect Jewish migrants coming from all over the world to the lands inhabited by Palestinians under the British Mandate to open new settlements. They used every method in the terrorist handbook to stop or destroy anyone who dared to get in their way. The members of this paramilitary organisation, who were involved in village raids, assassinations and massacres, later became pillars of the Israeli military and intelligence service. Elrom was one such pillar. But there was something else that made him even more important. Back in Langley, Dewey had heard the name Elrom a few times. Elrom was the mastermind behind an epic action they had all learned about. His team pulled something off that had never been achieved by an intelligence agency before. The state of Argentina had famously allowed numerous high-ranking Nazi officers who escaped after the Second World War to sneak into the country and take shelter there. In 1960, Mossad formed a unit called 'Bureau 06' headed by Elrom with the express purpose of capturing these Nazis, alive if possible. The idea was to try these Nazis publicly and get them to talk about the genocide they had conducted in a way that hadn't been heard before, and share these hearings throughout the world. They needed a high-ranking Nazi to realise this plan. Thanks to Elrom's attentive work, they didn't need to wait long.

Elrom headed up the operation to kidnap Adolf Eichmann, the highest-ranking Nazi officer ever caught alive after the War. The brilliantly executed kidnap operation had a lot of ramifications. For the first time, the world learned about the suffering of the Jews during the holocaust on the news, day after day. No one had ever considered what this genocide meant in such detail before. All of a sudden, even Jews living in the wider Arab peninsula started to view those who'd escaped Europe to settle in Israel differently. Elrom remained head of the Nazi hunt, and began to see the importance of the world's media in the planning and delivery of other hunts. The Eichmann trial helped legitimise Israel in the eyes of the world. It had other effects, one of which was to embolden the CIA in its own aggressive interventions overseas going forward. But it was the death of Elrom's only son that had brought this battled-hardened old man down. Having witnessed all kinds of slaughter in his own life, Elrom had tried everything to keep his son from joining the army. He feared the boy would not be as lucky as he had been, surviving so many scrapes, if he chose a similar path. Elrom had spent a lifetime losing friends, getting injured, and killing to prevent being killed. He had walked through blood in order to make it possible for his children to live in peace and freedom. He managed to keep his son out of harm's way through all kinds of means. Despite being a military pilot by national conscription training, his son was able to resign to become a civilian pilot before seeing combat, and managed to avoid punishment thanks, no doubt, to his father pulling strings. But death found him all the same, during a training flight with one of the world's safest planes. This was the end for Elrom. He did not know what to do with himself, after this loss. Prime Minister Golda Meir, who'd been a comrade-in-arms and a friend for nearly 50 years, asked the Foreign Minister to appoint him as Consul General to Istanbul. It was a place for him and Elsa to rebuild their lives, one last duty before his retirement.

You could only guess at Elrom's thinking for coming to Istanbul. Maybe he thought life would be easier abroad. Or maybe the idea of outliving his son just didn't feel right to him, and because of this, he didn't invest in additional protection when he knew he was being followed. Maybe he only informed the other agencies of the danger out of 50 years of professional habit. Perhaps dying wasn't so scary, for such a war-battered old man, but he couldn't face the idea of Elsa coming into danger. Elrom was an old-school spy and their time was coming to an end.

On weekdays, Markiz Patisserie was generally quiet in the mornings. Dewey reached forward for the caramel petit four he had saved till last. The impact of sugar on the brain was something he lived for. He had plenty of time for other stimulants, but nothing could rival sugar. To begin with, you could get it anywhere and everywhere. Secondly, the Turks knew this sweet business very well; you were never short of options. Thirdly it was legal, so no one could look down at you for eating the stuff. He still had an hour to kill before meeting Aron. Hiram had organised the meeting and they'd gone through the details together. Hiram would get into the large protocol car before it pulled up outside the Palazzo Corpi, home of the American Consulate in Tepebaşı, whereupon Dewey would get into it. The car would then travel from Taksim towards Nişantaşı – about a ten-minute journey. There Aron, the Deputy Consul General, would get into the car thinking only Hiram would be in it. Once inside Dewey would explain the reason for this strange meeting.

He tried to get the waiters' attention to ask for the bill. The older waiter nodded to signal he would bring it. Without thinking, Dewey gazed out the window and suddenly didn't know what to do. He could see Helga approaching the patisserie and she was with her husband. He knew him also; the three of them had met at the same time. Dewey's diplomat friend Meier, who worked for the West Germany Consulate, would regularly play tennis at the Hilton in Elmadağ and often played doubles with his wife against Helga and her husband, Hans. One day Meier's wife had to bail last minute so Meier asked Dewey to stand in as his partner. After a bit of coaxing, Dewey accepted. Just sitting in the unexpected tranquility of the Hilton's gardens would be pleasant, he concluded. Located in the busiest part of the city, the tennis courts in the hotel's gardens, shaded under tall plane trees, was like a hidden paradise. The most captivating sight that day, though, was the beautiful, former model, Helga. He had no memory of how the match ended that day, but he was convinced Helga had felt a spark between them, as he did. During the break, he made up his mind when and where their next meeting would take place, when he learned she played there at least three times a week while her husband was away on business. The Hilton became the location of most of their secret meetings. He hadn't seen Helga's husband since that first game. Now he was just waiting to pay his bill and at a loss what to do. Helga walked in and, after the shock of seeing Dewey, turned to her husband and whispered something. The waiter brought his bill, which he paid, leaving a generous tip as he always did. Hans and Helga began walking towards him. Not knowing what to do, his hand instinctively reached under his arm again. *Stop being so ridiculous*, he chided himself. From the smile stretching across Hans' face, he realised Helga had never told him about them. After a few, friendly words, he politely declined their offer to drink coffee together, and made his escape. Even out on the street, his heart was still beating like a teenager's. He gorged himself on the adrenaline rush, almost wishing he had been caught, as he dived into the Beyoğlu crowds.

His first days in the Istanbul office had been spent getting to know Turkey closely. He no longer wanted to look at the events from a terrace with a view of the Bosphorus. He wanted to be in it. He came with a mission after all: the country's youth were demanding freedom and equality and making their case heard more and more. They had to be stopped. The spectre of communism was everywhere. Any movement sprouting now must be plucked out immediately before it grew too big to pluck. They didn't want another Vietnam or Cuba on their hands. The Soviets had been a step ahead of them in the Middle East, socialist Arab governments had appeared first in Egypt then Iraq and Syria, but in Turkey, the US still held a lot of sway. Turkey was a key country for NATO and Europe. This was not just the view taken in Langley, Dewey believed it too, having spent so many years across Asia. The Counter-Terrorism Unit where he'd been trained, had been working on a plan for years. No longer would they stand by and let another country slide towards socialism. While the Cold War was still so febrile, countries didn't have the luxury of self-determination. The Soviets couldn't stop countries from sliding into socialism even if they wanted to. So you could almost call this a preventative strategy to avoid revolutions, and if it worked in Turkey, it could be implemented anywhere else, with minor adjustments. The world was full of students demanding more freedom, of course. But those in Turkey were different, organising workers, participating in trade unions, and joining with peasants at harvest time, while abandoning their studies in the city. Those who stayed on their campuses, organised a boycott against their own classes, some even convened alternative study groups to enlighten their fellow Turks with a free university. The students were also integrated into several of the main political parties, and went about blaming the previous generation, and renouncing the politics of the past for its passivity. They were betting on a fully independent Turkey.

For Dewey, the plan was an impeccable one. Phase One was to create a counter group against these students who would still look progressive and sympathetic in the eyes of the public. As part of this, nationalist and religious students who were not as organised as the leftists needed to be thoroughly drilled. The means for doing this were clear: by reviving the Special War Department originally formed under the auspices of the army, in conjunction with the CIA and NATO following Turkey's admission to NATO in 1952. For this job, they thought it appropriate to use high-ranking Turkish officers who had previously received special training in the US. In certain regions, these officers would provide ballistics training to nationalist youth brigades. Smear campaigns in the media against anyone representing the left were also integral to Phase One. Phase Two was to draw these protesting youths, who were entwined with scattered communities across the country, towards the centre and make them fight with the nationalist youth. The first phase of this plan had been completed after two years of hard work and considerable commitment of resources, largely successfully. They were now ready to launch the second phase.

For this, they first needed to provoke the leftist youth – to incite them into using the few guns they had their hands on and leave some bloody corpses in their wake. This was easier said than done. No matter what they did, the students refused to veer off course. Dewey had been waiting for the right moment and now at last it was approaching. Those students who'd been harassed by the state security forces began to leave the main political parties in their droves, and talk openly about alternative methods of revolution. This was the agency's chance. Some of the agent provocateurs seeded among them influenced these discussions and started to talk loudly about armed struggle. As a result, a group of students decided to travel to Bekaa Valley in Lebanon to receive combat training alongside Palestinian guerrilla fighters. The agency knew how many of them went, how they crossed the border and in which camp they trained. As they began to return to Turkey, they were hailed as heroes among their fellow students, triggering more people to make such journeys to the Palestinian camps. The agency didn't prevent them and they made sure the Turkish police didn't try to stop them either. They made good use of the fact that some, in the lower ranks of the army, supported the leftists.

It was simply a matter of waiting for the spark; once it came, the fire would be easy to fan. The moment any leftists committed a bloody act, the agency would insist the army top brass round up and arrest all the lower-ranking officers who'd supported the leftists previously. Then they would force the government to resign by putting pressure on them, via the same top brass who'd taken the last set of orders from them. Such provocations would continue after control passed over to the army. The list of the people to be arrested had been prepared weeks in advance.

The spark they were waiting for flickered into life on the 4th of March 1971. Deniz Gezmiş, the leader of the group that had thrown the soldiers of the 6th Fleet into the harbour back in 1968, had travelled to Palestinian camps with his friends and, on his return, started working among Ankara University students to launch an armed struggle. On the 4th March 1971, at around 1.30am, four American Navy soldiers on duty in Ankara were kidnapped by Deniz Gezmiş and his friends to launch their struggle. With this action, they declared the formation of a new force, the People's Liberation Army of Turkey (THKO). Deniz Gezmiş and his friends demanded a ransom of 400,000 dollars for the release of the soldiers. Dewey and his team in Istanbul didn't want to step on the toes of the CIA office in Ankara, but they also didn't want to miss a huge opportunity. President Nixon publicly stated that no ransom would ever be paid, but in secret, he gave instructions for the money to be handed over to resolve this one. Vietnam wasn't going well, and he didn't want the coffins of US soldiers from *other* parts of the world to appear on American TV on top of that. CIA command was against the federal government's decision to pay the ransom but their hands were tied. Dewey couldn't remain silent.

Taking his career into his hands, he sent an urgent telegram through to the head of the CIA. In it, he pointed to the existence of socialist soldiers among the Turkish army, saying this was a sign that the military has been waiting to instigate a *leftist* coup, and that they were about to strike. He also insisted that if the ransom money were paid it would be heralded as a victory by the THKO, and America – which didn't have the best reputation in Turkey – would be seen as fundamentally weak. But the telegram wasn't enough. He then issued orders to Turkish intelligence and police to conduct a series of snap raids across all the campuses of Ankara, with shoot-to-kill instructions. Dewey needed dead bodies. If a few heroic American soldiers were to die for this greater cause, then that was the price. Most, if not all, of Dewey's wishes came true. The press responded perfectly, describing the students as terrorists with blood on their hands. During the university raids, many students and academics were arrested and one student was killed. The protestors didn't use the guns in their arsenal despite the provocations. Gezmiş's group released the soldiers despite previously threatening to them if no ransom was paid. As it turned out, if they'd stood their ground for just two more days, they would have got their money, which had already reached Greece with a special courier, on its way to Ankara, when they decided to release the soldiers.

The release of the soldiers without a ransom brought the attention of the CIA headquarters and Nixon to the Turkey desk. Dewey and his team were suddenly awarded new powers from CIA command and began implementing the plans that had been drawn up many months before.

The American soldiers were released on the 8th March. By the next day, the 9th, scores of leftist military officers had been arrested, charged with planning to overthrow the government through a coup d'état. They didn't stop there. By the 12th of March they had organised a military coup d'état of their own, forcing the government to resign and taking control of the whole country. Now, for the agency, everything was clicking into place. Deniz Gezmiş and his friends were caught on the 15th. Nationwide arrests of ordinary citizens began immediately after the speech made by the new puppet Prime Minister Nihat Erim and broadcasted by TRT, the only national TV channel, on the 22nd April. The new prime minister, appointed by the military, stated in his speech, 'The measures we will take will hit their heads like a sledgehammer', and a state of emergency was declared in six cities including Istanbul, Ankara and Izmir. Meanwhile, operations were launched against leftist organisations regardless of their connection, or not, to Gezmiş's THKO. The Turkish Workers Party (TIP) and Revolutionary Trade Union Confederation (DİSK) were both closed down, and hundreds of leftists were arrested, tortured and imprisoned. Books were banned and burned en masse, strikes were criminalised, severe censorship was imposed on the press, and many independent newspapers were shut down. But these measures were not enough, far from enough. They had to get rid of the scourge of socialism for good.

A full two months after the coup, the students who they'd labelled 'terrorists with blood on their hands' still hadn't committed any killings. This didn't look good, and Dewey knew blood needed to be spilt soon. Only then could they justify imposing violence on every quarter that dared speak of socialism or independence from the US. This was why he was following so carefully the plan being entertained by a THKO splinter group to kidnap Ephraim Elrom, and doing everything he could to stop this plan from being foiled. He knew that if the kidnapping, which was to take place in Istanbul, were successful, he would be in control of everything. In just the third year in this post, he would become one of the unofficial leaders of the city. It was true, he was indeed a very important person, extremely important. And yet, being stared at threateningly by two unidentified students at such an important moment unnerved him.

Beyoğlu was crowded. As was his habit, he walked close to the shop windows, so that he could always check behind him in the reflection. Helga kept coming to his thoughts. So many things had happened that morning already, it wasn't a good sign. It was useful to be wary but he hated the thought of becoming paranoid, so he drove all the bad scenarios from his mind. Thinking about ways the Elrom kidnapping could still go wrong only made him sweat more.

So far, the plan had worked perfectly. It was now five days since Elrom's disappearance. The kidnappers sent a statement to the press, announcing their formation as a brand new organisation and explaining the reasons for the Consul General's abduction. The content of the statement and writing style got Dewey very excited:

> '...The deadline is three days from the release of this statement. If the demands are not met, Ephraim Elrom will be executed. (Deadline: 20.5.1971, until 5pm)
>
> – People's Liberation Party-Front of Turkey'

The statement contained some pretty ambitious demands. First, they didn't ask for a ransom – as a mark of their ideological determination. Secondly, they asked for the unconditional release of their friends who'd been arrested immediately before and after the coup. Lastly, they asked their statement to be read three times a day on national TV and radio. Their demands were impossible to meet. Clearly these guys were prepared to go all the way. They were not from the same group that had kidnapped the American soldiers. The kidnapping was really just a stunt to declare the formation of their new organisation. Nor were they prepared to negotiate. They knew exactly what would happen to them if they released him. They didn't want to appear naive like their friends. They knew now that they should only kidnap if they were willing to go all the way. The issue had been the single hottest talking point among students protestors for the last two months. Many criticised Deniz Gezmiş and his friends for releasing the American soldiers so readily in Ankara. They said people had lost trust in that particular set of leaders when they released the soldiers for nothing in return. Dewey followed the intelligence reports on these discussions in minute detail.

That's why he was certain this new group wasn't going to acquiesce and self-destruct the way THKO had, meaning the dead bodies he'd been waiting for would finally make their way into newspaper headlines.

There were several consulate buildings in Beyoğlu. Some of them were even on the high street. The Swedish consulate could be seen the moment you left the underground: a Scandinavian palace standing in the middle of a tranquil garden. A little further on, you would pass the USSR's centre of intelligence operations hiding behind towering walls. Whenever Dewey passed it, he couldn't stop himself peering through the gate, as if he would see someone up to no good. It was a senseless impulse, and not something an intelligence officer should be caught doing. He couldn't control himself, and even though he should have remained cold and aloof, his eyes still accidentally caught those of the security guard at the front gate. Today, he would have to pick up the pace just to overcome this impulse. To get to the US consulate he would have to take a side street which wasn't exactly the safest thoroughfare in the daytime. It wouldn't be an exaggeration to call it assassination-friendly: tall buildings bustled in on either side of a narrow, crooked lane. Being full of bars and nightclubs, streets like these were full of colour and life in the evenings, but silent and deserted by day.

He had been ready to pounce, as if it were only a matter of time before Elrom would be kidnapped. The moment he heard the news he called Hiram and instructed his contacts to initiate the raid. Hiram, as a representative of the National Intelligence Agency (MİT), was going to make a 'recommendation' to the newly installed prime minister to issue an urgent response against the agitators and their demands. He told Hiram to recommend that this statement be read out by the Prime Minister himself, for better effect. As it turned out, it was the Minister of the Interior who made the statement at 11pm that night, broadcast on national radio and TV. It was a strongly-worded statement declaring there would be no dialogue with the kidnappers. The great Turkish state did not negotiate with terrorists. It demanded the immediate and unconditional release of the hostage otherwise legislation would be passed to try Elrom's kidnappers and those who helped them of a crime punishable by death.

Now in Phase Two, an operation was underway to arrest hundreds of activists in every major city, working off the list prepared by MİT. The day after the kidnapping, 547 people including renowned writers, scientists, artists and academics were arrested. New lies were being served up by the media on an hourly basis, assuring the nation that every new batch of arrestees were all 'communists with blood on their hands'. Meanwhile, the Israeli government's first reaction was to establish a dialogue with the kidnappers. After all, Elrom was a close friend of Golda Meir's, and not someone to be sacrificed. Subsequently, CIA Director Richard Helms spoke on a secure line with the head of Mossad, and explained the US's new intervention strategy in relation to this crisis. Israel would benefit, in the long term, if they allowed this one sacrifice to be made, and coordinated with the CIA on this new strategy. The CIA provided files to the Israelis that demonstrated Bekaa Valley wasn't just host to Palestinian guerrilla fighters in training, but fighters from Italy, Germany, Spain and even Japan, all affiliated with new socialist movements in their home countries. The possibility of loss of life was now high, they added, so it would be better to plan to take advantage of that outcome. At this point, they added that Elrom was a national hero already, and with this last act, he could deliver a great final service to his country.

It was Meir's call. And she lived up to her 'Iron Lady' nickname. From that day on, she never took another phone call from Elrom's wife, Elsa, despite having previously spoken to her on a daily basis since the crisis began. The consulate staff could no longer give any answers to the understandable importuning of Elrom's wife. Elsa was now fighting for her husband's life. She knew that the aggressive language of the new government was only further endangering it. Seeing the reversal in the Israeli government's position, she cast about for new ways to save her husband. Meanwhile, a parallel development was taking place between the kidnappers and their hostage. Elrom knew all the protocols. In any hostage situation, the state would take every opportunity to engage in a dialogue, if only to distract the kidnappers and buy time. But it was as if the state, and the forces behind it, were happy to force the kidnappers' hands. At that point, a Plan B came to Elrom's mind, one that would spare everyone's lives. It was simple. Elsa came from a wealthy family that could easily put together a private ransom. Although money hadn't been asked for, Mahir Çayan and his fellow students could turn this into a win-win for the movement: a ransom would have been paid and the government wouldn't be able to use the incident for their propaganda. To do it they needed a secret back-channel to Elsa. It was obvious that staff at the Israeli Consulate couldn't be trusted at this point. Elrom told his kidnappers how to reach Elsa. A day after the deadline the new, puppet government declared that from that Friday onwards a 36-hour state of emergency would be put in place allowing 36,000 soldiers and police officers to conduct house-to-house searches to find the Consul General, 'alive or dead'. Both the kidnappers and Elrom knew what this meant, the security forces were planning to kill them all on sight.

They had to act quickly. Elrom gave them the phone number of Ishak, a family friend and chairman of the Jewish-Turkish Business Association. He believed they could safely reach Elsa through Ishak.

Just before Dewey reached Pera Street where the consulate was based, he caught the eye of a young man staring at him who promptly disappeared. He wasn't sure if it was just his paranoia or if he'd caught the man out. His heart pounded. The importance of the meeting with Aron – at which he'd explain in fine detail how to implement the kidnap plan he'd spent months preparing – was also playing on his nerves. Many things, it seemed, were getting to him that morning. Shame over Maggie. If Maggie had just reacted angrily, he would have been relieved; but the children came first, so Dewey now had to stew on it. Also regret. Seeing Helga this morning made him realise he didn't want to leave her.

Maybe he had been taking the spy thing too seriously. He couldn't explain his behaviour. Under such emotional stress, it was difficult to understand the nature of external threats. Normally, it would be obvious what to do, either he would change his course or throw himself into a crowd of pedestrians. Instead, he just kept walking, afraid to be late for his important meeting. All his training eluded him.

When Dewey had received intel that a sizeable amount of cash had been withdrawn from one of Elsa's family's accounts, following their making contact with Ishak, he realised underestimating these kids would be a mistake. But he still had time to correct things. All he needed to do was inform Aron and make sure the Israeli consulate intervened and stopped any transfer of cash. For safety, he and Hiram had a couple of other measures in place as well.

Such were his thoughts when he saw Hiram getting out of his car about 50 metres away. The car was not quite in front of the consulate, but a little down the street. Hiram had not seen Dewey yet, nor had he seen what Dewey could suddenly see was behind him: a tall, slight figure walking determinedly towards him. It was the taller of two youths who'd glared at him that morning. At that moment, as the young man reached under his arm, Dewey knew exactly what would happen next and, raising his hand, was about to shout to Hiram when he was startled by a sound that was far too close. The sound was that of a bullet clicking into the barrel of a Walther semi-automatic, a

9mm bullet to be precise. As he turned, he heard two shots – one from far off. That was the sound of a 9mm bullet being fired into the nape of Hiram's neck, no doubt from the gun of the tall youth standing behind him, who Dewey was still convinced was an amateur and really didn't know what he was doing. If he'd had more time to think he could have worked out what kind of weapon it was fired from but the damage caused by the Walther semi-automatic pointed at his face didn't allow him to use his brain any more.

He was killed because he was a very important person. The way he died was just more evidence of how important he was. His death was almost exactly as Dewey had imagined it. The setting chosen for the assassination was just the kind of place he would have picked. The only thing that took the shine off was that he died was at the hands of a student who'd probably never used a gun before. Moreover, his death was a shame because his great plan couldn't be completed. Mahir Çayan would go on to release the Counsel General, infuriating the new puppet government. CIA headquarters would suspend its new aggressive strategy until it could fully understand what had happened. The security guards of the Palazzo Corpi consulate would follow protocols strictly, locking all the doors and not confronting the two young men still in possession of weapons. The pair would run towards a second car waiting for them and within minutes disappear into the maze of steep, narrow streets that made up Kasımpaşa, one of Istanbul's poorest neighbourhoods. Those who witnessed the shootings would soon be coming back out from their hiding places and, with police sirens screeching in the distance, would be able to see that the two bodies on the ground, 50 metres apart, lay in exactly the same mid-reflex pose: reaching under their arms.

# Afterword: 12 March

## Ertuğrul Kürkçü

THE YEAR 1971-72 was in many senses a unique moment in the course of modern Turkish political history. It was a year of many firsts. 12 March 1971 saw the Turkish Armed Forces stage their first 'military coup by memorandum' – an ultimatum meant for the Speaker of the parliament but aired first by the army on state television, insinuating that the right-wing Prime Minister Süleyman Demirel should immediately resign and calling on parliament to set up a new government 'above party politics' in order to restore law and order, or else the army would take over. Demirel resigned.

26 March saw another first: Professor Nihat Erim, a prominent parliamentary deputy of the main opposition Republican People's Party (CHP) and self-described 'socialist', was summoned, with a wave of the Army's magic wand, to withdraw from his party and step forward as Turkey's first prime minister to oversee the first 'neutral' cross-party cabinet. On 26 April, against a backdrop of ongoing industrial and agrarian disputes, sending workers and farmers out onto the streets, student protests resisting the intimidation of the Grey Wolves, police raids on university campuses, and kidnappings of the members of wealthy Istanbul families by the urban guerrillas, martial law was declared in eleven of Turkey's 67 provinces, with the army taking over the administration of major urban areas and Kurdish regions. Civil society was silenced: trade union activities,

outdoor rallies, dissident publications, strikes and public protests were all banned. After five long years of class struggle for democratic and social rights, 36 million ordinary Turkish citizens had suddenly, with a single stroke, been sidelined. The country waited with bated breath to see how this standoff between democracy and dictatorship, between revolution and reaction, would play out. On 2 May, Erim made his first public statement revealing plans for a series of restrictive amendments to the 'liberal' Constitution of 1961 – aspects of which had become 'an unbearable luxury for Turkey'[1] in Erim's words. The coalition parties – still dominated by the fractured, right-wing Justice Party (AP) of the former prime minister now came together to shrug off the humiliation of having bowed to a 'memorandum' and worked collectively like a paper shredder on the 1961 Constitution, eliminating for good all the 'unbearable luxuries' that so offended the army's top brass.

On 17 May, another first: the Popular Front for the Liberation of Turkey (THKC) conducted the first ever attack on a foreign mission on Turkish soil, taking Israel's Head Consul in Istanbul, Ephraim Elrom, hostage in a new episode in the 'people's war against imperialist domination and counter-revolutionary tyranny' and called for the 'release of all revolutionaries already under arrest.'[2] The government responded with a massive crackdown that resulted in hundreds of students, academics, writers, trade unionists and Workers' Party activists (leftists and liberals alike) being detained and tortured. Consequently, on 22 May, Elrom became the first casualty of 'the people's war'. On 1 June, during the initial encounters between the counterinsurgency forces and the newly-formed guerrillas, prominent revolutionary leaders Hüseyin Cevahir and Sinan Cemgil were killed in Istanbul respectively, with the THKC leader Mahir Çayan being wounded and captured. On 29 November, five revolutionary leaders including Çayan escaped from an Istanbul military jail in another first: the first ever political prison break. On 26 March 1972: the first ever guerrilla attack on a NATO mission, with THKC and the People's Liberation Army of Turkey (THKO) guerrillas, led by Çayan, taking three British officers from 'Her Majesty's Secret Service' hostage in Ünye on the Black Sea coast in the hope of stopping the execution of three THKO leaders being held on death row. On 30 March, the army and counterinsurgency units surrounded the guerrillas in their hideout in Kızıldere village, near Niksar, Tokat and in the shoot-out that followed three hostages and ten revolutionaries lost their lives in the first ever massacre of a Turkish guerrilla unit. On 6 May, three revolutionaries – Deniz Gezmiş, Yusuf Aslan and Hüseyin İnan – were hanged, having been charged with leading a 'forcible attempt at altering, violating or abolishing the Constitution'[3] in an armed uprising against the Turkish state. The court's decision came into force with the endorsement of a parliamentary majority mainly comprising of former Prime Minister Demirel's Justice Party (AP) deputies. By the time martial law was lifted in March 1973 '1,584 persons had been convicted and 404 associations banned by Martial Law Courts. Over 2,000 others were still under trial or awaiting.'[4]

In the space of a year, Turkey had dramatically veered from an apparent course towards an open, democratic, pluralist society, as pursued through class struggle, towards instead the dark alleys of a 'national security state'. The strong and energetic youth protests of 1968, the agile working-class movement and ardent rural activism of farmers that had developed over the previous five years – urging for broader economic, political and social rights – were suddenly criminalised; the vibrant intellectual life of Turkey had been silenced at the tip of a bayonet. As power was increasingly transferred into the hands of the executive, the military once again ascended to the top of that executive. Public debate and popular participation in decision-making was only allowed – through the means of a beheaded parliament – if it conformed with the military's preferences. By the time martial law had been lifted in 1973, and the army had returned to its barracks, the coercive apparatus of the state had been disproportionately reinforced, effectively overriding civil society with the successive constitutional amendments.

Since then, there has been a constant dispute at home and abroad as to the real driving force behind the turn of events that resulted in the state's takeover of civil society in Turkey, in the early 1970s.

The liberal perspective could be summarised by Ali Gevgilili, columnist for the Istanbul-based daily newspaper *Milliyet:* 'Alongside the indisputable external dynamics of the transformation from the 12 March *coup* to the tragic 12 March *regime* exists the particular part played by the expectations, ignorance, agony and suffering of a generation of petty bourgeoisie trapped between Turkey's official ideology and the new left practices,'[5] Gevgilili wrote. In short, Gevgilili placed the blame for the army's reactionary takeover at the door of left-wing radicalism in the younger generation of revolutionaries. Their actions became a catalyst in stirring up social disturbances that ultimately cleared the way for the army to take over, he argued. 'The revolutionaries' urge for freedom is devoid of a material social basis reflected among the pillars of a modern industrial society,' Gevgilili added. 'It boils down to a kind of freedom fetishism that leads to nothing but a dead end.'

Granted the embryonic guerrilla movements played a significant part in accelerating the crackdown on social movements, but the wider course of events pointed in a different direction, I would argue, questioning Gevgilili's assumption that harmonious progress was an inevitable byproduct of the 'main pillars of modern industrial society' – i.e. the tensions between Turkey's working classes and its bourgeoisie under capitalism.

Indeed, it is worth retracing the events that led up to this terrible year, to better understand Hüseyin Karabey's story. Rewinding the clock back to 1969, long before guerrilla groups had started to emerge from the revolutionary youth movement, Turkey's economic and political order was already in crisis. The ruling Justice Party (AP), despite having secured the majority of the seats in the parliament in October '69 elections, lost a vote of confidence in parliament during the subsequent budget debate. A disagreement within the party over the government's plans to increase taxes on large landowners created a split that ran through the AP ranks. New measures to transfer capital from rural agriculturalists to urban industrialists caused a crack in the bloc of property owners' that had herded around Demirel's government since 1965. The National Order Party (MNP) – a forerunner of the current ruling Justice and Development Party (AKP) – established by Islamist Professor Necmettin Erbakan, attracted AP defectors, in particular small-to-medium-sized business owners and tradesmen from the provinces. On top of this, Ferruh Bozbeyli's short-lived Democratic Party created a separate political group within the parliament which further undermined Demirel's supremacy in conservative politics.

Although a long-time ally of the US, and someone who traded on his close personal ties with President Johnson, Demirel was, by the early '70s increasingly at loggerheads with Washington for his relatively autonomous foreign policy towards the Arab nations, his recognition of Palestine's right to self-determination, and his continued rejection of US demands that he ban opium farming – a major source of agricultural income in central and western Anatolia, a voter base for Demirel's Justice Party. This, combined with his government's impotence in quelling anti-American sentiments among the public and across the lower ranks of the armed forces, eventually cost Demirel heavily, resulting in a loss of US political confidence and a reduction in its economic aid to Turkey – a major source of the government's finances, second only to tax revenues. In the face of dire economic developments, the government had to speed up efforts to increase cooperation with the European Community, improve economic relations with the Soviet Union despite the ongoing Cold War, legislate a new tax law in order to double its tax revenue, and deliberately devalue the Turkish Lira to increase income from exports – all of which triggered further protests from intellectuals, workers, farmers, and public sector workers (including the army, police and civil service) in the months that followed.

The prime minister was trapped between a need to repel the wave of protests taking place and a constitution that protected people's rights to take part in such protests. In order to bypass these constitutional liberties, Demirel desperately adopted his security chiefs' recommendations to resort to an old formula of Eastern despots: 'Kill dogs with dogs'.[6] Demirel's 'dogs' to contain the revolutionary movement were the 'Grey Wolves', a covert network of ultra-fascist paramilitary gangs organised and trained by the former army colonel Alpaslan Türkeş, of the Nationalist Action Party (MHP).

According to Daniele Ganser, the author of *NATO's Secret Armies: Operation GLADIO and Terrorism in Western Europe*, Türkeş was the head of NATO's anti-communist 'stay-behind' operation in Turkey. As first acknowledged in 1990 by Italian Prime Minister Giulio Andreotti, says Ganser, 'a secret army existed in Italy and other countries across Western Europe that was part of the North Atlantic Treaty Organisation (NATO) [...] set up by the US secret service Central Intelligence Agency (CIA) and the British Secret Intelligence Service (MI6 or SIS) after the end of the Second World War to fight communism in Western Europe.'[7]

In order to integrate Turkey firmly within NATO, the US had to exploit the anti-communist leanings of the dominant and violent Pan-Turkism movement whose teachings were widely shared, in different tones, across Turkey's vast nationalist landscape. Just as the US intelligence strategy needed the consent of Pan-Turkism in order to integrate Turkey's intelligence and defence structures into NATO's anti-Soviet mission, so the Pan-Turkist movement in turn needed to use Turkey's NATO membership to its own advantage. Former Turkish Land Forces officer Alparslan Türkeş is believed to have established contacts with the CIA during his stay in the USA for military training in 1948, under whose orders he began setting up a secret anti-communist 'stay-behind' army in Turkey.[8] Türkeş, as a young first lieutenant during WWII, had been involved in anti-communist activism as part of the staunch pro-German current among Turkish military and bureaucratic elites at the time, and is believed to have become a Nazi contact person in Turkey.[9] As Turkey's ties with the US solidified, Türkeş travelled extensively between Turkey and the States, establishing intimate contacts both with the Pentagon and the CIA. Türkeş, as result of power struggles in the military junta that overthrew Adnan Menderes in 1960, was expelled from the army at the rank of colonel, and became the 'Başbuğ' – the Turkish equivalent of Führer – of the Nationalist Action Party (MHP).

According to GLADIO's simulations of a potential future Soviet invasion, 'the secret GLADIO soldiers under NATO command would have formed a so-called stay-behind network operating behind enemy lines [...]. The real and present danger, in the eyes of the secret war strategists in Washington and London, were the at-times numerically strong communist parties in the democracies of Western Europe [as well as the 'revolutionary movement' in the case of Turkey]. Hence the network, in the total absence of a Soviet invasion, took up arms in numerous countries and fought a secret war [of their own] against the political forces of the left. The secret armies, as the secondary sources now available suggest, were involved in a whole series of terrorist operations and human rights violations that they wrongly blamed on the communists in order to discredit the left at the polls. The operations always aimed at spreading maximum fear among the population and ranged from bomb massacres in trains and market squares (Italy), the use of systematic torture of opponents of the regime (Turkey), the support for right-wing coup d'états (Greece and Turkey), to the smashing of opposition groups (Portugal and Spain). As the secret armies were discovered, NATO, as well as the governments of the United States and Great Britain, refused to take a stand on what by then was alleged by the press to be 'the best-kept, and most damaging, political-military secret since World War II.'[10]

Hence, Türkeş's Grey Wolves trained for 'assassinations,

bombings, armed robbery, torture, attacks, kidnap, threats, provocation, militia training, hostage-taking, arson, sabotage, propaganda, disinformation, violence and extortion' as outlined in the Turkish army Field Manual ST 31-15 – a verbatim Turkish translation of the US Army Field Manual FM 31-15.[11] This secret army remained 'on duty' until 12 March,[12] attacking university campuses, kidnapping and torturing individual militants, executing with firing squads, and ambushing students – all the while under the protection of Demirel's police. Forcing the left to resist and organise its 'self-defence' through similar means. During the two years of deadly confrontation, many students – mostly leftist – lost their lives. University campuses became influence zones, bitterly divided between the 'Grey Wolves' and Revolutionaries.

Ironically, the inevitable end result of Demirel's deliberate security tactics ultimately became the establishment's justification for calling for an 'extraordinary regime' in order to end the 'brothers war'[13] with restrictive laws and a new illiberal constitution.

However, mass protest continued to rise notwithstanding the atrocities of the 'Grey Wolves'. Throughout the long hot summer of 1970, Turkey's major industrial hubs, farming communities, and public services were all fermenting with social unrest; boycotts, strikes, marches, and outdoor rallies were pouring angry farmers, revolutionary students, determined workers, non-commissioned officers, teachers, and nurses out onto the streets. Unrest was in the air.

Demirel sought to appease the soldiers and police with increased salaries but was determined to suppress workers' demands for wage increases as he needed the funds to reinvest in the automotive industry, an industry that benefited from Demirel's import substitution policies and, in return, put all its support behind his government. In June, Demirel tabled a series of amendments to the Trade Union Law designed to block the flow of workers signing up to the independent Revolutionary Trade Union Confederation (DİSK) and channelling the rising tide of unionisation towards the government-controlled Türk- İş – Turkey's first and oldest labour confederation organised along US-style trade-unionism guidelines.

DİSK unionists, and workers generally, responded energetically to the government's plans. On 15-16 June 1970, more than a hundred thousand workers across metropolitan Istanbul and Izmit took to the streets to protest. Police and army crackdown squads met with protestors and three workers and a police officer were killed in the ensuing clashes; the main international highways and government buildings were occupied by angry workers and at the end of the second day of clashes 'martial law' was declared in Istanbul and Izmit, and several workers' leaders jailed.

Turkey's working class had effectively rejected the 'harmony model' proposed by the government and the bourgeoisie. Small producers too, in almost all agricultural regions were out in the streets and major highways protesting against the falling prices of hazelnut, sunflower, tobacco, onion, garlic, tomato, sugar beet, etc., while the costs of production linked to imported agricultural essentials were on the rise.

A crisis had already erupted, meeting most, if not all, of Lenin's criteria for a revolutionary situation: 'the first symptom' of which arises 'when it is impossible for the ruling classes to maintain their rule without any change; when there is a crisis, in one form or another, among the 'upper classes', a crisis in the policy of the ruling class, leading to a fissure through which the discontent and indignation of the oppressed classes burst forth.'[14]

Indeed, an open debate on the prospects of an 'extraordinary regime' had already started in the mainstream press. In the absence of a TV network infrastructure and pluralist public radio, traditional print media – the only arena for open debate – veritably boiled with conflicting opinions on the pros and cons of a military takeover.

The army high command had already assimilated the 'social problem' of the last few years into its 'security agenda', as reflected by Armed Forces Chief of Staff, Four-star General

Memduh Tağmaç in a press statement following a high-level army command meeting in the aftermath of the 15-16th June workers' revolt. Known for his staunch opposition to an army takeover, in the past, General Tağmaç was now ringing the alarm bells for the old order: 'The currents in pursuit of social rights have surpassed the [needs for] economic development'[15] he was quoted in the press seven months before the 12th March.

The uncanny similarities between Tağmaç's statement and another analysis being offered on the other side of the Atlantic, by influential political scientist Samuel Huntington, suggests that Turkey's military top brass may have been briefed by their counterparts in the Pentagon as to civilian-military relations prior to what the American's regarded as a justified coup. Tağmaç's statement sounded like a direct 'quote' from Huntington's criticism of modernisation theories built on the assumption that economic and social progress inevitably leads to democratic stability.

In the first chapter of his 1968 book *Political Order in Changing Societies*, Huntington discusses possible causes for the increased number of US allies seemingly troubled with 'violence and instability' and concludes that 'it was in large part the product of rapid social change and the rapid mobilisation of new groups into politics, coupled with the slow development of political institutions.' Huntington closes his observations with an illiberal conclusion: 'The primary problem is not liberty but the creation of a legitimate public order.'[16]

Turkish army commanders had, of course, already made up their mind to tilt the playing field, long before guerrilla warfare was even being considered by the revolutionary movements. Rumours of an imminent military dictatorship did indeed accelerate the taking up of arms as a kind of last resort in defence of political liberties, but it was certainly that way round, not vice-versa, as the historical record would bear out.

According to witnesses' memoirs, General Tağmaç at a National Security Council meeting on 24 April 1970, openly discussed the possibility of a 'leftist' military takeover which would have gained the support of the lower ranks.[17] 'The leftist youth is positioned against the army; the higher ranks of the armed forces are depicted [by them] as servants of imperialism in line with the government,' Tağmaç argued, as recollected by Air Forces Commander, and Four-star General Muhsin Batur, one of the four authors of the 12th March memorandum, in his memoirs. 'Under these circumstances, no one can guarantee that 'the Armed Forces would not attempt a revolt' [...] The revolt this time will not be like that of 27th May 1960[18] but would be more like the Russian Revolution of 1917. The Constitution, the University and the National Broadcasting Company (TRT) laws should all be amended immediately.'[19]

The sheer scope of measures agreed on in this National Security Council meeting provides a clue to understanding the unparalleled increase in counter-revolutionary activity taking place *off the books* under the auspices of the 'Grey Wolves', in the months leading up to the 'soft coup' of 12 March 1971. The path to completely annihilating the revolutionary movement now lay clear, as the rival factions of the army top brass reconciled their differences in the face of possible 'revolution'. As the course of events demonstrated in the years that followed, there was no real threat for Turkey either from within or without. A revolution – communist or otherwise – would not have posed an existential threat, but merely a set of possible pathways towards social welfare and political liberties the country still doesn't enjoy 50 years later. But in the bipolar world of the Cold War, any hint of a legitimate, popular move towards revolution represented an existential, and therefore military, threat to the US and Turkey's fascists and ultra-nationalists.

Indeed, modern Turkish history could be imagined as a chain of interlinking counter-revolutions, each link reinforcing the idea of the monolithic Turkish 'nation-state'. It is an open question how much the Turkish military imported new tactics of brutality from the CIA, and how much it already had in its armoury, from its own imperialist and authoritarian past.

The history of modern revolutionary praxis in Asia Minor began, of course, with a tragedy – the defeat of the Armenian revolution and the genocide of up to 1.5 million Armenians between 1914 and 1918. Deep wounds were inflicted on the collective consciousness of both Turks and Armenians alike, wounds that would never heal unless cauterised somehow by a subsequent, successful revolution. Yet when the new republic of Turkey was declared in 1923, the entire Ottoman security apparatus was inherited along with the unique counterinsurgency experience gained by the Special Organisation [Teşkilat-ı Mahsusa], a special forces unit founded by the ruling Unity and Progress Party [İttihat ve Terakki Fırkası] of the constitutional monarchy. In spite of heinous crimes committed against humanity during the genocide, neither the organisation nor its leaders or henchmen ever met with any consequences.[20] The German army corps, fighting as an ally of the Ottoman Empire in the First World War, watched the mayhem unfolding with unflinching eyes.

Even during the War of Independence (1919-1923) that followed the collapse of the Ottoman Empire, when the nascent Turkey allied itself, for strategic reasons, with post-revolution Soviet Russia, the supposedly revolutionary Ankara government did not hesitate to ostracise the leader of the Turkish Communist Party, Mustafa Suphi, and his comrades, from the highest rostrum of power, the National Assembly. On 21 January 1921, founder of the Republic, Atatürk himself – then Speaker of the parliament – in a secret session of the assembly declared: 'Some degenerate, rampant sons of this nation, in connection with Russian Bolshevik government officials under the guise of doing public good, have founded a communist party led by Mustafa Suphi – not out of patriotism but more likely to curry favour with the leadership in Moscow who pay, protect and value those willing to make vain attempts at planting Russian Bolshevism into our country through several means.'[21] Unsurprisingly, a week after being charged by Atatürk, Mustafa Suphi and fourteen of his comrades were strangled to death on 28 January 1921 on a boat off Trabzon, in the Black Sea by a local gang leader previously employed in the Pontic genocide.[22]

Just as the birth of the Turkish bourgeoisie coincided with the bloody slaughter and expropriation of the Armenian people, the Turkish nation (and its sense of itself as a unitary nation-state) evolved at a time of bloody massacre and assimilation with regard to the Kurds, through the first twenty years of the Republic, costing tens of thousands of Kurdish lives.[23]

Following the Second World War, Turkey's allegiance to the US (and membership of NATO, with all its covert operations) represented an alliance it could understand; the blood-drenched derin devlet[24] apparatus nurtured from its imperialist past found a natural bedfellow in the New American World that Washington's own 'deep state' was building, complete with a global strategy and an international mandate: a licence to kill even its own kin in the name of America.

## Epilogue

The editors would like to clarify that Hüseyin Karabey's fictional CIA character 'Dewey' may bear some similarities to a real-life CIA officer stationed in Turkey at the time called Duane Ramsdell Clarridge, but he is entirely fictional. Unlike Karabey's Dewey, Clarridge was never assassinated. Instead he went on to become Deputy Chairman of the CIA's European Division, where he may have been involved in an incident similar to the Efrahim Elrom affair in Italy. In 1978, Italian Prime Minister Aldo Moro, was kidnapped by the Red Brigades and executed. During the 'Mani pulite' (clean hands) investigations of 1993, it was alleged that the CIA infiltrated the Red Brigades and killed Moro to discredit the communists and prevent them from coming to power. Clarridge served in Rome between 1979 and 1981 and was there when the failed assassination attempt against Pope John Paul II took place in the Vatican on 13 May 1981, by a former Grey Wolf member, Mehmet Ali Ağca. Moving back to Washington in August 1981, Clarridge became the head of the Latin America Division, and coordinated conspiracies against the Sandinista government in Nicaragua, recruiting in the process the guerrilla leader

Edén Pastora, nicknamed 'Commander Zero'. His time as head of the Latin America Division saw the invasion of Grenada and included, among other things, the administration of drug trafficking operations with Manuel Noriega, then CIA operative and Panama National Guard Chief of Staff. Between 1984 and 1986, Clarridge was head of the European Division and helped organise arms sales from Israel to Iran together with Lieutenant Commander Oliver North. His last post was Director of the Counterterrorism Center.

## Notes

1. Nihat Erim, quoted in *Milliyet Daily*, 2 May 1971, Istanbul.
2. 'Communique No. 1' by the THKC, 17 May 1971, reprinted in *Encyclopaedia of Socialism and Social Struggles*, Ed. Ertuğrul Kürkçü, vol. 7, Istanbul, İletişim Publishers, Istanbul 1988.
3. Justified by Article 146/1 of the Turkish Penal Code, which only actually calls for 'proportionate' force.
4. *The Rule of Law in Turkey and The European Convention on Human Rights, A Staff Study* by The International Commission of Jurists, page 15; https://www.icj.org/wp-content/uploads/2013/06/Turkey-rule-of-law-and-ECHR-thematic-report-1973-eng.pdf
5. Ali Gevgilili; *Türkiye'de 1971 Rejimi* (1971 Regime in Turkey), Milliyet Publishers 1973, excerpted in *Encyclopaedia of Socialism and Social Struggles*, vol. 7, p. 2174, 1988, Istanbul.
6. A popular interpretation of the Koranic discourse from the Surah al Anam, Verse 129: 'This is how we make the wrongdoers [destructive] allies of one another because of their misdeeds.'
7. Ganser, Daniele, *NATO's Secret Armies: Operation GLADIO and Terrorism in Western Europe,* Introduction.
8. *ibid.*, p. 226.
9. *ibid.*, p. 225.
10. *ibid.*, p. 2.
11. Ertuğrul Kürkçü; *X Örgütü* (Organisation X) https://m.bianet.org/bianet/diger/119164-x-orgutu
12. Sadly, 12 March was the beginning and not the end of the Gray Wolves' 'mission' on the southeastern flank of NATO. Having cost thousands of lives during the near civil war in 1977-80, they were officially employed by the Turkish counterinsurgency authorities as an

essential component of 'Turkey's war on Kurds' even after the end of the 'Cold War'. See, Ertuğrul Kürkçü, *Trapped in A Web of Covert Killers*, "Covert Action Quarterly (CAQ)", Summer 1997, No. 61, pp. 6-12., Washington D.C.; https://covertactionmagazine.com/wp-content/uploads/2020/01/CAQ61-1997-2.pdf.

13. 'Throwing the country into [...] a brothers war ['*kardeş kavgası*'] was one of the charges the military directed at the government in the original 12 March 'memorandum'. See. https://tr.wikisource.org/wiki/12_Mart_Muht per centC4 per centB1ras per centC4 per centB1

14. V.I. Lenin 'The Collapse of the Second International,' *Lenin Collected Works*, Progress Publishers, [197[4]], Moscow, Volume 21, pages 205-259.

15. *Milliyet Daily*, August 4, 1970, Istanbul.

16. Samuel P. Huntington; *Political Order in Changing Societies*, pp. 4-7, 1968, Yale University Press, Seventh Edition, London 1973.

17. Ümit Cizre; *AP-Ordu Ilişkileri Bir Ikilemin Anatomisi* (Justice Party-Army Relations: the Anatomy of a Dilemma), Iletişim Publishers, 2. Edition, Istanbul 2002, p.49.

18. The first coup d'état in the Republic of Turkey, staged by a group of 38 young Turkish military officers, led by General Cemal Gürsel, ousted the democratically elected Democrat Party, and subsequently tried and executed Prime Minister Adnan Menderes, Foreign Affairs Minister Fatin Rüştü Zorlu and Finance Minister Hasan Polatkan, on charges of 'high treason', 'misuse of public funds' and 'abrogation of the constitution'.

19. Muhsin Batur; *Anılar ve Görüşler 'Üç Dönemin Perde Arkası'* (Memoirs and Opinions: the Backstage to Three Eras), Milliyet Publishers, 3rd Edition, Istanbul 1985, p.189.

20. *See* Taner Akçam; *The Young Turks' Crime Against Humanity: The Armenian Genocide and Ethnic Cleansing in the Ottoman Empire*, Princeton University Press, 2012, for a detailed examination of the facts concerning the events.

21. Mustafa Kemal Paşa; *T. B. M. M. Gizli Celse Zabıtları* (Verbatim Records of the Secret Sittings, Grand National Assembly of Turkey) v.1, p. 326, January 21, 1921, Ankara.

22. The systematic killing of the Christian Ottoman Greek population of Anatolia, carried out during World War I and its aftermath (1914–1922) on the basis of their religion and ethnicity.

23. The most notorious genocide of this era was the carefully prepared and executed Dersim massacre under the pretext of quelling a 'rebellion', that was in fact a deliberately provoked local disturbance by the Turkish colonial rule in 1937-38. 13,806 people, mostly children and women were mercilessly killed as officially admitted by Prime Minister Tayyip Erdoğan on November 23, 2011 in the Turkish parliament, relying on classified official reports.

24. Deep state; a group of influential anti-democratic coalitions within the Turkish political system, consisting of high-level parties within the intelligence services (domestic and foreign), the Turkish military, security agencies, the judiciary, and mafia.

# Plan Z

Lina Meruane

Translated from the Spanish by Megan McDowell

*To Guido Arroyo, who knows so much about those years*

THEY WERE GOING TO *kill us all,* said the Mother. Her voice, cracked by the years, rose as she pressed her hands to her breast. She had thick fingers, long nails, unpainted but greedy lips that she licked to refresh. The Mother, her aged eyes lined in black, her short eyelashes. *They were going to kill us, they were going to kill us all,* she insisted. *You don't remember,* she said. *You were very little,* she said. *There's no reason you would know,* she went on in a maternal timbre, as if she were unaware that her daughter was fluent in the details of the past, that she had made the past her profession. That way she had of tensing an affection that already lived on tenterhooks, on the verge of disintegrating from disappointment or lack of roots or simply from the Daughter's exasperation at how her Mother still treated her as if she were four years old instead of forty-something. As soon as the Mother detected her Daughter's disinterest or the distance flitting across her face, she launched into it again, threw off some spark to revive the fire, saying, as she was saying now, *the Marxists had a plan and they would have slaughtered us.* She puffed out her chest, the flesh peeking voluptuously from her newly widowed neckline; she was silent for a moment, expectant, quivering, the gold bracelets tinkling on her wrist, the Mother searching, seeking out the evasive gaze of her Daughter, who, to escape the provocation, had knelt down to tie her sneakers. The Daughter was taking her time on the knots, as if they held a mystery of the world and she needed to resolve it. But the Daughter wasn't trying to untie any enigma; the Daughter distrusted interpretation and, for her, hard facts held sway, objective data, the veracity of documents, and not unsupported speculation or the rumours that the Mother wanted to pass off as true.

If the Daughter had announced that visit after several weeks of making excuses, it wasn't because she had any interest in that oft-repeated story. (Sooner or later, the Mother always started in again on that precious plan, and the Daughter found herself wondering if it wasn't the unequivocal sign of incipient senility or something worse, full-on dementia.) The Daughter had something to say to the Mother, something she hadn't said yet, something she didn't know how to say, because out of all the things that created friction between them, this thing the Daughter was coming to communicate could arouse a howl of indignation from that Mother, hers, who would always turn to drama in a pinch. The Daughter could no longer put off her news and its immediate consequences, but she had let lunch go by, waiting for the Mother to inquire. The Mother didn't even ask how she was or what she'd been up to, but talked instead about the regrettable health of the cousin on dialysis, the alcoholic colleague shut away in her house by neurotic daughters, the neighbour who was slowly dying from metastasis, the irritating forgetfulness of the aunt who asked the same thing over and over, *like a wind-up doll, poor thing,* and without a pause she moved on to her occasional lower back pain, her agonising bunions, the arthritis that was deforming her hands, *just look how ugly they've gotten,* and she talked about the afflictions of her maid who was old like her, or maybe younger, though Rosa looked old from the long workdays she had endured since childhood. The Mother had talked to her without a full stop (the way people who spend a lot of time without talking to anyone talk, thought the Daughter) and she hardly touched her food, while the Daughter tucked into a succulent cut of salmon with soy sauce and sesame seeds and mashed sweet potato and salad with avocado and walnuts and a slice of Rosa-baked bread and all culminating with some very sweet strawberries that the Mother declared light because they were sprinkled with sweetener. She had interrupted herself, the Mother, only to clarify that false sweetness, but the Daughter wasn't worried about her weight, the Daughter crowned her strawberries with cream and watched her Mother wrinkle her nose. Then she offered coffee, suggested they sit outside while they drank it. The Mother seemed to have completely forgotten there was a reason for that lunch and that chat on the terrace. (Mothers are so canny, observed the Daughter once she was sitting in the shade of the wide white awning.) She was expert in taking detours around things she didn't feel like hearing, and expert as well in keeping her Daughter's attention by linking successive family tragedies to national tragedies or calamities of any other nature. She didn't understand how the Mother had managed to move from arthritic hands and feet to the famously false Plan Z that had threatened to do away with them all. Once again, the Plan. She would let her talk, she told herself, finishing the double knot on her sneaker and rising from the uncomfortable position, feeling the Mother's brown eyes locked on her own, those fierce eyes of a solitary hawk using its curved beak to open her optic nerve, her encephalitic mass, her cranial bones, effortlessly peering right through the black locks on the back of the Daughter's head.

*Fortunately the military listened to us.* The Mother, her slackened face with too much flesh. *And thank God they did!* she raised her voice in English, then returned to the comfort of Spanish, more soberly, *the gringos understood how serious the matter was, and together we defended ourselves against the Marxists.* The Daughter noticed the strange appearance of the word Marxist in the Mother's wrinkled mouth, and she wondered if for once she was trying to be more measured, or at least more exact. She had always called them *upelientos*, and the Daughter discovered in that instant that she preferred *upeliento*, much as it was an insulting and degrading word, much as it combined the initials of the Popular Unity party with *peliento*: shaggy, tattered, miserable. And she preferred the contemptuous word, the Daughter did, because it declared upfront and unvarnished the Mother's hatred for all those men and especially the women who had voted for the government of Salvador Allende. *All those rattleboned, layabout women, seduced by socialism, convinced that some kind of white knight was going to pull them out of poverty and stick them in a palace while the whole country went to hell,* she had said on certain occasions, or else she said, more quietly, *they were going to take away everything we had earned through hard work and give it to the rabble who only knew how to hold out their hands.* She'd sit waiting for a reaction from the Daughter, who would produce a tense-lipped smile or grab her book-heavy backpack and get into her car and head down from the hilltop neighbourhood of fenced-in, guarded condominiums to her apartment in the crowded centre of Santiago, ironically whistling 'Las casitas del barrio alto' by the murdered Víctor Jara, or singing the 'Little Boxes' of the original English. That used to be what she did, make her exit humming without even saying goodbye; she'd done it often while the Father was still alive (if the Father's day-to-day could be called life, incapacitated for years, confined to a wheelchair, unable to move even his lips). She could depart and leave the Mother talking to her Aurelio, venting onto a husband who could no longer contradict her, nor for that matter agree. Back then, she wouldn't be left alone, the Mother, with the door slam echoing in her ear drums, but now that the Father was dead, those enraged exits could only accentuate the Mother's solitude. Because, though she was accompanied day and night, seven days a week and twelve months of the year, lifelong, by Rosa, she now felt that she had no one to talk to.

Maybe that's why she's skipping the epithets, to avoid

another altercation. The Mother must remember the last time very well, when she offered up her *upelientos*, when she belittled Allende's voters as *shabby communists*, and had received in return a *vieja momia, you should be ashamed to talk like that, they're all dead.* Her Daughter, her only daughter, her only child, always threw that in her face, how so many human beings had been murdered and then people like her went around suggesting that they must have done *something* to have disappeared (that phrase on repeat), that the left's disappeared leaders were just vacationing with their lovers in Europe (that other phrase), instead of reckoning with reality. The Daughter sometimes thought the Plan Z that her Mother had believed in and still believed in today and needed to believe in, the supposed Marxist plan to massacre the bourgeoisie, allowed her to pardon the Junta for its heavy hand (*genocidal* hand, the Daughter thought to herself). Then she understood that her Mother would never stop holding that plan dear, even when the very same colonels and advisors who had avowed its veracity eventually admitted it was a lie. The Mother claimed to have *seen* the documents that described the plan Allende drew up with the most extreme factions of the left, a plan for a self-coup that would that would lead inexorably to the murder of the Armed Forces' high command and the opposition leaders, after which one could expect an extensive inventory of people who would be headed for the firing squad. For some reason that remained a mystery to the Daughter, the Mother included herself, and her Daughter, in that imaginary list of victims. The Daughter was sick of telling her that it wasn't enough to *see* a document, to touch it, smell it, bite and taste it, not even enough to confirm the existence of a stamp certifying authenticity; you had to *compare* the information, *verify* sources, all those things she dedicated her life to researching in the archives and declassified documents from the period. That plan had been nothing but an idea the CIA proposed to the Military Junta, a way to justify the intervention that had received such bad press worldwide, with La Moneda Palace in flames and the president, socialist but democratic, dead inside it. She'd gotten tired of explaining that all those typed pages collected in the bizarre book that was the *Libro blanco*, those pages published by an incompetent historian (what an embarrassment to her profession, the Daughter complained), were nothing but falsified documents, coup-mongering propaganda to sell the massacre as civil war and to justify mass imprisonment, indiscriminate torture, the disappearance and murder of thousands of people without a single trial. The Daughter wanted to believe that Plan Z soothed her Mother's troubled conscience (that's what she told herself, that the Mother suffered from an unspeakable guilt, and that thought allowed her to forgive her, and even love her). That's why she steeled herself, protected by her lie-proof vest as she let her Mother talk. Now her eyes found distraction in the garden, some black thrushes that shone as if they'd just been shined with shoe polish, a shiny, dark tumult, six or seven little thrushes meticulously tearing at the grass and pecking the earth in search of worms.

*The truth*, continued the Mother, stubborn and undaunted, *the truth is that until 1970 Chile was a perfect country on a turbulent continent.* (The old myth of exceptionalism always excluded Allende from Chile's democratic oasis, thought the Daughter, still staring at the thrushes. As if Allende hadn't won the election legitimately, as if he hadn't respected the laws and every one of the censures and restrictions that a hostile Congress imposed on him before finally declaring him president.) *And the truth is that the coup saved us, even if you don't like to hear me say so, and even if many of the people who pleaded for a coup now deny it.* (The Daughter listened to this and thought without saying it that *the truth* was not what people believed or read in the newspapers, because, at least during the years of socialism, the newspapers and magazines and radio stations and two of the three TV channels were owned by the oligarchy and functioned as propaganda apparatuses for the opposition, telling half-truths that were not *the truth.*) The Mother saw that her daughter was again turning her attention towards the spacious and flowered garden that was her rigorous morning task, and she lit up remembering just then that the Daughter had something to tell her and perhaps this was the moment, and she said, as though to upbraid her, *you're very quiet today, is something wrong?* (Finally, a question, thought the Daughter, and she quivered as her head promptly emptied.) She nodded vaguely, murmuring, *I'm just a little tired.* It was an evasive reply that didn't rise to the level of a lie; the Daughter was incapable of reneging on the truth, and it was true that she had spent days packing up boxes for her move, boxes and boxes of books and also some clothes, her torn jeans, her ragged T-shirts and coats, sneakers, maybe a cotton dress, old underwear she didn't throw out because shopping for clothes was an exhausting waste of time. She was more exhausted by the Mother, though, more drained and furious after those visits, and now she had squandered the opportunity of her question.

She met the Mother's suspicious eyes, the same eyes as her own, because she, the Daughter, was a carbon copy of her Mother at her age. The Daughter was thin and she already knew that when she grew old she would still be gaunt and bony, but she would lose her waist and her behind would grow, and her breasts would be even more excessive than the ones she sported now, a little ashamed, and had since adolescence, and she could observe her Mother to foresee where her still discreet wrinkles would deepen. She knew that even if she wasn't with her Mother, even if her Mother died suddenly, even if the years and an eternity went by, she would go on seeing her every morning in the mirror. Not as an ephemeral silhouette but as a presence made flesh in her own body. *Gross,* she exclaimed suddenly. The thrushes' cries had pulled her from the mirror, an excited fluttering around the bird that had managed to pull from the earth a worm long as a root, dark, winding, fleshy and soft; the other birds had crowded around to peck at the prey, tearing it to pieces with their swift, sharp beaks. The Daughter closed her eyes, disgusted at the viscerality of bird life, and when she opened them again a few thrushes were flying off to disappear among the trees. *My, that's a nasty look,* said the Mother when she saw the Daughter's expression of disgust, which she was convinced was directed at her, always at her, even if she would never admit it. *Do you feel OK?* Care was an opportunity for closeness, the Mother knew it and used it whenever the chance arose. *Those birds eating worms*, muttered the Daughter, taciturn, to reply with something that was true even if the Mother knew she was hiding something, a boyfriend, a lover or something worse, the sickness of a pregnancy. *I know that girl as well as if I'd given birth to her,* said the murmuring Mother then, immediately realising it was absurd to use that expression because she actually had birthed the Daughter, and had raised her even while she regretted becoming a mother precisely in the year Allende was elected, and promised herself she would never get pregnant again. She had informed her husband in the hospital, cradling the baby with its bluish, swollen head in her arms, that she was not about to give any children to Marxism. She was sure they were going to take her Daughter away because that's what they did, they stole kids. And what a paradox to have defeated them but to have her Daughter become their stalwart champion. It was as if the midwives had brainwashed her there in the hospital, behind the Mother's back.

She vividly remembered one of the lectures she'd heard from that usurped Daughter, that susceptible and demanding Daughter that she, the Mother, had done nothing to deserve. That Daughter clutching her head, shaking her head, her straight hair swaying side to side, *please, Mom, there was no Plan Z or Plan X, and they weren't going to kill anyone. Allende had the left's few weapons taken away from them. And if he didn't manage to implement his social measures it's because an imperialist power was aligned against him. Remember, Mom, we were in the middle of the cold war, the United States was run by a Republican government that had financed Allende's right-wing opponent, in secret – maybe you don't even know that. Did you vote for Alessandri to keep Allende out of office?* The Mother hadn't answered the question; the Daughter seemed uninterested in her reply. *But maybe you do know that Nixon swore to strangle the Chilean economy – Make it scream! That's what he said, make the economy scream! Such hubris! All to keep Allende from winning the election, or, if he won, to force him to abandon his nationalist convictions and bend right over for the gringos. They cut off the financial assistance so many presidents had counted on. They didn't renew the bank loans Allende needed for his solidarity plan – his Plan S, Mom, not Z. And you remember how Kissinger said that he didn't see why they should allow, al-low,* and the Daughter had emphasised the verb, separating the syllables, *allow a country to become Marxist just because,* and she emphasised that just because, *just because its people are irresponsible. They were worried about the hundreds of millions of dollars they had invested here, and they weren't about to lose control of the copper, steel, iron, the media, the phone company! They practically owned the country and they didn't even know Chile or anything about Chile, they had no interest in Chile or in this continent, only in Cuba because they'd lost it, and Vietnam because they were in the process of losing it... They only cared about Chile when a socialist turned up on the ballot and their pockets started trembling, that is, they didn't care about Chile, they weren't afraid Allende would fail but that he would come out ahead, that his democratic revolution would work. The gringo plan was to overthrow him. As if they had the right to destroy our democracy in order to make us democratic! The hypocrisy!* The Mother had waved her hands to tell her Daughter to lower her voice but the Daughter went on, indignant. *Nixon gave a lot of money to the centre and ultra-right parties, the violent kids in Patria y Libertad, and he gave instructions to the CIA to convince the Armed Forces to rise up against Allende, and it took them three years to do it, to convince them, and they managed it because they had been training the military for years to fight against international communism, against the revolutionary guerrilla that we never had in Chile. You understand, Mom? An attack on the sovereignty of a skinny and flimsy country like ours!*

The Mother remembered that monologue, remembered having felt momentarily proud of her Daughter, who must be a great history teacher; it was clear she had studied conscientiously, that she had learned a few things even if she hadn't lived through those events she was talking about... if only she wasn't so vehement and sententious, if only there weren't such rage in her words; and she imagined that the biggest troublemakers among the students would interpret that rage as passion and social commitment and would admire her. The Mother leaned her head back to get some air; she was so aggressive, the Daughter, and that's why she was alone, alone and bitter like arugula. And since when did she hate the United States so much? An enormously rich and organised country, full of hardworking people who pulled themselves up by the bootstraps without complaining and ended up becoming millionaires. And those opulent cities with beaches of turquoise waters and outlet stores, full of elegant Cubans nostalgic for the island that had expelled them... How the Mother missed Miami. Since Aurelio's accident she hadn't had anyone to go with, and she wasn't about to invite her Daughter, definitely not her Daughter, because even if she accepted, which was unlikely, she would make life impossible with her endless disquisition about Cuba. She saw the Daughter's pedagogical hand rising up in her memory, her right hand, her long, ringless fingers that bent into a fist as she enumerated each and every one of the *imperialist interventions* on the continent. Pinky finger, the annexation of half the Mexican territory. Ring finger, the anti-Sandinista operation. Middle finger, Guatemalan genocide. Index finger, Cuba and the embargo and the failed Bay of Pigs followed by the Missile Crisis that almost blew the planet up. The Mother couldn't help but stare at her Daughter's rough, calloused elbow, she'll have to suggest a little lotion or her skin would end up cracked and bleeding, but the Daughter was accusing the gringos of *pushing the Cubans to align with the Soviets when they tried to put the squeeze on them, they took it upon themselves to turn a leftist revolution into a communist dictatorship, understand?* She was tiresome, the Daughter and her lectures. The Mother had dared to ask where she got all that stuff. *But, what do you mean where?* sputtered the Daughter, *I've spent years researching the cold war on our continent. Do you still not know what I do for a living?*

That's where it all began! the Mother realised, ignoring her Daughter's insolence. She had learned to hate the United States in college! The Mother had paid for that expensive education only so her Daughter could learn how to hate. She smoothed her green pleated skirt with her sweaty hands so as not to have to meet her Daughter's rage at the fact that she could be grateful to the United States for interfering in the domestic affairs of all those pathetic countries, hers included. They had to intervene, thought the Mother, recalling Kissinger, his face that of a diligent boy, his hair waved neatly back, his thick-framed glasses, shaking hands with Pinochet in uniform and without glasses, happy to have him as an ally. And the Mother remembered putting on her own fine, gold-rimmed glasses to read that endearing gringo's memoirs, which her Daughter had given her one Christmas so she could find out who that evil Kissinger really was. The Mother saw herself lying in bed with the giant tome at siesta time; she dozed off and the book fell onto her face, thwacked her forehead, yanked her from sleep, and she read another page full of letters that criss-crossed and intersected and grew blurry in spite of the glasses until the book again fell like a stone onto her face. That book was agony, the Mother laughed quietly, and it was her Daughter's own fault she never found out how the interventions had increased as the United States became a superpower. Why in the world would she give such a tiresome gift, and she smiled and wanted to laugh but gave a start instead when she looked across from her: the Daughter's thumb was waiting at the ready, because that finger, she spat, that suspended thumb was Chile. The Mother felt the vigour of a forty-something professor (how manly the Daughter was as a university teacher) explaining how Chile *was an opaque country for the United States because it defied the stereotypes of a banana republic, because it was more organised, more industrialised than the other countries in Latin America, because it had a significant and educated middle class and a high literacy rate. And Allende wasn't just anyone, he was a leader respected by his peers and adored by the people* (by some people, by the unwashed masses, the Mother retorted in her head), *and to top it off he hadn't seized power. The United States had to be especially careful if it didn't want to risk a credibility that was already suffering. And that's why,* the Daughter continued, her thumb still in the air (fat and erect, the Mother allowed herself that vulgarity), *not only had they tried to foment* a *military uprising in 1970, they were likely behind the assassination of General Schneider and the failed Tancazo coup in June of 73, as well as the successful coup in September.*

The Mother squinted her eyes as if her skepticism were caused by the sun and not the sermon she was receiving. *So,* she said with impatient irony, *everything that happened to us is the gringos' fault?* And in English, her voice rising falsely: *Give me a break! It's easy to place the blame on your tool,* she said, but immediately felt the saying sounded like something else if you didn't mention the bad carpenter. *It's all Daddy Gringo's fault, it's all your mother's fault! I didn't say that, Mom, don't be manipulative,* replied the Daughter drily. *You didn't say it now but you always say it,* retorted the Mother. *How I supported the Junta. How I lied to you while you were growing up and that's why you believed and even voted to keep Pinochet in power, as if you weren't a grown-up woman by then... And you only understood in college, where I worked so hard to send you only for you to be ashamed of us, of living in this house with the privileges we wouldn't have had under Allende, because salaries would have kept shrinking until we were in squalor* (that phrase of her Mother's) *and because inflation was sky-high* (that other one) *and because under Allende I would have lost my job, and without my job, after what happened to your father, we wouldn't have had enough, we would have been out in the street, living like bums, alongside the bums under some bridge or else with those friends of yours, the hippie-dippies with their guitars, their Chilote sweaters in winter, the ones who subsisted in poverty on the outskirts of Santiago and studied with a stingy pittance of a loan from the State...* With a haughty indifference that the Daughter didn't remember having seen in her, the Mother rang a bell and Rosa, encased in her sky blue apron with white trim, came to the glass door. The Mother asked her to bring out a pitcher of water – she was thirsty on that sweltering afternoon. And the Daughter nodded, understanding that this was her chance to air out and wash and dry all the dirty linen of the past. *Were you involved then?* asked the Daughter, feeling her mouth go dry, her tongue sticking to the roof of her mouth, *involved with the military in…? But of course not! Who do you think I am? Or was? I have no idea, Mom, you never talk about what you did beyond the fear you felt and about how Dad, not long before his stroke, organised with the neighbours to keep watch at night in case someone came to kill you.* And the Mother said *Yes, yes, they threatened us from the slums with megaphones,* and the Daughter, undaunted, *and also how you left the cars in the street like a barricade, with the brakes on and drums of gas that would explode and create a wall of fire to give you enough time.* And the Mother said, *Exactly, time to get away.* And the Daughter went on, *and I also know that you planted a giant cross flapping in the front yard of the house we had then, and that for many years after the coup, and I remember this, you put Chilean flags in all the windows that looked out on the street.*

*We were nobodies,* murmured the Mother, *we were just mothers and wives, what else could we do… You were the executive secretary at a company, right?* the Daughter interrupted. The Mother nodded: *it was a company that the UP was going to nationalise, and I knew my job would be gone with nationalisation and the little security we had would disappear. I know all that,* said the Daughter. *What else do you want to know, then? There's nothing else to tell,* said the Mother, noticing in surprise that the pitcher was already on the table along with two glasses. *I want to know what company it was.* The hot breeze had risen, blowing the Mother's hair as she looked up at the sky and excused herself, she had to go to the bathroom. *If you please, Mom. What company was it?* The Mother was already standing, but she sat down and said that the company was Teléfonos de Chile. *The ITT? The famous ITT of the gringos who financed the opposition? That one, yes,* stammered the Mother. *That company was Nixon's economic arm…* the Daughter began. *Those gringos were very generous with me, and when they closed down they gave me a handsome severance for all my services,* added the Mother, fearing the reaction from her anti-imperialist Daughter. *Mom, you have to tell me the truth, if you were complicit in diverting funds,* but the Mother interrupted, her voice pleading, *no, no, noooo, stop it! I was never in that business! I had nothing to do with that!* Her voice become a harsh wail. The Daughter sighed, rubbed her knees and thighs. It wasn't exactly business that the ITT did. The pitcher had slices of cucumber and lemon and she poured water for them both. *I'm sorry, Mom, I had to know.* And she saw that the Mother's eyes were damp, though she didn't know whether from sadness or anger or what, but surely it was irritation because now she was whispering, *and another thing, just so you know, since you want to know so bad.* The Mother emboldened. The Mother half-cocked. The Mother beside herself. *It wasn't the gringos who convinced the Armed Forces to intervene, abandoning their tradition of staying on the sidelines, it was Chilean women,* and she puffed out her chest, fallen in spite of her bra's metallic structure, *the brave women of this nation.*

Her Mother rubbed her old-lady eyelids and told of how she had been one of those women – those patriots – who had gone out to protest. This woman sitting before the Daughter was no longer the former young mother in the house of her past waiting in terror for the nocturnal *upelienta* horde, but rather one more woman among so many of the tottering upper class determined to march against the Popular Unity party and against the long official visit of Fidel Castro, for whom they felt real aversion. That woman was telling her how they'd organised through hundreds of phone calls and how they persuaded their indecisive girlfriends on entire afternoons of conversation, and how they all went out together in the capital's downtown streets on December 1st, 1971, precisely the day Castro was to return to Cuba after his triumphant entrance into a Santiago of avenues packed with people cheering for him, after tireless days traveling Chile from the saltpeter mines of the north to the coal mines in the south and the very tip of the legendary Strait of Magellan, all with Allende beside him. The Daughter listened, attentive and ill-tempered, even as she remembered a documentary from that time, remembered finding out that Fidel was tall and robust, but his Cuban blood meant he froze in the south, his parka with its furred hood wasn't enough for him, while Allende, who was older and smaller, wore only a suit and didn't seem to suffer at all. And she liked discovering then that Fidel wasn't the Castro her Mother spoke of: on his tour, he hadn't talked ad nauseam in each place, he stopped to listen to the workers and university students and also the female workers with a rare kind of respect. And she realised as she watched the screen that his assembly of nearly fifty thousand people at the National Stadium had been distorted, that sure, he spoke for an hour and two hours and five hours without stopping, without glancing at a piece of paper, and sure, there were people who cheered and clapped and cried and people who fell asleep and also people who left, but it wasn't because *not even the leftist Chileans could stand so much radical yackety-yak...* Studying the archive, the Daughter had learned that he was a great orator, sophisticated and captivating, but also moderate and cautious in his impressions of Allende, and that he had a sense of humour.

A long way from that humour now, the Daughter felt mortified. She was finding out after so many years that the Mother had pushed hundreds of women to star in a decisive milestone in Allende's fall. But she didn't want to miss the details of what the Mother was relating, because knowing the details, she understood, would perhaps allow her to distance herself and feel a less definitive guilt over what she had to tell her. And with unexpected relief she listened as her Mother told of marching through the streets to protest because Castro had stayed for a whole month (not a whole month, Mom, but she abstained, the Mother would have accused her of being like her Father, correcting even things that didn't matter, because if it wasn't a month it was 24 days, too long for a visit). *So little money in the country, and the government spent it on joyriding around. And why did Castro want to get so deep into what was happening in Chile? Was he planning on running for vice president or presidential advisor? Did he want to convince Allende to implement his dictatorship of the proletariat in Chile?* The Daughter knew the Mother was somewhat right about that; it was well known that when Castro left he was annoyed that he hadn't been able to convince Allende of *his* Marxist revolution, but neither could Nixon twist Allende's arm with his capitalist hand. *That speaks well of Allende,* the Daughter protested out loud. *Don't interrupt me, didn't you want me to tell you about the march?* murmured the Mother, wiping her forehead with her wrist.

The Daughter didn't tell her she'd seen photos of that protest in newspapers from the time, hundreds of ladies with pearl necklaces and earrings and young women in bell-bottomed pants and big sunglasses. She could picture the Mother with straightened hair, wearing herringbone and leather sandals, a frightened Rosa behind her. Because she supposed Rosa had been dragged to the march, though maybe she'd gone willingly because there were some poor housewives and working women who were against socialism. *You should have seen Rosita with her hair in the wind and her blue apron, a pot in one hand and the lid in the other, and you should have seen me, another empty pot raised in my porcelain hands; because that was our message, that we didn't have any food to fill our pots. ¡La izquierda!, ¡unida!, ¡nos tiene sin comida!,*[1] chanted the Mother, and she burst out in convulsive laughter. *With every word we hit the lids like they were cymbals, and we all shouted together because there was such scarcity, you had to wait in interminable lines for every product or turn to the black market with the little money we had. ¡Allende!, ¡escucha!, ¡mujeres somos muchas!*[2] *There were other phrases that made us laugh, like ¡Fidel!, ¡a la olla!, ¡aliñado con cebolla!*[3] *And the women from Javiera Carrera School howled ¡Allende!, ¡proceda!, ¡imite a Balmaceda!*[4] The Daughter would have liked to stick her fingers in her ears so she could think about whether it was true what she had read in a sensationalist paper, that 'the witches with pots and pans were shielded by thugs the Right hired to take Allende down.' (Shielded by thugs, she thought now; those thugs were members of Patria y Libertad who marched beside the women in suits and ties or in all black, equipped with chains and crowbars and wooden bats.) It turned into a hullabaloo, the Mother was saying. We were attacked by a troop of Marxists, they mocked us, threw rocks at us, and potatoes with razor blades went flying through the air, some women were wounded. Which of those feminine organisations had she been affiliated with? Was she mixed up with paramilitary groups? the Daughter wanted to ask. Wanted to know if the Mother's friend Pepe belonged to Patria y Libertad. What about her own father? No, she didn't want to know anything. She wanted the Mother to be quiet. She wanted to forget that whole story.

The Mother's verbosity bewildered her. *And we did so well with our pots-and-pans protest that we had the idea to go later and beat our pots in the faces of the military, and to throw feathers at them. Feathers! Did you say feathers?* the Daughter couldn't resist, *wasn't it corn?* And she arched her eyebrows with the empty glass in her hand and a slice of lemon between her teeth. *Feathers, of course it was feathers. We got tons of them from sleeping bags and pillows, and we went right down there to throw them at the barracks and at the generals' houses.* The Daughter swallowed her lemon. Feathers. It didn't seem right, it was very hard to find chickens on the black market, not to mention turkeys or ducks. Where would they find so many feathers? *I don't understand,* admitted the Daughter, and the Mother straightened up in her chair as if she were the teacher and the Daughter her student. *It was to tell them we thought they were chickens. To push them to act, and we got what we wanted,* said the Mother, triumphant. *You see now that it wasn't just the gringos?* she repeated, raising an eyebrow. *I never said it was just the US intervention,* the Daughter corrected her, seeing or imagining those yards snowy with down from all the chickens that were missing from tables. *The United States alone wouldn't have been able to do it, and the military alone wouldn't either. All Chileans were calling for the coup.* There was silence. *All Chileans, Mom! So this country belonged only to you? So the others didn't exist or didn't count? They had to be murdered so they would count less?*

howled the Daughter, slamming her glass onto the table and getting up from her chair. *You have a problem!* bellowed the Mother, in English again, watching her walk towards the door with her car keys in hand. *You too,* the Daughter pointed out sombrely, speaking English better than her Mother, with less of an accent, or with the American accent she had learned in the pricey private school full of children with inferiority complexes about being Chilean. But the Mother had won, she had gotten her riled up, managed to push her away. She was trembling from head to toe, and said, in English, *That's some shit.*

*Was that what you came to tell me?* the Mother muttered resentfully. The Daughter stopped, frowned, astonished that she'd almost forgotten. Fluffy white clouds were being shoved along by black storm clouds coming from the south and darkening the city. A downpour was coming, and the Daughter thought she was going to miss the smell of rain and wet earth and maybe even her Mother's garden. She turned her head back and saw the Mother had straightened up in her chair, sensing (mothers were so canny) that she was about to receive some bad news. *What did you come to tell me that was so urgent?* The Daughter felt the words suffocating her, she would have to say them to keep from drowning, and she went back to the terrace and sat down across from her Mother and murmured that she had finally received a university contract. *A contract, finally, dear!* the Mother said several times, knowing she should be happy for her Daughter but intuiting from her fearful expression that no. That she shouldn't be happy. The Daughter had accepted a professorship at the far-off University of Seattle. She had sold her apartment and sent her furniture by ship, and she already had a buyer for her car. She would leave in five days. She had come to say goodbye but hadn't left time for the goodbye. The Mother hunched over as if she'd been punched in the liver. *You're going to the United States? When you've done nothing but bad-mouth the gringos?* Her tongue seemed to be sparking. Her eyes flashed, because a contract was a lifetime and it was abandonment in the Mother's final years of old age. *The United States!* she repeated, pressing her lips together, feeling that she was going to collapse but leaping energetically from her chair to enter the house without looking back, murmuring, *If the Marxists didn't kill me with their plan, my daughter's not going to kill me with hers.*

## Notes

1. *The Left, united, would have us without food!* (Rhyming)
2. *Allende! Listen! We women are many!* (Rhyming)
3. *Fidel! Cooked in a pot! Dressed with onion!* (Rhyming)
4. *Allende! Go on! Imitate Balmaceda!* A reference to the aristocratic president of Chile, between 1886 and 1891, whose political disagreements with the Chilean congress led to the 1891 Civil War. Balmaceda fled the country during his term, and later killed himself.

# Afterword: Unhealed Wounds

## Francisco Dominguez

Middlesex University London

The fraught conversation between the Mother and Daughter in Lina Meruane's story captures the almost religious adherence of the country's middle class to a patently mendacious interpretation of the events leading to the bloody coup d'état that ousted President Salvador Allende in 1973.

The Mother still holds (50 years later!) to the explanation fabricated by the Pinochet-led military junta in the aftermath of the coup (in 1973 itself) of a 'Plan Zeta' (or Z) published in large quantities, widely distributed and publicised by the dictatorship charging the Allende government with the sinister intention to 'decapitate the military high command and (physically) eliminate all opposition to it'.

The Mother's view reflects the self-deception of substantial sections of the middle class of Chile that desperately wanted, then, and still now, to believe the decision taken by the military to overthrow Allende was a last, pre-emptive, life or death resort before 'the Marxists' killed them all. The front page of *La Tercera* (a right-wing newspaper with a wide circulation) on 15 September 1973 carried the headline: 'Either we destroyed them, or they destroyed us', shows the endurance and longevity of this false belief.

The Daughter, having been born in the same year as the coup, like many kids from middle-class families, grew up influenced by the Mother and the Father's (Aurelio) fears, prejudices and the self-righteousness of having 'saved' Chile from 'totalitarian Marxism' but, also as many middle-class offsprings, they became educated and were able to discern historical fact from political fabrication.

The writer's portrayal of the Mother reinforces the impression of somebody not just dominated by intense class prejudice but whose demeanour, attire and even physical appearance are coherent with such depiction: wearing expensive, jangling attention-seeking jewellery; starving herself neurotically to delay ageing; using a sweet, fake voice that's still charged with loaded political vocabulary; resorting to speaking in English; and deploying an overly theatrical behaviour, always playing the victim in order to get her way. Furthermore, the Mother's use of Chilean slang words – *rotos* and *upelientos* – conveys with great accuracy the strong middle-class contempt still felt to this day for the country's poor – the social, political and electoral base of Salvador Allende. Exactly the image I had during my youth of the *Viejas Ricas del Barrio Alto* (Rich Women of Affluent Neighbourhoods, in Chilean parlance).

The Daughter's deconstruction of the Mother's myth about the real intentions of Allende's Popular Unity government is as powerful as it is accurate. She is, after all, an academic specialist on the Cold War in Latin America, whilst the Mother has no arguments or evidence to question the Daughter's demolition of the narrative justifying the coup on the basis of Plan Z, except the incessant propagandistic repetition to herself of the threat represented by the *comunachos* (Chilean pejorative slang term for *comunistas* – communists) to society, to her life and that of her family and the families in her wealthy neighbourhood.

There was no Plan Z. Allende was democratically elected; a hostile political majority in Congress *did* impose all kinds of restrictions and limitations on Allende's programme to bring about structural change, and even that programme was confined to the limits allowed by the nation's bourgeois constitution which he fastidiously respected even to the point of imperilling the very revolutionary process; Nixon *did* order his secretary of state, Henry Kissinger, to make the economy scream to prevent Allende's election; Kissinger, on 27 June 1970, speaking on Chile *did* say to the US Forties Committee: 'I don't see why we need to stand by and watch a country go communist due to the irresponsibility of its own people. The issues are much too important for the Chilean voters to be left to decide for themselves.'[1] The US, in typical fashion and seeking to strangle the economy, *did* actively sabotage Chile's economy by ensuring no economic aid or financial credits were advanced to the country; and the US *did not* orchestrate the coup to save Chile's democracy but to prevent Allende's government programme from succeeding.

The election of an avowedly Marxist president presented the US with the rather intractable problem of destabilising and ousting a democratic government by undemocratic means, hence the necessity to hide behind Chile's political parties of the right and ultra-right as well as the emerging fascist shock troops (Patria y Libertad), whilst simultaneously financing them all (and very likely helping with their training).[2]

The same happened with Fidel's visit to Chile in 1971, which, as a young man, I remember as vividly as if it were yesterday. Imagine how Chile's right perceived the 'affront' of Allende welcoming the most feared Latin American revolutionary leader with full honours and the red carpet. Many of the welcome banners in cities, neighbourhoods, universities and rural areas that Fidel visited read something along the lines of 'Welcome to Chile: Second Free Territory of the Americas'. Worse, his planned short visit was extended to three weeks, time he used to visit the whole country from the far north to the far south (Chile, being such a thin country geographically, and culturally, has neither an east nor a west). Everywhere he went, he received a rapturous welcome, turning each stop of the tour into a major political event.

The right-wing media (which was most of the media) spewed volumes of vitriol against Castro, more out of fear than hatred, though with an abundance of the latter too. Their narrative claimed that Fidel had come to Chile to persuade Allende to embrace the Cuban revolutionary method and jettison his 'peaceful road to socialism'. However, the right's response to Fidel's visit did not confine itself to editorialising their dislike of the Cuban leader, they orchestrated demonstrations, of the 'empty pots' kind described in the story (where women banged pots and pans as they marched)[3] flanked by barely disguised paramilitary soldiers, as well as more violent public disorder: they deployed clearly trained paramilitary shock platoons to wreak havoc for several days up and down the nation, with their epicentre being Santiago, the capital city.

Though he uttered some carefully worded warnings about the fascist threat in Chile that was visible for everyone to see, Fidel was extremely cautious and highly experienced when it came to TV, radio and newspaper interviews, open discussions, speeches, and other public appearances at which he persistently emphasised that all nations in the continent, including Chile, would have to find their own nationally-specific road to socialism, and not just copy Cuba's way. His long farewell speech at a packed-out National Football Stadium, delivered on 2 December 1971 (of which I listened to every word, as I was there!), had an enormous impact when, though he emphasised the uniqueness of the Chilean revolution he warned that, in Chile, 'the reactionaries, the oligarchs, are much better prepared than in Cuba, much better organised and much better equipped to resist changes from an ideological viewpoint. They have created all the instruments to wage a battle on every front against the advancement of the process, a battle in the ideological field, in the political field, a battle against the masses.'[4] An assessment that turned out to be very accurate: indeed this very football stadium would later be turned into a concentration camp and a place to carry out torture and executions by the military dictatorship that came into power after the coup.

But, notwithstanding the hatred, vitriol and fear of the right wing and their media, Fidel was very personable, quite courteous and exceedingly polite both when speaking in public and when giving interviews or polemicising, as the Daughter in Meruane's story is later to discover: during his Chilean visit he was somebody capable of respectfully listening to workers, peasants, students, women and others, and of engaging in genuine dialogue with them; was undoubtedly a great orator, a sophisticated politician, charming, cautious, and endowed with a good sense of humour. Such perception of Fidel's persona had little to do with the stories the Mother had told her whilst growing up. Thus, the deconstruction of the Manichean version of the Mother's memories of the country's history extends beyond Chile's borders.

The intense hatred that suffused the political campaigning of the right wing, which the Mother, in recounting with relish and pride conveys, is well captured in the story, and, perhaps unbeknownst to her, the Mother's version loses the high moral ground. Otherwise, how can slogans such as 'Allende! Go on! Imitate Balmaceda!', for example, be morally defended or openly supported. This was in reference to Chile's president (1886-1891) who, like Allende, had to contend with strong obstruction from conservative forces to his enlightened developmental programme; forces that, barricaded behind a deeply hostile and aggressive majority in Congress, unleashed a civil war against Balmaceda in 1891 that led to his defeat. He sought refuge in the Argentinian embassy in Santiago where, demoralised and after writing his political testament, he committed suicide.[5] In other words, the message was, to come out of the crisis Chile found itself in in the early 1970s, Allende had to die: the demonstrations and pressure were in preparation for a civil war, if necessary, which ideally would lead to an induced self-assassination. In this context, the story's reference to the hired thugs and paramilitaries that 'protected' the women's marches underlines the scenario being coldly constructed and how much she is mortified by the knowledge that the Mother and her father had been actively involved in such abominable endeavours.

The monothematic conversations, discussions, and rows between the Mother and the Daughter, is a dialogue of the deaf since the Mother insists that 'the gringos understood how serious the matter was, and together we defended ourselves against the Marxists', contradicting herself by also asserting that 'It wasn't the gringos who convinced the armed forces to intervene, abandoning their tradition of staying on the sidelines, it was Chilean women,' who did, motivated by their fears of the Marxists' sinister objectives outlined in Plan Z (as subsequently 'confirmed' in *El Libro Blanco*[6] published by the military junta). Yet, though the Daughter proves that her Mother's version of the history surrounding the election and eventual ousting of Allende is false (and that the latter knows that this is the case), the Mother stubbornly holds on to the Plan Z explanation over 40 years later, even though the very military officers who had certified the ludicrous assertions in the aforementioned infamous book had publicly stated they were a lie, and Junta Member Gustavo Leigh, Air Force commander-in-chief, had admitted Plan Z 'never existed'.[7]

Like the Mother in Meruane's story, many Chileans of that generation need to continue to believe there was a Plan Z since it allows them to excuse and justify the military junta's perpetration of massacres, illegal mass imprisonment, indiscriminate torture, extrajudicial executions, murder and disappearances. What is at stake is the battle over Chile's social and historic memory, which, despite the growing and irrefutable evidence that the alleged sinister plan of the communists in 1973 was fake and had been fabricated to 'extirpate the Marxist cancer'[8] (in the infamous phrase of military junta member, Gustavo Leigh) from the face of Chile, it remains the dominant establishment narrative. The Daughter suggests as much, for the Plan Z helps the Mother to ameliorate an unspeakable guilt, a trauma that continues to morally paralyse those in the political class, economic elite and military officers and their families, who played direct or indirect roles in fomenting the coup, making them unable to go through the catharsis of confronting the truth.

The Mother's holding on to the myth of Plan Z and the so-called 'self-defence' of Chile's 'traditional democratic forces' against it, though unjustifiable is an understandable nationwide phenomenon; after all, as late as 2014, two key parties of the country's right – the Union Democrática Independiente (UDI) and Renovación Nacional (RN) – still had an official endorsement of the 1973 military coup written into their statutes. These statutes codified their support for a 'new political system' aimed at 'preventing demagoguery' and the return of the (Marxist) 'totalitarian threat'. Furthermore, it was only in 2014 when RN incorporated, for the very first time in their history, the principle of 'promoting human rights' as a party objective,[9] whilst the UDI only followed suit in 2018.[10] RN and UDI were the parties of government in 2010-14 and are governing Chile right now.

Imagine the impact this narrative has had on Chileans generally, considering how it has dominated so much of their consciousness domestically for over half a century (the campaign against the so-called 'Marxist threat' began in 1964 during the presidential election campaign in which Salvador Allende stood as a candidate). The narrative is still being pushed. As recently as 21 October 2019, after declaring a state of emergency that saw horrendous oppression of protestors during the 'Estallido Social' (Social Outburst) protests, Chile's President Sebastián Piñera subtly invoked the same threat when he said Chile was at war against 'a powerful, implacable enemy that respects nothing and nobody'.

Worse still, no major political parties in Chile have ever challenged or made any serious efforts to change the country's 1980 Constitution drafted by the extreme right, and promulgated under dictator Augusto Pinochet. The 2019 uprising (against privatisation, metro ticket price increases, government corruption and the escalating cost of living) has created the conditions for such a change, especially after the recent, dramatic victories against neoliberal 'pinochetista' forces in two referenda to not only draft and promulgate a constitution for an anti-neoliberal economic model but also a Constituent Convention to bring this about.[11]

When the Mother admits in her final outburst of self-righteous anger, that she helped the US multinational, ITT, for which she worked, diverting funds realising the company was earmarked for nationalisation, she is admitting to being part of a pivotal component in the coup. It has been known since 1970 that ITT was centrally involved in coup efforts, even before Allende's coming to office that ended with the assassination of Chile's armed forces commander-in-chief, Rene Schneider.

With the assassination of Schneider, Chile's elite crossed the Rubicon, thus unleashing a diabolical dynamic of polarisation, hatred, and violence aimed at causing chaos and a total dislocation of the country's democratic edifice that would end up with the bloody overthrow of Salvador Allende on 11 September 1973, a fateful Tuesday when Chile's democracy was destroyed by Pinochet's coup d'état. The coup involved the surrounding of the presidential palace by military tanks which opened fire, and the relentless bombing with pinpoint accuracy by British-made Hawker Hunter warplanes which set the palace aflame with the president inside. The inexorable denouement led to the cold-blooded assassination of Allende whose bullet-riddled body was secretly removed by the military later that day. Their Chilean henchmen had both fulfilled Nixon's wishes and heeded Kissinger's warning.

Through the Pinochet dictatorship, the US was able to impose a regime that abolished all freedoms and was obsessively dominated by the frantic witch-hunt of political and social leaders of the left (later extended to include Christian Democrats), the establishment of concentration camps, secret torture centres, and the deliberate and planned disappearance, assassination and execution of over 3,000 people. Apart from Allende himself, among the victims we find Chile's former president Eduardo Frei (1964-70); commander-in-chief of the country's armed forces, Carlos Prats and Allende's former foreign minister, Orlando Letelier (both by a car bomb ordered by Pinochet, one in Buenos Aires, the other in Washington DC); Nobel Prize for Literature winner, Pablo Neruda; folk singer, Victor Jara; hundreds of political leaders of left-wing parties; and thousands of trade unionists, students, activists, peasants, workers, women, teachers, lawyers, priests, nuns, and even children. The Pinochet dictatorship has left deep psychological and moral scars from which Chile has not yet healed.

These days, to paraphrase a famous dictum, Chileans are attempting to make their own history, but they do not make it exactly as they would like; they are making it under predetermined circumstances, inherited and transmitted from the past. 'The tradition of all dead generations weighs like a nightmare on the brains of the living.'[12] The battle for the rescue of the country's social memory is indeed an uphill battle. Let's hope the Chilean people will not be lumbered with the fate of Sisyphus in their pursuit of progress and can finally realise Salvador Allende's prediction in his last speech from the presidential palace: that workers in the future 'will overcome this dark and bitter moment when treason seeks to prevail [...] and that, sooner rather than later, the great avenues will open again where free [women and] men will walk to build a better society.'

## Notes

1. Anthony Lewis, 'The Kissinger Doctrine', *New York Times,* 27 Feb 1975.
2. US Senate Commission, known as the Church Commission issued the report, *Covert Action in Chile 1963-1973* providing abundant evidence of some (though not all) US covert activities during the whole period leading eventually to the 1973 coup (https://www.archives.gov/files/declassification/iscap/pdf/2010-009-doc17.pdf).
3. Conservative forces in Latin America have, on several occasions, mobilised women dressed in black, supposedly 'mourning for democracy', to protest against tyranny and totalitarianism, and to express discontent, often also marching with 'empty pots', in a variety of different countries whose governments were deemed hostile by the United States.
4. Castro Speech Data Base, Lanic, University of Texas, http://lanic.utexas.edu/project/castro/db/1971/19711202-1.html
5. One of the best research works done on this crisis in Chile's political evolution and the real national and foreign interests behind Balmaceda's undoing is Hernán Ramírez Necochea, *La Guerra Civil de 1891, Antecedentes Económicos,* Editorial Austral, 1951.
6. *The White Book on the Change of Government in Chile, 11 September 1973,* https://www.bcn.cl/Books/Libro_Blanco_del_cambio_de_Gobierno_en_Chile/index.html#p=1
7. Juan Cristóbal Guarello: *Plan Z,* 20 Aug 2013, https://web.archive.org/web/20130905215033/http://www.publimetro.cl/nota/politico/la-columna-de-juan-cristobal-guarello-plan-z/xIQmht!0JvkVUb2w3eEI/
8. Thomas C. Wright, *State Terrorism in Latin America: Chile, Argentina and International Human Rights,* Rowman & Littlefield Publishers Inc., 2007, p.53.
9. 'Consejo de RN elimina alusión al Golpe Militar de su declaración de principios', *El Mercurio,* 23 Nov 2014, https://www.emol.com/noticias/nacional/2014/11/22/691210/consejo-de-rn-elimina-alusion-al-golpe-militar-de-su-declaracion-de-principios.html
10. 'UDI aprueba cambio en declaración de principios e incluye defensa de Derechos Humanos', 24 Jul 2018, https://www.latercera.com/politica/noticia/udi-aprueba-cambio-declaracion-principios-e-incluye-defensa-derechos-humanos/255199/

11. Francisco Dominguez, 'The Battle for Chile', PRRUK, https://prruk.org/the-battle-for-chile/
12. Karl Marx, *The Eighteenth Brumaire of Louis Bonaparte,* Good Press, 2019.

# Scent of Life

## Wilfredo Mármol Amaya

Translated from the Spanish by Julio Barrios Zardetto

'My God! That reeks! My hands stink,' the man said to himself as he approached the bedside table at the far end of his humble shack patchworked together from metal sheets. Applying some lotion on his hands and spreading it over his face, neck and abdomen, it reminded him that bad smells, when perfumed, only smell worse.

Once again, as had happened so many times in the last 31 years, a strong pestilence had settled in his guts, heralding the ghosts that so haunted him. The obstinate need to listen to radio news about the celebrations commemorating the martyrdom of the murdered was another symptom of this somatisation, this physical manifestation that impregnated his existence with its stench. 'Damn smell!' the man repeated to himself. In the past, he had been a soldier, skilled in weapons of war in the country known as *El Pulgarcito de América*, America's Little Thumb.

*

One of those nights he turned on the radio and listened with a hatred that made his blood boil: 'It's now time for everyone to celebrate the martyrdom of our brothers! Their generous blood, which paved the way for a negotiated, political solution that ended the civil war, which brought an end to the violence and silenced the guns... brought social justice, land rights, and the defeat of militarism... and enabled the people's voice to be heard...'

Angrily he turned it off, his heart racing. These outpourings from 'social organisations' and 'civil societies' with 'broad participation of the youth' prompted him to light a cigarette. He turned his gaze to the sky; its cascading lights fed his nostalgia, his heart wanted to leave his chest.

In such moments he felt like crying, though he couldn't. He had learned that it was pointless. 'Eat shit!' he bellowed, with a cloud of smoke. 'Poor fools think they have won peace. They don't know that it is us who are always in control – the military establishment, hand in hand with our masters: the fourteen families that own the country and God.' As he stretched on the hammock, his faithful dogs lying by his side; they who out of a fondness for his physical presence kept their own bones alive, always watching over the insomniac owner, sniffing the dust as they guarded for any trace of food. The former soldier looked around him, imbibing the humble atmosphere of his surroundings, the poverty of it all: 'And the families of the plantation owners? They will always have the best paid jobs, the most profitable businesses... But for us?' mused the man, 'We get work and some tortilla with salt if we're lucky.' His complaining would devolve into bouts of shouting insults at the wall, until he was surprised again by that repugnant smell that came with his sudden, streaming sweat. 'For God's sake, that stink is coming from *me*!' he would remind himself. It always happened around this time of year. Maybe that was the reason no one wanted to talk to him, no one would even approach him. The village priest had told him that there is no remedy for what was happening to him. He talked about forgiveness and how it healed everything. 'Bullshit!' he said out loud. 'Just like everything else they say in mass; all that turn-the-other-cheek, love-thy-neighbour crap. It's all bullshit.'

★

A memory insisted its way into the former soldier's mind. It was May 4, 1983. He was serving as a 'prison assistant' in the now defunct National Police Headquarters in the heart of the capital. Hearing interrogations at all hours of the night, people being subjected to all kinds of abuse and torture. The prisoners were being investigated by the intelligence division, S-2, and were suspected of belonging to 'terrorist organisations'. Among those prisoners was the Lutheran Pastor, Medardo Gómez. In those days, the Director of the National Police was a colonel who held the post until 15 June 1984 and now works in higher education, at the university, the one on Arce Street. The former soldier remembered well what he heard that night from one of the interviewees:

'The student had asked our psychology professor, Luis Achaerandio, permission to address the whole class. He was a member of the FUR-30, and began to confidently enumerate the human rights abuses that, he said, the oligarchy, the criollos and imperialism generally were inflicting on the working class, peasants and his fellow students. The student was then interrupted by another member of the FUR-30 who suddenly burst into the room and handed him a piece of paper that had a message written on it. The student was surprised by what he read, and said in a broken voice, "See! See what the fascist military tyranny is capable of! They have just assassinated Monsignor Óscar Arnulfo Romero!' Fear had enveloped the students in the room and soon panic spread throughout the halls and classrooms of the university as all the students fled to the safety of their homes. As the students poured out of our classroom, the young man from the FUR-30 shouted words of encouragement in defiance of the terrible news about the Archbishop. He told us to have faith, this murder "would yield three Latin American saints, Monsignor Romero and the two other priests who had been murdered by the security forces: the beloved Cosme Spessotto Zamuner Mansuè, murdered on 14 June 1980 in San Juan Nonualco, Rutilio Grande, viciously murdered on 12 March 1977, on the roads just outside the El Paisnal municipality...'"

Resentfully, the former soldier still recalled every detail that FUR–30 student told them about the suspect that night. Most of all his name, which he uttered over and over: 'Allan Martell, Allan Martell...'

*

Many years had passed, but it was true, he had participated in the worst of the death squads' work over the course of the civil war's twelve long years. He had started as a member of a local paramilitary group working his way up to one of the elite of *Reacción Inmediata* (immediate reaction) infantry battalions, or BIRI, trained by military advisers from a certain country to the north: the one that left its mark on countless poor and underdeveloped countries – as *they* called them – around the world, denying and hiding their work as they did so.

But the former soldier did not forget those strategies of counterinsurgent warfare or 'low intensity warfare' as it was called. He had boasted about those memories to anyone who'd listen whenever images of the BIRI appeared on TV. The green and red berets, the painted faces, and of course the M-16s cradled in their arms. He had never ceased feeling proud of those images that glowed at the edges of his past glory. He dwelled especially on the times when, with his face daubed with frightful symbols, he took part in massacres. Some had been carried out against old people, or women – often pregnant or with their children in arms or holding their hands. It happened in El Calabozo, and in San Sebastián, not to mention the thousand or so murdered in El Mozote, or when the Air Force dropped 500 pounds of explosives on civilian communities it later claimed were guerrillas.[1] He knew how the army invaded, street by street, metre by metre, at gunpoint. 'Scorched earth' they called it, in the villages of these humble people, everything that moved was left for dead. In such operations, representatives from the Batallón de Sanidad Militar, trained in the Southern Command,[2] or personnel trained in the School of the Americas, sponsored by the northern country, would always be present until the job was done.

*

As if to mock the injured, women of the Comite pro soldado,[3] accompanied by doctors, psychologists, dentists and a priest they called a 'chaplin', would come scurrying into the battle space, carrying medicines and sweets to alleviate pain, whilst offering 'spiritual nourishment' to whoever managed to survive a battalion whose motto was: 'Remove the water from the fish!'

The former soldier focused his mental energies on the memories now raining down on him, in the right light he knew this past could empower him. They had been contributions to the nation itself, he told himself, to its institutions and… to the country's rightful owners.

It was often one specific moment that jumped into the former soldier's mind. That morning when dawn arrived with a sense that it would not be just any other day. The memory of it was dyed in saturating red. The scathing echo of the tiny Sergeant Valladares' voice, shouting: 'You and you! And you five at the end of the line! And you!' indicating Julian. 'Today we will form a BIRI to protect our country twenty-four hours a day. Our group will be in charge of identifying, locating and then cornering entire families. In the early, mornings we will raid and capture them, then remove them to a secluded location and... Checkmate! Y'all know the drill: Nip them in the bud!' From Sergeant Valladares' mouth came a new reality: our humble, paramilitary cell would transform itself and take charge of intimidating and disappearing political opposition of all kinds. 'From now on, there should never be any trace of us. We don't exist! Is that understood?' he barked, in a commanding, almost fatherly voice.

The municipality of San Martin, in the northwest corner of the capital, would be protected from any terrorist horde. This was their mission, one that would be applied by other battalions across the entire country. A dark man, his straight hair partially covering his face, a golden tooth in his mouth, short, bad-tempered, always anxious and distrustful, had been chosen by the owners of the country and their faithful representatives – the military establishment. His nickname: 'Chejazo'.

Years later these elite battalions were formally constituted and made official, financed by the taxpayers from the north.

*

In his brain an imperishable thought was illuminated for an instant. He was in a safe house in Santa Ana, at the precise moment when the founder of the death squads and of the right-wing party arrived. He was a retired major, a known quantity. He immediately gathered the troops together and began to address them in his own peculiarly energetic voice: 'You are this nation's finest sons. Your duty is to defend it with your life. We will not allow our country to fall into the hands of international communism – not for anything in the world. And you, "Misterio"' – he said to a soldier called Mauro Cornejo – 'you have the calling of a natural leader.'

'Yes Major!' Misterio answered.

The retired major saluted then walked away, leaving them with the same words he always used to close his TV broadcasts: 'May God bless you.' He left and headed to another safe house, somewhere else in the network of clandestine paramilitary groups that worked away in the darkness. During this time, his death squad operated out of Santa Ana, the second most important city in the country. It carried out its bloody assault on the very idea of human rights, outside any legal framework or respect for life, and yet within the place once known as 'el país de la sonrisa', the country of smiles.

★

These memories brought forth feelings that swelled the former soldier's ego. He felt rejuvenated by them. The sway of his hammock and the snoring of the dogs seemed to encourage him to keep weaving together his memories of that glorious civil war. It had lasted twelve years, leaving more than 80,000 dead, and over 8,000 missing; the names and the dates of these violations still etched in that monument in a park called Cuscatlán, from the Nahuatl word meaning, 'Land of precious things' – ironically once the name for the entire country.

★

His bellicose thoughts emboldened and revitalised him. It was then the former soldier recalled one of his fondest military adventures, a memory he kept lovingly locked away from his ordinary daily thoughts: 'Keep following the trail!' shouted the corporal in charge. They had seen an armed woman fleeing in the direction they were now headed; she was wounded. 'Blood tracks! Down there!' There had been numerous casualties for the military and they had been walking for five days in the mountains. Hungry and wanting someone to take it out on, they searched the ravine inch by inch. It was David, a soldier with ten years war experience and a member of the Atlacatl Battalion, with dreams of becoming a pastor of souls when the war ended, who shouted: 'There's the terenga!'[4] Signaling for the rest to advance on her, he added: 'Too bad she's wounded. Looks like she's not gonna make it, either.'

The girl was barely fifteen years old, with a wound across her chest that left her breasts sagging. 'She's a beauty!' one of the soldiers exclaimed as he approached, slowing down as it became evident that she still had a combat pistol on her waist. David left the scene. It disgusted him to see a teenage girl like that with no chance of defending herself. Weakly, she raised her hands, out of defensive instinct more than anything else.

David went to get water for her, to award one last sip to the fallen, mutilated, still breathing guerrilla.

But returning with the water, he could not process what he saw: a soldier, also from his old battalion, trained by the most civilised country in the world, was forcing himself on the girl, while another soldier, also young, held her arms above her head. David kept silent. He said nothing and felt nothing. Not a shudder passed through him; he didn't even need to swallow hard to clear his throat. It made him remember how on other occasions his fellow soldiers abused the wounded guerrillas, or even civilian women... If their bodies were still warm, the soldiers would line up to rape them. About three years after the war ended, one day, when David came down from the pulpit after recounting what he had witnessed, what had happened in that scene of war, he whispered to his brother in the congregation: 'I really don't know why I didn't feel anything that day, I didn't even need to swallow hard that day. While tonight, as I was giving the service, I could hardly speak for the knot in my throat.' He said all this as he shook hands and said goodnight to his congregation, he was after all their pastor.

⋆

It was then the former soldier, with his signature stench radiating from his skin, evoked the memory of those lost children who were often found wandering around after an operation. The military officers would take them in quietly to their garrisons, whereupon negotiations would begin with tireless lawyers around the world, to secure their safe passage abroad – a great money-earner for the commanders! The pestilence came back mercilessly, clouding the former soldier's thoughts, the stench of the dead accompanied by memories of others' pain.

⋆

Shards of memories were now hailing down in the former soldier's mind until he smelled again the aroma – 'What an unbearable stench!' – and his own utterance broke the spell of the memories that had so occupied the last 31 years of his life. He would cover his nose.

*

With each bead of sweat, the stench intensified. Times like these called for the temporary relief that alcohol and cigarettes brought to his soul. They were his faithful companions. He fell into a schizoid reverie that summoned the last days of the founder of the death squads, and of the right-wing party; the man who years later would rule the entire country, would privatise public services, take the pensions of working people into private hands. He became deeply nostalgic, old ideas of glory seem to wash over his entire being.

*

His mind fixed on a memory that he had been resisting till now. It was impossible to avoid it any longer. It was a press conference on February 12, 1992. Peace agreements that ended the war had just been signed. The former soldier had infiltrated the event, posing as an assistant for a commercial radio station. Archbishop Monsignor Arturo Rivera y Damas and his auxiliary Gregorio Rosa Chávez were there. They were answering questions: 'Mr. Archbishop, what is your church's reaction to the news that the retired major, the known quantity, has just died of cancer in a private hospital a few hundred metres from here?'

The Archbishop answered without hesitation: 'Hopefully he will find a generous judge.' The former soldier still recalled the stunned faces of the local and international journalists covering the press conference that day and how convinced they were not to risk any further questions. Then everyone was gone, only the ex-soldier was left sitting at the back of an empty room with an ache in his chest.

*

From his hammock he could still hear the radio. Again the invitation to the great pilgrimage of commemoration made him seethe with fury. But at the same time impotence set in. There's nothing he could do, the militarism that had defined his life was history...That is how the chill of the early morning found him. His blanket sweeping the floor with the rhythmic swing of the hammock. Bloody scenes still entertaining his attention and then those words, that curse which gnawed at his existence, uttered by one of the six priests, the one wearing a blue sports shirt, on that fateful night, just before the bullet that the soldier fired pierced his skull: 'You are worthless carrion,' said the priest who was also a specialist in psychology. Afterwards he remembered the man agonising on the ground until he stopped breathing. His body and face on the damp grass and his arms outstretched in front him as if reaching for that horrendous dawn. It happened not too far from the Arce neighborhood, inhabited exclusively by military officers, and under the vigilance of the Joint Chiefs of Staff.

*

This memory instilled in him insomnia... the pestilence pronouncing itself unbearable... impossible to resist. The saying that goes 'defects are like smells, the people around notice them more than the person who emits them' was not borne out in the case of the former soldier. The stench stuck to his body, as it had from the beginning of that month of commemoration for the martyrs of the UCA.[5]

The eve of the pilgrimage, of the great commemoration of martyrs that would bring thousands of young people together, finally deflated him... He couldn't take it any more, and the smell became more elusive and enigmatic to him. All the while the invitation announced again and again on the radio grew louder and louder, accompanied by the procession's songs of solidarity, and lanterns, no doubt, sporting candles of many colours carried in the hands of the crowd. The music, but especially the anthem of this cause, offended the former soldier: 'You... yes, you, don't look the other way! You have ears, you are no fish. I'm not talking to the folks beside you. I call on you! Who are you? What the hell are you doing with your life? What are you gonna do with yourself?' He turned off the radio with a single blow. That night, after twilight, he became more melancholic, emotional, resentful of his past.

A trail of strange sounds began to lull his soul. He became docile. He became afflicted by compassion and a sigh of hope traversed his being. The man turned pale, sadness levelling in him a single desire... He no longer wanted the life he had. It was not worth it any more. It was lacerating, like an endless storm. He unleashed a burst of fury and a deathly sob washed him with the desire not to remain dead while still breathing: 'By God it smells like death in here,' he muttered through his teeth. 'It smells like a curse.'

*

Weary of the stench that came out of his body the former soldier was taken by an insurmountable and profound sadness. He remembered the old cliché 'the only thing evil needs to succeed is for the good to do nothing', and immediately thought about the wealthy families for whom he had risked his neck throughout the war. He had been convinced of what they had led him to believe: that the war against the terengos was a war against communism. He thought: 'There is no doubt; there are people who are so poor that all they have is money, and they buy everything except the peace of mind that forgiveness offers... yes forgiveness... forgiveness...'

*

That is how dawn found him; sadness had taken him away with the divine promise of resurrection. The former soldier was found in his hammock, gazing at heaven with a smile on his lips. A misspelled note rested on his chest that read: 'Forgive me.' At his side, his skinny and hungry dogs, his faithful companions, still taking care of their master.

*

From the veteran's body now came the smell of orange blossoms. As if an entire pilgrimage that night had passed by, filling his tiny room with heaps of flowers. It smelled of wild flowers, the scent of life everywhere. It was the early morning of November 16.

## Notes

1. The US supplied these 500lb bombs for the Salvadoran Air Force, which they were not averse to dropping on civilian areas regularly, for instance during the Final offensive (Ofensiva Hasta el Tope) of November 1989.
2. Located in Doral, Florida in Greater Miami, the US Southern Command is one of the eleven unified combatant commands in the United States Department of Defense, and is responsible for providing contingency planning, operations, and security cooperation for Central and South America.
3. Pro-Soldier Committee.
4. An El Salvadorian word meaning 'silly' or 'stupid', or in this case as a noun, 'idiot'.
5. The martyrs of the UCA refers to the massacre that took place in 1989 in the University of Central America 'Simeon Cañas.'

# EL SALVADOR, 1981

# Afterword: Thou Shall Not Kill

## Raymond Bonner

YOU CAN SEE THE entire country of El Salvador from a helicopter, an American diplomat was fond of saying. That might be a slight exaggeration. But it is small. About the size of Massachusetts, a sliver larger than Wales. Population, three million back in the 1980s.

This was when the diminutive Central American nation became a major foreign policy concern for the United States, as much as Bosnia, Iraq, Syria, Afghanistan would years later. El Salvador had no oil, no gold, no silver, nor any other vital natural resources, yet it was one of the largest recipients of US military and economic aid, surpassed only by Israel, Egypt, and Turkey; the American embassy in San Salvador had almost as many diplomats, military attachés and CIA operatives as the one in New Delhi.

The reason: the Cold War. A civil war in El Salvador was pitting Marxist-led guerrillas against an alliance of the oligarchy and the military, which had ruled for generations. Washington supported the government, driven – as was typical of the time – by a fear of creeping communism.

The Soviet Union was still a union, the Berlin Wall was still standing, Soviet troops occupied Afghanistan. Closer to home, Cuba under Fidel Castro had firmly aligned itself with the Soviet Union, and stood as a model for revolutionaries around the world. In Nicaragua, El Salvador's immediate neighbour to the south, the Somoza family dictatorship that had ruled the country for generations, with loyal support from the United States, was overthrown by Marxist revolutionaries, the Sandinistas, in July 1979.

Washington feared El Salvador would be next.

'Very simply, guerrillas armed and supported by and through Cuba are attempting to impose a Marxist-Leninist dictatorship on the people of El Salvador,' President Ronald Reagan said in an address to the Organization of American States in 1982.[1] 'If we do not act promptly and decisively in defence of freedom, new Cubas will arise from the ruins of today's conflicts. We will face more totalitarian regimes tied militarily to the Soviet Union.'

With this apocalyptic vision, nothing stood in the way of American support, or the flow of military and economic aid. Not the assassination of an archbishop. Not the rape and murder of nuns. Not the daily execution of students, union leaders, and peasants. Not the worst massacre in modern Latin American history, in which nearly a thousand old men, women, and infant children were killed.

No doubt, the Soviet Union was hoping that if the Salvadoran leftists were victorious they would align with Moscow; and Cuba was providing some training and arms. But Havana and Moscow were not the causes of the revolution.

In March of 1980, on what turned out to be the eve of an all-out civil war, the American Ambassador in El Salvador, Robert White, sent a twenty-eight-page 'assessment' of the situation in El Salvador to Washington. It was reminiscent of George Kennan's famous Long Telegram from Moscow in 1946, which set out his views of the Soviet Union, and recommended a policy of containment.

'In El Salvador, the rich and powerful have systematically defrauded the poor and denied 80 per cent of the people any voice in the affairs of their county,' White wrote succinctly understanding why there was now a revolution brewing. 'There is no stopping this revolution,' he added bluntly.

'Above all, we must rid ourselves of the notion that the Cubans are playing an important role here.' Yes, Cuba was providing some weapons and training, but it was 'marginal'.

White believed in Carter's human rights policy, that support for human rights should be an element of America's foreign policy, but he wasn't blind to what a guerrilla victory might bring. 'An extremist communist takeover here, and by that I mean something just this side of the Pol Pot episode, is unfortunately, a real possibility due mainly to the intense hatred that has been created in this country among the masses by the insensitivity, blindness and brutality of the ruling elite, usually designated, "the oligarchy".'

America's challenge was to find an 'alternative to the Nicaraguan model.' Through political negotiations, not war, he believed.

White's analysis was profound and prescient – and was ignored by policymakers, in the White House and in Congress.

In the overwhelmingly Catholic country, the church had an outsized role in the revolution. Historically, it had been aligned with the elites and the government. When the Vatican named a 60-year old bishop, Óscar Arnulfo Romero, the archbishop of San Salvador, it was with the blessing of the oligarchy and the military, which considered him conservative and not controversial. But as the repression mounted, Romero began denouncing atrocities from the pulpit. The country's leading conservative newspaper now called him 'demagogic and violent', and accused him of preaching 'terrorism from his cathedral.'

On Sunday, March 23 of 1980, Archbishop Romero delivered a homily that rings through the ages – and probably sealed his fate. He addressed the country's soldiers: 'In the face of an order to kill given by a man, the law of God that says "thou shall not kill" must prevail. No soldier is obliged to obey an order contrary to the law of God.' The parishioners, mostly peasants and workers, erupted in applause. Then, in words that should be etched in granite, marble, steel, and preserved on tablets, he went on: '*In the name of God, in the name of this suffering people whose cries rise to heaven more loudly each day, I implore you, I beg you, I order you in the name of God: stop the repression.*'

The next day, while Romero was celebrating mass at the Divine Providence Hospital, a red Volkswagen drove through the gate and stopped outside the small chapel; the doors were open. A sniper pointed his high-powered rifle through a car window and fired a single shot. The car drove off, as Archbishop Romero lay on the floor in a pool of blood, worshippers screaming and crying.

It was the work of Roberto d'Aubuisson, a charismatic, chain-smoking, hard-drinking, fierce anti-communist who became one of the most infamous individuals of El Salvador's civil war. The day before Romero's assassination, d'Aubuisson had presided over a gathering in which soldiers had drawn straws for the 'honour' of killing the archbishop. Though cashiered from the army, d'Aubuisson ran 'death squads,' consisting of small groups of soldiers operating at night in civilian clothes. The CIA described d'Aubuisson as 'egocentric, reckless and perhaps mentally unstable.' Ambassador White was less measured, calling him a 'pathological killer'. While White was still Ambassador, the embassy shunned him. The Reagan administration would not.

One of the principal architects of the Reagan administration's policy in Central America was Elliott Abrams, a brash, smart, neoconservative, anti-communist hardliner. Asked if he considered d'Aubuisson an extremist, Abrams said he did not. He would have to have 'engaged in murder' before he would say that, Abrams said. He was, of course, of the archbishop and scores, if not hundreds, of innocent civilians. (D'Aubuisson died of lung cancer in 1992).

Romero's assassination was the spark that ignited the simmering revolution. Five guerrilla organisations reluctantly and loosely united under the banner of the Farabundo Marti National Liberation Front (FMLN, also known as the 'Frente').

The generals and the oligarchs popped champagne corks and fired their rifles in celebration when Reagan was elected president in November of 1980. They would no longer have to listen to lectures about human rights from the Carter administration.

Three weeks after Reagan's victory, heavily-armed men, their military boots showing beneath the cuffs of their civvies, stormed the campus of the Catholic San Jose High School, a few blocks from the American embassy, where opposition political leaders were meeting. Their mutilated, bullet-ridden bodies were found the next day near the scenic Lake Ilopango, where the wealthy waterskied. One man's face had been disfigured; another had had his left arm severed.

Ambassador White slumped in his chair upon learning about the killings. 'Who will I talk to now?' he asked, the lament etched in his voice. Gone was any hope of a negotiated political settlement.

Again, the incoming Reagan administration wasn't troubled. 'He who lives by the sword, dies by the sword,' said Jeane Kirkpatrick, Reagan's senior foreign policy adviser and his first ambassador to the United Nations. In her book, *Dictatorships and Double Standards* (1979), Kirkpatrick had assailed the Carter administration for its emphasis on human rights. If the Soviet Union could support dictatorships, why shouldn't the United States if they were pro-American, she argued.

The limits to which the Reagan administration would go in carrying out Kirkpatrick's philosophy would soon be tested.

Five days after the Salvadoran political leaders were murdered, soldiers intercepted a Toyota van carrying three Roman Catholic nuns and a lay missionary as they were leaving the international airport. The women were missionaries administering to the needs of impoverished peasants in rural areas - which made them subversives and communists in the eyes of the Salvadoran elite. The women were raped and murdered.

Pictures of the women being pulled out of a shallow, hastily-dug grave, their clothes torn, shocked the world's conscience. But not senior policymakers in Washington.

'The nuns were not just nuns,' said Kirkpatrick. 'The nuns were also political activists. We ought to be a little more clear about this than we usually are. They were political activists on behalf of the Frente.'[2]

Reagan's secretary of state, Alexander Haig, was equally calloused and cavalier. 'Perhaps the vehicle the nuns were riding in may have tried to run a roadblock or may have accidentally been perceived to have been doing so, and there may have been an exchange of gunfire,' he said during a congressional hearing.[3]

Haig ordered Ambassador White to send a cable saying that the Salvadoran military was investigating the crime. It wasn't. White refused. Haig fired him, putting him in an elite group of foreign service officers ever dismissed for standing by their principles.

White was replaced in El Salvador by Dean Hinton, a career diplomat who would dutifully carry out Reagan's policy.

The pictures of helicopters lifting off from the roof of the American embassy in Saigon, bringing the Vietnam War to an ignominious end, were a recent memory, and Congress, fearing 'another Vietnam,' put a severe limit on the number of troops that the White House could send to El Salvador. Further, as a condition on the continuation of military aid, the President was required to certify every six months that the Salvadoran military was making progress on human rights. As part of its attempt to wiggle through, if not circumvent, those restrictions, the Reagan administration trained and equipped the Atlacatl Battalion, an elite, rapid reaction, counterinsurgency force, whose members proudly wore red berets and carried American-made M-16s.

In December 1981, the battalion, whose officers and senior enlisted men had just finished their training by American Special Forces (Green Berets), conducted its first major operation, in the northwestern province of Morazon, a sparsely populated mountainous region where the leftist guerrillas had considerable support among the impoverished peasants.

What followed was one of the worst massacres in modern Latin American history, as the army conducted a 'scorched earth' operation. 'The Armed Forces executed all of those persons it came across: elderly adults, men, women, boys and girls, they killed animals, destroyed and burned plantations, homes, and devastated everything community-related,' judges on the Inter-American Court of Human Rights summarised it years later.[4]

A few peasants managed to flee into the hills before the soldiers arrived in their village. From their places in hiding, they heard young girls screaming as they were being raped, followed by rifle shots when they were executed. When the operation was over and those who had survived emerged from hiding, they found the bodies of relatives and friends. One 37-year-old woman was lying in her bed, next to her one-day-old son. She had been shot in the forehead; her son had been stabbed in the throat. '*Un nino muerto es un guerrilla menos*,' the soldiers had scrawled in blood on the wall of one simple house. 'One dead child is one less guerrilla.'

The soldiers gathered the residents of El Mozote into the dusty village square. Old men were taken away and executed, after being tortured for information about whether their sons were guerillas. Women were raped and executed. A large group of children, and a few women, were forced into the convent behind the church. From within the church, standing in a doorway, or through a window, soldiers fired their American-supplied M-16 rifles. For good measure, the soldiers set fire to the building; the falling beams crushed childrens' skulls. An exhumation years later identified the skeletal remains of 143 individuals. Almost all were younger than twelve; the average age, six years old. Some two hundred spent M-16 cartridges were found among the bodies, toys, dresses, booties, etc; markings showed they had been manufactured by the United States government.

The massacre was reported by the *New York Times* and *Washington Post*. Front page. Along with graphic photographs in the *Times* of dead bodies. (I was the *Times* reporter, Susan Meiselas, the photographer; the *Post* story was written by Alma Guillermoprieto).

In face of this depravity, how was the Reagan administration possibly going to certify that the Salvadoran government was making progress on improving human rights? It quickly, and easily, swung into cover-up mode.

'There is no evidence to confirm that government forces systematically massacred civilians in the operation zone,' Thomas Enders, assistant secretary of state for Inter-American Affairs, said in congressional testimony a few days after the articles appeared. Enders was experienced at dissembling and cover-ups in pursuit of American foreign policy objectives. A few years earlier, as the number two in the American embassy in Cambodia, Enders had personally selected the targets for American B-52s carrying out secret bombing raids in Cambodia, and then lied when one B-52 accidentally dropped its 20-tonne load on a small village, killing or wounding more than five hundred.

In denying a government massacre at El Mozote, Enders was relying on a cable from Deane Hinton, the American ambassador in El Salvador. The day after the articles in the *Times* and *Post*, Hinton sent officers from the embassy to investigate. They never reached El Mozote, which Hinton declined to note in his cable to Washington. Nor, did he tell Washington that his officers – based on their interviews with refugees from the war zone and with a priest – had concluded that there *had* been a massacre and that the Salvadoran army *was* probably responsible.

Instead, Hinton sought to lay the blame on the guerillas. They had done 'nothing to remove' the civilians 'from the path of the battle which they were aware was coming,' he wrote in his eight-page cable. He then suggested that the victims may have been caught in a crossfire, or as he put it, 'could have been subject to injury as a result of the combat.'

Elliot Abrams, from his position as the assistant secretary of state for human rights, dismissed the reports as 'guerrilla propaganda'.

The Reagan administration certified that El Salvador was 'making a concerted and significant effort to comply with internationally recognised human rights.' Congress accepted it, and approved more money. It was a charade, farcical. 'One more massacre, no more aid,' members of Congress said each time. Salvadoran generals and politicians laughed. They knew they were fighting America's war against communism.

The war in El Salvador continued throughout the decade of the '80s – more violence, more massacres, more assassinations. Finally, two events in 1989, only days apart, not directly linked, one abroad, one at home, brought all sides to the negotiating table. First came the tearing down of the Berlin Wall and the collapse of the Soviet Union. This deflated the Salvadoran revolutionaries. That same month, November 1989, they launched another 'final offensive', which failed. Concomitantly the collapse of the Soviet Union diminished fears in Washington that Central American communists were going to march through Mexico into Texas.

And a week after the world cheered the collapse of the wall in Berlin, there was another act of depraved butchery in San Salvador. In the early hours on 16 November 1989, soldiers from the notorious Atlacatl Battalion raided the campus of the Jesuit-run Central American University. The university's widely respected rector, Ignacio Ellacuría, and five other Jesuit priests were rounded up, forced to lie face down in the garden and shot. On the way out, the soldiers murdered the priests' cook, and her 15-year-old daughter to ensure there were no witnesses.

In a display of contemptuous hate almost impossible to fathom, the soldiers who killed the Jesuit priests fired into a portrait of Archbishop Romero.

Two days before the operation, d'Aubuisson, who still loomed large in Salvadoran politics a decade after ordering the assassination of Archbishop Romero, had railed against the Jesuit priests, accusing them of 'inventing lies, brainwashing UCA students, and of being responsible for their joining the FMLN,' the CIA reported.

It is difficult not to ask how many lives would have been spared if the United States had not accommodated d'Aubuisson and the Salvador military over the preceding decade, had not been so obsessed by a fear of communism, Cuba, the Soviet Union, had not seen a 'red under every bed.'

In January 1992, El Salvador's civil war, which had taken an estimated 75,000 lives, ended with the formal signing of a peace treaty. At the ceremony, El Salvador's president, Alfredo Cristiani, a wealthy conservative who was a member of d'Aubuisson's right-wing political party, shook hands with five guerrilla commanders, including Shafik Handal, who was general secretary of the Communist Party of El Salvador. President George H.W. Bush had supported the negotiations, and when Handal spoke about his hopes for a more 'respectful' relationship with the United States, Bush's Secretary of State, James A. Baker III, sat in the front row at the and seemed to nod approvingly. The United States had come a long way, and had perhaps even seen the folly of its policy.

## Notes

1. https://www.youtube.com/watch?v=SvX3GuYXqk0
2. *The Tampa Tribune*, 25 Dec 1980.
3. United Press International, 18 Mar 1981.
4. Inter-American Court of Human Rights. Case of The Massacres of El Mozote and Nearby Places v. El Salvador. Official Summary Issued by the Inter-American Court, Judgement of October 25, 2012, p. 2.

# Born Again

## Carol Zardetto

Translated from the Spanish by Julio Barrios Zardetto

THE RAISED STAFFS OF the elders appear as silhouettes against the last rays of sunlight. Through my camera lens, I struggle to capture the strength behind this collective gesture. We are in the Ixil triangle, a rugged terrain flanked by three ancient villages: Nebaj, Cotzal and Chajul. The elders are the keepers of intricate threads that bind these communities together, making them the only legitimate authority in the eyes of their people. Once the Ixil Mayans lived in isolation here, unperturbed by the passing ages. But those times are gone; isolation has become a rare commodity on this earth.

A crowd gathers at the central plaza of Nebaj. It is the eve of a bittersweet commemoration: two years ago, in a courtroom far away from here, Efraín Ríos Montt was sentenced. The strike of that gavel profoundly disrupted the racist order that has reigned in Guatemala for so long and validated the testimonies coming out of so many Ixil mouths. They came from little hamlets and villages, on their peasant feet, weary of dust and mountains, till they reached the cold marble of the city tribunal to testify.

Indigenous people sitting in the great halls of justice in the middle of the capital city. Indigenous people demanding justice in their language. Both signs of a disruption brought about by the daunting winds of change. And the accused, none other than the most refined emblem of military patriarchy, the revered whip that forever looms over the colonised mind. It was an affront to the elites who still slumber in Jurassic dreams;[1] unsettling as a stick thrust into an anthill.

I had been absent for over 30 years. Like a sigh they passed. Although I never confessed it to anyone, I never considered coming back. But then the unexpected happened. The news wrenched me back to Guatemala like a tunnel through time itself: the Ixil people had managed to bring Efraín Ríos Montt to trial. Who could have predicted it? I knew immediately that I had to witness this event. For someone like me, who had grown up in Guatemala during the war, it was an unthinkable event: I had to see it to believe it.

But it did happen two years ago. By then Ríos Montt was a brittle old man. He was over 80 when he received that great bundle of accusations thrown at him by the Ixil people; accusations that could be summarised in a single word: genocide. Behind thick lenses magnifying bloodshot eyes, he was made to sit and listen, without saying a word, to the seemingly endless testimonies of seemingly endless victims. Never had karma made so much sense.

He was not an ignorant man. On the contrary, he donned a strange intelligence, bordering on madness. He understood very well the mechanism that was unleashed under his reign, he had summed it up in a simple metaphor: scorched earth. This semiotic composition wasn't his own. He took it from the Bible, a traditional tool of power. The 'Great Jehovah of the Armies' was a great excuse, a magnificent parapet for the general. He found it convenient to repeat what his adulators said of him, the born-agains: he was like the very Nehemiah; the servant of God who, with a willing heart, would rebuild the eroded walls of Jerusalem. Those walls that separate – eternally and with iron judgement – the chosen ones from the rest. Jehovah himself, who the Evangelists had billed as the most zealous anti-communist of all, guided his terrible hand.

The indigenous woman now climbing the stage to address the crowd is the mayor of Nebaj. I swap to a longer lens. She speaks deliberately and clearly: 'We did what we had to do,' she explains. 'We testified before the Judges. We spoke the truth. We said what happened to us. Woe on them if they decided to play with justice. Woe on them if, in spite of the weight of evidence, they annulled the sentence. For us, the blame had been cast. For us, the sentence is alive, even if they tried to kill it.'

There was a shine to the faces in the plaza. Avidly I take their photographs, wanting to tell their story. Through them, I recognise that the victim who treads the long road of justice – over 30 years in this case – and drags his aggressor to the bench, stops being a victim and recaptures that little-talked-of power within us all: dignity. Ixils say that dignity is a sacred mantle. One that was violated profoundly by the scorched earth policy but has been restored by trudging the long walk of justice. All indigenous peoples know the healing power of that mythical journey.

These thoughts occupy me as I go through the pictures I've taken. I am here as a journalist, but more importantly, I am here as someone who remembers. The memory of Ríos Montt is etched in my mind like the contours of the earth, each geological layer marked by time. I was only a child when he first sought to be president, in 1974. I can still see the poster with his face on it, daubed in scarlet graffiti with the word *communist*. I remember it because, even if I didn't know the meaning of the word, I had learned to fear it. Communism was... diabolical. Ríos Montt was the candidate for the Christian Democratic Party in the middle of 30 years of ultra-right-wing military governments. It was a time of fraudulent elections. Though he was a general, the slight inclination to the left that this civilian party represented, never stood a chance. His followers were sure they had been robbed of victory. Despite claiming to denounce the result, he was bought off, accepting a post in the Guatemalan Embassy in Spain. Rumour had it his stay in Madrid was more or less a prolonged drinking spree. He lost himself in the raging sea of alcohol that suspends time for all those who journey through it.

Maybe being 'lost' was the cause. Maybe shipwrecked by the waves of alcoholism, he found salvation in the harbour of Evangelism. In any case, by the time the eighties came around Ríos Montt had taken shelter as a biblical teacher in a 'Born-again' Christian church, that in Guatemala assumed the simple name '*Verbo*'. The Spanish name concealed the fact that the promoters were gringos. They had come as volunteers in the aftermath of the earthquake that destroyed the country in 1976. They planted the seeds of 'the evangelism of prosperity', a perverse tentacle, with the power to influence public opinion akin to that of Hollywood movies. One of the most perverse things about it was the unexpected door through which it entered: culture.

My life was entwined with Ríos Montt's in that church. My boyfriend Armando and I had wanted to get married. I was on the verge of completing my degree in journalism and he was a freshly graduated engineer. Our plans had to be delayed due to our lack of money. We had to wait. Our 'waiting' was different from that of other young couples. We lived in Guatemala and that constituted a separate reality. Forging a future in the middle of the terror of a concealed war is something only those who have lived it can understand. Like good Guatemalans, we did all we could to ignore reality. Every day new executions were reported in the newspapers: lawyers, union members, university professors. Their bloody corpses appeared strewn about randomly in the streets. Others simply disappeared. In a vague way, we understood that it was somehow due to *reasons of state security*, though no investigations or legal proceedings were ever carried out to make those reasons clear. People shrouded their fear in the assumption that those killed 'must have been up to *something*'.

Romeo Lucas, the brutish general having his turn at being president in the late seventies, had no qualms about the bloodbath being out in the open. The implacable viciousness of his regime was a source of pride, displaying the kind of sadism that the ignoble often venerate under the euphemism, 'an iron fist'. Even the US government, with its adoration for those ignorant sadists so unscrupulously attentive to their every requirement, withdrew its support in response to Lucas' indiscriminate crimes. This gesture of disavowal made Romeo Lucas feel he could act freely, without the weight of political correctness.

When, in January 1980, a group of indigenous people occupied the Spanish Embassy to denounce the massacres that had occurred in the countryside, the flood waters began to rise. The government decided to invade the embassy, shrugging off the inviolability of diplomatic premises. The forced entry of the armed soldiers resulted in a terrifying fire that left 37 dead. The ambassador himself miraculously escaped, ushered out by the timely intervention of the Red Cross. The charred bodies of the occupants were removed from the debris, frozen in strange poses. Was it possible – I remember thinking, seeing the images on the newspapers – that those twisted chunks of charcoal had once been people?

The day of that raid, I was with a friend studying for our exams. Armando called me mid-afternoon and told me not to go out. The city was in uproar, though we were used to that. Not being able to go out due to disturbances was something that occurred with punctual regularity. And yet, despite the frequency of such brutal events, the feeling of anguish – the one that hits the stomach and is driven into memory like a thorn – never went away.

The political situation had been sucked into a vertiginous whirlpool. The burning of the Spanish Embassy was the drop that made the cup of Guatemala's carnage run over. Spain broke off diplomatic relations with the country. The military was now acting like a ruthless machine, openly and with impunity. The violence of burgeoning far-right paramilitary groups was also allowed to go unpunished. We, the ordinary people huddled together in the ever-smaller pockets of normality that remained.

One day, Armando told me that he had met up with Rafa, a friend from high school. He was the grandson of the patriarch of one of the handful of families that control the country. His grandfather had just died and Rafa was the heir. He had decided to build an office building by tearing down his old family house on Avenida de La Reforma. Armando couldn't contain his enthusiasm: if he got this commission, we could get married. We would make the leap out of hardship and into the other side. That place where the wealthy few and their acolytes live.

We soon found ourselves having lunch at Rafa's house with Silvia, his wife. He was clearly naive. Like many heirs, he had never worked and was confounded by the task of capitalising on his inheritance. He drank too much and would leave his wife to handle anything that actually merited attention. Silvia owned a flower shop and had the weary air of an alcoholic's wife, always waiting for the miracle that would set her free from the curse. There seemed to be a way to get through to them: they were members of a Pentecostal church. Soon the conversations turned to evangelistic endeavours. Silvia told us that they had been *born again*. That Armando and I had to accept Christ, if we wanted to be saved. To begin our journey they invited us to join them in the Sunday prayer service.

Given Armando's eagerness to go into business with Rafa, the following Sunday we went to a huge tent that the *Verbo* church had installed in a vacant lot on Avenida de La Reforma, a neighbourhood that guaranteed access to the people they were interested in: the rich. If the gospel in its early days promised to be good news for the poor, the tables were now turned: the god of 'the born-again' cared primarily for the rich.

Avenida de La Reforma was prime real estate. Clearly, the leaders of the church understood that in Guatemala people do not cross the frontiers of their neighbourhoods, as each one strictly delineates their membership to a particular class. A church on this avenue, therefore, was ideal for spreading the gospel of prosperity to the already prosperous. After all, that was the premise: If we became Christians – joyous tithe givers for the church – prosperity would rain back down on us, driven by the very force of gravity. We were, after all, God's children. So why not dream of having a Mercedes?

As Armando and Rafa's business relationship developed, the elders of the church pressured us to consolidate our evangelical commitment. We soon realised that they were running more than just Sunday services. They had a powerful network of influence formed among the families of believers. Their prayer breakfasts for *hombres del evangelio completo* (men committed to the Gospels) brought together the city's most prosperous capitalists to whom Armando wanted to cling, like a barnacle on the side of the most sturdy ship sailing through turbulent, war-torn waters. In return for this safe passage, barnacles like Armando offered loyalty to the causes of the wealthy.

Silvia and Rafa consulted all financial decisions with 'their' pastor, a red-haired and bearded gringo they called Pete. It was obvious that he had been a hippie. This was evidenced by his habitual sandals, his addiction to indigenous textiles, and the air of intimate complicity that quickly emerges between any two people who have previously experimented with hallucinogens. Of course, Pete would never miss an opportunity to testify how he had left that life behind. He had seen the light in Eureka, California. At a local ranch an idea had come up: they would start the *Gospel Outreach* congregation to spread the word. Convinced, he had been baptised in water and fire, and had volunteered to travel to Guatemala in 1976, when the earthquake hit.

Now Pete was in charge of a group of church families. It turned out that Armando had to be *approved* before he could do business with Rafa. He was persuaded to be baptised and accept Jesus as his saviour. We also had to bring the wedding forward, a fundamental requirement of becoming a member of the Christian community. The pair of us had to sit through a detailed interrogation whereby Pete pried into every minutia of our lives, as was necessary to fit us into the map of members of his 'cell'.

From that day on, things seemed to flow. Armando received an unexpected phone call from Gabriel Motalvo, one of the unreachables, a powerful oligarch. He was interested in financing Rafa's construction project. Social visits to Rafa's house began to feature Gabriel and his wife Virginia; they were much older than us and extraordinarily wealthy. The sheer artificiality of our mingling with these people seemed to go unnoticed. We tried our hardest to pretend it didn't bother us. Armando was clear that his only purpose in condescending with this elaborate process was to obtain the management of Rafa's project. In my case, I just went along with it, ushered there by the walls of impossibility that blocked all other routes. I was barely twenty years old and didn't know better.

In the summer of 1981, when we were finally married, Pete officiated the ceremony and the church choir sang beautiful hymns in Hebrew. The 'brothers' and 'sisters' danced, set free by the fire of the divine presence, as King David himself did in his mystical outbursts. For our friends and family, accustomed to the rigid Catholic rituals, the service was enticingly eccentric. They expected something like this from us. We had been part of the hippie paradise that, at the end of the 70s, dreamed of peace and love on the shores of Lake Atitlán. The Verbo church had a well-defined hierarchy. The elders and preachers were conspicuous. I never saw Efraín Ríos Montt among them, though. They say he was a Sunday school teacher at this point, the humblest of vocations. In any case, what I did learn firsthand was the pervasive dynamic of that community, where we all let ourselves be convinced that the solution to every problem would come from our privileged connection with the divine. We were the chosen people. The new Israel. 'Speaking in tongues' – the sobbing praises and general hysteria of moments 'when the spirit rained on us' – became the necessary embrace we needed to forget what was happening outside.

During the last days of the Romeo Lucas government, the war felt like a hellish chainsaw cutting through everything. It was a well-known secret the generals were keeping the country in a state of perpetual instability as a matter of day-to-day business. In recent years the military high command had undertaken projects of pharaonic proportions. Many only existed on paper (although the money that reached the pockets of those involved was real). Others were soaked in blood, like the Chixoy hydroelectric plant, erected over the rubble of Río Negro, a village whose inhabitants, refusing to be relocated, had been massacred. The government's game was one of perverse ambivalence: the chaos was both unsustainable and necessary for the gorging on money that wars allow.

After celebrating another fraudulent election on 23 March 1982, the city awoke under the weight of all-too-familiar news: a group of soldiers had carried out a coup. This event was accompanied by the same trappings as previous such occasions: tanks in Central Park, helicopters flying over the city, announcements on national radio and television (often using the same theme music as previous coups) – like a bad screenwriter rehashing the rhetoric of a worn-out narrative.

Ríos Montt had been a teacher and director of the military academy, among other things. His students remembered him well. His histrionic gestures always attracted followers and the imagination he put into them was prodigal. He was a bold chameleon, capable of changing with the winds of time, and skilfully putting himself in the shoes of whatever character the situation demanded. He had previously offered to impersonate a leftist leader. Now he had inherited the mission of liquidating a war of insurrection led by a Marxist guerrilla movement. Inconsistent, you say? Yes, till the day of his death!

Despite being retired as a military man, and preferring life these days as a born-again Christian and a Sunday teacher dedicated to children, Ríos Montt's first move was to re-adopt full military uniform. His jet-black hair (recently dyed), thick moustache (largely grey), exaggerated gestures and way of speaking – which continually rose and fell for dramatic effect – were all entirely consistent with the countenance of a preacher. When he raised his voice, his bellowing filled the room. Was he mad? Should a madman be allowed to wear that camouflaged uniform? Should he be allowed to be in command a country? It didn't matter! We were just relieved for the change in power.

Ríos Montt's connection with the Verbo church was not forgotten in this turning point in his life. The morning of the coup, he did not arrive alone at the National Palace. One of the highest-ranking elders in the church assisted him as he took his seat in the presidential chair. In his first speech, the new head of state made it clear: he was going to fill that position as God had designated him to it. 'For it is only He who gives and takes authority,' he said with solemn certainty. The notion was outrageous to everyone, even for the other coup leaders. Was the Evangelical Church ascending to power? Back then the country was still mostly Catholic.

Verbo's leadership was convinced that this unexpected turn of events was prophetic evidence of their mission: to make Guatemala the New Jerusalem. To rebuild the walls as Nehemiah had done. They well knew that containing communism in Latin America exceeded the capacity of armies. It was necessary to penetrate minds and sow, from there, the truth of things. The God that was to be venerated was not a humanistic Jesus who called for brotherly love and dedication to the poor. For wasn't that version of Jesus – the one who said it was easier for a camel to pass through the eye of a needle than for a rich man to enter the kingdom of heaven – responsible for the perversion of the followers of the Liberation Theology? This Jehovah would fulfil the needs imposed by the times: the church and capitalism would find a way to embrace each other. Instead of driving the merchants out of the temple, the temple had to be converted into a market. In a primordial gesture that appealed to his divine mandate, Ríos Montt began by renaming the country: 'Nueva Guatemala'. He surrounded himself with church-affiliated counsellors who had unlimited access to his ear, feeding him biblical prophecies and metaphors designed to prove the piety of his actions.

Perhaps the torrent of memories from those times that now rushes through my head requires too many words. It's really just a synthesis of imagery; a film sequence that lasts just a few moments. In the realm of the mind, history and memory become easily entangled, in a dreamlike remix. Right now, back in the plaza, the mayor has concluded the commemoration ceremony. The marimba plays one last tune and our hosts invite us to walk to a nearby field. Night has fallen.

In the centre of the field, an Ajq'ij initiates the fire ceremony by tracing a cross of destiny in sugar on the ground. Next, he sets down tallow candles of every colour, flowers, and different kinds of incense, raw sugar cane and cocoa seeds. His assistants then follow suit, leaving offerings of their own. Then, he instructs one of them to light the fire. A litany summoning the power of the Nahuales unfolds like a canvas woven with voices. I am transfixed by the look on their faces. A few hours earlier, in the plaza, they looked shiny and polished. Inscrutable, as if made of stone. Around the flames, they open up like seeds that burst in the heat. Many cry, their faces drawn, hunched over, like melting candles.

Beyond the titanic struggle to find justice, beyond the joy of the conviction being commemorated tonight, the burning embers of pain are quite alive. Many of the faces that now glow in the light of the fire saw horrendous things. Others grew up listening to the stories of that wretched time, now referred to by the elders as simply 'when the violence came'. Coming from their lips, 'the violence' sounds like something very far from human; as if they spoke of a terrible beast. One that pounced on them, ready to eat them alive, rape the women, raze the fields. One that chased villagers up into the mountains where they roamed terrified, carrying nothing, where survival was a matter of eating roots and burying your children where they died, in graves that were never to be found again. The earth was stuffed with bones without tombstones to remember them.

All the dead whose bodies were lost, scattered outside military detachments or out in the fields and mountains, are now present. I had seen their skeletons in the grotesque photographs that forensic experts took of mass graves, shown at the trial. Now, their souls approach the flickering light of the flames, alive as they once were. They are still wearing the same jackets, or the same huipils they wore in their previous lives. The fire is an invitation to remember them all and weep.

I have no one to remember. None of my dead were killed by war. But in the midst of the flames, one of my many demons emerges: I see the face of Ríos Montt. He has taken off his combat fatigues, and wears a white, tailored suit. He has two masks. That of the strong man who restores order; that of the preacher on television on Sunday nights. With that shaky, untuned voice, he demands impeccable morality from each one of us. It is our daily sins that have destroyed Guatemala; our adulteries, our drunkenness, our neglect of parental duties. If only we changed our hearts... If only we changed our thoughts... the country would overcome its woes.

'I don't steal, I don't lie, I don't abuse.' This slogan, this moral capsule got turned into a symbol: a hand with three fingers raised. Many Guatemalans came to loath him. Oddly it was not due to the hundreds of massacres he allowed that led most to hate him. It was the Sunday sermons. It was his pointing, accusatory finger typical of so many preachers.

Behind the extravagant moralistic displays that served as a great theatrical curtain, a hideous creature was hatching. The military leadership devised a counterinsurgency strategy. That 'final battle', was branded with a practical, almost Buddhist sounding metaphor: 'taking the water away of the fish.' Under the premise that the indigenous populations gave logistical support (food and supplies) to the various guerrilla groups, the most efficient way to annihilate their military capacity would be to annihilate those villages. Nothing should remain alive. The Ixil triangle was marked as a 'red zone' because it was there that the EGP – the Guerrilla Army of the Poor – had deployed most of its forces.

The notion of 'leaving nothing alive' would have been unthinkable were it not for one initial condition, in abundant supply: racism. Indigenous people or mestizo peasants mainly inhabited the towns and villages that would be affected. They were all profoundly poor. The army operated as a function of the needs of wealthy farmers and capitalists: 'white' people. The decision to turn the army on the people was not absurd. The logic of extermination is not unusual when it operates hand-in-hand with racism. The peasants had officially become 'the internal enemy'. The guns were not aimed at the armed guerrillas, but against ordinary villagers. Soldiers were to avoid killing women and children... 'whenever it was possible.'

Military dossiers had been projected onto large screens during the hearings. Documents of war, full of the details that I can now recite verbatim. In the end, those details, so meticulously unravelled, triggered the collective trauma that became the experience of that trial.

One shouldn't fall for the false impression that Ríos Montt was cunning, capable of terrible designs. It is more appropriate to conjure a different picture: Ronald Reagan visits Honduras in December 1982. Ríos Montt travels to meet with him. The counterinsurgency strategy for Central America is discussed, and in the process, Reagan is impressed by this born-again from Guatemala, Ríos Montt. And that's how he'll sell him back to the American people: 'a good Christian'. The US government had clear knowledge of the military strategies being executed in Guatemala, and of the potential impact of Montt's strategy on the civilian population. But the human consequences that Reagan's advisers warned him about were of little matter, and instead, he stepped on the accelerator. And what Reagan was unable to do upfront to shore up the efforts of the Guatemalan Army, he did through the back door: using their reliable lapdog, Israel.[2]

Back among the flames, Gabriel Montalvo's face emerges, his warped features make him look rabid and cadaverous.

During the trial, as the representative chosen by the oligarchy to protest the accusations against the general, he made vehement statements defending Ríos Montt, even attempting to justify the worst crimes: the murder of children and women: 'The guerrilla strategy was supported by the whole community: children and women played a part in the war. They all worked as one body.' They were repeating what their American advisers, hardened and embittered by Vietnam, had told them. It was about replicating that model.

Ríos Montt and his body of advisers had publicly promoted their plans with a simple catchphrase: 'bullets and beans'. If the peasants surrendered to the army and agreed to be transferred to 'model villages' – their euphemism of choice for a kind of concentration camp – they would receive food in exchange for strenuous, unpaid work such as opening trails among the mountains with picks and shovels. If they did not, they would be held responsible for their choice. The soldiers had very precise orders for those who didn't surrender. Such orders were ascribed a simple label: 'scorched earth'. Not even dogs should be left alive.

With a combination of public and covert activity, Ríos Montt quickly pacified the country. The random assassinations of dissidents on the streets of our cities ended, while the killing in the countryside continued, unreported. For people like us, living in the capital, life began to enter a kind of normality, fragile though it was, like the skin of an onion. But too many were still dying or disappearing to pay for this normality. I used the city's new-found peace to finish my studies. Armando got a job in the government. From one Sunday to the next we gradually drifted away from the church – his business interest with Rafa having failed to flourish. Finally, the marriage collapsed into an empty vortex, and I resolved to get out of there. It wasn't hard to get a scholarship for a masters abroad.

Yes, I had to run away. I wanted to amputate the country from my mind and I nearly achieved it. Ironically, now that I'm back I feel there's no escape from it. I'm trapped by the obstinate and obsessive need to open up all the secret coffers of the war. It is a cruel pleasure: for 30 long years, all this information had been concealed behind a dark curtain, draped over everything. Anyone who sought to look behind it, and find out what happened to a loved one, would be killed. Today archives are being opened, war strategies are publicly discussed, Washington is declassifying documents. Clinton even apologised. And I feel overwhelmed. I lived in the midst of it all unknowing and the revelations dumbfound me.

Back at my hotel, I try to sleep. But the movie projector inside my head won't stop. When I was growing up, we were terrified of the army, the police, and the clandestine groups that attacked with boundless violence. They were untouchable, immune, terrible gods. People died and disappeared at their hands, like sand that just slips away. Ríos Montt was the last link in the chain. I can't stop thinking about that old man looking a little ridiculous at the hearings. The trial was the result of a gigantic community effort. It was put together with extraordinary patience. Witnessing it alone was exhausting, like feeling the skin of my country, inch by inch, reaching for every dark crevice. Experts discussed the technical aspects. The famous word 'genocide', for example. Politicians rigged the word with obstacles. It is not a simple matter of punishing those who pile up thousands of dead, as one might think it is. It is about fulfilling requirements and conditions built into words. Like filling out a boring form. That's how bureaucrats kill justice: with words.

But the core of the proceedings lay not in the technicalities or the trickery of the lawyers. It lay in the testimonies. Different people approached the bench to tell their story. They put into words questions that are too complex or cruel for us to answer: What does it mean to be raped by 30 men? What is it like to be six years old and see a group of soldiers execute your father? What happens inside a human being who is taken to a concentration camp and forced to sing the national anthem every day after his son was murdered by the government? How does it feel to see all the men in your community locked up in a church and set on fire? In all the testimonies there was the same feeling of impotency: words were not enough. We were all pierced by those memories. To this day, they cut us, lacerate us.

I took note of the presence of the US ambassador, each day from my seat in the public gallery. He didn't miss a single hearing. Nothing is quite as volatile as North American loyalties. One minute they are raising a monster, the next they are disposing of it: killing or condemning it, whichever is more convenient. As I sat there in court, I kept asking myself: was Ríos Montt the only culprit? Was he not just one of the cogs in an extremely complicated mechanism? Hiding behind the army were the wealthy oligarchs, empowered by rancid and deep-seated racism. Behind the oligarchs was Washington, with all of its demands. Behind Washington were the interests of the privileged citizens of the First World, the primary benefactors of raw capitalism. Finally, behind that, I guess, a self-justifying, pharisaic religiosity that, in this part of the world, paraded as evangelism. All these logical explanations fit inside each other like Chinese boxes. Each one carrying its own piece of the blame. But condemning the entirety of responsible parties, or an entity as abstract as 'the system' is impossible. Ríos Montt was not solely guilty. He served as a synthesis, a symbol of the condemnation that lay at the door of everyone responsible. As it appeared to me, that trial was metaphorically, and literally, a great act of insurrection.

When Judge Yassmin Barrios read out the sentence, those of us present in the courtroom were struck by amazement. Even now, lying in my hotel bed, I bristle as I remember. People were applauding, crying, hugging, singing. Everyone's personal histories came rushing back to them in that room. The exhausted sadness, the unforgettable horror. The people bellowed in unison the newly-minted slogan: *My heart is Ixil!*

Ríos Montt's conviction was a scandal for members of the elite. They understood that symbolically they were included in the verdict and moved quickly to defend themselves: We are not genocidal, they insisted. The sentence reached them as if it had called them out by name, one by one. Ten days later, the Constitutional Court obeyed the implicit demands made in the irate statements published in the major newspapers. The sentence was annulled. The system had not been able to bear the weight of those truths, the healing power of justice. They scrambled to cover their sudden nakedness with precarious new robes but it was late. Words are like milk. Once spilt, they cannot be taken back. The conviction had released the words that genocide had been committed in Guatemala. And those words could never be erased.

Dawn is breaking above Nebaj and I haven't been able to sleep. I don't need rest. History is a length of tangled yarn and each of us needs to untangle the piece that we get to live and witness.

As I draw back the shutters, I can see people beginning to congregate again in the main plaza. Today we will walk together in a solemn march to the nearby village of Cotzal. There, the inhabitants of the three villages will meet. As people gather for the march I see some of them carrying old portraits, they are the images of their dead. Adding to the ceremonial atmosphere, they also bear bouquets of flowers and candles. A child carries a portrait behind him so big that it almost covers his whole back. It is of his grandfather, someone he never met but has learned to love. The march is accompanied by a band of women with drums: they set an implacable rhythm for that bright red caterpillar that fills the street and advances with difficulty, impeded by every narrow passage. Everyone wears the regional costume. Hence the cacophony of red.

We walk to a large fallow field where an army base used to stand. There are several open ditches in the ground, covered over with black plastic: excavations of mass graves, where fragments of skeletons are still being removed. Ultimately, the most damning evidence came from here: from graves like these, and the thousands of skeletons found in them; from the forensic work that links the bones with the accounts of missing people and executions; from the investigations linking the bones with families in mourning. The testimonies could have been dismissed as lies, or given other explanations. But bones coming out of mass graves and pieced together with other evidence, don't know how to lie.

I note how many young people and children are here today in Cotzal. Most of those present are not yet 30. So it is the elders who speak. They tell their stories from memory like living books written to guard our past. The young and the children have come to learn, to connect their own existences to those of their elders, bringing full meaning to the word 'history'.

Everything happens in a language that I do not understand. And that gap between my understanding and their lives has not stopped hurting since I returned. In any case, what I see is consolation. It dilutes my sadness with joy, like when the sun mixes with the rain. A people who could not be exterminated try to understand. They are here 30 years later, young, strong and growing in dignity. 'The Violence', that nameless animal, has passed, as all things pass. And these survivors have managed to transcend the death it brought: they have truly been born again.

## Notes

1. A reference to the famously short story by the Guatamalan author Augusto Monterroso, tiled 'El Dinosaurio' ('The Dinosaur'), published in *Obras completas (Y otros cuentos)*, the entirety of which reads: Cuando despertó, el dinosaurio todavía estaba allí. ('When he awoke, the dinosaur was still there.')
2. Throughout Central America in the 1970s and 80s, the Israeli military acted as a proxy for the United States, providing military training, intelligence support, weapons, aircraft and military personnel for US-backed regimes in the region. This was particularly true in Guatemala after 1977, when US support became subject to constraints stemming Congressional opposition to the Guatemalan government's human rights practices. This support included up to 300 Israeli advisers on the ground, 39 per cent of Guatemala's weapons imports between 1975 and 1979, the off-the-books loan of 10 UH-1H 'Huey' helicopters, and even a computer system installed in an annexe behind the presidential palace in 1980, that used data analysis to monitor electrical and water usage as a means of pinpointing the coordinates of potential guerrilla safe houses.

# Afterword: Genocide or Communism?

## Julio Barrios Zardetto

*In the 1970s all of the democracies that existed in Latin America were ended, all the opportunities to carry out change through legal means were aborted.[...] The tragic thing is that we have defined pro-American in almost anti-democratic terms, the countries we have the best relations with are the least democratic.*

– Jonh Dinges, Central America Correspondent, *Washington Post*, 1982.[1]

BETWEEN 1960 AND 1996, the people of Guatemala lived through 36 long years of civil war, during which the vast majority of casualties were civilians, and, by conservative estimates, around 200,000 people were killed or forcefully 'disappeared'.[2] Genocide and war crimes (particularly against the indigenous Maya people) were committed, generations were scarred by violence, and truly baffling horrors were systematically perpetrated by government forces. Officially, it was a domestic war against communism. Unofficially, through the CIA's funding of the Guatemalan army, it was just another act in the US's global battle against 'the communist menace', the main stage for which, according to President Reagan, was now Central America.

Guatemala has a long colonial past, but its real history reaches much further back than the Hispanic presence. Consequently, about half of Guatemalans presently speak one of twenty plus indigenous languages other than Spanish. Ancient practices and beliefs are still vital in these indigenous communities. Their ancestors were the 'raw materials' the Spaniards came to reap in Guatemala, forming estates that held entire villages in indentured servitude where the locals became slaves to the land-barons in exchange for negligibly small parcels of their own land to grow food for their own families. The oligarchic plantation structure changed very little over the centuries, even after independence from Spain in 1821 and independence from Mexico in 1938. Historically there had never seemed to be any room for social or economic reform. The clearest illustration of this inequity is the fact that until as late as 1945, there were laws that legalised forced labour, by which indigenous people and peasants were obligated to abide, either for the benefit of large plantations or for the building of state infrastructure.[3]

In October 1944,[4] there was a revolution in Guatemala that for the first time brought about free elections; and from them, a civilian government was elected. This new government inaugurated an era known as the Democratic Spring. Lasting for just ten years, and a total of just two (democratically elected) governments, it began to build Guatemala as a modern state. One of the cornerstone policies of this modernising project was a much-needed land reform policy that would expropriate fallow lands from only the biggest owners. This last policy affected the interest of the US-owned United Fruit Company that had important shareholders in the US government like the Dulles brothers, one (John Foster Dulles) as head of the State Department and the other (Allen Dulles) as head of the CIA. A coup was carried out by the CIA, in June 1954, starting in what became known in the US as 'Operation PBSUCCESS', which saw the deployment of hundreds of CIA-trained soldiers, aerial attacks (using American planes), a naval blockade, and the use of heavy psychological warfare (including a radio station that broadcast anti-government propaganda and reporting on military events favourable to the rebellion, claiming to be genuine news) which successfully intimidated the Guatemalan Army into refusing to fight back.

Following the coup, the government and legislature were disbanded, communist leaders arrested, and the commander of the invasion General Castillo Armas became president. Hundreds of Guatemalans were rounded up and killed, in an operation meticulously planned by the CIA beforehand in the event of the coup being successful (as revealed by documents obtained by the National Security Archive).[5]

This failed attempt to forge a modern, democratic state through social reforms sowed the seeds of civil war, and its failure perpetuated systems of institutionalised racism (towards indigenous people and the peasantry in general), systemic injustice, political privileges, and economic exploitation. The nascent democratic spirit and its institutions were overridden and suffocated by the repressive power of the traditional alliance between a military class and a very conservative oligarchy now clad in the apparatus of the state. The civil war began in 1960, as a direct result of the 1954 intervention. By this time, the Cold War paradigm dominated geopolitical strategies and anti-communism ideologies became the dominant philosophy of the US and its sphere of influence.

In the case of Central America, during the Kennedy administration, the anti-communist support came packaged as 'the Alliance for Progress', an aid programme that encouraged infrastructure and economic growth in the region, but focused predominantly on the military training of officers and troops in counterinsurgency tactics and promoted the adoption of the National Security Doctrine. This was a scheme which installed protocols in the region's military institutions to prepare them to wage irregular wars: infiltration, mass surveillance, interrogation, torture, psychological warfare and terror tactics.

An insurgency or resistance movement began with a small group of young officers, though it never developed into anything like a unified campaign. The resistance grew not through a series of progressive military victories or the support of communist countries such as Cuba or the USSR, but as a grassroots reaction to the repression that had gripped the country at so many levels. Throughout the civil war, any sort of dissent against the authorities could mean death. Opposition parties, worker unions, farmers' cooperatives, rural humanitarian aid groups (especially Catholic-led ones), student organisations, and collective initiatives of all kinds were potentially subject to codified bans and the assassination of their leadership. Any intent to push reform or demand accountability (on anything from a disappeared person case to government corruption) was dealt with swiftly and violently. This strict regime of intolerance benefited only one segment of the population. For everyone else, there were very few options besides rebellion.

In 1977, trying to promote a human rights-oriented foreign policy, President Carter cut off direct military aid to Guatemala, although intelligence and diplomatic support for the government was mostly maintained. By contrast, the subsequent Reagan administration (1981-89) went to great lengths to support the counterinsurgency struggles in Central America even if, in some cases, it meant using illegal means and known criminals to ensure a steady stream of guns and money to anti-communist movements in the region.[6]

As Reagan himself said to a famous joint session of Congress in 1983: 'The national security of all the Americas is at stake in Central America. If we cannot defend ourselves there, we cannot expect to prevail elsewhere. Our credibility would collapse, our alliances would crumble, and the safety of our homeland would be put in jeopardy.'[7]

In the year before Reagan's election, in Nicaragua (five hundred kilometres to the southeast of Guatemala) the long-time dictator and staunch US ally, Anastasio Somoza, was overthrown by the Sandinista Movement. In the wake of this revolution, the Nicaraguan resistance set out to establish a socialist state aligned with Cuba and the USSR. El Salvador's capital city was surrounded by regions supporting the FMLN (El Salvador's social revolutionary movement) and that country seemed on the brink of following suit. Guatemala was not Reagan's priority, but his foreign policy mandated the reestablishing of direct military aid.[8] This policy was based on Jeane Kirkpatrick's doctrine of 'Dictatorships and Double Standards', one that promoted 'authoritarian' regimes because they were useful for fighting against the left.[9] After being propped up with foreign aid, once the foreign policy goals had been met, they could be toppled in favour of democracy. It asserted that Marxist regimes were 'totalitarian' by virtue of being Marxist, that they couldn't be negotiated with, and therefore had to be torn down pre-emptively. Guatemala, however, and by association its new dictator Ríos Montt, needed first to redeem themselves in the eyes of the international community and particularly the US Congress, if they were to resume receiving military aid from abroad.[10]

Although Ríos Montt had been installed by a military coup in March 1982 for domestic reasons – to stabilise the country following the escalation of violence during President Romeo Lucas Garcia's regime (1978-82), whose 'scorched earth' policy towards the insurrection led to unprecedented paramilitary chaos in both cities and the countryside – Ríos Montt's appeal to the US lay in his 'holy' war against communism. Unlike his predecessor Lucas, Ríos Montt waged this war almost exclusively in the countryside, far away from the nervous urban middle classes, and most importantly far away from national and international journalists, and the embassies.

The US Embassy set out to help Reagan bring Guatemala back into the fold. Though testimonies and evidence of massacres started to find their way to the US Embassy, the ambassador Frederic L. Chapin treated them with suspicion and his diplomatic mission did little to actively uncover what was really happening. When the clamours of the victims became too loud to ignore, Chapin sought to sow doubts internationally by discrediting the NGOs that were reporting on behalf of the victims as communist propagandists. Declassified documents have now cleared up any doubt as to what the embassy knew regarding the massacres taking place in the countryside: For example, one declassified CIA intelligence document from February 1982 (approved for release in 1998), stated: 'The well-documented belief by the army that the entire Ixil[11] population is pro-EGP[12] has created a situation in which the Army can be expected to give no quarter to combatants and non-combatants alike.'

While Catholicism was still officially Guatemala's main religion, its networks had suffered greatly from repression as many rural priests had been associated with the Liberation Theology movement that sympathised with the poor and, in some cases, supported insurrection. Many priests had been assassinated. If anyone asked, at least in the countryside, it was better to be identified as Evangelical than to be associated with potentially seditious Catholicism. Pentecostal Protestantism was on the rise, filling in part the void left by the persecuted Catholic priests, but also due to intense missionary work following the 1976 earthquake.

Reagan and Ríos Montt shared a common power base: the 'religious right' or the conservative evangelicals whose political agenda had used anti-communism as a primary banner to rally under. In the US, some of these Christian conservatives had formed a group called the Moral Majority, to help get Reagan elected in the first place. But this was just one of many such groups jumping into the political arena and successfully revitalising the Republican Party at the time. Central to the religious right's discourse was opposition to communism as a matter of faith. Based on the premise that communism and Christianity not only didn't mix but were sworn enemies, they justified support for dictatorships abroad as long as they fought the 'communists'. This label was thrown around broadly against any perceived threat to these dictatorships and resulted in the death of many activists, students, children and even babies who couldn't possibly have yet been infected by 'communism'. Within these US religious sects, Ríos Montt was known and supported. One televangelist declared that Ríos Montt was 'sent from God to fulfil [His] prophesy,' while another evangelist pastor called him 'the David of the New Testament.' It's hard to tell for sure, but according to US Embassy reports, Ríos Montt himself seemed to believe he was sent from God, that his authority was extended directly from Him.[13]

As Zardetto's story argues, the Ríos Montt that ran for president in 1974 was not, at least in public, the same man that became dictator in 1982. By the early 80s, he had become a born-again Christian with a mission to create a 'New Guatemala', a nation that would be Christian, disciplined, conservative and above all would love and respect authority. He set out to spread these values by addressing the country through an endless series of radio and TV broadcasts in which he would preach on such subjects as discipline, marital obligations, good conduct, and how it was everyone's God-given duty to purge the evil of communism from their hearts and from the nation. To some, his discourses may have appeared histrionic, even laughable, but in the hundreds of new, Pentecostal churches around the country, his lectures clearly resonated. It gave a morale boost to the army and to a government whose strength had been more military than moral up until this point.

Propaganda depicting communists as devils was distributed in the countryside. And 'devils', of course, need to be extinguished. Equating communism with evil in this way led to another sinister step, whereupon some indigenous populations were considered to be communist, and therefore evil, in their entirety, thus excusing, and even sanctioning, the inevitable ethnic cleansing these communities suffered in the predominantly indigenous highlands. It's actually written into the internal operational document, *Victoria '82* (the codename for the Ríos Montt's new counterinsurgency programme), stating that indigenous people of a certain ethnicity (Ixil people) could be considered to be de facto participants of the insurgency (EGP). The underlying, obvious message being that they were all (men, women and children) enemies to eradicate. This document was an important piece of evidence in the case that brought Ríos Montt to justice, it indicated that a whole population was defined not by their choices or politics but by their ethnic identity, thereby sanctioning their systematic extermination.

The common tactic shared by all participants in this genocide – from political organisations like Jerry Falwell's Moral Majority, through Nixon and Reagan's foreign policy, to Lucas' and Ríos

Montt's scorched earth enforcement – was the simple rhetoric of *us* and *them.* It builds on a deep-rooted belief that the *other* poses an existential threat to your life, even your soul. In Guatemala, this rhetoric has attempted to erase the historic grievances of a society moulded by colonialism, the marginalisation of indigenous people and a governing, ancienne régime-style elite that stifled any attempt at reform. Considering the entire span of modern Guatemalan history, the aborted revolution of 1944–1954 represents the only moment when there was a concerted effort by the government to transform a banana republic, for want of a better phrase, with a colonialist economic structure, into a modern democratic state with a capitalist economy. The US intervention, far from warding off global communism, succeeded in wrecking a nascent democracy by propping up decadent, murderous elites that left no channels for dissent or reform. In doing so, it left people little alternative but rebellion. This oligarchic structure still stands today. By any standard, Guatemala is one of the most unequal countries in Latin America, with one of the highest rates of chronic malnutrition and violence, a combination that is creating an exodus of migrants that find no option but the dangerous road to the north, whatever those risks may be.

The 2013 ruling of genocide[14] or indeed any accusation of wrongdoing by the Guatemalan Army is still very contentious. The religious/anti-communist rhetoric is still relatively strong. Nevertheless, the ruling of genocide that resulted in a life sentence for Ríos Montt was a turning point, pitting the historically disempowered Mayan people against one of the most powerful men in Guatemalan politics. And, for the first time, they won. Ríos Montt's conviction came with heavy historical implications: genocide entails a racist structure that enabled it. It was a ruling therefore on Guatemalan society and its history, and is inevitably seeping into the way Guatemalans understand their history, allowing entirely new narratives from the perspective of indigenous experiences to be built. Narratives that have so far been missing.

## Notes

1. John Dinges, *Reagan's Wars in Central America*. (Alternative Radio, Boulder, 1982).
2. The Commission for Historical Clarification. *Guatemala: Memory of Silence, Tz'Inil Na 'Tab 'Al: Report of the Commission for Historical Clarification, Conclusions and Recommendations.* (Guatemala: CEH, 1998), 21.
3. Ley de Vagancia (Vagrancy Law) and Ley de Vialidad (Highway Law).
4. The 1944 revolution began in earnest on 25 June, when a peaceful demonstration of female schoolteachers was suppressed by government troops during which one teacher, Maria Chinchilla, was killed. A week later, on 1 July, amidst a general strike and nationwide protests, the dictator for the last fourteen years, Jorge Ubico, resigned hoping to hand over power to a former subordinate he could control. His first choice for that, General Roderico Anzueto, proved unpopular as he was a Nazi; his second choice was a triumvirate of former majors, one which, Federico Ponce Vaides (still under Ubico's command), forced Congress at gunpoint to vote for him to be provisional president. On 19 October, a small group of students and soldiers led by former military professor and exile, Jacobo Árbenz, stormed the National Palace, forcing Ponce into exile and declaring a commitment to hold free elections before the end of the year.
5. Ruth Blakeley. *State Terrorism and Neoliberalism: The North in the South* (Routledge, 2009), p92.
6. The Iran-Contra affair.
7. Ronald Reagan, Address on Central America to Congress, April 27, 1983.
8. Guatemala was buying weapons from Israel and Argentina, but only the US could supply much-needed helicopter parts.
9. 'Dictatorships and Double Standards' was the title of an essay published by Jeane Kirkpatrick in the November 1979 issue of *Commentary Magazine* which criticised the foreign policy of the Carter administration, and was credited with leading directly to Kirkpatrick becoming an adviser to Ronald Reagan and thus her appointment as United States Ambassador to the United Nations.
10. Virginia Garrard-Burnett, *Terror in the Land of the Holy Spirit: Guatemala Under General Efraín Ríos Montt, 1982-1983* (Oxford

University Press, 2010), p190.
11. The largest of the indigenous Maya communities in Guatemala.
12. EGP: Ejército Guerrillero de los Pobres (Guerrilla Army of the Poor).
13. Virginia Garrard-Burnett, *Terror in the Land of the Holy Spirit: Guatemala Under General Efrain Rios Montt, 1982-1983* (Oxford University Press, 2010).
14. Though the ruling was temporarily overturned it eventually came to the same conclusion with a new tribunal in 2018.

# The Gathering Voice

Jacob Ross

Ada Bowen sat on the high chair in her kitchen, her elbows on the windowsill, facing the restive waters of Dolphin Bay. A reddish moon hung on the edge of the horizon, about to dip into the sea – a sign of heavy rains to come.

Out there on the Western Main Road that cut through Dolphin village, the thunder of engines shook the dark. She imagined young soldiers of the new Military Council, jam-packed in little Lada Niva jeeps, hurrying north towards Sauteurs, or south to St Georges where all the trouble was.

Then silence folded over Dolphin once again, and all that remained were the snoring of the high winds in the Fédon hills, and the rhythmic thrashing of the sea.

She'd lived through two shoot-on-sight curfews before but this one felt much worse – as if time had stopped, and the darkness in which she sat now would never end.

Her head felt heavy from lack of sleep, her mind numb from pacing the floorboards and the beach, because this was the third night after the killings and Daniel, her one boy-child, hadn't come home.

Her thoughts dragged her back to Wednesday afternoon when the words of the man who called himself 'The General' broke through the 9 o'clock news, his voice gravelly and gruff.

Every statement he made stirred up pictures in her head – images that had been planted there by all the rumours that reached Dolphin earlier in the day.

... *the Prime Minister... not willing to talk...* Those words brought to mind a tall brown man, with a thundering voice – rich with cadence and defiance – chained to a bed in a house above St Georges. She visualised his woman beside him, ignoring the soldiers' order to walk away and leave him to his fate.

... *a crowd...* She saw children in her mind, spilling out of their schools onto the streets; storming the house above St Georges, and the jubilation and frenzy as they broke past the soldiers, set the Prime Minister free and carried him to the old stone fort that looked down on the hospital.

*The Revolutionary Armed Forces were forced to storm the fort,* the General said. The six people they'd stood against a wall and shot had brought this on themselves. He named the Prime Minister first, then added another five. And, he told them finally, there were some others.

By 'some others' Ada supposed The General meant the dozens of school children who tried to escape the machine-guns by leaping from the high walls of the old stone fort in St Georges, dying where they landed on the rocks below.

Daniel, she knew, would not be among them.

An early-morning wind stirred the waters of the bay – a sudden shuffle and rise of chilly air that rattled the sea grape leaves and brought with it the fresh, unadulterated odours of the ocean.

On an ordinary day, this would be her getting-ready time: gathering her gear, fitting her Seagull engines to her boat and setting out a couple of hours before the men were up. A habit she had forced on herself during her early years of fishing when she needed to protect herself from the spite of Dolphin men.

Now here she was this 'fore-day morning shivering at her window, waiting for Daniel.

*

She must have dozed off. The shuffle of footsteps on the sand snapped her out of it. Leaning out, she glimpsed the gangling shape emerging from the alleyway, burdened by that long canvas bag Daniel always took with him to militia training. She rose to her feet watching him plod along the shoreline to the rocky northern end of the bay. For a while Daniel seemed to merge with the giant boulders, then separate abruptly from their darkness. She went to the kitchen and lit the three-burner gas stove, her hands fumbling with the matches. She placed a pot on the hob.

There was scratching at the door. She hurried across the floorboards and pulled it open. The chill rushed in along with the chafing of the sea.

Her son hung on the threshold, his back against the early-morning gloom. He was taller than her now, whip-slim, his shoulders curved forward. For a moment her breath caught in her throat, thinking he was still carrying the bag.

'How you got here?' she said conscious of the pulsing in her head, the dryness in her mouth.

He gestured in the direction of the road and stepped past her. She hadn't heard a vehicle arrive or leave.

She filled a bowl with the soup she had just warmed and set it on the table. Daniel stared at it, then raised his eyes at her – a flicker of a glance before he looked away. Still a boy, she thought, with those smooth girlish cheeks, the soft curve of his jawline, the loose uncertain mouth – although the rest of him was full of muscles now which she put down to those months of militia training. Or maybe he'd got the muscularity from her.

'You been away three days. You didn think I was goin to worry?' she said.

He rubbed his head and shrugged.

She flicked a finger at the bowl. 'You not hungry?'

He shook his head. Suddenly her son looked as if he'd aged overnight.

'All that nastiness that happen in Town, you know anyfing about it?' Her gaze dropped to the pistol he wore tucked into his waist. A Makarov he'd called it the first evening he brought it home. He'd said the name as if he'd just been handed a winning ticket. And from the time they gave her son that little gun, he walked straighter, began to stare down older men, and to openly trace the shape of young women with his eyes.

She would have preferred anything from him now, even the sour-faced, rude-mouth backchat that he threw at her sometimes but not this silence he'd brought home with him.

'I talking to you,' she said.

'I dunno, Ma. I just a militiaman. I –'

'You not no militia *man.*' Ada bit down on the last word. 'You just fifteen and you still in school. I did never want you to mix with people who make you carry gun. Now look what they gone and done! Where you wuz when all that killin happen?'

'Where I was s'posed to be.'

'And where was that?'

'What the hell you tryin to say, Ma?' His eyes were fierce on her face. 'Jeezas Christ! That's what my mother think ov me?'

'I have to ask. If people round here even think that you – we... I have to ask!'

'Have to!' He erupted from his chair, threw himself at the door and dragged it open. The sound of his feet was heavy on the sand. She heard the flat kerplunk of water and knew he'd thrown himself into the sea. A childhood habit. When Daniel wanted something that she refused to get him, or when he could no longer bear the weight of whatever was distressing him, he took to the water.

Ada pushed the window open. He was up to his neck. That coughing could have been the waves hitting the sand if it were more rhythmic and less prolonged. It was her son wringing out the hurt inside him. Crying in a way that *she* hadn't been able to. Until now.

By the time he returned, she'd dried her eyes and calmed herself. He'd stripped off the wet clothes at the doorstep; stood in the hallway swaying, his eyes red and swollen, not caring about his nakedness. She went to his room, returned with a towel and tossed it at him.

'Go sleep,' she said, directing a stiffened finger at the pistol on the table. 'Get rid ov it. You don't have nothing to do with no Revolution no more.'

He went off to bed without a word.

Ada stepped out into the stillness of the early morning. She felt lighter – wanted to weep with relief, seeing how deep the hurt had been for Daniel too.

A fine thread of light was rimming the eastern peaks of the Belvedere Mountains. In a couple of hours the sun would peel off the shadows from the foothills and light up the sea. But for now, most of the houses – a tight regiment of galvanised roofs that led from the beach to the very edge of the Western Main Road – were still locked down in sleep. She could hear the shuffles and sighs of life in them: fretful toddlers demanding to be fed; the slur of women's voices drifting along the narrow alleyways; Santana's new baby-girl, feverish and fretful; Alice's crazy boy-child, Tarvi, already up this time-a-morning, pounding their floorboards with his heels. Sounds which, she knew, no shoot-on-sight curfew in the world could suppress.

Beyond that there was nothing – just the heavy quiet that had fallen on the island.

A cluster of twenty-footers nodded on the foreshore, packed with fishing tackle: ring nets, a fish pot here and there, demijohns, plastic buckets and bait holds. Her craft, *Ori*, was empty, its two Seagull engines safe inside her house. She ran assessing eyes along the boat – dark blue in daylight with a white leaping dolphin painted on the port side. The big red float she used to mark out her fishpot territory was secured to the bow cleat by a plastic rope.

Their boats had been sitting there three days – from the Wednesday afternoon when news of the killings reached them. The shock of it had drawn them out of their houses and directed them to the beach. The whole village: women with infants on their shoulders; toddlers hanging onto the tail end of their mother's dresses; shirtless men with tar-coated fingers, or hands closed around hammers, or trowels, or net-needles – every one of them converging on Dolphin Bay, not a word between them.

They'd cast under-eyed glances at Jason the giant shopkeeper, wanting him to help them make sense of this disaster. What demon had possessed these men – who laughed and hugged and nudged each other at their rallies and celebrations – to make them turn their guns on each other, sudden-so?

But Jason's head was tilted upwards – a dreamy gaze that took in the sky, the sea and the blue-black hills rearing up behind them – staring, it seemed, at everything and nothing at the same time. Ada thought she knew why even a book-reading man like Jason could find no words for the heaviness that had settled over them. It felt so much worse than helplessness, so much dirtier than shame.

Still, Daniel was home with her now. She hadn't heard the grumble of a vehicle arriving, or the quick tap of a departing horn. Perhaps he'd walked the twenty miles from St Georges? She didn't think so; not with that big ole canvas bag.

*

Night had begun to creep down the foothills when Alice dropped by. Heavy-set and lumbering, her friend had the delicate, uncreased face of a child. 'Where's Danny Boy?' she said, easing herself down on the steps.

'Inside,' Ada said. 'He not sleeping.' It was an invitation to Alice to go check for herself.

Alice shook her head. 'He awright?'

'He so-so!'

With nothing to do, she'd spent the whole Saturday tending to Daniel as if he were struck down by an illness. He looked as if he were – the stunned eyes, the slowness of his movements. She'd wiped away the sheen of sweat that coated his face and shoulders; cooked him the food he liked – red snappers steamed in coconut milk; callaloo leaves with the shredded flesh of blue crabs. She'd even waded the shallows of the north end of the bay, harvested sea urchins, seasoned and baked the mango-yellow eggs, then sat beside him on the bed and watched him eat.

'Danny Boy awright?' Alice asked again. She didn't seem interested in an answer. Her eyes were on a pack of gulls squabbling over the water. Her hands were restless in her lap.

'What's botherin' you, Alice?'

'Ada, I keep asking meself, why they had to kill de Chief? Becuz is like we dunno what to do now.' She pressed a palm against her throat, the fat cheeks quivering. 'If the General and iz people so damn vex with him for something that he done, they could've beat him up; they could've even break he foot, but to shoot him down like that an–an–all–them–people…'

'That's what botherin you?'

'You didn hear the radio?' Alice said.

'I been busy with Daniel. What the radio say?'

'Ada I 'fraid,' she whimpered. 'I so damn 'fraid.'

'What the radio say, Alice?'

Alice pushed herself to her feet. 'I glad your boy-child come home. Jason say he givin away free drinks in his shop.'

'When?'

'Right now.'

'Right now is curfew time,' Ada said.

'Jason know that too. You coming?' Alice didn't wait for her reply.

*

*Free drinks!* Her heart flipped over.

Four years ago, Jason had offered free drinks too. That was when, in the grey hours of a mid-March morning – a Tuesday she believed – Dolphin woke to the rattle of gunfire. And, of course, the first thing she did was reach for the radio and switch it on. A voice pitched high and fast was raging through the plastic speaker. It informed them that they had a new government, that the army had surrendered and they were ordering all police to remain in their stations and await further instructions.

Here in Dolphin, in the long concrete building behind the crumbling Catholic Church, the police replied with gunshots.

The standoff stretched into late morning. And as the day heated up, young-people began to appear from everywhere, some arriving on the mud tracks that led down from the villages in the foothills; others from Victoria Town further up the coast.

She would never forget the quickening in her blood at the sight of a teenage girl dressed for school in a pressed white shirt, with ribbons to match, and a deep blue skirt, walking into the church, bringing out the old white priest and shooing him off.

They assembled in clusters of four or five. Took shelter from the barking guns behind the walls of the church buildings with piles of stone at their feet. They'd turned up in Dolphin with a new language – just movements of the head and hands.

Three young men had gone through the alleyway to the boats anchored in the bay. They returned with demijohns and buckets, strolled over to the courtyard of the Esso petrol station, broke the locks that secured the pumps, and filled up the containers. They returned to their group.

It had all made sense to her at the time. It still did. It was like something a pusson don't expect but once you see it happening, you find yourself prepared for it. Becuz those were the children born into the long dark night of terror in which she had found a way to make a life for herself and bring up her boy-child.

Those young-people knew no life other than the spite of

the police, controlled by the man who believed he owned the island. They had broken bones to show for it; beatings and abductions; the arrest and disappearance of their companions. They'd marked out these policemen with names that told you what each one did to you when they lifted you off the road and took you somewhere secret: Strangler, Steel Rod, Raperman, Gunbutt, Iron Toe, Whiplash. Hangman.

So! There wasn't a man inside that police station who didn't know his time had come.

She remembered congregating with the fishing men and women of Dolphin at the front of Jason's shop. The big shopkeeper had laid a row of unopened soft drink bottles on the counter. He left his bottle opener in his drawer.

No one touched the drinks and Jason looked relieved. 'We don't want no blood here,' Jason said. 'We don't want nobody spoil Dolphin reputation.'

'Dolphin done have bad reputation awready,' Screwface mumbled. 'We can't make it worse. I say burn their arse.'

'I see why you say that,' Jason told him, his eyes pausing on Screwface's distorted jaw. 'But common sense tell me you don't burn people alive, not even if them is dog. Is why we have to stop this. Who' inside the station now?'

'All of them, I fink.' Leroy said. 'Except Steel Rod.'

'Where Steel Rod gone?'

'By his woman – where else?'

She remembered Jason pressing his chin down on his chest, his cheeks puffed out, the hairs on his upper lip agitated by his breath. When he raised his head he was smiling. 'I get the answer from your answer, Leroy. Find their wimmen and bring them here. If their mother not around bring the grandmother.' He paused a while, his shoulders twitching. 'Their child-mother too, and make sure she bring the children.'

'And if they don't want to come?' Leroy wanted to know.

Jason showed Leroy his teeth. 'Tell them the truth, Leroy! Tell them we got a whole heap ov young-people in Dolphin

Junction ready to burn down the police station with their man inside. Tell them to stay home if they want their man to roast.'

Jason's eyes had gone wide, as if he were already seeing the burning men.

'Hold on!' He'd raised an arm, left the shop and strolled over to the youths, his shirt unbuttoned, his barrel belly exposed.

In the hot morning light, their faces were expressionless as stones while the shopkeeper stood before them, busy making gestures. The girl glanced at the small watch on her wrist then turned to the others. She tapped her watch and said something to Jason. Jason nodded and strolled back to the shop.

'I ask them for two hours,' he'd said. 'They give me one. Best I could do.'

She remembered that morning, four years ago, as if it happened yesterday. It was the longest, hottest hour of her life – from the time Leroy hit the road in his uncle's pickup truck, while Santana cut a fast white path to Victoria, in his boat.

The youths remained exactly as Jason left them, rigid and unmoving like statues on the asphalt. The world grew very, very quiet. She could hear the crackle of galvanised roofs expanding in the heat, the shivering fronds of the single coconut tree on the tip of the precipice above the south end of the bay, the high bright cries of chicken hawks circling above the Fédon hills.

The hour passed and Jason hurried over to the youths, this time begging with his whole body, the perspiration glossing his throat and chest, his cotton shirt limp with sweat.

Leroy made a story of it afterwards. Had the whole of Dolphin crying with laughter for months when he recalled the time the mothers and grandmothers descended on the village *from nowhere*, head-wraps tying down unruly hair, faces set like hoe blades, arms directed like cocked rifles at the bolted doors and windows of the police station, rebuking their men, ordering them to drop their weapons and come outta the blaastid station, or else... 'Shoot me! Kill me! Me! – your own mother, because you done born with curse already! And when you finish shoot me, shoot your blaastid child-mother *and* your own children! Is blight you have! Is like hell not hot enough for you, so you want to burn twice! Bring y'arse out here!'

Even the young people who'd come to smoke them out were subdued by the raking voices.

And all the while there was Jason choking with laughter as the men left their guns and walked out of the building. 'Bloodless coup!' he'd shouted. 'That's a world record! And is Dolphin people make it happen.'

He'd turned to Ada grinning. 'Is woman who rule de world! Y'all just dunno it yet.'

Now here was Jason, four years later, offering them free drinks. Again!

Before she set out for Jason's shop, Ada pressed a cheek against the crack of Daniel's bedroom door. He was on his back staring at the ceiling, the light from the kerosene lamp yellowing his face. She pushed the front door open, reached down towards the corner and retrieved her holstered gaff. She slung the small canvas bag on her shoulder and stepped into the late evening.

A sickly moon hung low over the Fédon hills – a smear of brightness smothered by the rolling mists up there. The sky above it had gone so purple it was almost black. It made her think of childhood stories about a young horseman, the colour of polished nutmegs, up there in that high white place of wind and rocks. Old People called it *vilaj-la anho van-a* – the village above the wind. There were tales of Dolphin women climbing the fern covered slopes to find the horseman and harvest his seed to give new birth to ancient gods.

A shallow concrete gutter was all that separated Jason's shop from the main road. He'd named his place, The Parlour – a long flat-roofed building inherited from his father, a stonemason. Plastic strip curtains hid most of the space behind the bar – a long gloomy room where Dolphin men waged drunken battles with dominoes, dice and darts before taking the rest of the war home to their women.

Behind the counter, a battalion of rum bottles sat on shelves that climbed all the way up to the ceiling – some of them winking fabulous shades of yellow, pink and blue in the light of the gas lamp he'd hung from the rafter. At the far left of the space, more shelves with dry goods.

The shop was heaving with the cough and rumble of men. Women crowded the entrance, arms folded across their chests, nervous eyes switching to and from either end of the main road. No children except Tarvi – Alice's haunted ten-year-old boy-child, tough as a wood knot, quick as a fly and just as impossible to swat away.

Jason was brushing the surface of the counter with his bare palms, his cleaning cloth on his shoulder. Ada couldn't figure out when Dolphin started turning to the big shopkeeper. He was tight as a whelk with his money. He rented his house and slept in his shop. Would harass a man to death for every single penny owed him. And yet he would readily dip into his bag of rice, sugar or dried milk and his barrel of salted meat to give to a hungry woman and her child, sometimes taking the parcel to her doorstep and leaving it there.

'The way I see it,' he said, 'we got a hurricane coming. Any time now it going to hit.'

'Jason! You call people here in curfew time to give dem parable? Talk plain, man!' That was Boose – brusque as usual and damn impatient.

'What I saying is…' Jason lifted his big radio off the shelf behind him and laid it heavily on the counter. That radio was a thing of wonder. Black metal, bristling with knobs and dials and switches. Two forward facing metal handles. On the front speaker grill in silver lettering, the word Grundig. Six glass windows. Printed in white, just below the first window, Sattelit 3400.

Jason talked about his radio as if it were a living thing. Stella, he said, plugged him into the world. It brought him voices from places on the planet he hadn't known existed. It gave him the ears of God. In fact, if God spoke at all, whatever message he got for this shitty world, it would come through this Grundig Satellit.

'They coming,' Tarvi shouted.

'Who coming?' Jason said.

'Soljers, I hearin de jitney.'

In the sudden silence, they heard a low throbbing in the air.

'Everybody inside,' Jason said. 'Move back, fellas. Give them woman room.' He reached up and slid back the strip curtains.

The men moved further back into the long room. Ada crowded in with the other women.

Jason raised the lid of his big cooler and began laying bottles of soft drinks, three at a time, on the counter. Young Cissy slipped past him and with rapid fluid movements, began handing out the bottles of Fanta, Coke and Sprite while Leroy, with the same quick efficiency, laid dominoes and draught boards on the tables.

By the time the vehicles stopped outside everyone was holding a drink. Ada stayed beside the door, her gaze shifting between Jason and the entrance.

'Relax,' Jason mouthed.

A slim-boned youth, the peak of his cap pulled low over his forehead, pushed in his head then stepped in. Good looking. Serious face. Crisp uniform. The usual Makarov on his hip. The two behind him looked even younger.

'Busy night, fellas; not so?' Jason said.

'Comrade, y'all didn' hear the General' orders on the radio?'

'Everybody hear it,' Jason twirled his cleaning cloth. '"Stay inside. Anybody demonstrate or disturb the peace will be shot on sight" Right?'

He dropped his cleaning cloth on the counter. 'Take a look, young-fella. All ov us inside. And none ov us demonstrating or disturbing the General' peace.'

'Is orders we following, sir.'

'Same orders y'all follow to kill de Commander-in-Chief and –'

'Boose, shut your fuckin mouth!' Jason's voice was a thunderclap across the room. He wiped his brows with the back of his hand then opened his palms at the soldiers. The big man's chest was heaving. 'Is I who invite everybody here to tell them what the General not telling us. That he gone and give Reagan excuse to pound we arse into the sea. I ain got no doubt that Yankee army coming to invade us. Them Cubano saying it; them Russian saying it. I hearing it on sideband radio from Florida and Miami. Even Adams, that fuckin Bajan crook talking about it too.'

'We know dat,' the young man said. He sounded almost boastful.

Jason leaned forward squinting as if he could barely see the youth. 'And that don't worry you?'

'Nuh!'

Jason scanned the room. 'Lemme tell y'all what not worryin this young-fella here. Battleship name Guam that Reagan send to murder Arabman in Lebanon – he turn it round and sendin it here instead. That battleship almost same size as this island, y'all hear? It carryin fighter plane and helicopter on it. Radio say, they even sending nuclear submarine becuz,' Jason raised a finger. 'Ain got no way they going let the littlest country in the world cut their arse and get away with it. Before that happen, they will blow up the island and kill every fuckin one ov us. Specially since Beirutman been bombing their arse like crazy. Is a lynchin them want, to feel good about themself again. And we give them excuse. How I know?' Jason jabbed a finger at his radio, 'God voice tell me.'

Tarvi had come to stand in front of Jason. The boy was staring up at him with open mouth and wide startled eyes, his lips mimicking the movement of Jason's mouth. Jason noticed him and something in him subsided. He rested a hand on Tarvi's head and the boy nuzzled into him.

The young soldiers turned to leave, the slim one cocking his chin at the room. 'Is we duty to defend the Revo –'

'The Revo dead, young-fella. Last Wednesday y'all kill it,' Jason threw back.

'The order still stand,' the young man said.

'And while it standing, we sitting down right here.'

The vehicle was still out there. Ada could hear the metallic clicking of the engine as it cooled.

A sleepy voice, thick as tar, floated from the back of the room. 'Jason that was provocation.'

'I dunno about you, Fisheye, but I tired ov being afraid.'

Jason passed his cloth across the radio, lifted it and replaced it on the shelf.

The room subsided into murmurs. Alice was whispering something to Meena. The nervousness Ada had seen in her earlier was still there. If anything, Jason's words had made it worse. She was fanning her face with both hands and muttering what sounded like a prayer.

With her shoulder against the door frame, Ada threw a long sidewise glance at the room. The nearest faces were almost bleached out by the white light of the gas lamp. The gloom in the far corners at the back had reduced the bodies back there to shadow and shape.

She'd never lost her wariness of these men; the cruelty behind those eyes; their appetite for revenge; the stupid little things they were capable of killing for. Prompted by those thoughts, she paused on the broad shoulders of Kaba, Daniel's uncle. Kaba had his big head lowered, the thick shoulders hunched forward, aware, no doubt, of her presence.

It worried her that the jeep was still out there. Mebbe they'd radioed for help to clear out Jason's shop? She lowered her head and cocked her ears. The soldiers' words came to her in snatches – *crazy big fella ...chupid people...deal with him...*

A voice cut in, querulous and impatient. 'I thought Jazzman say Trigger not living far.'

*Jazzman –*

Oh God! She muttered, and launched herself out of the shop. The heads of the militiamen shot up as she swung past them, crossed the road and took the stony alley towards the beach, barely managing to keep her balance. She emerged gasping; stopped abruptly at the sight of Daniel in the doorway, the light of the gas lamp spilling past his slim frame onto the man at the foot of her step. Jazzman, rigid as an oar in his army uniform, staring up into her son's face – this man who never looked her in the eyes, who would call out her boychild from her house any hour of the night or day with just a whistle from the road, or the curl of a finger. She hated him for the fluttering unease he stirred in her, the danger she sensed in this soljerman to whom her son was drawn like a gar fish to the tip of a baited hook.

Ada stood a few yards from the mouth of the alleyway, her heart tripping over; held there by a terrible, frightened fascination. What was it in that voice that had such power over her son? She could pick it out from a crowd of thousands, even in her sleep – staccato and pulsing. But she'd also heard it drop low, and guttural and breathy. She pictured Jazzman's wet unsmiling mouth, his big brown eyes, the tapering arms thick at the shoulders, slim-wristed at the end.

Daniel turned away from the door and went into the house. The man shuffled sideways, took two steps back and became a shadow against the side of the house.

He seemed to sense her presence. He edged once again into the pool of light at the bottom of the steps and began peering into the darkness at the thundering beach behind him.

She was less than ten oar-lengths from Jazzman, conscious of the weight of the sheathed gaff hanging on her shoulder, and it came to her with a sudden brutal clarity that tonight she was going to kill this man if he tried to take away her son.

Daniel returned to the doorway in his militia gear, fumbling with the buttons of his khaki shirt. Finished, he reached down to tie the laces of his boots.

'Where you going?' she called.

He straightened up as if he had been struck. Ada stepped out of the shadows and lengthened her stride towards the man. He stepped back, his eyes on the unsheathed gaff.

A gull-cry came from Daniel, 'Ma!'

'You not taking my fuckin son nowhere with you,' she said.

'I just inform Trig – erm, Daniel that we facing an invasion and –'

'Is y'all who call them. Fuck outta my yard. Go fight invasion with your fam'ly, not with my child.'

She swung her arm at Daniel. 'Inside!'

He looked at the man.

'Inside,' she snarled.

'Do what your mother say,' Jazzman said. He lifted a hand, made a small circular movement with his head, then left with quick silent strides across the clearing. There came the crunch and rattle of pebbles in the alleyway.

Ada was shivering when she faced Daniel in the house. 'In all my life, Daniel, I ever raise my hand at you? I ever maltreat you?' She was ashamed of the way she sounded – choked and plaintive.

'He could ha shoot you, Ma!' he said, sullen faced, his eyes brimming with resentment.

'I tell you this, Daniel, if you try to leave this house tonight – I – I –'

'He could'ha shoot you!' he repeated.

She took a breath and swallowed. 'And what you would'ha done, Daniel?' She asked quietly, with trembling lips because she really, really wanted to know.

Daniel pulled off his shirt, then his boots and retreated into his bedroom.

She stood in the hallway, her head lowered, ears tuned into the sounds on the main road. An engine grated into life, tyres yelped. The drone of the vehicle faded southwards. Then all was quiet.

*

Ada pulled two pillows off her bed, dropped them on the floor and sat facing her open bedroom door. She could get some rest this way but the discomfort would keep her hovering on the edge of sleep, without falling in completely.

She closed her eyes and tried to calm herself. What Jason said to those young soldiers tonight about the next disaster that was about to descend on them had made it clearer and more real to her than the radio could have ever done. Invasion – *like a hurricane.* She should have told Jason that it could never be like a hurricane. With a hurricane a pusson know what to expect and how to prepare for it. With a hurricane the sea give a pusson notice in advance. By the deep-water creatures it vomits on the beach. The sea changes its voice. Ocean birds arrive and populate the hillsides and the trees.

You feel it – in the suffocation as the ocean sucks in its breath, leaving you with little air to breathe. Then there is the pressure on the eardrums that might last a coupla days.

Faced with that, you do what sensible people do: you take your boat off the water, drag it under your house or anchor it to a tree or rock. You drive a few extra pounds of nails into your roof, batten down your windows, bolt your door and wait for the coming rage.

And when it done, yuh walk out into a mash-up, scrub-down world. Yuh walk into a clean day. Yuh start all over again.

Now Alice's words surfaced in her mind, *We dunno what to do,* and for a moment Ada felt the throbbing terror that had taken hold of her friend. How do you prepare yourself for what Jason said was coming? Where did you find the strength? Where was the gathering voice to rouse the island, bring them all together so they could stand and face it? Three days ago, on the old stone fort in St George's, The General and his friends had destroyed it.

*

She'd been dreaming of dolphins when she snapped out of her doze.

She realised that she'd fallen asleep.

She remained on the floor, her breath shallow, blinking at the fluttering flame of the kerosene lamp on her bedside table. Daylight poured in through the half-open front door. She sprang to her feet and rushed to Daniel's room. The bed lay empty; the single cotton sheet under which he slept was a grey tangle on the floor.

Now she was out of the house and running towards the alleyway, the ends of her night dress gathered in her hands. A sound – flat and sharp like a snapped oar – halted her and turned her round. It was Man-Man, her mute cousin, up to his knees in the brightening water; his Rasta lox heaped on top his head like a crown of thorns. He swung a long arm seaward. It took a while before she spotted the red float, like a bead of blood on the heaving water, then her son's head a little way ahead of it. Ada looked at her craft, even though she knew her float would not be there. Daniel was now arcing inland towards Roland Bay, three miles down the coast.

'Help me!' she cried, turning back towards the house, her mind on the two outboard engines in her room. Man-Man brought his palms together again. Now, his arm was directing her eyes towards the road that overlooked Roland Bay. He mimed a steering wheel, dropped his left hand and shifted a gear. Up there, through the roadside greenery she caught the glint of a vehicle.

A hard wind rose off the sea and threw sand in her face. Ada lowered herself on the sand and began calling. And the sound that came from her must have been terrible because it started off the dogs, then the chickens, and Santana's lil baby-girl next door.

And now, from the edges of her vision the women were scrambling from their houses running along the beach towards her, stooped at the edge of the water, facing the ocean and screaming her boy-child's name.

# Afterword: Remembering the 'Revo'

## Dr Brian Meeks
Brown University

THE MORNING OF THE US-led invasion of Grenada on 25 October 1983 is indelibly marked in my memory, etched on the core of my being. I am Jamaican, but lived in revolutionary Grenada and early that morning, from the far-away comfort of my parents' home in Kingston, immediately recognised the voice of the Radio Free Grenada broadcaster Edwin Frank as he called pleadingly for popular resistance: '...United States paratroopers have invaded Grenada with helicopter gunships! All Grenadians report immediately to your militia bases! Block all roads and obstruct the enemy's progress...'

Frank's voice was so familiar, as I had worked with him in the tiny Grenadian media fraternity for two years, he at Radio Free Grenada and I as sometime editor for the national newspaper the *Free West Indian*. I had left Grenada a month before from the small Pearl's Airport, precariously positioned against the sea on the eastern shore of the island, to travel home in order to begin my PhD work on the Grenada Revolution. My expectation was to return the following summer, in order to record and try to explain the social and political changes that were taking place, entirely anticipating that the revolutionary transformation that began in 1979, would be continuing ahead at full steam. Nothing prepared me for what was about to occur.

Not many weeks before, I had been in a meeting with Prime Minister Maurice Bishop and Deputy PM Bernard

Coard along with a number of New Jewel Movement (NJM) comrades. The discussion was around how to best deliver a public education program we had started a few months earlier. It was on Grenadian and Caribbean history and politics, and the main text was a little book by the American journalist Cathy Sunshine and its name, *Grenada: the Peaceful Revolution*, suggested its content. The discussion was lively and animated and featured the usual Caribbean banter of jokes and personal jabs that was typical of the many interactions I had seen between Bernard and Maurice. There was no hint of animosity nor of rancor. Thinking back on those last months, I do recall, however, an odd question I was asked by two party members one hot August morning on the steps outside the NJM party headquarters on Lucas Street. Deep in conversation before being distracted by my presence, they stopped in mid-sentence and asked 'Comrade, what are the qualities you respect in a leader?' I was more than a little startled and don't remember what I answered, but I do recall finding it very strange as, until then, I could think of no good reason for it. Maurice Bishop was, as far as anyone could tell, the unrivalled leader of the Grenadian Revolution from its inception on 13 March 1979 through all the rapid, hectic years that had passed since then.

It had been a tumultuous and unforgettable four and a half years of revolutionary rule, following the overthrow of the corrupt regime of strongman, mystic and UFO-lover Eric Gairy. There were, indeed, naysayers, who drew attention to the often-arbitrary detention of numerous people – so-called 'counters' – perceived as activists or simply as being hostile to the People's Revolutionary Government (PRG). But somewhat contrary to this narrative, there had been little shedding of blood when power was taken and the NJM had been careful not to dismiss civil servants from office just because of their support for the Gairy regime. Opponents also pointed to the closure of the *Torchlight* newspaper under PRG accusations that it was involved in a destabilisation campaign and saw this as an ominous sign that the NJM was heading in a Cuban direction, significantly bolstered by the Cuban military and economic support for the country and the close personal relationship between Bishop and Fidel Castro.

However, when I first landed in Grenada in the summer of 1981, it seemed to me that a significant, perhaps even overwhelming, majority of Grenadians were of a different mind and gave their passionate support to Bishop and the 'Revo' as they fondly called it. I saw this in August, 1981 in the Queen's Park, the public pavilion just outside of St George's. Almost every calypso in the annual Calypso King Competition was political and all lauded the direction of the country. Grenada was 'moving fast', the National Airport project, started under the People's Revolutionary Government (PRG) with help from the Cubans, was making the country proud; Little Grenada was no longer the butt-end of jokes in the Eastern Caribbean because of Gairy, but was making progress, and in the words of the popular revolutionary chant, Grenada was moving 'Forward Ever and Backward Never!' Rapid social and economic change was under way. A maternity leave law was in the making along with new gender equality laws, and jobs at the Airport site and in dozens of infrastructural and housing projects were leading to unemployment falling to unprecedented levels. The annual Budget Debates would soon begin, allowing tens of thousands of citizens to play some role in discussing and formulating policy for annual revenue and expenditure, through trade unions, professional associations and the nascent community organisations for popular participation – the Parish Councils. I saw this grassroots enthusiasm and support most evidently in the 1982 'Heroes of the Homeland' military manoeuvre – a popular mobilisation of the armed militia in the face of repeated hostile utterances from the Reagan administration and subsequent US military exercises in and around the Puerto Rican island of Vieques in early 1982. This mock US invasion, aimed at rescuing imaginary US hostages from fictional Caribbean islands called 'Amber and the Amberdines' (involving 120,000 US military personnel, 250 ships and over 1,000 planes), was not just a training exercise, but a thinly veiled reference (and threat) to Grenada and the Grenadines. In response, Grenada's 'Heroes of the Homeland' manoeuvre saw tens of thousands of militia supporters gather over that weekend, enduring testing drills over the mountains, and slogging through mosquito-infested mangroves on the coast in preparation for what was at the time expected to be mercenary-led invasion. This response culminated in an island-wide motorcade of packed military vehicles with participants and supporters lining the roads and chanting, 'The manoovah, will never ovah!' Not one irresponsible shot was fired; not one person was injured. The Revolution from what I could see in 1982, despite the presence of clear detractors, seemed to be safe and secure, protected by the solid support of the poor and working people.

But there was a deep and unseen fissure at the heart of this tender political process. A wooden and dogmatic application of 'Leninism' as an organisational strategy by the Party, insisted on the maintenance of a small, elite vanguard party with a core of tried and tested members – Lenin's strategy for the Bolsheviks of 'better fewer, but better' in the peculiar conditions of Tsarist Russia. This tiny cadre was unable to bear the administrative strain of both running itself, the country and a revolution. Members were physically collapsing under the strain, and the pressure was felt most keenly by female party members, who, in addition to party, state and often militia responsibilities, invariably shouldered primary roles in the raising of their children. These stresses were also reflected at the very top in emerging differences between Bishop and Coard over administrative duties – their division of labour and of authority – and undermined what had previously been a cordial, even fraternal relationship. In 1982 Bernard Coard resigned from the Political Bureau, the highest, if hidden organ of the Party and by extension the entire process, though retaining his official position as Minister of Finance and Deputy Prime Minister. He had expressed frustration over some decisions that had been taken as well as its lack of organisational efficiency – a critique that was inevitably directed at the Bureau's Chairman, Maurice Bishop. However, the response of the Political Bureau to this unanticipated decision, was, rather than rethink the entire organisational strategy, to intensify 'Leninism', in other words, double down on work, party discipline and the requirements for membership. The inevitable (at least in hindsight) result, was further collapse and demoralisation, leading, in early 1983 to a not unsurprising decision to call on Coard, the acknowledged organisational and tactical leader, to rejoin the Bureau, but this time in an elevated position of Joint Leader with Bishop. 'Joint Leadership' was not an unknown feature in the history of the New Jewel Movement. It had started in 1973 out of the merger of two organisations, the Movement for the Assemblies of the People (MAP) and the Joint Endeavor for Welfare, Education and Liberation (JEWEL). Bishop was head of MAP and Unison Whiteman led JEWEL. At first there had been a sharing of leadership, though by 1976, Bishop was the undoubted head of the NJM. Then, in the years leading up to the 1979 taking of power and beyond, Bishop and Coard worked in tandem in an unspoken sharing of decision-making and power. However, after March 13, with Bishop as Prime Minister and both his national and international profile enhanced as the leader of the Grenadian Revolution, the old balance had been upended. Within the Party, members could imagine juggling with the geometry of leadership – Bishop's charisma, wedded to Coard's organisational strengths – to improve its ability to address grave national and international problems. But outside the Party, (as, indeed, for Bishop himself) this could only be perceived as an unprecedented and unnecessary demotion of the one and only respected leader, Maurice Bishop.

This is exactly how things unraveled and many of the tragic events have been captured in great detail elsewhere. In short, Bishop at first agreed with the decision, followed by rejoicing among the gathered comrades; but then he traveled on official business to Eastern Europe and Cuba and on return, rescinded his decision, leading to consternation in the Party. Shortly thereafter, a rumour hit the street that Bernard Coard and his wife Phyllis were plotting to kill Maurice. When the leadership sought to find out where this dangerous and damaging rumour came from, a close member of Bishop's security detail testified that it was Maurice himself who had started the rumour; Maurice refused to respond to this accusation, leading to a fatal decision to place him under house arrest, which brought the entire standoff for the first time to an immediately enraged public. In the days following, large popular demonstrations began, leading on October 19 to a huge march that freed Bishop from detention at his home. The crowd, now with Bishop at the front, headed to the main military installation in St George's – Fort Rupert – and without resistance, took it over. A military contingent of the People's Revolutionary Army arrived at the Fort to retake it and came under fire, leading to a bloody exchange, eventually recapturing the Fort and taking Bishop, Jacqueline Creft and some of his closest supporters prisoner. Then, in a cruel and infamous moment, Bishop, Creft, Unison Whiteman and others among Bishop's closest supporters, were placed against a wall of the Fort and shot.

The killing of Maurice Bishop and his associates, alienated the NJM from the vast majority of Grenadians of whatever political persuasion and removed the political basis for PRG rule. This provided the opportunity for the US-led invasion, which had been in the planning at least since Ronald Reagan's inauguration in 1981, when he referred to the Airport Project as a threat to US national interests, and had been rehearsed to perfection in the previously mentioned 'Amber and the Amberdines' military exercise. Without the support of the united population and with the Commonwealth Caribbean divided over whether to facilitate or oppose US intervention, an invasion was inevitable. In the United Nations, the overwhelming majority opposed it as a breach of international law; but with the fig leaf of a few Caribbean supporters, the US felt fully confident to launch her war machine. In the early morning of October 25, 1983, it came, with 6,000 US troops, strongly supported by aircraft carriers and the overwhelming weapons and paraphernalia of a superpower. After six days of relentless bombardment and fierce resistance from the PRA and some contingents of the militia – a totally unanticipated surprise to the US forces – the Grenadian Revolution ended. Former leaders of the country, including Bernard Coard and his wife Phyllis, were rounded up, displayed with blindfolds and half-naked, like common criminals and ultimately, all members of the Central Committee of the NJM (despite some not having been in the country or sick in hospital at the time of the conflict) were conveniently charged with conspiracy in the killing of Maurice Bishop and his allies. In the nearly four decades that have cascaded since those dark times, the Grenadian prisoners have been tried under deeply flawed circumstances, condemned to death, pardoned at the last moment and ultimately, in 2011, freed from prison. Much of the literature written on the Revolution, has focused on these last days, the clash of personalities, the inner party struggle and the tragic denouement, leading to Bishop's death.

Yet, there is another story to be written, which is hidden behind the crisis of October, of young women and men attempting to tell their own story, of ordinary Grenadians in their community groups, parish councils and militia squadrons, giving new meaning through popular participation to the deeper Caribbean history of resistance against slavery and colonialism and of attempting, if ultimately failing, to challenge and add their own page to notions of sovereignty, freedom and liberation through their everyday support of the Revo and in the last desperate, rearguard resistance against invasion. This half of the Grenada Revolution, partly captured in Jacob Ross's poignant story, is still to be fully told.

# One Hell of a Shot

## Gioconda Belli

MY BOOTS ARE WET. My shirt is wet. My pants and socks are wet, and I can't take any of them off. When you are at war, camped in the jungle, you set up your hammock at night and keep all your clothes on, whether or not they're dry. You don't take anything off. No sir. You must be ready to get up and go. Armed and kitted out in a flash. Sleeping with my boots and clothes on is one of the hardest things I have had to get used to since I was recruited to fight the Contras. Before this I have slept in my birthday suit ever since I can remember. In my hometown, San Carlos, next to the San Juan River, it is so fucking hot you can cook an egg on the roof. My mother always worried that if an earthquake struck, I would end up naked in the street. I did a few times, until she laid out an old tablecloth over a chair near the door so that I could grab it on the go and cover my privates. I miss my mother, her cooking especially. I am on the skinny side but not for lack of food. Fortunately, I was strong to start with. War and hunger go together. We are always hungry.

I should go to sleep. It is always a struggle for me, no matter how tired I am. My mind insists on taking me back home every night. I see the street of the pharmacy where I worked as an assistant. I want to become a doctor. I liked to see people come by, after they were cured, to thank m boss. They get so emotional, women especially. My boss is a doctor of sorts. Short, big moustache, the white overcoat always spotless. I never saw someone who paid more attention to his appearance. 'Trust is part of the cure,' he would say. He was my inspiration to become a doctor. I had it all planned. After my conscription, if I survived, I would ask to be sent to university. Maybe the Party would send me to Cuba. I would be 21 by the time I finished military service. At seventeen, I had voted already. The Revolution ruled that if, at sixteen, you could be recruited for military service and die for your country, then you certainly had the right to vote. I didn't know if I would ever vote again. I have seen so many *compañeros* die during the five months I have been posted to the Gaspar García Laviana light infantry battalion.

My buddy Byron and I were picked up by the army the same day. I didn't like war, but there was no chance of hiding, escaping and crossing the river into Costa Rica, like some of my friends had done. You needed money to do that and my mother had none. Every day she worked washing and ironing clothes at the mayor's house. My poor mother. No doubt she was missing me right now. She always went to bed at eight at night. When I was little, I used to fall asleep listening to her saying Ave Marias and the Lord's Prayer as she slid the prayer beads of the rosary between her fingers. I wish I had brought a rosary with me, but she could not give me the only one she owned. Instead she had a small wooden cross made for me by Chema, our neighbour, the carpenter. I wore it around my neck tied with a strip of leather. I had never been very religious, but in battle I prayed. I think the cross had magic powers. I held it when I took cover from the bullets whizzing right above my head.

I was dreaming that a gigantic wasp was about to bite my head. She had a long gold sword for a tail, and she was about to plunge it in my ear when I woke terrified, my hands shielding my head. Before I knew it, I had sat up on the hammock and grabbed my AK. Dawn was beginning to break through the dark jungle. Hundreds of birds had begun to get excited. Birds were incredibly noisy at sunrise. Tourists that went up the San Juan river couldn't stop talking about the quantity of birds they heard. They thought it was amazing. Not me, man. I wished they would shut up and let me sleep at least another half hour. I laid back in my hammock, eyes closed. That was the first time I heard the plane. It had probably flown over us and turned into a wasp in my dreams, but now the sound was faint. It had to be far by now.

Why did we walk so much? My buddy Byron and I would curse our luck to have ended up in a small infantry force patrolling an area near our home turf. Contras, led by the ex-Sandinista Edén Pastora, operated in the region. I had admired Pastora, as a kid, but his army was as much of a sham as he was; still the gringos nurtured it. They supplied them with weapons, food and uniforms that they dropped from the air. It was hard for me to understand why Pastora, who had led a commando that took Managua's National Palace in 1978 and who my mother loved – so handsome, she would say, so brave – had betrayed the revolution. Traitors were the worst kind of people, and he was such a show-off. Often at night, we heard him on the radio. The sombre commander of our battalion turned it on so that we could hear the stupid things he said. To go from revolutionary to CIA stooge was unforgivable. I hated him even more for being the reason we had to walk for hours in the heavy September rains, sliding about in the mud, tortured by mosquitoes in swamps under thick vegetation. Another thing I didn't understand from rich tourists was their fascination with nature. God Almighty! In Nicaragua, we spend our lives running away from it. Sure, the sight of a river among trees is pretty from a distance, but to be in it twenty-four-seven was another thing. I preferred to see the outside from inside, from Don Lucas's bar at the edge of the port, for instance. But tourists, they go looking for danger. It was their thing, to walk in the jungle, 'hiking' they called it. They were willing to risk snake bites and whatever just to see a big tree, or a goddamn monkey. Incomprehensible.

The main item I was carrying was an SA7, something I had been especially trained to operate. It was ten pounds unarmed, almost fifteen with the projectile inside – a long, green Soviet-made, surface-to-air missile, shaped like a thick bamboo pole. To me it felt as if I was carrying the Holy Cross. It was attached to a harness I slid my arms through that kept it square across my back. It made my movements clumsy. At the training camp, the commander always commended me on the care I took to keep it clean, the battery charged. I had liked the instructor. He was thorough and friendly, a good storyteller who professed to love books and teaching. He liked that I planned to become a doctor after the war. By contrast, Lieutenant Serafin Mendoza, who was our Battalion's commander, was one of those people who think authority demands a tough, inscrutable pose. He rarely smiled, and he took it upon himself to make my life difficult. Being wiry and skinny with a mop of dark hair that fell across my forehead, he took me to be weak, being a fan of banter; he thought me ridiculous, having a pinky finger that was crooked; he made fun of the way I ate. He tried his best to humiliate me and put me down. Byron was convinced it must have been because I reminded him of someone he hated. The morale of our ten-man squad was not particularly good thanks to him. His harsh exterior hid an insecure, indecisive, and scared leader. I didn't fear him, but I was careful not to provoke him.

We had been marching from El Tule in the direction of the San Juan River. It had stopped raining and the afternoon was cool under a cloudy sky. Byron and I were at the rear of the line advancing through a clearing. There was a hut we figured belonged to the owner of that patch of land. I was thinking it was strange not to see any smoke at that time of day when normally families would begin cooking dinner and making tortillas. Then we heard a shot.

We spread out through the bushes finding cover while we got our AKs locked and loaded. Another shot came from the hut. We were at a disadvantage in that open space, trying to hide behind the scrawny shrubs in the clearing. It was clear to me we had to make a run towards the thicker part of the forest on our left and try to approach the shooters from the rear of the hut. After a third shot, I heard our guys at the front returning fire. It was easy to tell there were not many enemies firing at us. No doubt the first shot had come from whoever was guarding the access to the hut. More men were probably inside it. I told Byron to cover me while I ran towards the rear. There were shots fired from the shack but already the rest of our troop had seen my intentions and were covering me while they advanced towards the front of the hut.

As I approached the back, I saw two Contras trying to sneak out. They also saw me. Startled I pulled the trigger. It was them or me. The weight of the surface-to-air missile on my back almost made me lose my balance. It was fortunate. It took my mind off any pity I might have otherwise felt for the two guys I was spraying with bullets, my heart's racing was what made me react so quickly, not giving them a chance.

Byron went to check if the woods were clear, meanwhile Lieutenant Mendoza walked with two men into the hut to make sure nobody else was hiding in there. He came back and patted me on the back. 'Well done, Flaco,' he said, 'and you didn't fall on the SAM either!' He had barely turned his back to join the others when I began shaking uncontrollably. My legs felt like rubber and I had to sit on a log. Byron saw what was happening to me. The others were busy collecting the weapons the dead Contras had left and checking their pockets. It had been the first time I had killed anybody face to face and I couldn't believe it. I couldn't look at the bodies. I felt nauseous. Byron sat next to me and gave me a hug. It was brief, but I could tell he understood what I was feeling. Friendship is a good, deep thing, I thought, holding back tears – no way I was going to let anyone see me cry! Byron and I had been together throughout the war, but we were rarely as close as we had been in our hometown. There were moments when I thought the experience was going to distance us forever. I was glad to be wrong.

'Come on, girls,' Lieutenant Mendoza called, when he saw us together. It pissed me off. He was pretending to be immune to what we had all just been through. His back so straight, his chest pushed out like a rooster's.

Then we heard the plane.

'Take cover!' Mendoza yelled.

I moved near a bush but didn't hide. Instead I signaled to Byron to help me arm the weapon. Took us ten seconds. He mounted the SAM on my shoulder. I had been waiting for an opportunity and this could be it. I felt the adrenalin rush, my body alert and tense. With Byron's help I was ready in position in less than a minute. It was nearly dusk. Storm clouds, mixed together with cumulus ones, darkened the yellowish light. We kept hearing the plane, but it was hard to tell whether it was coming or going or to see it through the rain clouds. Come on, come on fucking clouds! I kept thinking, praying.

I heard Mendoza coming my way, saying something about not wasting an expensive missile. I would never make the shot. I was a wimp. Flaco! he shouted. I paid no attention, my eyes fixed on the sky. A cloud moved and then I saw the flickering light, the wing of the plane flying low. I didn't think twice. The trigger was pulled and the missile slipped its surly bonds. Byron stood beside me gaping upwards. I knew it was a good shot. I knew my aim was true. The plane was flying at no more than 700 feet, and the missile would seek the heat of the engine. Time stopped. The jungle noises stopped. Mendoza stopped. My heart felt as if it too had stopped, and I grabbed the cross at my neck and held it tight. The cloud had obscured the plane again. When we saw the fireball it was as if in slow motion, rippling out across the sky, bending it. We just stood and watched, spellbound. The next thing we saw was a parachute opening up high above the jungle canopy. Someone had managed to jump out, someone we had to capture. The plane dived and there was another explosion as it hit the ground. Everybody screamed in unison. We started jumping and hugging each other and laughing. I saw Mendoza walking towards me. I saw a smile, the first big fucking smile I'd ever seen on that face of his. He gave me a strong, victorious handshake: 'That was one hell of shot! One hell of a shot!' He kept saying it, over and over. I had never felt so good.

As the excitement subsided, it dawned on us that the Contras we had disturbed must have been waiting there for the drop. We had to get to the downed plane quickly.

'What about the guy who parachuted?' Byron asked.

We split into two groups, five of us with Mendoza would go find the crash site, the other five would go look for the parachutist. If they couldn't find him before nightfall, they were to stay wherever they could to spend the night and keep looking in the morning.

Mendoza, Byron, I, and the rest didn't have far to walk. We found the plane about one and half kilometres from our position. It was a big aircraft, a cargo model C123 that I later learned had been used in Vietnam. The sight of it horrified us. It stank of gasoline and charred flesh. There were three blackened bodies in the cabin. The plane had snapped in the middle and was teeming with supplies, much of which was scattered around the crash site: backpacks, boots, food rations. When the flames died down, which didn't take long, Mendoza made some of the guys walk into the smoke-filled body of the plane, covering their faces with bandanas, and take out ammunition and guns so they wouldn't light up and be lost. We recovered 60 AKs and a ton of ammunition. *I shot this plane down*, I kept thinking, staring at it, sprawled across the crash site. The enormous belly of the thing had become separated from the cockpit. I kept watch as two of the guys entered it to drag the bodies out. There was a short flight of steps leading up to the cabin. I looked at the dead when they were laid out next to the plane. I didn't feel the same way as with the Contras. I had done this from a distance. I had not seen any of them die right in front of me. It felt weird but I wasn't sorry. This was a gringo plane, a CIA aircraft for sure. I felt proud, I walked around it as if it belonged to me. I began to imagine myself as a hero back in my hometown. I would be in the paper. I imagined my mother attaching it to the wall of our house, telling everybody about her son's achievement.

Mendoza had radioed the regional command centre. A helicopter would be coming in the morning, he told us. It would bring photographers and journalists to see the site. He was excited and talkative. 'This is a huge deal, guys. This is proof that the CIA has been flying into Nicaragua to drop supplies to the Contras. This will really embarrass the Reagan administration. Big fuck up, big fuck up for them!' We took turns that night to guard the fallen plane. It became really cold and the mosquitoes were feasting on us, but the worst thing was the smell. Byron and I barely slept. We talked about all kinds of things.

At daybreak, Mendoza and two men went to look for Raul and the others, to make sure they had found the survivor.

The sun was overhead when we heard them approaching. I will never forget the sight. Raul, who was short and skinny was pulling behind him a blond, burly, blue-eyed giant with just a tiny piece of black cord that he'd used to tie his hands. The man looked dirty, tired, but seemed harmless, humble even, like a tame old horse. We walked back to the clearing. The journalists were expecting us at the hut where I had shot the Contras. The helicopter had landed. The photographer from *Barricada*, the FSLN's newspaper caught up with us before anybody else. He was the one who took that famous picture, the one that made the cover of newspapers all over the world.

We were flown to Managua in the helicopter. Byron, Raul and I were decorated by the head of the Army, General Humberto Ortega that same morning. The military from the high command were all there, laughing, congratulating themselves as if they had done the deed. They barely paid attention to us.

There was a special edition of the newspaper we got to see before we went home on the helicopter for a two-day leave.

Byron, Raul, and I were sitting in an air-conditioned waiting room at the High Command's office, when General Ortega's secretary came in with copies of it. She set it on the table in front of us. The photograph that the whole world would see took up most of the front page. There was Raul pulling the gringo that fell from the sky on the end of a piece of string. There was Byron walking behind.

'What the hell! Where am I?' I blurted out.

'There, there you are!' said Byron pointing. 'Don't you remember? You were walking by Hasenfus's side. Look, look!'[1]

I looked. In the photograph all I could see of myself was a sliver of arm, a sliver of leg, and the top of the SAM launcher peeking out behind the back of the gringo.

## Note

1. Photograph reproduced here: https://images.dailykos.com/images/309813/story_image/hasenfus.jpg?1476037358

# NICARAGUA, 1986

## Afterword: A Turning Point

Victor Figueroa Clark

THIS STORY TAKES PLACE in the midst of one of the most complex conflicts of the twentieth century, one that was part of, but extended beyond, the Cold War. For both sides, the war was part of a much bigger picture, involving revolutionary struggles in El Salvador and Guatemala, and the global 'correlation of forces' between socialism and imperialism. The revolution, and the United States' counter-revolutionary war, subsumed an indigenous-mestizo conflict, a rural-urban conflict, and an atheistic-religious conflict. It turbo-charged the development of a transnational alliance of anti-communist groups that brought together fascists and liberals, dictators and drug dealers, Zionists and Wahabbites, and stretched as far afield as South Korea. But the revolution also saw a flowering of socialist internationalism. This internationalism went from that of progressive Catholics, such as the Spanish priest Gaspar García Laviana, through to Western social-democrat brigadistas and also included members of ETA and the Baader–Meinhof, as well as the thousands of Latin Americans who fought for the revolution and aided its construction. At root, it was the war of the world's most powerful state against one of its poorest.

As Hobsbawn noted, revolutions create nations, and Nicaragua today is the creation of two major struggles against US imperialism. Firstly, that of Augusto César Sandino, the General of Free Men, who in Chilean poet Gabriela Mistral's words led his 'small crazy army' against the occupying US marines. Sandino was undefeated, but he was murdered during peace talks with the US-backed government at the behest of the US Ambassador. Secondly, that of the Frente Sandinista de Liberación Nacional (FSLN)'s later revolution in Sandino's name. Neither war was solely Nicaraguan, they inspired volunteers and supporters from across Latin America, who then took their revolutionary inspiration home with them. Nicaragua's struggles were therefore also episodes in the larger nation-building struggle of the people of Latin America, the Bolivarian dream of a single sovereign nation living in justice.

The 'Frente' created modern Nicaragua, but any political movement contains factions derived from sometimes minute, sometimes major differences in perspective and priority. Charismatic leaders and agreement over goals and methods reduce these differences, exile exacerbates them. Success brings new challenges and newcomers who have had little time to internalise the organisational ideology and culture. The 'Frente' had less than 200 surviving members in 1977, but grew to thousands in 1979. After the revolutionary victory, the FSLN institutionalised its factions, installing a collective leadership and giving each faction control over different areas of government. They largely held together through the difficulties of the 1980s, but defeat precedes division, and 1990 saw electoral defeat and shortly afterwards the collapse of the socialist world that had sustained Nicaragua. The 'Frente' suffered division, and within the 'Frente' disagreements emerged over how the Party should meet the challenges of a post-Cold War era, and the FSLN acrimoniously split.

But let us begin at the beginning.

On 19 July 1979, Sandinista guerrillas streamed into Managua and other towns and cities across Nicaragua as the National Guard followed General Somoza in fleeing the country. Everywhere the Sandinistas were greeted by cheering crowds. People cried tears of happiness and witnesses remember an intense collective joy. Behind the Sandinistas were two failed offensives in late 1977 and late 1978, and three months of heavy fighting from May-July 1979. In its efforts to stay in power the Somoza regime had killed some 40-50 thousand people. Many were young people shot as presumed rebels, or civilians killed as the air force bombed rebel neighbourhoods. The cities, particularly Managua, were already heavily damaged by the 1972 earthquake. Foreign debt amounted to over a billion dollars.

The Sandinistas did not need to destroy a state in order to make their revolution, they needed to build one. But the scale of the challenge was immense, and it encompassed every sphere. There was no healthcare system and no nationwide education system. There were tens of thousands forced to beg for a living, many more dwelling in shanty towns. There were thousands of armed militia members and criminal gangs who rejected central control. The little infrastructure that existed was heavily damaged. The economy had broken down. By July 1979 Nicaragua was, in the words of Costa Rican President Carazo Odio, 'a nation destroyed.' The US embassy agreed, 'It will be some time before the GRN has a grip on the enormous and complex problems it faces.'[1]

But the US was not going to sit back and let the Sandinista Government of National Reconstruction (GRN) get on with the job. Within six months the Carter administration had authorised funding for the political opposition in Nicaragua. At the same time, the US began building up a 'paramilitary strike force' made up of former members of the National Guard, anti-Castro Cubans, Guatemalan military personnel, and mercenaries.[2] The efforts of the CIA's Cuban renegades brought the backing of the Argentinian dictatorship, who sent instructors and equipment. Meanwhile, US policy sought to pit Sandinista moderates against the rest, and as hopes for a political takeover by moderate elements faded, they moved towards pushing Edén Pastora, the former commander of the Sandinista southern front and an avowed social democrat, into leading a coup. This never happened, and Pastora left Nicaragua in July 1981, saying that he was going to continue the revolutionary struggle elsewhere.

Sporadic military opposition to the Sandinista government began that same year, with peasant militias who disliked the atheism of Sandinista activists. These were suspicious of the cooperatives being set up, and were infuriated by sometimes arrogant and heavy-handed Sandinista officials from the cities who were trying to disarm them. But these groups were more of an irritation than a threat. The real danger came with the first wave of Contra attacks in December 1981. These Contras were largely made up of former 'Guardia' (National Guard), and they had all the support they needed from the US and other governments. Their initial focus mirrored the Sandinista strategy. They would seize a piece of territory, establish a provisional government and call for assistance from the United States. Fighting was fierce along the Honduran border, but the Contras failed to seize the territory they sought. Throughout 1982 and 1983 their capacity and numbers grew from a handful to around fourteen thousand men. By 1983 the small, ill-equipped Sandinista army (Ejército Popular Sandinista, also known as the EPS) was being overwhelmed by well-trained, well-armed Contras with state-of-the-art communications and support from US intelligence. Sandinista civilians in the rural areas of Nicaragua's north paid a heavy price in blood as the brutal Contras sought them out.

But the former National Guard weren't the only rebels. By early 1982, Edén Pastora was in Costa Rica where he helped set up an organisation called ARDE (which means 'it blazes' in Spanish). For many Sandinistas then and now, Pastora was simply a traitor. When I interviewed Pastora in 2008-9, he claimed that his actions had been agreed with the Sandinista leadership, and that his mission was to set up a force that would neutralise US efforts to create a Southern Contra front. 'If we don't do this, the gringos will fill that space with Guardia,' he told them. In other words, Pastora claimed to be a double agent. But equally that may have also just been Pastora being Pastora, offering a version of the truth that best suited him at the time.

Pastora died in June 2020, but he was a man notorious for ego and his knack for conspiracy. As one of his bodyguards told me, with Pastora, 'Anything is possible'. Unless the documents he promised would vindicate him arise, the most we can say is that he never betrayed his own 'social-democratic' and patriotic version of Sandinismo. Playing all sides is a dangerous game, and the Sandinista Interior Ministry (or was it the CIA?) almost killed Pastora in May 1984. If we judge Pastora by his actions, there is no doubt that the CIA grew increasingly frustrated with his lack of action and his constant criticism of the FDN Contras in Honduras. Shortly before the assassination attempt, the CIA has issued Pastora with an ultimatum, either join the FDN and start fighting or we cut the money.[3] Pastora was eventually replaced by junior commanders linked to the CIA and went back to shark fishing in Costa Rica. He was not an active Contra at the time Hasenfus' aircraft was shot down when the EPS reported that ARDE, '...is in difficult conditions, and at the moment they are practically limited to surviving'.[4] According to EPS documents from the time, it was not supplying ARDE, but the FDN's 'Jorge Salazar' Task Force under the command of a Contra called 'Franklin'.[5]

The Sandinistas knew that the US would be hostile, and they had initially thought of keeping a small army of about 15,000, but with large militia reserves ready if necessary. It was these reserves that were being increasingly called into action by the end of 1982. The EPS command decided to set up new units called 'Irregular Warfare Battalions' or BLI, as well as reluctantly instituting conscription. The BLI became the backbone of the Sandinista struggle against the Contras, acquiring a legendary status that still resonates in Nicaragua today. Each BLI had about 300-500 men, most of whom were conscripts. The officers, like Lieutenant Mendez in the story, were usually young men who had volunteered from the old guerrilla units, and had been rushed through a year-long training course run mainly by Chilean officers of the Cuban army. A handful had been trained in Cuba itself. Most had only recently learned to read, and although they were experienced and brave fighters (*rungueros* in Nicaraguan slang), they were not yet very skilled at the technical side of war. The soldiers themselves were usually barely literate and most came from absolute poverty. They had four months of training before going out on operations, and often spent much of their time hiking up and down mountains ambushing or being ambushed by Contras, or chasing them back towards Honduras (or less often, Costa Rica). These troops bore the brunt of the Contra war. It was they who by the mid-1980s had taken the strategic initiative, smashing the Contra invasion in July 1986 and chasing the Contras back to their bases in Honduras. It is quite incredible that they were able to do this despite the level of US direct and indirect support – US naval groups on both coasts, constant US military exercises involving thousands of US troops to the north, overflights by US spycraft, and attacks by US agents on the ground.

The Reagan administration also did its best to whitewash the Contras. They put civilians nominally in charge, and they accused the Sandinistas of human rights abuses. But the truth on the ground was simple. The US was engaged in a war of terror with Nicaragua. In May, the International Court of Justice held that the US had violated international law by backing the Contras and mining Nicaragua's harbours. Atrocity after atrocity led to widespread international condemnation that no amount of propaganda could shift. Uriel Vanegas, a Contra commander, later admitted that the FDN 'was fighting for the interests of a power, the United States, that used us as cannon fodder.'[6] All this made direct US support increasingly difficult. In November 1984, the Sandinistas won an open election (despite the CIA's move to discredit the result by having one of the opposition alliances, headed by Arturo Cruz Senior, withdraw from the election at the last minute). Towards the end of 1984, US Congress finally forbade any further military support of the Contras. But Reagan was not going to be stopped by the law, he ordered his National Security Council (NSC) to continue supporting the Contras.

The CIA had used clandestine methods to fund illegal aspects of the war in Vietnam, and under NSC direction they used this experience to begin a complex operation to funnel illicit funds to the Contras in secret. This involved private networks funnelling money to the Contras from wealthy donors from all over the world who in return got other favours. More money came from the sale of Colombian cocaine in the US, with the networks spreading as far afield as Bolivia and Chile. Then the US also funnelled money to the Contras from the sale of weapons to Iran, in what became known as the Iran-Contra scandal.[7] Hasenfus' plane was a concrete product of this operation. It was paid for with Saudi money, its operations were directed by Cuban CIA agents in El Salvadorian airbases, and planes like it were directly involved in drug trafficking.

Then in 1985-1986 Reagan went on an all-out offensive to get Congress to approve a $100 million 'humanitarian package' of support for the Contras. Finally approved in October 1986, the money kept the Contras afloat, and lined the pockets of their commanders, but military failure meant that the US now took more direct control of operations, which alienated many of the rebels. Morale fell, and some groups took the government amnesty. The Contras made up numbers by widespread kidnapping, a brutal form of conscription.

The shooting down of Hasenfus' aircraft was a key moment in the war. The aircraft was not only being flown by US crew, but it was carrying flight logs and other documents. Hasenfus himself was cooperative when interviewed by the Sandinistas and journalists. The picture that emerged helped lead to the Iran-Contra scandal and was an important political victory for Nicaragua.

Belli's story shows how one simple event can distil the essence of a historical moment. The past lives within the present, and nowhere more so than in Nicaragua, where most of the surviving participants of the Sandinista revolution are still alive and well, partly because they were so young when it took place, and partly because the FSLN has been back in government since 2006. Although an accurate retelling of a moment in time, aspects of present political tensions might also be read into it, in my view. The story unfolds within a tense relationship between the bullying Lt. Mendez and the men. The Sandinista 'top brass' too are distant and uncaring, and as an illustration of the way in which ordinary people were and are ignored or forgotten, the narrator, Jose Fernando Canales, is obscured in the photograph published in *Barricada*. The current political overtones are also present in the way Pastora is introduced into the story. Pastora, who died in June 2020, was certainly a *bête noire* of the Sandinistan Renovation Movement (MRS) who split from the FSLN in the 1990s. They hated his 1980s betrayal, but mostly they hated his support of and allegiance to Daniel Ortega's government after 2007, particularly the way he and other historic Sandinistas mobilised armed veterans to defend it during the violent protests of 2018.

The soldiers who shot down Hasenfus' aircraft were members of one of eight 'Light Hunter Battalions' created in early 1986. The relationship between the officers and men in these small irregular units was usually good, and there were solid reasons for this. The officers were usually very young, and from the same social background as their men. They had usually fought as guerrillas. Unlike officers in Western armies, Sandinista officers lacked privileges – they shared the same conditions and food as their men, so much so that EPS documents stated that it was an important issue affecting officer morale, and in preventing soldiers from too zealously seeking promotion. The command relationship was often quite informal, soldiers called their officers 'compañero', and if troops felt any injustice they would often complain collectively, or would speak to the political officer. Physical punishments were forbidden, and generally efforts were made to ensure 'conscious discipline' - a form of self-discipline created by awareness of the need for, and meaning of, every action. Even desertions were only punished by return to the original unit and perhaps being tasked to carry a mortar tripod. At most, disobedient troops might have their trousers cut short, a form of minor humiliation, and greater discomfort when on operations. But the best units made great efforts to encourage 'socialist emulation', rewarding courage and diligence with small gifts or pennants, and having their actions reported on 'Radio La Cachorra', a radio station dedicated to the irregular warfare units. All units had political officers whose job was to keep troops informed and help resolve any problems the soldiers might have. Morale and faith in the revolution were usually high, at least while on operations, and troops generally had a clear idea of what they were fighting for.

On 8 October 1986, the three soldiers Raul Acevedo, Byron Montiel and Jose Fernando Canales were flown to Managua and were awarded the highest honour of the EPS by General Humberto Ortega. They were then flown to Cuba and then on to other socialist countries where they were also honoured. There were dozens of photos of Hasenfus being taken prisoner, and in many of them Fernando is clearly visible. In fact, as the man who shot down the plane, he became a celebrity. He later studied medicine in Cuba and today he is an epidemiologist in his hometown. The two are still supportive of the Sandinista government, and in a recent interview Byron Montiel said, 'We are struggling to continue the legacy of our General Sandino, of Zeledon, of Carlos Fonseca, of Tomas Borge, and all the heroes and martyrs. We have to be strong, because the only alternative that we have is the Sandinista National Liberation Front.'[8]

## Notes

1. 'The GRN Confronts a Shattered Economy – Some Impressions of the First Days', Confidential Cable, 25 July 1979, Digital National Security Archive, Nicaragua Collection, Item NI00998.
2. Dissent Paper on El Salvador and Central America, DOS 11/06/80, 23 January 1981.
3. Multiple sources including 'Crisis for the Contras' *The Guardian (US),* 13 June 1984.
4. EPS Document, 'Sintesis del desarrollo de la c/r en la V RM', 1986.
5. EPS Document, 'Informe especial estructura y estado de fuerzas c/r', June 1987.
6. Revista Envio 'Contra decline continues: will peace follow?' number 77, November 1987.
7. Report of the Congressional Committees Investigating the Iran-Contra Affair, November 1987.
8. Testimony and photographs available at: https://redvolucion.net/2019/10/05/eugene-hasenfus-el-mercenario-que-abastecio-a-la-contra/

# Soramin's Diary

## Ahmet Halûk Ünal

Translated from the Turkish by Nicholas Glastonbury

*For Nurê, with my utmost respect and love*

*6 October 98*

'A PURE WHITE CAT emerged from the water. One of its eyes was green, the other blue; in its mouth it had a river carp.

It approached the fox waiting nearby, leaving the fish at its feet. Then they began to eat it together, one from the head, the other from the tail.'

'You're teasing me, cats don't go in the water.' I looked in his eyes and said it loudly so that the others could also hear. It happened exactly as I wanted, and they all turned to look at us.

A smile spread across Tolhildan's[1] face; he looked at his friends and proclaimed, 'Soramin doesn't believe in the cat's solidarity with the fox. She's interrogating me.'

They all let out a laugh in unison.

Çiyager added, 'I can vouch for what he says, Soramin;[2] we were together when we saw them both in the valley, passing by the bank of the river. I was surprised, too.' Then Ferhat, our walking encyclopaedia, said that Van cats are the only kind that hunts fish. In the winter, the fox feeds the both of them, stealing geese and chickens from the henhouse. It's spectacular solidarity, isn't it?

'How can I see it?'

'You don't have to go far. Do you still not understand, daughter, that some of them are foxes and some of them are cats?' my mum laughed.

'She's giving us food like this so we don't hang around the henhouse,' Tolhildan said, erupting in laughter. They all laughed heartily at his joke.

They would come to the village often; we knew them all.

After we moved to this hamlet, our friends hadn't come to visit for years.

Then, last night, my older brother came home saying we were going to have visitors.

'The kids from the mountain.'

*What kind of people are they?* I wondered.

We girls were so excited.

My older sister, my older brother, my mum and my dad remained calm.

They arrived when darkness fell.

We lined up at the front door.

They shook everyone's hands one by one and came in.

Normally men and women would sit separately in our house, but strangely, when the guerrillas are here, Dad never enforces that rule, and the women can come into the living room.

Dad would say, 'Whatever the PKK does is moral.' That's why he didn't make the men and women stay separate.

When they're here he acts one way, but when they leave, he acts in a completely different way.

Dad was against communism. He rejected it. But he read a lot. He would read Bediüzzaman,[3] and always urged us to question what we read.

'Apo,' he would say, 'isn't a godless or faithless man. Did he ever say there is no god? That's your interpretation. And it's an unfair one at that.'

The guerrillas could turn my dictator dad into such a good person – how could I not like them?

Mum had spent two days preparing. She had made a veritable feast.

They sat on the cushions on the living room floor. They kept their guns by their sides the whole time.

When Dad gestured them towards the table, one of them said, 'The children should eat first, then us.' No matter how many times Mum and Dad insisted, they didn't approach the table.

Leyla, Ceylan and I were dazzled by all those foods we only saw on holidays, and only sometimes at that. When we'd had our fill and got up, they began to eat.

When the men began cleaning up the table, Dad grew uneasy. 'Why would you do such a thing?' he said. When they replied, 'Why *wouldn't* we? It's our pleasure,' he was embarrassed.

They were always speaking in accordance with Apo, and I was so glad to see him defeated.

I feel so happy and safe when the hevals – the comrades – come around.

In the village where I was born, Turkish soldiers would often come at night.

They would round us all up in the village square, strip the men completely naked, and then beat them up.

A few times they stripped the women too. I don't even want to remember it.

Being insulted, beaten, sworn at, and cursed: they were all things I learned from the soldiers.

They even named their dogs things like 'Kıro,[4] Kurdo,' and when they gathered us in the village square they would call their dogs. They found it funniest to set their dogs on the naked men.

The last time they came to the village was when they burnt down all our houses.

I ran and hid behind one of the houses.

One soldier took a beam from a hayloft and leaned one end

against a mound in the earth and the other against the door of Rojin's house.

Rojin, her mum, her dad and her siblings were inside.

Screams, sounds like choking, coughing, I was so afraid I was trembling like a leaf.

The soldier moved to the next house to set it on fire.

I couldn't restrain myself, they were burning alive. I ran, I tried to push the beam. The soldier heard my voice; he turned around, and our eyes met. He ran up to me, raised his gun, and stood there staring at me, his eyes filled with fear and hate, but he didn't shoot me for some reason. Then he ran off.

I managed, barely, to push the beam away from the mound. I fainted. Rojin's dad carried me in his arms to the square.

'It wasn't just us, they burned down all the surrounding villages!' my older sister cried. I can't stand crying.

Close to morning the whole village had gathered everything they could save from the fire and scattered in all directions... Some fled to cities, some to other villages, and some, like us, to hamlets.

*8 October 98*

My name is Sekine, but everybody calls me Soramin. It's the name of a woman who's very important to the kids of the mountain. They gave me that name because I'm a redhead like her. Most people, if you ask them, don't know me as Sekine but as Soramin.

The hamlet we came to is on the skirt of a mountain, beside an endless forest.

Our in-laws, my older brothers, my uncles and their families all make up nine houses. Two of the houses are empty, because my oldest uncles went to the city.

None of us have been able to get over the terror of that night.

My second-oldest sister kept saying they burned down more than three thousand villages that night, crying as she explained. Three thousand, a number I hadn't yet learned. I already mentioned that I can't stand crying.

But I would run off all the time, and daydream in the forest, beside the brook. The forest is like heaven to me. I share the forest with countless other creatures.

Bears, wolves, foxes, hawks, mountain goats, doves, swallows. Pine trees, oak trees. Plants and trees whose names I don't yet know. There are even yılkı horses in the forest.

I love horses...

Poor families who can't afford to feed their horses set them loose as yılkı horses in winter. Only the strong, the sturdy, survive. Come spring they round up the survivors and tie them back up in their stables.

The yılkı horses roam in herds, and you can't approach them, much less ride them.

I've tried, of course, so many times. I'd come home covered in scrapes and bruises. I'd be scolded for even the smallest of scrapes.

If only they knew that I was actually a yılkı horse too.

I've never gone to school. There's no school in the hamlet where we live. Since we're just nine houses the place is too small for a school. There's a regional boarding school in town. They send the boys there. Girls can't go.

Which is fine, because I learned how to read and write thanks to my older brother. Now I even have a diary. My brother says I'm doing a great job. He looks at what I write in it, and the other day he said, 'Maybe one day you'll be a writer, and we'll come to your book signings.'

Apparently when writers' books are published they have signings and readers come and have their books signed.

In my dream that night I became a writer. The whole village lined up for my signature, each of them holding my book.

The uncle I don't like came and stood in front of my table, yelling 'Don't read it, don't believe anything she wrote, little girls can't become writers...'

I woke up in a cold sweat.

The beast had even made his way into my dreams. Supposedly I was setting a bad example for his daughters.

*10 October 98*

For us, it's tradition that as soon as you turn twelve you have to cover up. At that point, even in the hamlet, it's forbidden for you to go outside with your hair and face uncovered, or to play with the boys.

I never got used to the veils.

Mum's been begging and pleading with me for days on end, holding the black sheet; when she gives up, my oldest sister gives it a shot.

They're set on making me wear it. Impossible. I can't walk around in that weird sheet.

Would they tie a bird's wings?

If I don't wear it, they say, it's a sin.

There are so many things that I can't stand and God demands I do them all.

If things continue like this, it seems, I won't just be cross with Dad and my oldest sister, but with God too.

In our house, you have the hardest conversations with Dad, and then you get your slap from my sister.

Dad wouldn't hurt a fly, but my older sister would happily beat you within an inch of your life.

With every passing day the distance between me and Dad grew.

None of the things he imposes on me make any sense. Insults and slaps won't kill me, but those coverings, having to go around in them…

Slowly I began to understand them all, but the one thing I didn't understand was why Dad was one way around the hevals and another way when they're gone.

I think life ought to be how it is when the hevals are around.

When they came, he would never tell me to 'stop, hush, sit,

cover your hair, cross your legs, you just don't get it'; instead, he'd start with 'What do you think, Soramin? I'm getting some water from the kitchen, do you want any?'

They always went on about what Serok Apo, Leader Apo, would say about women.

I love Apo so much, and he's the only backbone I have when facing Dad.

Whenever Dad and I argue, I always list off everything I've heard from the hevals, and he starts swearing like the Turkish soldiers do and shoos me away.

Even if some of my older sisters think the way I do, they're afraid of Dad and my oldest sister's malice and never say a word. Since my older brothers aren't at home they can't protect me from them.

Once I told them about what was going on and asked for their help. 'You're right, but I can't help you,' my brother said, patting my hair. I guess I have to deal with this problem all on my own.

I was so disappointed, but I'm still grateful to my older brothers.

I owe the fact that I can read and write to the books they gave me in secret every time they came home.

My oldest brother would take some time off and teach me how to read and write.

What they brought were Turkish grammar books. When I reached a certain level, he gave me two story books, one called *Jonathan Livingston Seagull* and one called *Little Black Fish*. I read both of them over and over so many times I practically memorised them.

I'll tell you those stories sometime, heval diary.

My brother told me that Kurdish grammar books were forbidden, and that until we win our freedom, the only books we'll ever find will be Turkish ones. 'Knowledge is knowledge, no matter if it's in Turkish or in Kurdish,' he would say.

When we get our freedom and establish Kurdistan, we're apparently going to build the world's biggest Kurdish library.

But we've got to hold our horses, after all, good things come to those who wait.

I don't think Apo knows about this problem with the lack of Kurdish books, because if he did, he'd find a solution.

I learned how to keep a diary from Tolhildan. He said it's very common for the guerrillas to keep diaries. Not only does it improve your reading and writing, but you can really pour your heart out, like you're talking to a good friend who will keep your secrets.

Apparently, the hevals collected all the martyrs' diaries in a library. I wonder if I'll get to see that library one day.

*12 October 98*

Today I discovered that in the neighbouring hamlets there are horses tied up in stables that haven't been put out to yılkı for the winter. I convinced my cousins that we should sneak in and steal them. I love horses so much. Horses are uncontrollable.

They always argue whether animals have feelings, but I think they do. They recognise love.

They don't run away from me. They won't let themselves be reined in. You have to ride them without a saddle, bareback.

When you're on a horse riding at full gallop, you feel the wind. You hold onto it by the mane.

You have to become one with the horse. You feel it get tired, feel it sweat.

I've always loved horses. It's my biggest dream, still, to have a horse.

We rode until evening, and then we left the horses where we got them and went home.

At home they were making hurried preparations.

The 'kids from the mountain' were going to come. I was jumping for joy.

Everyone gathered in the sofa;[5] Mum and my sisters had set the table; like a wedding banquet, they had us eat first and then ate themselves.

Like all Kurds' houses, our house has two antennas, one tuned to the Turks and one tuned to our broadcasts.

This time, things are different for some reason; there's no joking, nobody's sharing their memories, nobody's reading parts of their diaries.

They came to watch TV. They're restless.

I realised that the issue being discussed on the TV that was bothering them had to do with Apo.

All of a sudden there was an explosion in the distance.

My sister turned off the lights right away.

Tolhildan pushed me behind the couch.

They took their guns and went to the windows. A couple of them went outside. The explosions receded in the distance and then stopped altogether.

They came in from outside.

'The bastards, they're dropping bombs at random left and right. I think we should go back, just in case. Hacı, excuse us,' he stammered. They always address Dad as Hacı.

'Godspeed,' Dad said, and stood up to send them off.

Jiyan[6] hugged me and kissed me. Tolhildan patted me on the head.

'What happened to Apo?' I asked, looking him in the eyes.

'I'll explain next time we come. Don't be sad, nothing will happen to him.' They vanished into the dark night.

My sisters are snoring away, the day's now breaking, and I still haven't been able to fall asleep. If something happens to Apo, how will I deal with Dad?

*20 October 98*

'Your daughter makes off with our horses every day,' they finally said, confronting Dad.

When he got home he was fuming. He left no insult unsaid.

He turned to my oldest sister and mum and yelled, 'If I see her leave the house, I want you to know you're going to be the ones to pay the price.'

I went to our room, I was so angry.

My oldest sister came and hissed between her teeth like a snake. 'I'm not going to beat you today out of respect for Dad, but come tomorrow, you'll see.' She slammed the door and left.

Mum came in and ran her fingers through my hair and held me, comforting me like she always does. I knew that she never agreed with what Dad said but that her fear left her helpless. She was caught between us.

They watched TV again for hours, completely silent.

With her same pigheadedness my oldest sister locked me into the room.

Lock me in as much as you want, but I can hear you when I put my ear to the door, you pig.

On the Kurdish channels they're saying Apo has to leave Syria because Turkey's threatening war, and that he went to Greece.

Heval diary, why do the Turks hate Apo? I should ask Jiyan. I'm sure she knows.

*22 October 98*

I've been imprisoned in our room for two days.

I haven't been able to go out. From here I can hear the sounds my friends make when they're playing outside. They shout and scream as they play, almost like they want me in particular to hear.

How many more days can I bear this? I don't know.

I have to find a solution.

Tell me, then, what do you think I should do?

*24 October 98*

They aren't even letting me watch TV. It's a nightmare.

I thought of something I heard from the kids from the mountain.

Their friends in prison apparently resist by going on death fasts. I wonder if that'd work here at home?

You don't eat anything, you can only drink water. Given

what a glutton I am, how many days can I go hungry?

What would Apo say about this?

Apo's got bigger problems than me right now anyway.

I asked one of my sisters, Ceylan; America forced him to leave Syria, to leave the lands where he was safe. Apparently they don't want us to establish Kurdistan. Apparently they think it's bad for him to stay in Syria.

So he went to Greece, a place that he trusts. But it snowed on the mountains he trusted. Of course it snowed. What business do you have in a foreign country when you could head to our mountains?

*25 October 98*

I made my decision.

When mum brought my breakfast in the morning, I told her.

'I'm on a death fast now, I'm not going to eat.'

She didn't take me seriously at first, I think. She probably thought it was just another of my crazy notions.

But when she came back hours later and saw that I hadn't touched my food, she understood how serious I was.

I can't explain how astonished she was. She whined for hours. She cried, she begged, she pleaded. When she realised I wouldn't budge, she left the room and slammed the door.

Then my older sisters came, and they whined a lot too.

I told them that I couldn't bear to be imprisoned, that I was determined to keep up my death fast unless they lifted my punishment. Helpless, they left too.

Finally my oldest sister came in and she beat me bad. She tried to force the food into my mouth.

Eventually she threw in the towel as well.

Mum made my favourite food for dinner.

Is it possible to pause your death fast and then resume it again later?

But what if mum cooks my favourite foods every day?

I decided not to pause.

Eventually they told Dad. I can hear his angry voice from the sofa, I think this time he's going to beat me himself. I'm waiting…

But my stomach has been aching so badly, I'm dying of hunger.

At night I put my ear to the door, trying to listen. That's how I forget my hunger, at least a little bit. But it's not always something that cheers me up.

Apo's traveling from country to country.

The people making him promises aren't keeping their promises.

'It's betrayal to not keep a promise you make,' Jiyan once said. 'A promise is a matter of honour.'

*27 October 98*

My head started spinning and I started to feel sick to my stomach again.

They can probably hear the aching and grumbling of my stomach from the sofa.

Seems it's not easy to be a kid from the mountain.

But I won't give in. If I were to give in, who knows what would happen?

Suddenly the door opened and mum came in. We looked each other in the eye. She stared at me for awhile and then left, leaving the door open.

At first I didn't understand. What did this all mean?

But since the door was open, I left the room too.

I'm exhausted. My body's like jelly.

I noticed that no one was around, so I left the house too.

I inhaled the cold air over and over.

I don't remember what happened after that. Apparently I collapsed right there.

When I came to, I was lying in bed. Mum was sitting beside me, crying. My sisters sat on the floor in front of the bed, watching me in silence, with little smiles on their faces. When I opened my eyes two of them ran up and hugged me.

They grabbed the tray with a dürüm and ayran from my bedside table and put it on my lap. Leyla whispered into my ear, 'You won,' as she passed me the tray.

Was flatbread always this delicious?

After I ate more than my fill I got out of bed. 'How's Apo doing?' I asked.

They looked at each other, and Leyla said, 'He's good.'

Savouring the taste of my victory, I left the house as everyone continued to glance at one another in silence.

I walked over to where the children were playing. But I didn't feel like joining them.

They looked far too childish to me.

*1 November 98*

First we shovelled snow. Then Dad sent me to graze the sheep.

This was one of the jobs nobody liked doing. Since my sisters were in their bridal age they were forbidden from doing it. When my brothers were home they made them do it. But when they're at school the task is left to me.

But actually, I love doing it.

Taking my uncle's horse and his big sled, I go to the cave where we pile up the bales of hay in the autumn and load them onto the sled.

My brother and I found this cave together. A bear lived inside it. There were lots of caves around, but this one was best suited for us.

Brother bear could make a den in one of the other caves.

We chased it off without hurting it.

We covered the floor of the cave with straw and mud.

Now we had a storeroom where we could store our bales of hay in winter and where we could leave provisions for the guerrillas.

The bales are heavy and difficult to load onto the sled. But

I can't get enough of riding the horse.

I check the place where we leave provisions for the guerrillas.

If the provisions are gone, we have to replenish them.

First I draw the sled with the horse, bringing it back to the stable, then I let the sheep out of the stable and gather them up in front of the bales. Then I take the sled and go sledding with the boys.

My uncle's daughters see me and join in. Dozens of us kids, screaming and shouting as we sled.

Since I don't stay with the sheep, of course sometimes they go drink from the stream without my noticing. But in fact it's my job to take them to the stream when they've had their fill.

If a wolf got one of them, Dad would break my bones.

But thankfully, Turko never leaves their side. When he senses danger he begins barking immediately. He's a wolfhound, black as coal.

I can't tell you how much we love him.

The most dangerous thing is fog. The fog rolls in here quite often.

Wolves and foxes like to hunt in the fog. If the fog rolls in when the sheep are on their own at the stream, there's nothing you can do because you can't see past the tip of your nose.

*2 November 98*

Heval diary, I want to tell you about my new decision.

I decided to start teaching the kids of my relatives how to read and write.

They really ought to read the books I've read. They ought to stand up to their dads. They ought to wonder about where the river ends, like the *Little Black Fish*.

But anyway, I don't know how I'm going to do it. I don't have pencils, books, erasers, notebooks. Even if I asked the villagers for money they wouldn't give it to me.

Besides, how am I going to get the little girls to come?

Because I absolutely have to bring my uncle's daughters in particular. The pig won't let them, I know. But I will find a way.

I decided I'm going to ask my brothers for help.

They come home on the weekends.

I finally got news of Apo; they say he's in Russia. He went there from Greece. I saw Greece and Russia for the first time on TV. They're like fairy-tale countries.

But everyone in the family looks so sad. He's traveling the world, why are they unhappy?

*1 January 99*

As a birthday gift my brother gave me a bunch of alphabet books, pencils, paper, notebooks, erasers, and chalk. All his friends set up a commune and gathered money. The gift is from all of them.

1 January isn't just my birthday; all the kids in the hamlet were born on 1 January.

My brother said 'All Kurds were born on the first of January.'

Everyone laughed, but I don't understand the joke?

*2 January 99*

The number of little girls in the village is very large.

But my experience in the village slowly began to tear down the veil for them.

I became an example. In their wisdom, all the families decided to loosen up, so as not to burn all their bridges.

Teaching Turkish had now become an important goal for me.

Some of my uncles from the hamlet had given in early to state repression in the 90s and migrated. I decided to use one of the houses they left empty as the schoolhouse.

We painted the back of an old wardrobe black to use as a chalkboard. We made the desks from fruit crates. Everyone brought their own cushions to sit on from home.

When the villagers first heard about it, they laughed. They didn't take me seriously.

I abandoned all my chores. I devoted myself to the school.

In my school speaking Kurdish is forbidden.

They will speak Turkish in order to learn it.

Each student brings a bundle of wood from home. That's how we keep warm.

The villagers come and look, and they see that I'm teaching reading and writing. They're pleased.

If they're learning to read and write, they think, they're not doing something bad.

Sometimes they sent their kids off to shepherd, and I would go and bring them to school instead. Their dads would come and argue with me.

My brothers started a book campaign in town, and even the government heard about it.

One of the girls set up a school in her hamlet to teach Turkish. They were very pleased.

They told Dad, 'We'll visit soon and give her some gifts. We support her.'

*3 January 99*

All the girls come without exception.

Even the uncle who I thought hated me sent his daughters.

I'm going to teach Turkish!

He doesn't know that if his daughters learn to read and write and start reading books, they won't believe a single one of his lies any more.

That's how I'll get my revenge.

*7 January 99*

Lessons are going well. The girls are eager to learn.

When Turkish lessons are over, I tell them about Jonathan the seagull, and about the little black fish.

Every night now we watch TV without making a sound.

Apo keeps travelling to countries whose names I'm hearing for the first time.

My family's unhappiness seems to be rising every day.

They dropped bombs across the fields at random again.

*16 January 99*

The kids from the mountain have stopped coming. They've withdrawn to their winter quarters. They won't come again until spring.

The only thing we listen to at home now is the TV news. They don't turn on music, shows, or anything else.

My oldest sister is constantly weaving lace. All day she weaves her lace as they listen to the news.

The snow is as tall as a person. We have to clear the roads every day, so we can go from one house to the other.

At least the job of feeding the sheep still falls to me, so I can avoid making lace and sled instead.

Apo keeps wandering from country to country.

Do none of them want Apo?

Why didn't he go to our mountains, join the guerrillas? I don't understand.

Because the guerrillas would have protected him.

When I said so, Dad scolded me again. I just don't get it, he told me, why would I know better than Apo what to do.

*20 January 99*

Last night something amazing happened.

There was a knock at our door in the middle of the night. Dad went and opened it.

We could hear someone at the door, shaking the snow off themselves and whispering to him.

Soon who comes inside but heval Jiyan. I ran to her and threw my arms around her neck.

She's going to stay with us for a while, and if the soldiers come we'll say she's our aunt's daughter.

I have so much to tell her.

We sat in our bedroom till morning while I talked and she listened.

In fact I wanted to ask her lots of things about Apo. But I decided to save that all for later. Better that she learns what I've been up to since she left.

I told her about the school, about Turkish lessons, about the daughters of the uncle I despise, about my brothers' book commune, I told her about everything.

Then I let her read a few pages of my diary. Jiyan looked at me again, that same expression I love on her face.

*25 January 99*

Jiyan takes careful notes all day of everything they're saying about Apo on the news.

Then at night she leaves with those papers and returns a while later without them.

When I asked, she told me, 'The less you know, the better.'

'When I'm a guerrilla you're not going to be able to say things like that to me,' I said, standing up. I was so angry. Am I a child?

Enraged, I went to toss some wood in the stove. When I closed the stove's lid and turned around, our eyes met. Even Mum doesn't look at me with the kind of love and admiration that Jiyan does. I don't know how to say it, but it's like she's smiling not just from her face but from inside.

I ran to her and hugged her. She held me tight.

Apo is apparently in Tajikistan. In a city called Bishkek. He's healthy. So why is everyone so sad?

For a while she was quiet as she looked me in the eyes. 'We're worried about his safety, that's why,' she said. 'The enemy could injure him.'

I couldn't think of anything to say.

*28 January 99*

I decided to surprise Jiyan.

I learned how to set traps from my brother.

You take the laundry tub from the house and decide where to set the trap. You tie a string to a stick. Then you turn the tub upside down and balance the stick between the tub and the ground. One end of the tub is up in the air and the other is on the ground. You scatter some wheat by the open end of the tub and underneath the tub too. The sparrows start to eat the wheat outside, and then the wheat underneath. Once they've gone all the way in you pull the string and the stick falls, and they're stuck inside the tub. I can catch dozens of them.

I can't explain how tasty sparrow meat is.

Anyway, it's forbidden to hunt other animals. Deer, mountain goats, bears, boars, it's forbidden to hunt all of them. We don't even kill wolves or foxes. We just scare them off. The guerrillas forbid it.

I plucked and cleaned all the sparrows I caught, and after I wrapped them in a rag I brought them home and put them in front of Jiyan.

'I caught these for you.'

She was so surprised. She began to laugh.

Mum let out a little scream. Leyla and Ceylan were laughing too. My oldest sister was obstinate as usual.

'How could you dare to kill so many things,' she hissed.

'I'm going to cook them for Jiyan,' I hissed back.

'Thank you, but don't you know that it's forbidden to hunt animals?' Jiyan said, taking my face in her hands. She was still smiling. At least she wasn't mad.

'I know, one night heval Çiyager listed off all the forbidden animals. I didn't hear sparrows in the list.'

'How could Çiyager know there was a hunter like you in these mountains? I'll warn him so he'll know to add sparrows to the list next time.'

'What do you mean, you're not going to eat them?' I frowned.

'Of course we'll eat them, my dear, it was our mistake.' This time she let out a hearty laugh.

I ran to the kitchen. It'll be a feast tonight.

I'm so happy. I'm lying down in Jiyan's lap. She's patting my hair. We're watching the news about Apo.

They started shooting off bombs again at random from the gendarme station.

We turned out the lights and waited for it to end. Jiyan lied down on top of me again until it stopped.

Yesterday one of the bombs fell on a house in the neighbouring village. The monsters killed the whole family.

Today they've been saying everywhere that the guerrillas did it.

*29 January 99*

My older sisters are whispering with Jiyan, frantically discussing something.

When I approached them they stopped talking.

What could they be discussing in secret from me?

Maybe it's as Jiyan said, the less I know, the better.

Still, the curiosity irritates me.

Leyla can't stand up to me. Tomorrow I'll learn what's happening from her.

*2 February 99*

Jiyan's totally out of sorts. She hasn't played around with me for a few days.

Apo went to Kenya. I guess it's worse for him to be in some countries than in others.

How do they distinguish between them? I don't get it.

*13 February 99*

Tonight it was urgent that Jiyan return to her friends.

*14 February 99*

All us kids went to gather rosehip in the forest.

We gathered so much. On the way back there was a black rag hanging from the roof of my uncle's house.

I figured that someone in the hamlet had died.

I came home and my brothers were there. My oldest brother looked so sullen. My other brother was crying.

The TV was on, and I suddenly saw Apo, handcuffed, blindfolded, surrounded on both sides by men in balaclavas. I looked at Mum.

'They caught Apo. They're handing him over to the Turkish state; they're going to hang him.' That's all she managed to say.

So today we hung black rags outside of all the houses in the hamlet.

Near evening, Leyla and Ceylan disappeared. Where did they go? I was sure it had something to do with what they were whispering with Jiyan about.

I saw Dad cry for the first time. Mum always cries anyway.

Dad called, and me, Mum, and my oldest sister gathered around the stove.

He said that my sisters went to stay with my uncles in Istanbul, that they were going to find work there. They encouraged my brothers to go back to school early in the morning. Soldiers might come at any moment.

My oldest sister got up, angry, and went to her room.

Mum kept crying.

There seemed to be something fishy going on, so…

'Did they join up?' I asked Dad in a whisper.

He got so enraged I can't explain it. If he heard anything like that from me ever again, he said, he would break my bones.

I was so afraid. I've never seen him so angry.

*15 February 99*

My sisters are still away.

Mum keeps crying.

The random bombings continue all night.

The forest begins to burn.

Everyone waits in a safe corner of the house with the lights off for it to end.

The soldiers are apparently celebrating Apo's capture and his being turned over to the state.

All the TV channels show are pictures of Apo handcuffed and blindfolded over and over.

I can't stand crying.

My sister's diary comes to an end on the fifteenth of February.

On the sixteenth, she was killed by a mortar shell that exploded beside her as she took the sheep to the stream.

She was a special kid. Such a special kid. Had the enemies spared her, what might she have become?

The whole school came to her funeral. The whole village, in fact.

After we buried Soramin, I joined up.

I brought Soramin's diary with me to the mountains. I want all the hevals to know who she is. I'm going to put her diary alongside all the other martyred guerrillas' diaries.

Who knows: perhaps a writer will find it, will tell her story, write her novel; perhaps a director will make a film. They're the real wealth of our people. Let their legends and their tales be told.

## Notes

1. A Kurdish word meaning 'vengeance.'
2. In Kurdish, 'Sora min' means 'my redhead'.
3. Said Nursî (sometimes referred to as Bediüzzaman) was a Kurdish Muslim scholar, exegete, and writer. He has written about Islam and his work, Risale-i Nur, which interprets 300 verses of the Quran, has been translated into more than fifty languages.
4. A Kurdish word meaning 'boy' that's also used in Turkish to mean 'moron' or 'idiot'.
5. The large room at the entrance to the house used as a living room. This is where the stove burns and all the other rooms' doors open onto this room.
6. A Kurdish word meaning 'life.'

## 'KURDISTAN', 1999

# Afterword: Patriam Non Grata

## Meral Çiçek

On 20 February 1999, *The New York Times* reported on its front page, 'US Helped Turkey Find and Capture Kurd Rebel'.[1] A senior American official described how the US had worked for four months to capture the leader of the Kurdistan Workers' Party (PKK), Abdullah Öcalan – 'Apo' as he is known to the Kurds – and to hand him over to the Turkish authorities. Only days before, this open secret was officially denied by the Clinton administration. 'The United States did not apprehend or transfer Öcalan, or transport him to Turkey,' said State Department spokesman James Foley. 'In other words, US personnel did not participate in any of those actions that I just described.'[2]

In reality, the US intelligence service had not just been involved, it had been the puppet-master of the entire four-month operation, an operation Kurds refer to 'Uluslararası Komplo (the International Conspiracy)'.[3] As the first truly independent socialist, anti-imperialist Kurdish liberation movement, the PKK has been a thorn in the US's side ever since its foundation in the 1970s. Originally formed by Öcalan himself, the PKK does not recognise itself as a nationalist movement but as a revolutionary dynamic that aims to unite the Kurdish liberation struggle with the wider anti-capitalist class struggle and, on this basis, it strives to create alliances in the region against both reactionary nearby regimes (supported and backed by the US) as well as foreign interventionism generally.

As such, it has been confronted with counter-revolutionary attacks since its founding. The international conspiracy against Abdullah Öcalan was perhaps only the climax of those attacks.

So, what exactly happened in this four-month operation?

By the autumn of 1998 the Syrian regime, under Hafez al-Assad, was becoming increasingly weighed down by military, political and economic pressure from the US, NATO, Israel and Turkey. Buckling under this pressure, the Baathist regime eventually demanded Öcalan, who had been leading his movement from Damascus since 1993,[4] leave the country as soon as possible. He had two options: relocate to the mountains where the PKK guerrilla forces were based (and by doing so, draw even heavier fire onto the military wing of his movement), or deliver himself – as a symbol of the wider Kurdish question – into the hands of the international community and seek a peaceful political solution from them. He decided on the latter and left Syria on 9 October 1998 on a plane bound for Greece.[5]

At the airport in Athens, he was not met by the MP Kostas Baduvas as arranged, but by Savvas Kalenteridis and Yannis Stavrakakis, both high-level officials of the Greek intelligence agency EYP. Öcalan later would say, 'In the persons of Costas Simitis, Baduvas, Stavrakakis and Kalenteridis, the US and NATO were effectively taking me into custody.' The Greek intelligence officials did not allow him to leave the airport and told him to leave the country. The same day, Öcalan left Greece on a special plane chartered by the Greek foreign ministry, with Kalenteridis on board, heading for Moscow.[6]

The US administration piped up publicly for the first time on 4 November only when Russia's Duma decided to accept Öcalan's request for political asylum, despite a new oil deal between Russia and Turkey. James Rubin, spokesman for the State Department told the press on 5 November, 'We have asked the Russian government to investigate whether PKK leader Öcalan is in Russia, and to take the necessary steps to expel, deport or extradite him immediately.'[7] Thereupon, Russia decided that Öcalan should leave. Washington set all the political, diplomatic and trade machinery in motion to prevent Öcalan from finding shelter.

This time Öcalan headed for Italy, a place of significant support for the Kurdish cause. He arrived in Rome on 12 November. On 24 November, President Clinton called the Italian Prime Minister Massimo D'Alema personally, and insisted that they declare him 'persona non grata'. Öcalan stated that he was prepared to leave the country if another solution could be found. But not a single Western country was prepared to accept him. All of them closed their doors. Eventually, on 6 January 1999, he returned to Russia on a special aircraft chartered by the Italian prime ministry. Russia accepted as Italy had promised in return to lift its blockade of the $8 million first instalment of IMF aid owed to Moscow.

Yet Russian security officials visiting Öcalan the next day delivered this message from their prime minister Yevgeny Primakov: 'Our government does not allow you to stay here. You need to leave Russia within three days, and we shall determine where you go.'[8] Three days later, Russian officials forced him to board a cargo plane and deported him to Tajikistan, where he was held for eight days in a house in a remote village without any contact with the outside world. Afterwards, he was returned to Moscow and told that they were going to send him to Syria. Syria meanwhile had made a deal with Turkey to turn Öcalan over to Ankara if he ever returned to the country.

Instead, Öcalan flew to Athens on 29 January with a special aircraft chartered by the retired Greek admiral, Antonis Naxakis. But again he was welcomed with threats by intelligence officials. After a short excursion to Minsk, he arrived on the island of Corfu, where the US military has a base. The next morning, the Greek foreign minister Theodoros Pangalos called Nicholas Burns, the US Ambassador in Athens, and informed him of the arrival of Öcalan. Burns answered: 'Okay, get him out of Greece, don't mind the rest.'[9]

The Greek officials told Öcalan that he would be taken to a safe African country in order to arrange his relocation to South Africa. What they meant by a 'safe country' was Kenya, where the CIA had its African headquarters. In the early-morning hours of 2 February, Öcalan was flown from a secret military airport in Corfu to Nairobi. There he was welcomed by the Greek Ambassador in Kenya, George Kostoulas. Meanwhile the next day, an Israeli intelligence delegation led by David Ivry, the director of Israel's National Security Council, went to Ankara to meet with officials from the Turkish foreign ministry, intelligence service, and the general staff's special operations department.

On the evening of 4 February, the CIA representative in Ankara came to the headquarters of Turkey's National Intelligence Organisation *(Millî İstihbarat Teşkilatı)*, or MİT. The American agent made a very important offer to MİT-head Şenkal Atasagun: the CIA was ready to conduct an operation to capture Öcalan and hand him over to Turkey. Atasagun lost no time and directly informed the Turkish Prime Minister Bülent Ecevit. Later Ecevit would say: 'I still don't understand why they have given us Öcalan.'[10] The four men at the very top of the Turkish state directly came together for an emergency meeting: President Süleyman Demirel, Prime Minister Bülent Ecevit, Chief of General Staff Hüseyin Kıvrıkoğlu and MİT-head Şenkal Atasagun.

The operation was put into action. The US and Turkey signed a secret deal. Öcalan would be captured alive and handed over on condition of a 'fair trial'. Both sides had come to a mutual understanding. The rest was delegated to the operations centre. But US officials kept a firm hand on the tiller. The content of the operation, the weapons used, and the selection of the squad would be under the command of the CIA. MİT would propose candidates for the squad. Once selected, it was taken to a training camp in Ankara. They were not told any details about the operation and simply waited there for the green light. In the meantime, the CIA gathered blow-by-blow updates on Öcalan's exact route from Greek intelligence.

The squad of nine soldiers left Turkey on 10 February from Istanbul, on a private aircraft, rented from a Turkish businessman at the cost of $200,000. They landed at the Entebbe airport in Uganda, checked in at the Lake Victoria Hotel, and awaited news from Kenya.

On the morning of 15 February, Kenyan state officials met with officials from the Greek embassy. At this point, the Greek ambassador told Öcalan that his time was up and that he had to leave the embassy building where he'd been staying. Öcalan asked for one more day but Ambassador Kostoulas answered, 'I cannot guarantee what might happen at night.' Some hours later the head of Kenya's Criminal Investigations Department, Noah Arap Too, arrived at the Greek embassy with a convoy of five government cars. They told Öcalan that he could fly to Amsterdam. Although Öcalan stated that he would not leave the building without an official guarantee, the Kenyan intelligence officials threatened him, saying, 'The aircraft is ready, you need to leave right away. Night draws on. We cannot guarantee what might happen at night.'

Öcalan resisted. Thereupon Kalenteridis offered his assurances, in the name of the Greek state, that he would be safe. Öcalan had no choice. After intense further negotiations at the embassy, Öcalan boarded a Kenyan government vehicle without his aides or any Greek official. He was driven to the airport and placed on the waiting plane, whereupon Turkish agents boarded, seized, shackled, gagged and blindfolded him.

He was returned to Turkey and subjected to a what can only be described as a show trial. A week after his capture, Öcalan's family sent dozens of lawyers to meet with him, all of whom were denied access. Three attorneys from the Netherlands flew to Istanbul on 16 February to take part in Öcalan's defence, but were sent home a day later, after being detained for questioning overnight at Istanbul airport. The Turkish foreign ministry said the Dutch lawyers were not permitted to enter the country because they had acted 'like PKK militants' and 'because they intend to cause provocation and sensation and have no intention to act as lawyers.' Öcalan was consequently questioned by Turkish officials for ten days without any access to lawyers. On 25 February he was finally able to meet two lawyers (Ahmet Okçuoğlu and Hatice Korkut), but they were only allowed to spend twenty minutes with Öcalan, were only allowed to ask him about his health, and could only do so in the presence of a judge.

The trial start date was set as 31 May 1999. Only on 7 May did Öcalan's lawyers get permission to see the thousands of pages of his case file but were not allowed their own copy of it. They therefore had to copy the file, by hand, which took until 15 May. Later meetings with their client were limited to one hour, and several appointments were cancelled due to 'bad weather' or other spurious reasons. Öcalan's lawyers were unaware of what his charges might be and received the formal indictment only after excerpts of it had already been presented to the press. The guilty verdict, on charges of treason and separatism, was announced on 29 June, which many believe was a deliberate message to the Kurds – 29 June being the anniversary of the hanging of Sheikh Said and 47 of his followers in 1925, as punishment for their rebellion against the Turkish state in Diyarbakir. After the conviction, Amnesty International called for an immediate retrial and Human Rights Watch questioned the fact that witnesses brought by the defence had not been heard at the trial.

Öcalan was sentenced to death but the penalty was reduced to life in prison in 2002 after Turkey abolished the death penalty. To this day, over twenty years later, he is held in solitary confinement on the prison island of Imrali in the Sea of Marmara. The island was specially prepared for his incarceration, being evacuated just days before his capture.[11] Öcalan has been held in total isolation as the sole prisoner on the island for more than ten years. At the moment, there are three other political prisoners on the island but their opportunities to interact are highly restricted.

Just as the operation to kidnap Öcalan was unprecedented, so too are the conditions and nature of his detention. For most of the duration of his incarceration, basic human rights like communication with the outside world, access to lawyers and family visits have been withheld – with tacit approval of the European Council's Committee for the Prevention of Torture (CPT), whose alleged mission is to stand *against* physical and psychological torture. But despite all the inhumane and illegal measures taken to isolate him, his radical democratic thinking continues to inspire people fighting for a free life around the world.

Öcalan himself describes the CIA-led NATO operation to capture him as part (or even the start) of a 'Third World War', whose sporadic, intermittent and largely proxy-fought battles have one goal: to restructure and reorganise the Middle East. In his view, nobody other than the CIA is capable of undertaking such a restructuring. To end with his words:

> The strategy to occupy Iraq is closely linked with the operation to hand me over. [....] The same applies to the occupation of Afghanistan. More precisely one of the key steps, indeed the first one in realising the Big Middle East Project, was the operation against me. It was not for nothing that just before he died Ecevit said: 'I still don't understand why they have given us Öcalan.' Just as the First World War was started with the assassination of the Austrian crown prince by a Serb nationalist, the Third World War started with the operation against me.[12]

## Notes

1. https://www.nytimes.com/1999/02/20/world/us-helped-turkey-find-and-capture-kurd-rebel.html
2. US Department of State Daily Press Briefing, February 16, 1999, https://1997-2001.state.gov/briefings/9902/990216db.html
3. Turkish: Uluslararası Komplo
4. Öcalan had to leave Turkey due to state repression and the risk of imprisonment in July 1979. He crossed the border to Kobane illegally and, from Syria, developed relations with leftist revolutionary movements in Lebanon. Öcalan developed relations with the Palestinian movement at the end of 1979 and in 1980 they start to get training in the Beqaa Valley of Lebanon, where many Lebanese and Palestinian movements had their military camps.
5. In the 1990s, Greece hosted a high number of Kurdish political refugees from the Turkish part of Kurdistan. The Kurdish refugees in the Lavrion Refugee Camp organised themselves politically, socially, economical and culturally. Consequently, informal relations began to emerge between elements of the Greek state and the Kurdish liberation movement, which had a diplomatic representative in Athens.
6. Russia is home to a large Kurdish diaspora, originally from the Turkish part of Kurdistan. During the Russo-Ottoman wars of 1826-1828 and 1877-78, some Kurdish tribes fought on the Russian side. This is the reason the Ottoman Empire exiled many Kurds, especially from the Serhat region which bordered on the Russian Empire.
7. https://1997-2001.state.gov/briefings/9811/981105db.html
8. Taken from Öcalan, Abdullah, *Prison Writings*
9. Murat Yetkin, *Kürt Kapanı: Şam'dan İmralı'ya Öcalan [The Kurdish Trap: Öcalan from Damascus to İmrali]*, Remzi Publishing House, Istanbul 2004.
10. Interview with the Turkish daily newspaper *Sabah*, 13 April 2005: http://arsiv.sabah.com.tr/2005/04/13/gnd101.html
11. The island prison of Imrali had previously held, among others, Adnan Menderes, who had been the prime minister during the coup of 27 May 1960 and was sentenced to death and executed on the island on 17 September 1961.
12. Abdullah Öcalan, *Kürt Sorunu ve Demokratik Ulus* Çözümü*: Kültürel Soykırım Kıskacında Kürtleri Savunmak [The Kurdish Question and the Democratic Nation Solution: Defending the Kurds in The Grip of Cultural Genocide]*, Mezopotamya Yayınları, April 2012.

AFGHANISTAN

# Surkhi

## Fariba Nawa

I'M NAKED UNDER THE sheets when the housekeeper walks in, causing me to jolt up and cover my breasts.

'*Baray*!' I yell. 'Get out!'

'*Mazerat*,' she mumbles apologetically, shutting the door behind her, but I imagine her whispering something else – *sag shoi*, probably. Dog washer. Coming from America, calling herself a repatriate, landing a job as a consultant that pays 200 times what she earns as a housekeeper, and all in the name of rebuilding Afghanistan. Dog washer. Dishonouring the very word Afghan by sleeping with a man she's not even married to. They come here to save us, she's probably thinking, instead they shame us.

The first time I heard this curse, I was pacing around the ministry of education, waiting for a friend to meet me. As I walked, a middle-aged man with yellow, crooked teeth on a bicycle began to circle me, looking me up and down, from my polarised sunglasses and floral headscarf combo to my Nike Air sneakers.

'O *sag shoi*, is that what you were doing before America came to Afghanistan? You think you're better than us, but you were just a dog washer in America and you get to be queen here. Take off those glasses so I can look at you,' he sneered and spat on the ground, then rode away.

Red blotches start to pucker on my skin – it's normal when

I feel stress. Right now, the rash is a welcome distraction from the shame. It lets me start paying for it early.

The door opens again and it's Sekander, my boyfriend, another dog washer, in a grey suit and red tie.

'Raha, come down, breakfast is ready. *Tambal shodi*, you're getting lazy. Get up! You gotta go to work.' he orders, his voice gruff.

Then he sees the rash on my chest and arms, and his tone changes to concerned.

'What happened this time? Did you have another nightmare?'

'*Neh*, no, Najla walked in without knocking.'

'Shit. We need to tell the help in this house to respect our privacy. She's going to go blab it to the whole kitchen staff and guards now.'

'Well, it's easy for you.'

'Relax. You don't know what she's thinking. Maybe she's like, "Damn, she must have had some good sex last night. Wish I could have some of that instead of the old man I was forced to marry who can't perform any more".' Sekander chuckles at his own joke.

I manage a fake smile.

'If you want to live in Afghanistan, you gotta be yourself inside the house. Outside, I know you play the good girl you have to be. Come on, I'm hungry. Let's eat!'

I get dressed in my Afghan good-girl outfit: a loose grey pantsuit with the coat down to my knees and a black headscarf wrapped tightly around my neck. Downstairs is a reminder of the golden cage Sekander occupies, a luxurious shared living room serving the two-storey complex currently housing six consultants working with Kirkthorpe, one of the largest contractors assigned to build the country's infrastructure. It's like a bar down here: satellite TV, velvet-lined couches, an open cabinet of spirits and beers, boxes full of fat Texan cigars. Outside a gardener with torn slippers tends to the pink roses, singing an Ahmed Zahir song. But no one can hear him, all the windows are blast-proof just like the bunker installed in the basement: suicide-attack-ready. Down there in the dark, there are shelves stacked with tinned food and all kinds of corners and crevices any kid would love to explore. The house is situated in the leafy Wazir Akbar Khan neighbourhood where well-healed Kabulis once danced to The Beatles drinking Russian whisky.

I don't live here.

I'm just the girlfriend who sleeps over sometimes. My guesthouse has a skinny, unarmed guard, a back-up generator that hasn't worked in years, and no one remotely resembling a gardener or a cook. But I'm still a consultant. I was a lecturer in New York and came here to teach teachers about creative learning. The Americans still pay my salary.

I take my seat at the wooden dining table, hiding my blotchy hands under it. Sekander answers a call from his office and leaves for the other room. Jack, a former Navy Seal now an engineer, reads from the copy of *The New York Times*: '"No group has so far taken responsibility for the attack" – who writes this shit!' he scoffs in a strong Virginian drawl. 'Why are they waiting for an official press release before stating the obvious?' He tosses the paper across the table and reaches for the TV remote.

'Shouldn't we eat first?' I ask, knowing how loud he likes to watch his *Fox News*.

'Alright,' Jack shrugs. 'I wonder if the death count went up. One of the guys at work said he saw more bodies than reported at the Dienerd office. I think I'll work from home today. Maybe there's a second bomb planned.'

Dienerd was another foreign contractor here to train police. The Taliban bombed their headquarters just a few miles away yesterday.

The tall, quiet figure of Lars joins us at the table, hungry as always, at the same moment that Khadija, the cook, appears balancing a tray of breakfasts: scrambled eggs for Jack; eggs flavoured with onions, tomatoes and peppers for Sekander and I; and a cheese omelette for Lars.

'At last!' Lars claps his hands. 'I hope she's made it with the Danablu I gave her.'

She smiles at the men then casts her eyes down when I try to smile back at her. My pulse quickens. She knows. Khadija always said *Salaam* to me in the past. Of course, they all probably guessed weeks ago: my late-night visits to Sekander's room. But... the shame creeps through my blood, and I can sense the redness down to my spine.

'I have to go to work. Tell Sekander I'll call him later,' I abandon the food and make for the door, jump into one of the company vans that seem to always be waiting for us outside.

Traffic is backed up all along the newly paved Wazir Akbar Khan Road. Humvees have become commonplace on Kabul streets. Armed guards stand or sit in thin wooden booths in front of foreign guesthouses and government offices. Helicopters roar across the mountain-rimmed skyline every few days. They sound like the Russian ones that used to buzz over the city on their bombing raids out to the villages when I was growing up, while my mother turned up the radio, drowning them out with Indian ghazals.

The American helicopters are louder though, even the blasts of insurgent IEDs can't drown them out sometimes. I've learned to recognise these blasts, as they always come in clusters. I learn them like the drumbeat of a rock song, and it's a drummer I imagine when I hear them. If I'm home and the windows start to shake, I hover against the corner of the wall in my sparse room, and rock back and forth, imagining I'm the drummer until the noise stops.

The city was built for half a million people before the wars ravaged its elaborate gardens and peaceful hillsides. Now it's home to almost five million, dishevelled but resilient. New four-storey mansions pop up all the time, shaped liked wedding cakes with tinted windows – opium palaces – the homes of warlords and drug barons.

The van stops; there's no room to move as traffic is backed up as far as the eye can see.

Hafeez, the driver, speaks to a colleague on his phone. 'There's been an attack on Chicken Street,' he explains. 'It's still ongoing. We're not going anywhere for a while.'

'Open the door. I'll walk to work. It's fine,' I insist.

'You're going to walk through the police barriers and all the blood?'

'Just open the door!' I shout, unable to stay still any longer.

I need to walk or run to breathe. My feet feel heavy as I begin to jog slowly around the parked cars and police barricades, covering my nose and mouth with my headscarf to avoid the smoke and fresh scent of death. The blood is scattered on the black pavement, a torso lies on one side of me, a head on the other. I turn left on a side street then pick up the pace. I don't know where I am until a boy with a dirt-streaked face points at me.

'*Sorkh shodi*,' he clamours. 'You're blushing.'

I stop and catch my reflection on a parked Nissan SUV with tinted windows. The rash has spread to my face. I catch my breath and grab my mobile phone from my purse.

'Sekander, I need your help. I need my allergy medication but it's in my room, and I'm late for work. I saw the blood again, a… a head.' My voice falters.

'Hey, Raha, *qandem*, calm down. Hafeez told me you ran off down Chicken Street. I can't come. I'm tied up here but I'll come later. Just call in sick and go home.'

Tears prick my eyes and my cheeks sting. As I walk, the kebab vendor playing Bollywood music on his phone, fanning his grill, stares. The *shiriakh* ice cream-maker glares. A middle-aged woman in a chiffon white headscarf catches up with me. She pulls my sleeve with her coarse, brown hands. '*Khoobasti, bachem*?' she says. 'You okay? You look sick.'

I hold her hand tightly. 'I need my allergy pills and a taxi,' I whisper.

She hails a cab, tells the driver to take me where I need to go safely.

★

It's after seven and the sun is already setting when Sekander shows up with a Kirkthorpe SUV at my guesthouse. The company has many cars. He stops to have a cigarette with the guard. I watch him from the window, envying his freedom, the ease and entitlement with which he can walk, talk and dress. I wonder if he ever feels shame like I do, the shame of being a woman.

He hurries upstairs toward my room after his cigarette, calling my name in an authoritative tone.

I open my door and pull him inside so that my housemates don't see us. We hug and kiss. He touches my face. 'The rash is gone. You don't look like a *lablaboo* anymore,' he says, comparing me to a beetroot. 'You have dinner ready?'

'Ah, no. I kind of had a hard day, you know. I'm not in the mood to cook. I thought you would have eaten already.'

'Sassy Raha tonight! Babe, I need a woman who knows how to cook. You know how I appreciate that.'

'Okay, I can make pasta but there's no sauce or tomatoes, so you'll have to settle with purée.'

I head to the kitchen and make a loud clatter of the saucepans.

'You know, I know you're a feminist and all, but not knowing how to cook isn't a good thing,' he says with annoyance.

'I'm cooking, aren't I? So how was your day anyway? Were you able to convince the minister to adopt your anti-corruption strategy?'

★

Sekander is also here from New York. We grew up in Queens in the same community of Afghans in the Flushing neighbourhood. Our parents know each other, both families fled to '*Amrika*' during the Soviet invasion. My parents opened a small grocery store; his parents started a fast-food restaurant selling fried chicken. Sekander and I first met at a Queens College event about Afghan women when the Taliban seized power. He argued with the speaker, a journalist who had just returned from Kabul, that Afghan women don't need help from the West. They know how to fight their own battles. I defended the journalist. They needed allies to fight for their basic human rights, I contended, because our own men were killing their women. Sekander said I was too westernised. I called him sexist. But we had one thing in common even back then: a nostalgia for a homeland replete with other people's memories and bittersweet idealism. 'Afghanistan was a wounded child who didn't trust outsiders,' I said at that meeting, and we were something in between. We were always something in between, even now as the cultural translators and mediators, as an American educated version of what Afghanistan could be, versed in the local languages – the only ones who could help.

For Afghan-Americans, September 11 was a way to confront that immigrant idealism. Maybe the Americans seizing an abandoned Afghanistan could give us a chance to reclaim it again. The Taliban were not a grassroots Afghan movement. They were boys brainwashed by Saudi's and Pakistan's version of Salaffi Islam, and they had to be stopped. They were a modern symptom of both Soviet and 'McJihad' (Saudi-American) imperialism. Maybe people like us, descendants of the Afghan technocrats and intellectuals who the Soviets exiled, could stop the Taliban and keep America in check. Just maybe. I realised history wasn't on my side, but nostalgia refutes reason.

I quit my job in Queens and booked a ticket to Kabul two weeks after the Americans ousted the Taliban. Sekander came shortly after. Our paths crossed again six months later at a party in another big, expensive Kabul house, where a cover band played 80s American rock songs, a blonde expat on a white messiah mission jumped out of a cake dressed as Madonna and everyone was drunk on bootleg vodka. One journalist with a spaghetti-strap dress took off her shoes as she grabbed her aid worker boyfriend, who looked like he was dressed for the beach, and climbed on top of him as he sat with a full glass in his hand and started kissing him for all to see. An Afghan translator took that as a signal to fondle his boss, a redhead military consultant in black heels, on her behind. She slapped his hand and walked away to dance with a woman. A swimming pool with chipped concrete unused for years was filled with water, and a man in Speedos and a woman in a bikini dived in, splashing the dancing guests. It was free theatre for the neighbours sitting on top of the concrete wall watching a lifestyle they had only glimpsed before in movies bought on the black market. They were transfixed as we stumbled across the dance floor. Sekander and I forgot our old enmity and began a relationship based on urgency. Being alive in Kabul wasn't to be taken for granted; we were part of the war scene of foreign correspondents and aid workers, conflict-hoppers and war-tourists, living out high-adrenaline, high-paying careers. Only we thought we were different, Sekander and I, our connection to the homeland made us special and our relationship unbreakable. Or so I thought.

*

'The minister listened and said he'd think about it. I don't have much hope,' Sekander replies.

'You've got a hard job, especially since your employer is stealing from the same money they want to make sure doesn't get into the hands of corrupt Afghans,' I scoffed.

'Not this one again.'

'You mean the one about the HR office churning out invoices for ghost employees?'

'You should know better than to repeat baseless rumours, Raha. If it weren't for my employer, none of the roads and clinics would be built.'

'Sorry, I don't mean to piss you off, but you'll be more pissed off when you're literally the last person in town to realise it.'

'Let's just enjoy tonight's extravaganza!'

I serve him a plate of the tired-looking spaghetti. Sekander looks at it and gives me his 'I'll take two bites of this' grin.

'So babe, I have to tell you something,' Sekander mumbles, his eyes fixed on the pasta. 'My parents are coming to Pakistan and want me to meet up with them for a little break in Karachi. I know it's kind of sudden, but we're going to stay with my cousins there and it'll be good for me to get out of here for a bit.'

'How long?' I ask, knowing that his parents' visit may have ulterior motives.

'A few weeks, not sure yet, depends on how much time I can take off. When I return, we can go on another five-star vacation to Dubai. You know, for some quality time together?' Sekander pushes the plate away and holds my hand.

I pull back.

'We've been together for two years, and you still haven't told your parents. My mom has been expecting a marriage proposal from your parents for months. We can't live like this in Kabul any more. I'm in danger going on the way we are. Any one of the guards or gardeners could attack me for being a degenerate. Don't you understand what risks I'm taking being with you like this?' I start to lose control of my voice. 'What are we doing with this relationship?'

'Okay, calm down. I'll talk to them on this trip. I promise. I know you deserve better, but are you sure you want to spend the rest of your life with such a sexist brute?' He tries a sheepish smile.

Sekander pulls me gently onto his lap and caresses my arm. 'Let's watch one of your 80s movies. I'm leaving tomorrow afternoon, so let's have fun tonight!'

I bring my laptop and we watch *Pretty in Pink* in bed. I cuddle Sekander tightly as we both drift off to sleep.

The next day, he rushes out. I feel a distant void. I turn on Radio Arman and move around the apartment as if in slow motion. The host is talking about couples who dare to love and shun arranged marriages.

'*Dostan, akhir nadara*,' Friends, it doesn't last, he whispers like a sage, then switches to humour. 'Let your parents choose for you. That way, if it doesn't work out, you can blame them.'

I switch the station to news. Coalition air raids have killed more civilians in the countryside.

'The Taliban are getting stronger in our village. They have shut down the girl school because they say it was built by infidels,' one villager is telling the reporter. 'Then the Americans bomb from the air and end up killing more people than the Taliban did.'

The Taliban have released a foreign journalist they were holding hostage but killed his Afghan translator. Kabul should prepare itself for more suicide missions.

I switch off the radio and pour a packet of Nescafé into a chipped cup with hot water, knock it back, then head out to work.

Two weeks later, Sekander calls from Karachi.

'Hi, Raha. I hope you're well.'

The formal tone is already my answer.

'*Salaam*. I hope you're well too. How are your parents?' I keep equally polite.

'They are good. I can't talk long because there's a lot of family here.'

'Okay, then tell me what you have to say.'

'It's not going to work between us. We're too different, Raha. I've been thinking a lot about this and I don't think it would last.'

The rash tingles like newly smoked opium entering the body. I'm taking the call at my desk with five others in a cramped office. I clutch the phone and smile at my colleague who is eyeing me curiously. I excuse myself and drag my feet to the garden.

'How can you do this? I gave you all of me. I told you everything about myself. I told my family. How can you… Why?' I murmur in so much anguish that it hurts.

'Well, if you can bear the specifics, I just can't accept that you've been with other men so casually. I mean you have to understand our mentality as Afghan men, we just can't accept that. You should not have told me. It's dishonourable,' Sekander says, like he's firing an insubordinate employee.

'Are you fucking kidding me?' I scream, making sure I don't pepper in any Farsi in my sentences of rage. That way only the English speakers in the office will understand. 'You've been with more women than I have and some of them are my friends! What about Khatera? You've been married and divorced, and I don't hold that against you. How dare you!'

The anger feels icy, soothing, but the rash is rushing up my neck, and my *dil*, my heart is shredding. He is painting me red with shame, and I want so badly to stop him.

'What about my safety, my *naam*, the reputation that is my life here? What do I tell my mother, who has been planning our wedding? How will she show her face among our community in Queens?'

I ask him these questions but I don't hear what he says. I just hear the betrayal trailing through every step of my journey to this homeland. The bitterness is ripe. I hang up, then drop down into the white garden chair that sits amidst the tulips.

For the next month, I throw my attention into work, avoiding questions about Sekander's return from friends and colleagues. I cry nightly and scratch the rash deliberately so that it will leave scars. My mother calls one evening after another suicide attack that has made the American news. I'm home on my bed, watching *Platoon*.

'Raha, come home. There's no point being there,' she says in her special, wise voice. 'It's a lost cause, Amrika will leave a mess and you can't fix it. Your dad and I know, and you'll eventually find out. We miss you.'

'This is my home now. I'm not going anywhere. I miss you too, *Madar*, but I feel like I'm doing something that matters. Why doesn't that register or matter to you?'

'Fine, *bachaim*, God save you,' she says fatefully. Then there's a pause.

'You know, don't you? You know what he did?' I ask, frightened.

'Yes, his *khalas* have been spreading the word in the stores and at the mosque, at weddings. They're telling everyone you're the slut he couldn't marry. I don't show my face much around Flushing these days,' she says matter-of-factly.

'I'm so sorry, Mom. I'm so, so sorry. I really made a mess,' I put the phone on speaker and weep into my blanket.

'Don't do that to yourself, Raha. I know they are lying. I know you're still *paak*, innocent of such lies they are spreading. That's all that matters to me.'

My mother is only comfortable denying truths she cannot accept, like my lost virginity.

'Did his parents come back from Pakistan?' I ask.

'Not yet. They're just finishing up the post-wedding parties. I hear she's not all that pretty. She's dark-skinned and uneducated and, of course, half Pakistani, which makes it even more appalling.'

'Whose wedding?' I ask.

'Oh *Khoda*, God, I thought you knew.'

My traditional and often racist mother who loves me deeply stops to think of the pain she has inflicted on me with her news.

'Sekander's parents went to Pakistan to marry him to that cousin he always talks about, the one he claims has pined for him since childhood. It was all planned here before they left. You and I were the only ones who didn't know. *Khair basha, bachaim*, it's going to be okay.'

Those are her only words of comfort.

I'm numb, then relieved. I no longer have to love.

'Madar, the next *khwastgar,* the next suitor that comes asking for my hand, you decide whether I should marry him. I don't care. You know best.'

My mother responds but I don't hear. Helicopters are buzzing past my home en route to win over Afghan hearts and minds.

## AFGHANISTAN, 2001-2021

# Afterword: Empire Privatised

## Dr Neil Faulkner

THE FIRST BOMB CAUSED panic. Two more were timed to detonate as the kids poured from the school gates. The street was left strewn with books, backpacks, and bits of bodies, small and smouldering. They killed 85. Others were alive, black and bloody, writhing and groaning. Another 150.

The target was a girls' school in the Hazara district on the edge of Kabul, a sprawl of brick and mud houses ranged along dirt tracks. The Hazaras are Persian-speaking and mainly Shia. Persecuted for centuries, they are especially poor in a country where almost everyone is poor.

Why were their children targeted on 8 May? Because they spoke the wrong language. Because they were the wrong sort of Muslim. Because they were girls who did not know their place and wanted an education.

Just another atrocity in Afghanistan's long litany of atrocities since the fighting began more than 40 years ago. The identity of the killers is secondary. Probably not the Taliban. Perhaps Islamic State. Or some yet more deranged sub-faction. The bigger question is, what conditions give rise to such comprehensive social breakdown, such murderous mass psychosis? What tragic history has elicited such madness? What forces have conjured a world in which men believe they do God's work in blowing up schoolchildren?

Afghanistan's current agony began as long ago as 1979. That

is when the Russians invaded the country to prop up a beleaguered, nominally-communist client regime in Kabul.

The young Afghan apparatchiks meant well. Educated, professional, middle class, they favoured such obvious reforms as piped water and schooling for girls in one of the poorest countries on earth. It was a Stalinist vision: socialism from above; socialism because we know best. But they did mean well.

The village traditionalists – elders, patriarchs, bigoted old men, however one wants to describe them – blocked the reforms. And it was this, the reactionary resistance of the old rural Afghanistan, that triggered the Soviet invasion in December 1979.

Then it was hopeless. The resistance turned into a conflagration – a guerrilla insurgency of Islamic *mujahideen* that transformed Afghanistan into Russia's Vietnam.

The client regime was doomed. When the feminists are on the side of the bombing planes, they have committed political suicide. There is no such thing as socialism from above. The emancipation of the working class has to be the act *of* the working class. Tanks with red flags on are just tanks. You cannot bomb and burn people into socialism.

In another way, it was not Vietnam. The National Liberation Front had never been socialist – whatever it claimed – but it had been for the peasants against the landlords. The Viet Cong had been the armed wing of a revolutionary peasantry. The *mujahideen* were reaction incarnate: instead of rolling forwards to national independence, economic development, and social reform, they wanted to roll backwards to an imagined medieval past.

So the CIA was content to back them. US funding soared from $30 million in 1981 to $280 million in 1985. The combination of Islamist insurgency and US arms broke the Soviet occupation. Russian troop withdrawals began in spring 1988 and were completed a year later.

But warlord militias can be unreliable proxies. By the end of the 1980s, it was not only the Soviet army that was broken, but also the Afghan state. All stable centralised power was gone. Instead, there were regionally based warlords – loaded with high-tech weaponry, captured from the Russians or gifted by the States – competing for power and preference. Most wore their religion lightly. Not so the Taliban, whose cult of guns and prayers won them a growing following among the rootless male youth of a failed state. They took control of most of the country in 1996 – with the backing of powerful Islamist forces inside Pakistan – and looked set soon to grab the lot.

Afghanistan owes its global importance to its location. It is a geopolitical platform in the heart of Central Asia. That is why it was contested between Britain and Russia in the late nineteenth century, and again between Russia and the US in the late twentieth. In 2001, therefore, having failed to establish a client regime of their own in Kabul, the United States invaded Afghanistan, backed by the British and some others, just as the Soviets had done.

The Afghans have a saying: our enemies have the watches, but we have the time. From Alexander the Great to George W. Bush, the Afghans have eventually seen the back of every foreign invader. But the cost can be eye-wateringly high. And Afghanistan is usually only ever part of something broader.

9/11 provided US imperialism with an excuse to go onto the offensive. The US is the single greatest threat to peace in the world today. This is because the US is in decline economically, yet remains dominant militarily. The self-proclaimed 'War on Terror' is, in one sense, a global projection of US military power in an attempt to shore up a crumbling imperial hegemony. Across Central Asia and the Middle East, in particular, the aim after 9/11 was to steal a march on geopolitical rivals and secure military bases for the indefinite defence of privileged US access to oil and gas reserves. The cost would be around a million dead, a swathe of mayhem from Kabul to Yemen, and a dozen intractable insurgencies.

This 'War on Terror' has been portrayed as a Manichean 'clash of civilisations', a struggle between Islam and the West. It is nothing of the sort. It is a struggle of imperialist capital for control of scarce global resources. But it derives much of its ideological character from political developments inside the Middle East since 1979.

Islam is a religious confession, no more inherently political than Christianity, Hinduism, or Buddhism. It can give expression to a wide range of class interests and political attitudes. 'Islamism', or 'Islamic fundamentalism', or 'political Islam' is not, therefore, a single, cohesive, organised force. The label encompasses movements that range from the tribal patriarchs of the Taliban and the Islamic fascists of Al-Qaeda to radical resistance organisations like Hezbollah in Lebanon and Hamas in the Gaza Strip. Indeed, Islamism's lack of definition is part of its appeal. It seems able to offer a home to anyone opposed to imperialism, dictatorship, and impoverishment. It has the apparent capacity to unite the young professional, the unemployed graduate, the market stallholder, the street-peddler, and the village mullah in a single mass movement.

Islamism's appeal has been enhanced by the failure of other, secular traditions – that of Arab nationalism, the old communist parties, the Palestinian guerrilla groups, and many others. The Iranian Revolution of 1979 seemed to represent a new way forward. A mass movement of millions had overthrown a vicious, heavily armed, US-backed dictator, the Shah. The reality is that the Left in Iran was smashed as much as the Shah was, by a counter-revolutionary Islamist movement. The workers, the women, and the national minorities went down to defeat. But this reactionary essence of Islamism was obscured by the anti-imperialist rhetoric and posturing of the new regime in Tehran.

Good enemies to have, the Islamists. For they are no real threat to the rule of capital, yet can be cast as the alien 'Other', as stereotypical 'Orientals' – benighted, malevolent, a violent menace lurking in the shadows. How would the American Empire have successfully recast itself, after the collapse of the Soviet Union, but for 'the international Islamic conspiracy' invented by its security wonks and in-house publicists?

It is not so bad, this New World Disorder. Not for the lords of capital and the war machines that do their bidding. Too much order is bad for business. War pays.

Capitalism has been dependent on high levels of arms expenditure since the Second World War. In the context of the Cold War, US President Eisenhower spoke of 'the military-industrial complex' – state contracts to private firms to make military hardware. The Fall of the Berlin Wall was bad news for the arms manufacturers. Fortunately, the 'War on Terror' was not long coming. It was ideal: a war that never ends; a war that is self-feeding; a war in which each round of violence triggers further escalation, 'mission creep', rising demand for guns.

This dependence of the system on arms expenditure – like its dependence on debt and speculation – has deep roots in a long-term crisis of over-accumulation and under-consumption. In a world where the richest one per cent own half the world's wealth and the poorest 80 per cent have to get by on a five per cent share, there is a chronic lack of demand in the system. That is why the cash reserves of the 2,000 biggest non-financial corporations increased from $6.6 trillion in 2010 to $14.2 trillion in 2020. The world is awash with surplus capital seeking profitable investment. State arms contracts are an essential part of the system's life-support.

We now have a military-police-prison-security-surveillance complex amounting to what William I. Robinson calls a 'Global Police State'. US arms expenditure has tripled since 2000 and is now around $1 trillion a year. The profits of the US arms suppliers have quadrupled in that time. Increasingly, too, private corporations supply the personnel – the soldiers, police, and guards – with an estimated 20 million people now working in private security firms worldwide.

The Biden Administration has now pulled out. The mayhem around Kabul airport – the desperation of thousands tainted by association with the Western occupation forces trying to escape the Taliban – looks like a classic 'end of empire' scene. Not really.

The Islamic reactionaries are back in control in Afghanistan. The Islamic fascists internationally will be emboldened. But the Western powers will simply continue their War on Terror by other means. And the merchants of death will keep on getting richer.

The massive injection of state funds into 'militarised accumulation' ripples across the global system. Take the oil corporations. Estimated consumption of fuel by the US military? A million barrels a day. Take the construction firms. The total value of contracts issued following the US occupation of Afghanistan? A billion dollars. And these military-related contracts create further chains of accumulation reaching into every corner of the system, from the hamburgers consumed by military personnel on an army base to the digitalised surveillance systems of the secret state. It is a permanent war economy.

Afghanistan has been at war, more or less, for more than 40 years. No one who matters thinks this a problem. Before the Taliban takeover, the country was full of mercenaries and contractors making a killing. Someone blew up a market or a maternity hospital, and that was like a free commercial for G4S. Feeling unsafe? Worried about that pipeline? Employees getting anxious? Let G4S set your mind at rest. With operations in more than 90 countries and more than half a million employees across the world, G4S are the security experts you need in a troubled world.

The Afghan dystopia is only an extreme example of an escalating global social crisis. It is the archetypal failed state, destroyed by war, gun-running, drug dealing, and mass displacement, pulled apart by foreign armies and warlord militias, preyed upon by every sort of gangster and profiteer. It is an image, painted in the starkest of colours, of a world gone mad as corporate capital and the war machines that serve it propel us towards an abyss of social and ecological breakdown.

# A Gentle Breath in His Ear

## Gabriel Ángel

Translated from the Spanish by Adam Feinstein

BEFORE DROPPING OFF TO sleep, Simón had been thinking over many things in his past. Something in his character had singled him out from the other youths in Valledupar. Yes, he'd always loved accordion music and going out on the town, as well as enjoying his conquests over the local beauties, making sure he had a great time with the girls while at the same time always trying to avoid getting too seriously entangled with them. But what he hadn't done was throw himself head first into just studying with the sole aim of accumulating money. There were more important things in life.

Like building a better society, for example, where humanity meant more than, and took priority over, making a profit. Where wealth was not the exclusive property of an élite group, but belonged to everyone instead. Where governments were not acting on behalf of a privileged minority but rather were in the service of the vast majority of workers. Where no one suffered from hunger or ignorance. Those were the convictions which had landed him in that jail in the United States.

From respected manager of a bank to inmate sentenced to sixty years behind bars in the maximum-security prison in Florence. He recalled his first days as a guerrilla, in the Santa Marta mountains, alongside his comrades who, like him, had sought refuge up in the hills before the dirty war which took the lives of hundreds of opposition leaders. Sixteen years later, after his stint as the organisation's spokesman at the El Caguán peace talks, with the renewal of the war and while he was carrying out a mission in Quito, he'd been captured and handed over to the Colombian government.

In the end, he was extradited to the USA, falsely accused of drug trafficking. He remembered how overjoyed he'd felt when, after several trials, they were unable to convict him. And his immense indignation when they charged him again, this time with plotting to kidnap American nationals, and finally managed to sentence him. Just as sleep finally got the better of him, he recalled his closest friends around the table at El Caguán: black Biojó, Julián Conrado, Marianita Páez. When he thought about Marianita, it brought a tender smile to his lips. He learned they'd killed her in a shoot-out. She was so pretty, so seductively playful.

When exactly he fell asleep, he couldn't say. Time no longer held any meaning for him. Lying face down on his narrow black mattress, he felt a gentle breath waking him in his left ear. He had the impression that a new dream was starting within the first one. He'd grown used to this succession of dreams which kept him from becoming bored during his nights in prison, unexpected changes of place and situation which he always enjoyed.

Awake, each day was identical to the one before. But when he fell asleep, he could experience different situations. It was as if his life had become the exact opposite of that of all other mortals. For all other human beings, novelty began when you woke up each morning, whereas for him, anything new occurred only when he was asleep.

He wondered whether the breath he'd felt might not be the gentle fluttering of a blue butterfly, those enormous butterflies he'd loved seeing flying around the forest years earlier. For a moment, he wanted to be transported back to his life of marches and encampments which had so enchanted him and from which he had been so absurdly snatched away. And yet, instead of the fluttering, he thought he could make out the sound of soft, friendly, familiar laughter echoing in his ear, followed by a gentle voice whispering playfully to him: 'Commander, Commander Simón Trinidad, what a huge honour to see you again.'

Simón knew instantly who was doing the talking. For the past fifteen years, he'd been shut away in that prison built in the middle of the desert, without anyone, other than the security personnel, saying a single word to him. And they always spoke in English, in a remote, mocking tone. But this was an affectionate voice, which could only come from a woman guerrilla, a comrade-in-arms, and someone who was very close to him because of the intimate tone she was using. *La Nana*, she called herself, Marianita, the only person who felt at liberty to address him in such a teasing manner.

Her unexpected presence came as such a fascinating surprise that he felt unable to move an inch. He was afraid that, if he shifted position, the spell would be shattered and he'd wake up abruptly to the distressing white light of his cell. Suddenly, a flash of lucidity ran through his head. If Marianita had indeed managed to slip into his cell, she couldn't possibly have escaped the attention of the cameras capturing every moment. She was bound to be discovered.

He had to warn her. He opened his eyes and twisted his body so he could look her in the face. Of course it was her. With that mischievous smile and those eyes glowing with life. She was wearing a military uniform and a leather jacket in which Simón could make out the black shimmer of a calibre 7.65 Beretta pistol. Something truly inconceivable in that place.

Mariana laughed when she saw the look of astonishment in his eyes, and as she did so, her full head of black hair appeared to celebrate his delight. Immediately, before he could stop her, her short arms and slender body joined his in a powerful, emotional embrace.

'They'll see us,' Simón exclaimed in alarm. 'They'll come for you and drag you away in chains. You don't know what they're like in here.' To which Marianita was only able to reply, her voice breaking with happiness: 'Don't worry, Simón, they'll never find out.'

Simón decided to straighten up so that he was now sitting on the bed, which, in actual fact, was no more than a concrete plank attached to the concrete wall. Hugging Mariana, his startled eyes raced around the cell. Two yards by three-and-a-half, with a sort of table connected to the wall and a poor imitation of a bench, also concrete, facing the wall. Just beyond that, the toilet bowl and a small sink above it. At the far end: the bars which separated the cell from the corridor and the door. The little black-and-white television set was in its usual place. He hated switching it on; he'd never liked religious hymns or ceremonies.

Marianita asked him whether he remembered Casona and, without a moment's hesitation, Simón said, 'Yes.' In fact, it held pleasant memories for him. It was the last place they'd seen each other, where they'd lived – as if in a bubble – through the early stages of the Plan Patriota against the FARC's Eastern Bloc. It was situated on the banks of Caño Lobos, deep in the Yari forest, fairly close to the encampments where Manuel Marulanda Vélez and Comrade Jorge Briceño (*El Mono*) were housed.

Marianita made herself comfortable on the edge of the bed. Simón tried to lean back against the hard wall. They ended up sitting next to one another, but Simón had a good view of her. 'We went through some unforgettable months there,' she said. 'You and Lucero lived in a little house. Your buddy and *La Negra* lived in another small house. Just a few yards away. I was with Antonio Nariño's lot in the downstairs bedrooms. We had only recently arrived from Cundinamarca. The troops had finally forced us out, after one hell of a series of shootouts.'

'Yes, that's when we really started to experience a new type of war,' remembered Simón. He recalled that, during his stay in Magdalena Medio, around the time of the search squad that was hunting down Pablo Escobar after he escaped from La Catedral prison, the sky would suddenly light up at night with an intense reddish glow which meant they could see the lay of the land, despite the colouring, as if it were daytime. Planes and helicopters were checking for the possible presence of drug traffickers down below.

'It was the most sophisticated thing we'd seen, until the Plan Patriota, of course.' This was one of the chapters of the so-called Plan Colombia, under which President Pastrana threw the doors wide open to the Americans to intervene in the internal conflict.

'Yes, that was what we started to live through in Casona,' Marianita remembered. 'Then, day by day, they began to appear – we called them balloons. Dazzling lights in the sky, day and night, like big luminous stars, carrying out the most peculiar movements without the sound of any engine propelling them. Sometimes, they'd stay in the same spot for half an hour and then move on elsewhere. We never found out what they were.'

'Gringo devices,' Simón replied. 'The guys from the Southern Bloc managed to shoot down a small plane every now and then, and it turned out to be a glider, apparently guided by remote control. They found all kinds of crap inside, cameras, heat detectors. I saw the photos they sent. They said they were dropped by planes flying much higher up, with the aim of locating encampments and roads in the forest.'

'Yes,' said Marianita. 'And guerrilla committees also started coming across cameras in the bushes. The helicopters flew just above the treetops and a soldier would lean out quickly and attach the cameras to the branches. Then they flew off again without our even noticing. Their aim was to film the passage of guerrilla units so they could confirm their location. That was a pretty ridiculous idea. Given the size of the jungle.'

Simón smiled at the memory before adding: 'My buddy said it was all just business. Maybe a question of how many cameras, balloons and other devices the gringos could sell to the Colombian Army. What mattered was not how useful they really were but how many dollars they could rake in. Some did turn out to be useful, like those night-vision goggles they distributed to every active soldier. There were thousands of men in the mobile patrols and brigades, so providing them with goggles brought in money and helped because it allowed them to attack us at night.'

'On top of that, they had another use,' he went on. 'In the long run, I ended up a prisoner, many feet below ground, as a direct consequence of those devices the gringos introduced into the war.'

'I don't get you,' said Mariana.

'When the guys from the Southern Bloc shot down the light aircraft from which the three American contractors were carrying out aerial espionage – and I remember that we talked about that on various culture shows in Casona, which was hundreds of miles from where the event took place – no one imagined I'd end up being sentenced on a trumped-up charge of having ordered the kidnappings. Those planes were tracking the signals from the devices and cameras we'd taken from the crash site. That's what I mean.'

Marianita said nothing for a moment. 'It was true, the facts and their effects mingled so closely in the war that they ended up producing unimaginable consequences. It could be fatal to leave certain things to chance. We thought their objective was to locate our encampments in the jungle, to pass on their precise position to the fighter bombers. It never occurred to anybody that one of our units capturing some spies would land you in this hellhole.'

'That's right,' Simón nodded. 'It was around then that the bombardments started, a practice we'd seen very little of. That was the three Americans' job. I remember *La Panda*. She was a pretty girl. She may have been the very first victim of the practice. She was wounded in the first bombardment. The boys tried to get her out. But then more bombs started raining down, forcing them to leave her there. We never did find out what happened to her.'

'But we also gained some advantages, Simón. Some of the bombs ended up buried in the ground without exploding. When the worst was over, we dug them up, defused them and then extracted the TNT. You were already in prison when the most intense fighting of the war was going on. When everything flared up, they would bomb and then leave. Later on, after the bombardment, the helicopters arrived and when they'd finished machine-gunning the whole area, hundreds of soldiers parachuted down. That was their way of attacking us. But using the TNT, we made mines to stem the advance of their troops. The gringo way of waging war met its match when it ran into those mines. They stopped the advance.'

Simón nodded. Then he asked: 'Marianita, did you realise, when they arrested me in Quito, the men who came to the house to capture me were gringos? They were the ones who arranged everything.'

'They arranged everything,' she replied, 'all the way from Marquetalia up to right now, to what's happening today. They're to blame for everything.'

Simón looked down and said nothing. He thought about how television, the press and radio always presented those who defended 'law and order' as heroes, over and above the atrocities they committed in the name of that slogan. Apparently, it was true what they always said: it was only victors who got to write memoirs and record history. He'd thought long and hard about this. Here was his first opportunity to talk it over with someone, and yet he held back.

Instead, he asked: 'Did you come here just to talk about Casona?'

'Actually, that was just an excuse to get to what I really wanted to tell you,' Mariana replied. 'She came through Casona, the girl, your daughter, on her way to Ecuador with her grandmother. They were escaping their own country, their own land. People had tried to kill them several times. I personally saw how happy everyone was when they turned up and how terribly sad they felt when she and her grandmother had to leave again. They were going into exile. There was nowhere safe for them in Colombia.'

Simón winced in a grimace of pain. His eyes filled with tears which he tried to conceal by bowing his head again. When he was finally able to speak, he said:

'We saw her again in Quito. A couple of happy days before I was captured. She'd come back with her grandmother. They were watching us the whole time without our realising it. Then they transferred me to Colombia, and a year later to the high-security jail at Cómbita, Uribe arranged for my extradition. Lucerito had not seen her again, either, until the day she went to visit her in her encampment, in the Putumayo. We loved our daughter so much.'

Simón buried his chin in his chest again for a few moments. Then he continued:

'I've always believed that, ever since I was captured, they planned to follow the girl to attack the rest of us when they felt it was the right moment. Years later, they contracted an intelligence agent. His job was to get her to fall in love with him. That was how he learned she was thinking of visiting her mum. And he handed her a present. It had a tracking chip in it. That same night, they bombed the encampment. They showed no mercy. Everyone was killed. Lucerito, the girl, every single one.'

'Chips and other tricks like that are exactly how the gringos operate,' Mariana said, stumbling over her words, trying her best not to be overcome by tears. 'They managed to plant a chip on Comrade Jorge Briceño, *El Mono*, as well, in his encampment, in a pair of boots. That's how they were able to be so precise the night they bombed it.'

Then Simón unexpectedly changed the subject:

'But how did you manage to get in here, Nanita? How did the guard not notice you? I really must write this dream down. I don't want to forget it as soon as I wake up, the way I do with most of my dreams. You know, I saw you once in a dream dressed all in red, entering a church to get married to my buddy. This must be another dream like that one.'

Marianita replied with a hint of nostalgia in her voice: 'I always dreamed this would come true, Simón. But it was impossible. Life is so hard. But please believe me, this is not a dream. Do you really think there's anywhere the FARC can't find a way into? Anything we've planned, we've succeeded in doing. That's why I came: Comrade Manuel and Comrade Jorge organised it.'

To convince him, Marianita added: 'You know what, Simón? They can bomb the rebels, kill them, bad-mouth as many as they want. But what they can never do is wipe out our ideas. The ideas go on, the ideas are still alive. They must survive somewhere, mustn't they?'

'Of course they're alive,' Simón agreed. 'The ideas live on in those who continue the struggle, however that war is waged. With whatever new weapons are necessary. They live on in the survivors, in the people, in the classes who protest against injustice.'

'In the dead, too,' Nana pointed out. Don't forget I was shot in the head, at point-blank range. We're going to leave a doppelgänger here. It'll look as though you've died. That will make them happy. But you're coming with me. The old guard need you. They want to talk to you, they have another mission for you. A critically important one.'

Then, oddly, she asked him what went through his head when he felt her breath in his ear. Simón said straight off that he thought it must be a blue butterfly. 'The kind we'd see flying around in the forest,' he added. 'Does that mean anything? Does it mean you are longing for something?' she asked. 'Yes,' he said. 'The marches, the encampments, life as a guerrilla.'

No sooner had he said those words than Simón found himself following Marianita along a narrow path surrounded by enormous trees. In front of them lay a wooden bridge which seemed familiar. 'This looks just like Casona,' he said. 'It does,' she answered, 'but we're up in the Rocky Mountains, overlooking the desert. You'll see. There's such a lot of work that needs doing.'

As she walked along, she couldn't help laughing at the idea her breath in Simón's ear had conjured up in his mind. Earlier, twenty years earlier, when she arrived in secret at his buddy's hideout, lifted the mosquito net and breathed in his ear, he would turn to her and say: 'A tiger, I'm being attacked by a tiger and he looks hungry.' Then she would reassure him that nothing bad was going to happen to him, and she'd lie down gently and lovingly at his side. One of these days, they're going to send me to get *him* too, she thought, with a smile, then turned round to Simón to point out a broken plank.

At that same moment, looking over from the other side of the bridge, Simón stared as if he couldn't believe his eyes. Lucerito, with her short hair, her radiant face and her well-toned body, was running towards him accompanied by a pretty, fair-haired girl with green eyes and white skin.

COLOMBIA, 2002

# Afterword: From Plan Lazo to False Positives


## Daniel Kovalik

University of Pittsburgh School of Law


As I WRITE THESE words, Colombia is on fire. Colombians are protesting throughout the country, initially against tax increases, and now more generally against a right-wing government which has imposed draconian neo-liberal economic policies that have made Colombia one of the most unequal societies on earth, and which has been slaughtering those who have dared dissent. The Colombian state's crackdown has been brutal. At the time of this writing [May 2021], at least 379 protesters have been forcibly disappeared since protests began, less than two weeks ago, and scores have been shot dead in the streets.[1]

Colombia is currently voicing publicly what many of us have known for years – that the present government is a brutal one protected by military and paramilitary forces which engage in mass killings and disappearances to prevent progressive social change. Colombia leads the Americas in terms of disappeared people, with over 90,000, according to the International Committee of the Red Cross.[2] It also leads the world in terms of forcibly displaced people, at well over 8 million.[3] Meanwhile, scores of social leaders – including trade unionists, human rights leaders, indigenous and Afro-Colombian leaders and even Catholic priests advocating for the poor – are killed every year. Indeed, around 450 such social leaders have been killed since the signing of the Colombian Peace Agreement in 2016.[4]

And yet, despite all of this, one would be forgiven for not knowing this given the scant coverage of Colombia's human rights situation by the mainstream press.

Of course, all of this was according to plan – specifically, the plan laid out by the United States back in 1962 – two years before the FARC[5] guerillas were even officially constituted. As a report by Human Rights Watch explains:[6]

> [Colombian] General Ruiz became army commander in 1960. By 1962, he had brought in US Special Forces to train Colombian officers in cold war counterinsurgency. Colombian officers also began training at US bases. That year, a US Army Special Warfare team visited Colombia to help refine *Plan Lazo*, a new counterinsurgency strategy General Ruiz was drafting. US advisers proposed that the United States 'select civilian and military personnel for clandestine training in resistance operations in case they are needed later.' Led by Gen. William P. Yarborough, the team further recommended that this structure 'be used to perform counter-agent and counter-propaganda functions and as necessary execute paramilitary, sabotage and/or terrorist activities against known communist proponents. It should be backed by the United States.'

Judging by the events that followed, the US recommendations were implemented enthusiastically through Plan Lazo, formally adopted by the Colombian military on July 1, 1962. While the military presented Plan Lazo to the public as a 'hearts-and-minds' campaign to win support through public works and campaigns to improve the conditions that they believed fed armed subversion, privately it incorporated the Yarborough team's principal recommendations. Armed civilians — called 'civil defence,' 'self-defence,' or 'population organisation operations,' among other terms — were expected to work directly with troops.

Noam Chomsky further explains the purposes and methods of Yarborough's plan for Colombia, which grew out of President John F. Kennedy's newly-minted National Security Doctrine. As Chomsky relates:

> The president of the Colombian Permanent Committee for Human Rights, former Minister of Foreign Affairs Alfredo Vasquez Carrizosa, writes that it is 'poverty and insufficient land reform' that 'have made Colombia one of the most tragic countries of Latin America,' though as elsewhere, 'violence has been exacerbated by external factors,' primarily the initiatives of the Kennedy administration, which 'took great pains to transform our regular armies into counterinsurgency brigades,' ushering in 'what is known in Latin America as the National Security Doctrine,' which is not concerned with 'defence against an external enemy' but rather 'the internal enemy.' The new 'strategy of the death squads' accords the military 'the right to fight and to exterminate social workers, trade unionists, men and women who are not supportive of the establishment, and who are assumed to be communist extremists.'[7]

Meanwhile, the FARC began in earnest in 1964 after the US-backed napalm attack by the Colombian military upon the independent peasant republic in Marquetalia, Colombia. The civil conflict in Colombia continued almost without pause since that time until a peace agreement was signed in 2016. One pause in the war did take place in the 1980s when the FARC agreed to an earlier peace agreement in which it laid down its arms in return for the right to run political candidates through the Patriotic Union (UP) party. This peace agreement ultimately ended as the result of the Colombian military-paramilitary murder of thousands of UP candidates and supporters.

The US's paramilitary (aka 'death squad') strategy in Colombia, combined with its billions of dollars of lethal aid to the military that works with these death squads have contributed greatly to the massive human rights disaster which has destroyed the lives of millions in Colombia since the early 1960s. More specially, according to Colombia's own Victim's Unit, as of 2014, seven million Colombians fell victim to Colombia's armed conflict.[8]

It is a notable fact that, according to Colombia's own Victims Unit report, 'the majority of victimisation occurred after 2000, peaking in 2002 at 744,799 victims.'[9] It is not coincidental that 'Plan Colombia', or 'Plan Washington' as many Colombians have called it, was inaugurated by President Bill Clinton in 2000, thus escalating the conflict to new heights and new levels of barbarity. Plan Colombia is the plan pursuant to which the US has given Colombia over $8 billion of mostly military and police assistance.

As Amnesty International has explained, these monies have only fuelled Colombia's human rights crisis:[10]

> Colombia has been one of the largest recipients of US military aid for well over a decade and the largest in the Western Hemisphere. [...] Yet torture, massacres, 'disappearances' and killings of non-combatants are widespread and collusion between the armed forces and paramilitary groups continues to this day. [...]
>
> 'Plan Colombia' – the name for the US aid package since 2000, was created as a strategy to combat drugs and contribute to peace, mainly through military means. [...]
>
> Despite overwhelming evidence of continued failure to protect human rights the State Department has continued to certify Colombia as fit to receive aid. The US has continued a policy of throwing 'fuel on the fire' of already widespread human rights violations, collusion with illegal paramilitary groups and near-total impunity.
>
> Furthermore, after 10 years and over $8 billion of US assistance to Colombia, US policy has failed to reduce availability or use of cocaine in the US, and Colombia's

> human rights record remains deeply troubling. Despite this, the State Department continues to certify military aid to Colombia, even after reviewing the country's human rights record.

What Amnesty International did not mention is that Plan Colombia was initiated in the midst of peace talks between the Colombian government and FARC guerillas, and actually played a key role in derailing these talks,[11] and with them the chances for peace for some time to come.

One particularly gruesome phenomenon that flowed directly from Plan Colombia was the 'false positive' scandal in which thousands of innocent civilians were killed by the Colombian military which then tried to pass them off as guerillas killed in battle.

Thus, Human Rights Watch (HRW) issued a report[12] citing 'extensive previously unpublished evidence [which] implicates many Colombian army generals and colonels in widespread and systematic extrajudicial killings of civilians between 2002 and 2008.' HRW notes that Colombian 'prosecutors are investigating at least 3,000 of these cases, in which army troops, under pressure to boost body counts in their war against armed guerrilla groups, killed civilians, and reported them as combat fatalities.' Jose Miguel Vivanco, executive Americas director of HRW, described these killings, known as the 'false positive' killings, as 'one of the worst episodes of mass atrocity in the Western Hemisphere in recent years.'

There are reports by other groups, such as the Fellowship of Reconciliation (FOR), which put the number of victims of this slaughter at closer to 6,000. The damning report released by FOR[13] demonstrates how there is a direct correlation between US military funding and training, particularly at the School of the Americas (aka WHINSEC), at Fort Benning, Georgia, and the incidence of human rights abuses, including 'false positive' killings. To wit, the report concluded that 'of the 25 Colombian

WHINSEC instructors and graduates for which any subsequent information was available, 12 of them – 48 per cent – had either been charged with a serious crime or commanded units whose members had reportedly committed multiple extrajudicial killings.'

Moreover, FOR reports that 'some of the officers with the largest number of civilian killings committed under their command (Generals Lasprilla Villamizar, Rodriguez Clavijo, and Montoya, and Colonel Mejia) received significantly more US training on average than other officers' during the high-water mark of the 'false positive' scandal.

The most salient aspect of the 'false positive' scandal for Americans is that the Colombian military has been encouraging the high body count, and therefore murdering civilians to acquire it, in order to justify continued military aid from the United States which, since 2000, has given that military over $9 billion and counting to wage its counterinsurgency war. In other words, it is the United States which is truly behind the 'body count syndrome' at the heart of the 'false positive scandal.' And, it cannot be said that the US has somehow been encouraging body counts unwittingly, for it has been very aware of this phenomenon for many years.

As an illuminating account by Michael Evans at the National Security Archive explains,[14] recently de-classified US documents show that 'the CIA and senior US diplomats were aware as early as 1994 that US-backed Colombian security forces engaged in "death squad tactics", cooperated with drug-running paramilitary groups, and encouraged a "body count syndrome..."' Yet, despite long-standing knowledge of such crimes, the US not only continued but indeed massively increased its military aid to Colombia.[15]

A 2016 exposé in *The New York Times* entitled 'The Secret History of Colombia's Paramilitaries & The US War on Drugs' contained useful evidence as to the US's true views towards the Colombian death squads and their massive war crimes and human rights abuses.[16] The gist of the *NYT* story was that, beginning in 2008, the US has extradited 'several dozen' top paramilitary leaders, thereby helping them to evade a transitional justice process which would have held them accountable for their war crimes and crimes against humanity. They have been brought to the US where they have been tried for drug-related offences only and given lenient sentences of 10 years in prison on average. And, even more incredibly, 'for some, there is a special dividend at the end of their incarceration. Though wanted by Colombian authorities, two have won permission to stay in the United States, and their families have joined them. There are more seeking the same haven, and still others are expected to follow suit.'

That these paramilitaries – 40 in all that the *NYT* investigated – are being given such preferential treatment is shocking given the magnitude of their crimes. For example, paramilitary leader Salvatore Mancuso, 'who the government said "may well be one of the most prolific cocaine traffickers ever prosecuted in a United States District Court,"' has been found by Colombian courts to be 'responsible for the death or disappearance of more than 1,000 people.' Yet, as a result of his cooperation with US authorities, Mr Mancuso 'will spend little more than 12 years behind bars in the US'

Another paramilitary, the one the article focused on most, is Hernan Giraldo Serna, and he committed '1800 serious human rights violations with over 4,000 victims'. Mr Giraldo was known as 'The Drill' because of his reputation for raping young girls, some as young as nine years old. Indeed, he has been 'labelled [...] "the biggest sexual predator of paramilitarism."' While being prosecuted in the US for drug-related crimes only, Mr Giraldo too is being shielded by the US from prosecution back in Colombia for his most atrocious crimes.

Meanwhile, the treatment of ex-FARC leaders and combatants could not be more different. Thus, as the Colombian state did in the 1980s after the first peace accord with the FARC, it is currently actively hunting down and killing disarmed FARC members. All in all, over 250 ex-FARC combatants have been killed since the laying down of arms in 2017.[17] And, those FARC members who have been captured and imprisoned – such as the protagonist of Gabriel Angel's story, the real-life FARC peace negotiator Simón Trinidad – are being subject to the most inhumane treatment such as torture and extended solitary confinement.

So, what is going on here? The *NYT* gave a couple of reasons for why the US would single out right-wing paramilitaries – who the US State Department itself has 'designated [as] terrorists responsible for massacres, forced disappearances and the displacement of entire villages' – for 'relatively lenient treatment' while ex-FARC combatants are killed and tortured.

First, it correctly explains that former President Alvaro Uribe, the most prominent and outspoken opponent of the peace deal between the Colombian government and the FARC guerillas, asked the US to extradite these paramilitary leaders because, back home in Colombia, they had begun 'confessing not only their war crimes but also their ties to his allies and relatives.' The *NYT* also wrote off the US treatment of these paramilitaries as the US giving priority to its war on drugs 'over Colombia's efforts to confront crimes against humanity that had scarred a generation.'

Unfortunately, these explanations let the US off the hook too easily, for they do not tell the whole story behind the US's relationship with Colombia and its death squads.

The real reason is that the US also shares an ideology with both Uribe and his paramilitary friends, and that it has wanted to prevent the paramilitaries from not only confessing to their links with Uribe, but also from confessing their links to the US military, intelligence and corporations.

The *NYT*, while ultimately pulling its punches here, at least touches upon this issue when it states that 'the paramilitaries, while opponents in the war on drugs, were technically on the same side as the Colombian and American governments in the civil war.' But 'technically' is not *le mot juste;* rather, it is an imprecise and mushy term used to understate the true relationship of the paramilitaries with the US The paramilitaries have not just been 'technically' on the side of the US and Colombian governments; rather, they have been objectively and subjectively on their side, and indeed an integral part of the US/ Colombia counterinsurgency programme in Colombia for decades.

The potential confession of paramilitary leaders to their links with the US and Colombia, as well as to US multinationals, was as much of a threat to the US as their confessions were to Colombian President Alvaro Uribe. And that is why the US extradited the top paramilitary leaders and treated them with kid gloves.

As just one example, paramilitary leader Salvatore Mancuso told investigators nearly 10 years ago that it was not only fruit conglomerate Chiquita that provided financial support to the paramilitaries (this is already known because Chiquita pled guilty to such conduct and received a small, $25 million fine for doing so), but also companies like Del Monte and Dole.[18] However, given that Mancuso was never put on trial (the *NYT* notes that none of the paramilitary leaders has) but instead was given a light sentence based upon a plea deal, such statements have never gone on the court record, were never pursued by authorities and have largely been forgotten.

And so, the US, in the interest of covering up its own complicity in Colombia's paramilitary death spree, has guaranteed that the worst of crimes committed in Colombia have been given impunity, ensuring that such crimes will be repeated in the future.

## Notes


1. Lobo, Andrea. 'Colombia's mass protests continue Amid REPORTED "disappearance" of 379 Demonstrators,' *World Socialist Web*, 7 May 2021. https://www.wsws.org/en/articles/2021/05/08/colo-m08.html
2. Moloney, Anastasia. 'Silence Surrounds Colombia's 92,000 Disappeared – ICRC,' *Reuters*, August 29, 2014. https://www.reuters.com/article/us-foundation-colombia-missing/silence-surrounds-colombias-92000-disappeared-icrc-idUSKBN0GT22520140829
3. European Civil Protection and Humanitarian Aid Operations, Colombia Fact Sheet, 2021. https://ec.europa.eu/echo/where/latin-america-caribbean/colombia_en
4. *Id.*
5. FARC, also sometimes FARC-EP: Fuerzas Armadas Revolucionarias de Colombia—Ejército del Pueblo (The Revolutionary Armed Forces of Colombia-People's Army).
6. 'The History of the Military-Paramilitary Partnership,' *Human Rights Watch*, 1996. https://www.hrw.org/reports/1996/killer2.htm
7. Chomsky, Noam. 'Noam Chomsky on Colombia,' *Znet*, 24 Apr 2004. http://colombiasupport.net/archive/200004/znet-chomsky-0424.html
8. Wing, David. 'Number of Colombia's Victims of Colombia's Conflict Surpasses 7 Million,' *Colombia Reports,* 18 Nov 2014. https://colombiareports.com/number-victims-colombias-conflict-surpassed-7-million/
9. *Id.*
10. Kovalik, Daniel, 'The Wages of Plan Colombia Have Been Death,' *Telesur*, 3 Feb. 2016. https://www.telesurenglish.net/opinion/The-Wages-of-Plan-Colombia-Have-Been-Death-20160203-0009.html
11. Leech, Garry. *Killing Peace: Colombia's Conflict and the Failure of US intervention*, (Information etwork of the Americas, 1 Apr 2002).
12. 'Colombia Top Brass Linked to Extrajudicial Executions,' *Human Rights Watch,* 24 Jun 2015. https://www.hrw.org/news/2015/06/24/colombia-top-brass-linked-extrajudicial-executions
13. 'The Rise and Fall of "False Positive" Killings in Colombia: The Role of US Military Assistance, 2000 2010, A Report by the Fellowship of Reconciliation and Colombia Europe US Human Rights Observatory,' *Fellowship of Reconciliation,* May, 2014.

https://static1.squarespace.com/static/54961aebe4b0e6ee1855f20a/t/5bcb47b68165f55241ef07d4/1540048846084/Rise-Fall-False-Positives-US-Military-Assistance.pdf
14. Evans, Michael. '"Body Count Mentalities," Colombia's "False Positives" Scandal, Declassified Documents Describe History of Abuses by Colombian Army,' *National Security Archive Electronic Briefing Book No. 266,* 7 Jan 2009, https://nsarchive2.gwu.edu/NSAEBB/NSAEBB266/index.htm
15. Whitney, Jr., W.T. & Schepers, Emile. 'Urgent Need to Change US Colombia Policy,' *People's World,* 19 Nov 2009. https://www.peoplesworld.org/article/urgent-need-to-change-u-s-colombia-policy/
16. Sontag, Deborah. 'Justice Interrupted: The Secret History of Colombia's Paramilitaries & The US War on Drugs,' *The New York Times*, 11 Sep 2016. http://www.nytimes.com/2016/09/11/world/americas/colombia-cocaine-human-rights.html?_r=0
17. Grattan, Steven. 'Killings of Colombia Ex-FARC fighters persists amid Peace Process,' *Al Jazeera,* 18 Jan 2021. https://www.aljazeera.com/news/2021/1/18/killings-of-colombia-ex-farc-fighters-persist-amid-peace-process
18. CT Liberal, 'Chiquita, Dole and Del Monte Financed Murderous Militias,' *Daily Kos*, 19 May 2007. http://www.dailykos.com/story/2007/5/19/336518/-

# Babylon

## Hassan Blasim

Translated from the Arabic by Jonathan Wright

*The object of terrorism is terrorism. The object of oppression is oppression. The object of torture is torture. The object of murder is murder. The object of power is power. Now do you begin to understand me?* – George Orwell, *1984*

I WASN'T SURPRISED TO see him in the Südblock café. I'd seen him being interviewed on DW TV and knew he'd come to Berlin as a refugee a year earlier. I looked at his face and watched his gestures with curiosity. His eyes were fixed on the screen of his laptop. He had earphones in and looked up from time to time as if to make sure that everything around him was as it should be. He might have been having another look at his media interviews on YouTube. There was hardly a Western or Arab media organisation that hadn't interviewed this 'torture celebrity' called Khaled Ali. I knew his story by heart. The Americans had chained him to the bars of his cell for days, beaten him, threatened him, humiliated him, stripped him naked, sexually abused him, taken pictures of him, tortured him with music and waterboarding, and terrorised him with dogs. He still had pains in one shoulder, his ribs and his left leg.

I thought of saying hello. I wanted to have a chat with him, but I was worried I might start to get angry. I didn't really know why, maybe it was envy. Can you envy another person because you think their tragedy was more tragic and more interesting than your own? I went out to have a cigarette on the terrace, then went back to my flat near the café.

He didn't show up the next day, but he did come back to the café two days later. He opened his laptop, put on his headphones and started to stare at the screen again. I was playing Minecraft on my phone. I had built a beach house, planted some barley and watermelons, made a chicken coop and a pen for the sheep. I needed to get hold of some bones to tame some wild dogs in the woods nearby. I grabbed my sword and wandered around among the pine trees. Darkness fell and a zombie attacked me. I ran away. I made my bed quickly and went to sleep. The light went out and the night zombies disappeared.

I logged out of the game, stood up and headed towards him. 'How are you, Khaled? I'm Adnan and I'm Iraqi,' I said.

'Hi,' he replied, taken aback, and put out his hand to shake mine. He asked if we had met before.

'No, you don't know me,' I said, 'but of course there's no one who doesn't know you. You're very famous, and in a sense one could say we're colleagues.'

'How do you mean? Colleagues? I don't understand,' he said.

'I was in Abu Ghraib prison too, but you're a star and I'm a nobody, like an extra in a film.'

He seemed upset that I was speaking so cryptically, so I changed the subject and told him I lived nearby in Kreuzberg and that I knew him from his media appearances. I added that I had come to Germany in the 1990s. We spoke about the climate and he told me he'd started renting a flat in Kreuzberg a few weeks ago. I gave him my phone number and said I hoped we could meet up from time to time. I assured him I was a regular customer at the café. He thanked me and promised he would call. After that, he didn't show up at the café for two weeks. I regretted the way I had spoken to him. I might have been impolite, or maybe I had frightened him off.

I thought about Khaled a lot over those two weeks. I went back to all the interviews with him on YouTube, although I had already seen almost all of them. I looked for him on Facebook and Instagram, but he didn't seem to have active accounts. The story he repeated to the media was that he had worked in the Ministry of Oil. After the Americans occupied Baghdad, they wanted to show the world that Iraqis welcomed the democracy they had brought, and that people were happy with the change. But Iraqis were divided over the Americans – some people rejoiced and called it liberation, while others were angry and called it occupation. Khaled Ali was angry and offended when he saw American tanks and troops patrolling the streets of Baghdad. He went to one of the hotels where foreign journalists stayed and asked them to come on a tour with him and see the reality of the occupation. First, he took them to the Iraqi National Museum, which had been looted of rare, priceless antiquities from the Mesopotamian civilisations because the US forces had left the building unguarded. Then he took them out near the airport to see the dead bodies of some Iraqi soldiers that had been left in the street. He tried to explain to the journalists that the US Army had used internationally prohibited weapons in what was known as the battle of the airport.

The spokesman for the US Army based in the journalists' hotel, himself an army officer, reported Khaled's activities. Two days later Khaled was driving home with his young daughter when he noticed some Humvees following him. As they reached the street where he lived, a group of US soldiers climbed out and surrounded his car. Through a loudspeaker they told him to get out of the vehicle and take off his clothes. They arrested him and took him to Abu Ghraib prison. There were hundreds of prisoners there. They put him in a small dirty toilet and tied him up. An interrogator and a translator sat by the toilet door and started to question him. They asked him which organisation was supporting his activities. He told them he had organised the tour for the journalists on his own initiative out of a sense of duty to his country. They took him to the isolation cells allocated to what they called the big fish. They chained him to the cell door naked and left him there for three days, with very little food or water, until his strength flagged. When the warders gave out blankets, the prisoners made holes in the middle of the blankets by rubbing them on the ground, and then wore them as ponchos. Khaled said that the more prisoners arrived the more hurried the electric shock sessions would be. Khaled was made to stand on a wooden crate wearing his blanket and with a bag over his head, his fingers connected to electrical cables, as in the picture that was leaked out of Abu Ghraib and later became famous in the media.

In his interviews, Khaled talked about sexual humiliation and his surprise at the number of pictures they took of the prisoners, especially when they were naked in demeaning positions. He said they would threaten to publish the pictures in order to blackmail the prisoners. Once, when they were giving Khaled electric shocks, he bit his tongue and blood started pouring out of his mouth. They stopped the torture and called the doctor, who opened Khaled's mouth with a shoe and sprayed water inside. Then the doctor told them they could continue with the torture because the blood was just from a tongue wound and not from his stomach.

In one of the cells in Abu Ghraib, Khaled met a former Iraqi oil minister and, according to one version of the story, the Americans brought in the imam of a mosque from Falluja, together with the man's brothers, sons and other relatives. They made the imam put on a bikini, poured water onto the floor and ran an electric current through the water. Then they put on some music so that it looked like the imam was dancing in front of his relatives.

In the prison, Khaled said, there were also judges, university professors and physicists. After the photographs caused such an outcry in the international media, the International Committee of the Red Cross asked the occupying forces to allow a Red Cross visit to the prison. After that, the jailers tried to bribe the prisoners with better treatment and better food if they didn't reveal what was really happening inside the prison. They told the prisoners that the Red Cross would stay two hours and then go, while they would have to stay with their jailers for many months and maybe years. But the Americans were not content with simply bribing and threatening the prisoners. They arranged a complicated hoax to trick them. They took them into a hall and people wearing Red Cross badges then came in and the guards withdrew. The prisoners started talking about the torture, starvation, and sexual and psychological abuse they were being subjected to, in the belief that they were talking to real Red Cross staff. Then suddenly the guards came in laughing and it turned out that the Red Cross staff were just prison staff dressed up for the occasion.

Khaled and his group finally managed to meet the Red Cross team. Khaled was released a few days later, along with some prisoners who had health problems. They took them off in an open truck and dumped them in the street wearing nothing but blankets. Khaled said he had kept his blanket and had submitted it to the American lawyers who volunteered to file a lawsuit against the US Army for human rights violations in the prison. Khaled tried to set up a group to defend the Abu Ghraib prisoners, but he was threatened by militias linked to the religious parties to which the Americans had handed power. Khaled fled to Jordan and continued his activism, then he applied for asylum through the United Nations and was accepted as a refugee in Germany.

A few weeks after Khaled disappeared from the Südblock café, I was in the library looking up some references when I received a text message from him. He apologised for not having contacted him and said he had had some trouble with his health but was now slightly better. He wanted us to meet. I invited him to dinner at my flat. He agreed and I sent him the address.

I could hardly make space for a guest in my place. I was living in a small room that opened onto a small kitchen and a bathroom. There were books everywhere, on the shelves on the walls and in piles all over the place. I cleared the papers and wine bottles off the table and pushed it back towards the window, which was also blocked by books. For five years, I had been trying to finish a project – writing a trilogy on the theme of how the West has destroyed the world. But the more I looked into the subject, the more complicated it became, or maybe the truth is that I didn't have a gift for summarising and had never written a book before. I did, however, have a strong desire to write because I had been an avid reader since I was young, and was angry with the injustices in the world. If I had been more sure of my talents the project might have made better progress. I was thinking that the topic needed a whole research institute dedicated to it that could compile evidence for all the destruction that the West is responsible for around the world.

Khaled turned up with a bottle of red wine. 'What do you say we take a raincheck on the wine, if that's alright?' I said. 'I have an excellent bottle of arak that a friend brought me from Baghdad.' He helped me lay out the mezes on the table – chickpeas, a cucumber and yoghurt dip, pomegranate seeds, broad beans and crisps. My books piqued Khaled's interest. He picked up his glass and started to examine some of the titles. Then he asked, 'So which year were you in Abu Ghraib?'

'From the early 1980s,' I said.

'You must have been a communist then!' he said.

'True. How did you guess?' I answered with a smile.

After a long and irritating silence, he said, 'From the books. The communists in Iraq were always educated and read a lot. They had a powerful influence on civil society in Iraq, especially in the 60s and 70s.'

He drank half his glass, pulled out a book and added, 'But the communists were idealistic, in a simple religious society.'

'Were you a Baathist?' I asked him.

He flipped through the pages of the book for a while, then said, 'All Iraqis were Baathists, whether or not they wanted to be.'

He was the opposite of how he appeared in the interviews. He was soft-spoken and didn't talk fast, as most Iraqis do. But in his interviews, he spoke without taking a breath, and on many occasions, he would interrupt the interviewer before they had finished their question. He seemed afraid of forgetting the details of what he wanted to say. In interviews, he spoke as if he were making a confession under intimidation or torture. He put the book back in place and sat down, repeating the title of the book: *Today We Drop Bombs, Tomorrow We Build Bridges*. 'It sounds like poetry,' he added. I agreed with him but assured him the book had nothing to do with poetry, but rather with shameful facts. I told him that the book was about the reasons why foreign aid organisations become the casualties of war, as accomplices in Euro-American foreign policy. In the past, the word 'humanitarian' was used to describe civilian assistance to victims of natural or man-made disasters, but the military and the politicians now use it to put a spin on their own activities. So when America or Russia bomb a country, they say they are hitting strategic targets for humanitarian purposes, or that they're sending in troops and planes on a humanitarian mission.

'How long did you spend in Abu Ghraib?' I asked.

'Sixty days. And you?'

'Seven years and 49 days.'

'You mean right through the Iran-Iraq war,' he said. 'At least you escaped the horror of the war,' he added snidely. 'I was an Infantryman on the front lines and I saw my friends burnt to cinders or ripped apart by bombs and missiles. You had a miraculous escape!'

I opened the window to smoke and said, 'Sorry but you don't know the real Abu Ghraib.' He didn't reply to my remark – just put salt on the pomegranate and said that European pomegranates didn't have any real taste, and that real pomegranates came from Shahraban in Diyala province. I agreed with him on that and made a remark about nostalgia for the flavours of our country, saying that they were just illusions, memories that served no purpose other than to torment the imagination. I finished off the rest of my drink in one swig.

'What did you mean when you told me at our first meeting that I was a celebrity and you were a nobody?' Khaled asked.

I laughed and told him I had only been joking. 'Listen,' I continued, 'imagine Abu Ghraib prison as a film an hour and a half long. The film would start with a black background with the words 'Abu Ghraib prison was built in the 1950s by a British contracting company.' Then for the first hour and 25 minutes of the film, all the audience would see would be a dark screen and total silence. Then for the last five minutes of the film pictures of you and the other inmates under the Americans would appear. The film would end and that would be the story of Abu Ghraib.'

'I get it,' he said. 'This time you're not joking, I think. Your point is the media doesn't talk about the prison's past.'

I went to the bathroom, had a piss standing with the door open and continued to talk: 'The Westerners who destroyed our country, as well as certain other countries in the region, are obsessed with Hollywood stories. They've ignored the real horror of Abu Ghraib and focused all their energies on what happened in the prison when the Americans were there.'

I flushed the toilet, washed my hands, cut up a lemon, put it in a bowl, sat down next to him and went on talking. 'Why do you think the West is interested in the story of Abu Ghraib under the Americans, for example? Superficially they seem to want evidence that America and Britain were brutal when they occupied and destroyed Iraq. But tell me, honestly, that's such hypocrisy! Does the West need any more evidence of the massacres committed by its armies and by its multinationals, through control of international politics and contempt for other people? In reality, there's stacks of evidence for the crimes they have committed over the centuries. But the truth is that they don't have real courts or lawyers and their justice is selective; it's a sham. The photos from Abu Ghraib are an easy story for the West to digest. I mean, it's easy to understand, but the story of Abu Ghraib under Saddam Hussein would seem too complicated for them, too hard to understand. It doesn't have the flavour of Hollywood. But two US soldiers, a man and a woman, have their picture taken behind a pile of naked bodies, and hallelujah! They've got the perfect Hollywood shot. It can be reproduced in the cinema, in books and in the media. Do the people in the West know that in the time of Saddam Hussein, Abu Ghraib prison was surrounded by mass graves because of the enormous number of people who were executed there, after being raped and tortured. In the Arab tradition, the caliph would launch military expeditions and the poets would write poems about his exploits and his heroism. These days, the West kills with bombs and smart missiles, then they write stories to fill TV serials and Netflix documentaries. The barbarity and hypocrisy of the world hasn't changed since ancient times. It's only the slogans and the justifications that have changed.'

I was annoyed by the looks Khaled gave me while I was speaking. His body language suggested he was familiar with what I was saying and thought it was predictable, or at least that's what I felt.

'As far as they are concerned,' I concluded, 'the stories we tell, we the victims of the brutality of this capitalist West, are just the rubbish left over from their brutality and selfishness, and like recycled rubbish, some of which has economic value, our tragedy can be recycled, like the photos from Abu Ghraib, in the form of films, serials and works of literary fiction, and then they're buried forever in the gloomy vaults of oblivion.'

Khaled continued to browse through the book titles. In a voice clearly affected by the arak, he said, 'How were you arrested?'

'It's a long story,' I said. 'Okay, listen. I'll keep it short for you. I don't know. Are you really interested in hearing it?'

'Of course. Why not?'

'I was a student at the Institute of Technology and I was twenty-three. As you know, the Baathists annihilated the communists with the help of the West in the Cold War, and there was almost nothing left of the party. Some members were killed and others went into exile. The few of us who stayed in the country did very little – just swapped news and shared books. But the Baathists wouldn't leave us in peace. Most of the people in my family were communists, and my aunts and uncles were executed by the Baathist security people. I was carrying a message to a communist comrade when I was arrested. They interrogated me in the Public Security building, and you know what the interrogation and torture were like there. Then they sent me to trial and after four hours, they sentenced me to death. They took me to Abu Ghraib and put me and eight other men in a cell two metres by one metre. The 49 days I spent in that cell awaiting execution was the harshest and most terrifying time in my life. The room was like a grave and we were crammed into it – communists, Islamists and Kurds. You can imagine what it's like to be waiting for death in a miserable cell like that. We took turns to sleep, with some of us standing while the others lay on the ground because the room was so small. We shat in a bucket and the food was atrocious. Whenever someone was executed they would bring someone else to the cell.

'The person I remember best was a young man called Falah. He had studied English literature in London as part of an exchange programme. Maybe you remember that when the war with Iran broke out, the government ordered all students abroad and other expatriates to come back and serve in the army. At first, Falah was reluctant to come home, but they summoned his father to Public Security and threatened him. Falah had to return and join the army, but after fighting in the famous battle of the River Jassem, which was especially brutal, he decided to desert and go back to London. During his escape attempt, he passed through Kurdistan, where he was arrested and sentenced to death. Falah amused us by acting out scenes from Shakespeare plays. He assigned us parts and taught us our lines. I still remember how he laughed when one day he was giving out roles in Hamlet and all the prisoners in the cell refused to play Ophelia because it was a woman's role. In the end, I agreed to play Ophelia. They came at ten o'clock in the morning to tell prisoners they were due for execution, and they took them to the gallows at five o'clock in the afternoon. During his seven-hour wait, Falah spoke to us about the history of theatre, from ancient Greece to the present day. Finally we embraced Falah, one by one, and he addressed us by the names of the characters we were playing. 'So long, Ophelia,' he said to me. 'Farewell, Horatio,' he said as he hugged a young man from the Islamic Daawa party. Then he went off to the gallows with the warders, saying, 'To be or not to be,' and with tears in his eyes.

'It was like a miracle when my death sentence was rescinded and commuted to a prison term. They moved me to the rehabilitation cell, where the security services were in charge. You're Iraqi, so you know what 'rehabilitation' means: torture and abuse, and I went through it day after day for seven long years.'

We finished off the bottle of arak and opened the wine. Khaled told me he went to a psychiatrist regularly and was amazed that I hadn't bothered about my own mental health in all the years I had been in Germany. I pointed to the bookshelf close to him. 'See that book? My therapy is in there,' I said.

He turned around and pulled out *Children of the Days* by Eduardo Galeano.

'No, the book to the right of that one,' I said.

He took out the other book and said, 'Ah yes, you mean *Papillon*. I know it.' Then he read the name of the author, Henri Charrière. 'But I never knew the name of the author,' he added. 'I mean I knew the book from the film, with Dustin Hoffman and Steve McQueen.'

He passed *Papillon* to me and I took a gram of cocaine out from between the pages. I cut myself a line and he said he would try some and that it would be his first time. He asked me how strong it was. I made a short line for him and he snorted it, then drank from his glass of wine.

I played some Nick Cave from my laptop, and he looked uncomfortable. I asked him if he was okay. He told me he couldn't bear listening to Western music. He didn't understand it in the first place and his memories of torture by loud music in Abu Ghraib prevented him from relating or relaxing to any Western music. I closed the laptop, and he told me how they used to tie his hands behind his back, put his head between loudspeakers and play heavy metal. He said that after they stopped playing the music, his head would ring for weeks. He still felt sick and thought he was going to vomit when he heard heavy metal. 'They played loud music for hours,' he said. 'It was like a strange creature had forced its way into your ears and then your brain and then all the cells in your body,' he added. 'As if every cell in your body was being hijacked and destroyed by the constant vibrations that went on for hours, sometimes all night. Do you know what I mean?'

He looked up at the ceiling, then asked if he could snort another line of coke. After I cut him one, he suddenly said, apparently in all seriousness, 'At least you were with Iraqis in Abu Ghraib.'

I was incredulous. 'So you don't mind an Iraqi abusing you, but if an American does it, it's more humiliating!' I said. I changed the subject and told him we wouldn't be able to sleep easily after the stimulants. I asked him if he'd like to go for a walk in the Berlin night or go to a nightclub. It was about two o'clock in the morning. With the cocaine, Khaled seemed to have reverted to the way he spoke in his interviews. He started speaking rapidly and answered me more assertively. He let out everything that was inside him, all at once and without prior warning. He said something to the effect that I obviously seemed to support the American occupation. His evidence was that the communists had taken part in the Iraqi government after the invasion and that if it wasn't for treacherous Iraqis, the Americans wouldn't have been able to occupy the country in the first place. He launched into a long monologue about the achievements of the Baathist regime in health and education, comparing the current state of Iraq, at the mercy of the religious parties, with the state it was in under Saddam Hussein.

Eventually, he stopped talking and I managed to get a word in. 'It's quite clear you supported the Baathist criminals and you benefitted from the Saddam regime in some way.' An argument broke out between us, with an exchange of angry accusations. He wanted to leave but I grabbed him by the shoulder. He swung around and punched me on my nose, which started to bleed. He was flustered and started apologising profusely. He said he still panicked if someone grabbed him unexpectedly, because of the trauma of being tortured in Abu Ghraib. He apologised again. I went into the bathroom and stuffed some cotton wool up my nose. Then I heard the front door opening, and the prisoner was gone.

I regretted having invited him. But I realised I had been rude to him and had maliciously pushed him to breaking point. I changed my shirt, which had bloodstains on it, and went out. I wandered around the neighbourhood, then went to a nightclub and stayed till dawn. I went to a Turkish restaurant and ate some kebabs, bought some orange juice and went to the park nearby. It was summer and the weather was magical and refreshing.

I noticed someone was lying in the middle of the park. Then suddenly I realised it was Khaled Ali, the prisoner. I hurried over to him. I was worried something bad might have happened to him because of the cocaine. He was lying there staring at the sky with a blank look in his eyes. I lay down on the grass nearby, apologised to him and asked if he was okay. He apologised to me too, then said, 'Who are we?'

'Prisoners from the land of hypocrisy,' I said.

Then he repeated his question: 'Who are we?'

'A couple of idiots, drunks, cocaine snorters,' he said, in reply to his own question.

I laughed, and then we both broke into a long bout of laughter.

'Have you heard of a musician called David Gray?' Khaled asked.

'The name rings a bell,' I said. 'What about him?'

'For months I've been searching the Internet for a way to get in touch with him,' he said. 'And a few days ago I managed to find his phone number.'

'I don't understand,' I said.

'Once during the music torture, they played heavy metal for hours. Then suddenly one of them put on a song called 'Babylon'. It was like a lifeline for me after the heavy metal. Although they played the song for hours, it gave me some relief, a break. They only played it that one time. I don't understand English. So, with my hands tied, and my head between two loudspeakers, I was trying to make up new words for the song from my imagination. I hoped they would leave the same song on and not go back to the heavy metal. Babylon stuck in my memory and when I got to Germany I started looking for David Gray.'

'So you want to get in touch with him?'

'I don't know,' said Khaled. 'Maybe. I read a newspaper article that says he's apologised to the victims for the Americans using his music as a method of torture.'

'Well let's call him,' I said enthusiastically, and sat down.

Khaled sat down too. 'Now?' he asked. 'No, no.'

'For God's sake.' I said. 'There's not much of a time difference between London and Berlin. I know it's still early but at least we can check if the phone number works.'

Khaled took out his phone hesitantly. I urged him on, and asked him to put the phone on speaker so that I could help translate for him if David Gray or anyone else answered.

Sitting in the park, with just the sound of the birds in the distance, impatiently and in suspense, we listened to the phone ringing. Then David Gray picked up. He didn't sound as if he had just woken up. His tone was clear and steady but a little puzzled. I introduced myself, told him a very short version of Khaled's story and said Khaled wanted to speak to him. Gray asked us where we were calling from. I explained to him and he was silent for quite a while, then he asked to speak to Khaled.

'Hi David, my name's Khaled,' Khaled said in English, clearly embarrassed.

'Hi, I'm sorry about that happened,' Gray said. 'You know, I did an interview about this and spoke about ...'

'Yes. yes,' said Khaled, cutting in. 'I know, I read the interview. Thank you.'

'Really sorry.'

'I liked your song.'

'Thanks, sorry, you know…'

'No need to be sorry. I'll never forget your song. I should be thanking you.'

'Oh man, thanks, you know.'

It was the strangest and most awkward phone conversation I've ever heard. David Gray asked Khaled to call if he needed anything. Khaled was happy, but also a little bewildered. The conversation hadn't lasted more than ten minutes. I took my headphones out of my pocket, put them in my ears and listened to 'Babylon' on YouTube. I had never heard the song before. I shut my eyes and lay back on the grass, trying to imagine Khaled's head between the loudspeakers in Abu Ghraib. But my memory soon began to produce images of Abu Ghraib as it was when I was a prisoner on death row.

'Are you listening to 'Babylon'?' Khaled asked.

'Yes, sorry,' I said.

'No problem, but let me listen with you.'

'Are you sure?'

'Yes, thanks, don't worry.'

'Okay, sorry again, for being a dick to you.'

'No, thank you for the evening and the *Papillon* cocaine.'

I unplugged the headphones from of the phone. A tiny bird landed close to us, picked up something in its beak and then flew up into a nearby tree. And then the only sound was 'Babylon', sung by David Gray:

*Friday night, I'm going nowhere*

*All the lights are changing green to red…*

# Afterword: The Invisible Government

## Chris Hedges

IN APRIL 2004 THE investigative reporter Seymour Hersh, who had exposed the massacre at My Lai during the war in Vietnam, published a 4,000-word story in the *New Yorker* magazine titled 'Torture at Abu Ghraib.' The exposé, based on a secret army investigation that included lurid photographic and video evidence, documented how US prison guards, military police, intelligence operatives and private contractors routinely abused, humiliated, beat, raped and tortured prisoners held at the Abu Ghraib prison twenty miles outside of Baghdad.

Prisoners were forced to strip and then often bound, gagged and raped. They were beaten with clubs, broom handles and chairs. They were attacked by guard dogs. They were sodomised with broom handles and phosphorous tubes. They were dragged across the prison floor by a rope tied to their penises. Chemical lights were snapped open and the phosphoric liquid was poured over their naked bodies. They were doused with cold water while naked in their cells. They were forced to strip and climb on top of each other to form a human pyramid where they were photographed with guards grinning beside them. They were subjected to 'sound disorientation techniques,' heavy metal music that was blasted at high decibels at detainees for 24 hours a day. Hooded men had electrical wires attached to their bodies and were shocked. Guards took selfies of themselves smiling with victims they had tortured to death, the corpses wrapped in cellophane and packed in ice. Prisoners were forced to masturbate into the mouths of other prisoners. One photograph shows the walls of a room splattered in blood. Private Lynndie England, who is seen in a photograph with a cigarette dangling from her mouth, gives a thumbs-up sign as she points at the genitals of a young Iraqi, who is naked and has a sandbag over his head, as he masturbates. Hersh lamented that he did not have access to 2,000 of the most disturbing photographs and videos, including images of children being sodomised and male and female prisoners being raped by US guards.

'Women were sending letters to their husbands from Abu Ghraib saying, 'Please come and kill me, because of what's happened,' Hersh told me. 'These women were arrested with young boys. The boys were filmed as they were sodomised by guards. In the soundtrack the boys are shrieking.'

The several thousand prisoners held in Abu Ghraib, which included women and children, had been picked up at random in military sweeps, at highway checkpoints or during night raids on homes. 'They fell,' Hersh wrote, 'into three loosely defined categories: common criminals; security detainees suspected of 'crimes against the coalition'; and a small number of suspected 'high-value' leaders of the insurgency against the coalition forces.'

The Red Cross estimated that between 70 and 90 per cent of the prisoners at Abu Ghraib, which was a notoriously brutal prison under the regime of Saddam Hussein, were mistakenly detained and had no connection with the insurgency.

Eleven low-ranking US soldiers were eventually convicted of crimes stemming from detainee abuse at Abu Ghraib. Most received a few months in prison, with the exception of one who received a three-year sentence, one who was sentenced to prison for eight and a half years and another who received a ten-year sentence.

The architects of the US torture program in the CIA and the military, which runs black sites around the globe where this kind of torture and abuse is routine, however, were never charged with a crime. Those who directed and oversaw the vast torture program in black sites, along with other war crimes – George W. Bush, Dick Cheney, Donald Rumsfeld, former CIA Director George Tenet, Condoleezza Rice and John Ashcroft – were immunised. The lawyers who made legal what under international and domestic law is illegal, including John Rizzo, the former acting general counsel for the CIA, Alberto Gonzales, Jay Bybee, David Addington, William J. Haynes and John Yoo were not held accountable. The senior military leaders, including Gen. David Petraeus, who oversaw the formation of death squads in Iraq and widespread torture in Iraqi prisons, were also absolved.

The leadership was absolved because in the United States there are two forms of government. There is the visible government – the White House, Congress, the courts, state legislatures and governorships – and the invisible government, or deep state, where anonymous technocrats, intelligence operatives, generals, bankers, corporations and lobbyists manage foreign and domestic policy regardless of which political party holds power.

The most important organs in the invisible government are the nation's bloated and unaccountable military and intelligence agencies. They are the vanguard of the invisible government. They oversee a vast 'black world', tasked with maintaining the invisible government's lock on power. They spy on and smear domestic and foreign critics, fix elections, bribe, extort, torture, assassinate and flood the airwaves with 'black propaganda'. They are impervious to the chaos and human destruction they leave in their wake. Disasters, social upheavals, economic collapses, massive suffering, death and rabid anti-American blowback have grown out of the invisible government's overthrow of democratically elected governments in Iran, Guatemala and Chile and the wars it fostered in Vietnam, Afghanistan, Iraq, Libya and Syria.

There are brief, periodic glimpses of the moral squalor and ineptitude that define this shadow world, such as the hearings on intelligence operations in the 1970s led by Senator Frank Church, the leaked report and photos made public by Hersh about Abu Ghraib, and the revelations of Iraqi war crimes by WikiLeaks. Those who expose the inner workings of the deep state, including Edward Snowden and Julian Assange, are persecuted, silenced and sometimes 'disappeared.' Seymour Hersh is now blacklisted from most US publications, including the *New Yorker*.

The torture techniques made public at Abu Ghraib are not new. They were pioneered, with the help of hundreds of ex-Nazis recruited into the American and West German intelligence services, by the Central Intelligence Agency in the decades after World War II. Then, as now, people were kidnapped, tortured and often executed.

The medical experiments carried out by the Nazis in concentration camps, where chemical and biological warfare projects murdered thousands of helpless victims, including children, with agents such as the gas sarin, along with those carried out by the Japanese in the occupied Chinese region of Manchuria, were seized and used by US intelligence agencies against its hapless victims. Many of the war criminals who had overseen these medical experiments were recruited to work for US intelligence services and the military. No criminal, including Kurt Blome, who had overseen the Nazis' research into biological warfare, was too heinous or sadistic for the United States to welcome and use.[1] Shiro Ishii, who between 1936 and 1942 killed as many as 12,000 captured Chinese soldiers, anti-Japanese partisans, Koreans, Mongolians, prisoners, mental patients and, by some accounts, American prisoners of war in medical experiments on behalf of the Japanese government, was considered a highly valued asset by US intelligence.

In Pingfan, Manchuria, Ishii oversaw a four-square-mile complex, called Unit 731, that housed 3,000 scientists and other employees. As Stephen Kinzer writes, the victims 'were exposed to poison gas so that their lungs could later be removed and studied; slowly roasted by electricity to determine voltages needed to produce death; hung upside down to study the progress of natural choking; locked into high-pressure chambers until their eyes popped out; spun in centrifuges; infected with anthrax, syphilis, plague, cholera, and other diseases; forcibly impregnated to provide infants for vivisection; bound to stakes to be incinerated by soldiers testing flamethrowers; and slowly frozen to observe the progress of hypothermia. Air was injected into victims' veins to provoke embolisms; animal blood was injected to see what effect it would have. Some were dissected alive, or had limbs amputated so attendants could monitor their slow deaths by bleeding and gangrene. According to a US Army report that was later declassified, groups of men, women, and children were tied to stakes so that 'their legs and buttocks were bared and exposed to shrapnel from anthrax bombs exploded yards away,' then monitored to see how long they lived – which was never more than a week. Ishii required a constant flow of human organs, meaning a steady need for 'logs', the euphemism for victims.'

After each experiment, 'Ishii's microbiologists would meticulously remove tissue samples and mount them on slides for study,' Kinzer writes. 'Technicians used their research to prepare poisoned chocolate and chewing gum, as well as hairpins and fountain pens rigged with toxin-coated needles for use in close-quarters killing. In industrial-scale laboratories, they bred plague-infested fleas and manufactured tons of anthrax that were placed in bomb casings and used to kill thousands of Chinese civilians.'

These types of experiments would soon be replicated by the CIA in a top-secret programme, MK-ULTRA, with the assistance of Ishii and an assortment of ex-Nazis.[2] The experiments were directed by Sidney Gottlieb, an elusive, quirky and powerful operative in the CIA who in his quest for mind control – something he and others in the CIA had convinced themselves the Soviets had mastered – oversaw medical experiments that had been originated by his German and Japanese collaborators. The torture sessions often permanently shattered the minds of his subjects. Victims, as now, were kidnapped – today this is called 'extraordinary rendition' – and sent to clandestine centres around the globe – now known as 'black sites' – or were picked from the prison population abroad and at home. Those forced into taking part in these experiments included impoverished African Americans at the Addiction Research Center in Lexington, Kentucky. Many of the victims were labelled 'expendables,' meaning they could be murdered after the experiments and disappeared. The corpses were usually burned. Anyone who was powerless, or could be made powerless, was a potential target. Children with learning difficulties at the Walter E. Fernald State School in Massachusetts, for example, were fed cereal laced with uranium and radioactive calcium and their induced sicknesses were monitored. Gottlieb oversaw the administering of LSD and other drugs to induce psychotic states at the federal prison in Atlanta and a youth correctional facility in Bordentown, N.J. None of his subjects consented to being a human guinea pig, and many ended up psychologically impaired for life.

Prisoners, the CIA eventually concluded, were best broken through extreme isolation and sensory deprivation. These techniques, pioneered by CIA-funded research at McGill University in Canada, were laid out in a 1964 manual titled 'KUBARK Counter-Intelligence Interrogation.' KUBARK is the CIA's cryptonym for itself. The 128-page manual was not fully declassified until 2014. It was the primary resource used by CIA interrogators in the 1960s, including in Vietnam, where at least 20,000 captured Vietnamese were killed, often after being tortured. An updated version of the manual called 'Human Resources Exploitation Training Manual' came out in 1983. These forms of torture, which include shackling, sleep deprivation, electroshock, sexual and physical humiliation, prolonged cramped confinement, and hooding for disorientation and sensory deprivation, became routine after 9/11 in American intelligence black sites at home and abroad. CIA psychologists, like Gottlieb's earlier stable of mad scientists and torturers, monitor and perfect these techniques to ensure complete psychological collapse and a childlike dependence on the interrogator.

There is a direct line from Gottlieb and the origins of the CIA to Abu Ghraib, especially since the invisible government shrouds the activities of intelligence agencies from congressional oversight and public scrutiny. There was nothing new in the Abu Ghraib revelations. Abuse and torture are institutionalised. When the savage visage of the invisible government is briefly made public a few insignificant actors are always sacrificed to appease public opinion. The sordid machinery of torture, and those who oversee it, continue to this day to consume its human prey.

GAZA

# The Pact

## Talal Abu Shawish

Translated from the Arabic by Basma Ghalayini

Sondos took a few sips of the milk that her mother had brought her. Very cautiously, she approached the western window overlooking the sea, and peeked through the blinds at the Peace Resort that faced onto the beach. It seemed strange, frightening even.

This was her favourite window. A few years ago, Sondos had watched a Miss Gaza contest from it, taking place at the resort below, as well as other plays and musical concerts, put on by various companies, local, Arab and foreign. One summer she had even gone down into the resort and wandered through the stalls of an International Book Fair being held there with her mother. The venue stayed the same, even if its purpose changed.

She often invited her friend Dima to join her at her favourite window, to enjoy the cultural and entertainment activities being held on the resort's grounds. At sunrise and sunset, they would also follow the movements of the fishermen in the harbour just beyond the resort.

Recently, mornings hadn't been the same. She tried to understand, but the changes taking place around her didn't make any sense.

She asked her mother many times, who she knew would give her answers.

'In order to be given understandable and specific answers, we must first find the right question!'

She had heard her mother mumbling these words with tightened lips as she looked out on what was happening below: dozens of armed men were spread out over every corner of the resort's grounds; their clothes, their weapons, the way they moved, all different somehow to those at the checkpoints and army buildings Sondos passed every day with Dima on her way to school.

You could hear the chaos, clamour, cheering and shooting from time to time and see the cars transporting men, weapons and food every few hours. The Peace Resort, which had been intended for recreational activities, had been transformed into a military barracks where everyone seemed to be preparing for a big event.

The doorbell rang for a long time without pause, making everyone tense. It was her friend Dima's way of sounding it. Quickly Sondos grabbed her bag, said goodbye to her mother, who was busy cleaning the kitchen, and left for school.

Out on the streets, the atmosphere was unnerving. Everyone who would normally be out by this time had hesitated, waiting for others to start moving first. School children were the first to pump blood back into the streets' arteries, along with a few private cars belonging to parents keen to accompany their children to school personally, given the tension that had gripped the city recently.

Her mother or father could have done the same, but Sondos had refused despite the fear she felt when passing by the military buildings or emergency checkpoints on the road. Every time her parents had tried to do so, she had replied: 'There are hundreds of students who come to school on their own, Mama! On foot, I am no better than them!'

Sporadic shots tore through the tension that hung in the morning air. With each rattle of gunfire, the girls froze for a moment, then dived to the nearest wall for shelter; the sound of screeching car tyres didn't make things any better.

Sondos did not understand how the streets had suddenly awoken from the deafening silence a few moments before. Some commotion was taking place in front of one of the tallest buildings on her street and ambulance sirens echoed on all sides. A large number of military vehicles quickly surrounded the building while curious faces appeared at the windows of neighbouring buildings.

The two girls looked at each other knowingly. As quickly as they could, they started making their way back to the house and before they had covered the distance, Sondos' mother appeared, running towards them, having heard about what happened on local radio. The moment they were safe in the flat, she called Dima's mother to reassure her.

'Mama, what happened?'

Her mother couldn't answer right away.

'Stay away from the western window, and I'll make you a hot drink.'

Sondos warily approached the window and peeked through the blinds at the resort. The noises were louder than ever; she heard thunderous chants rising up, glorifying their leader and his pledge of revenge. She looked in the direction of the tall building where the commotion had taken place; everyone had disappeared as quickly as they had appeared. The street had returned to its state of silent anticipation, only interrupted by sporadic gunshots coming from different corners of this all-too tense city.

Her mother arrived with two cups of tea and some slices of mana'eesh. Loud music blasted from the radio in a way all Gazans were accustomed to, followed by the voice of a presenter announcing to people already on edge 'Breaking News' about the assassination of an activist from one side, the kidnapping of someone else from the other, an attack on a government website here, the storming of the basement of a mosque there. The headlines were endless. Her mother jumped up to change the channel, Sondos shrieked:

'Mama, please. We want to know the reason we couldn't go to school today!' Her mother was not trying to hide the news from her; it spread quickly and would soon be talked about by everyone; they'd talk about little else until the next one. But she preferred to explain the news to the girls in her own way, and only after she'd checked the facts first. She also wanted to spare her the scare-mongering that accompanies local news, as broadcast by radio stations whose loyalties were distributed evenly between the opposing sides.

The voice on the radio blasts: 'An official source has reported that the body of a government soldier has arrived at the hospital after being thrown from the fourteenth floor of a building having been bound and blindfolded.'

'Oh, Umm Mohammed!' Dima said, 'I *did* see them carrying a body to the ambulance!'

'But why?' Sondos exclaimed. 'Why would they throw a helpless person, bound and blindfolded, from the roof of a building?!' She flung a piece of the pastry across the room. Then she ran to her mother and threw her head onto her shoulder bursting into tears, Dima joining them, sobbing quietly on and off, in a way that didn't completely stop until Dima's mother came to pick her up.

The day passed slowly. Everyone was waiting to see what form of revenge would be exacted the following morning. Sondos' mother, who had rung her clinic to say she couldn't go in that day, tried to keep the girl busy with baking. Sondos helped her quietly, shocked. The image of what happened stuck in her head.

She couldn't stop thinking about the seconds that would have passed in the time it took for that person to fall fourteen floors before colliding with the ground.

In the evening, her mother asked her to sleep next to her in the back room. They could still hear the chants of the gunmen's commander coming through the western window. Her mother tried to distract her by stroking her hair in a repetitive motion, knowing the chants were bringing back memories of the day. An ambitious young man, born in the Khan Yunis refugee camp, the commander's star had risen in record time. He rapidly climbed the military ladder to occupy the most important security position in the government. Sondos's mother's thoughts were cut short by a rumbling sound from the loudspeakers in the 'Military Resort'.

'Death Squad Monsters. Attention!'

The response was loud: 'Monsters, monsters, monsters!'

Sondos' body shook and woke up from a restless sleep. The chanting continued through the loudspeakers. Without turning to her mother, she asked: 'Mama, why do they call themselves "Death Squad"?'

'Sleep now, habibti. We will talk tomorrow.'

Quietly, she soothed her daughter back to sleep by gently patting her back.

*Death Squad? You idiot.* She went back to her thoughts and started recalling what she had heard about this commander whose name the men kept chanting well after midnight. Just two days ago, she had watched a video showing some of his men holding a number of political opponents hostage. They appeared chained and blindfolded, as his men tortured them savagely; beating and kicking them, stretching them and forcing them to chant his name and insult their own leaders one by one!

*My God! How can a person be forced to chant the name of his own killer!* she thought. *What would such a man do if circumstances changed and allowed him to retaliate?! What kind of leadership perpetuates this bloody circle?! How can this infernal gate ever be closed?!*

She noticed a tremor passing over Sondos in her sleep. Calmly, she pulled the blanket over the girl's body then continued her painful reflections.

He had founded a student movement when he was a teenager, this commander. He was smart and knew exactly what he wanted; he refrained from competing or coming into conflict with anyone in the beginning, and instead showed great reverence to all his superiors. He applied his leadership skills to the student movement, knowing the importance of students and their future roles. The occupation deported him from Palestine, but this gave him many opportunities that helped him rise in the ranks, even in exile, and appear alongside great leaders at international press conferences, seminars and other key events.

He was elegant, tactful, and eloquent. He learnt the speeches of his leaders by heart, repeating them at any given opportunity.

He started to accompany his political leader on his travels to European countries and then to the United States, and although the people of the East create their icons, believing they will never die, in the West eventually they realise everything must eventually change so we should not wait for happenstance to surprise us randomly. Careful plans should be made to confront any new occurrence. People were convinced that the star of a historical leader would not fade before a new leader appeared who would shed light into the previously dark corners.

In order to convince people to embrace the new, seismic events needed to take place to create shock and astonishment resulting in people being convinced that the newcomer was the saviour they waited for, the messiah!

*And now they're chanting his name*, Sondos's mother thought, *and the atmosphere he dreamed for so long to create hangs over the Strip's towns, villages and refugee camps.*

Against her will, her thoughts turned to the details of the morning before.

*They could not have kidnapped him and thrown him from the roof of a high-rise building without torturing him first. How did his family receive the news of his death?*

*How can they ever get closure, knowing that the Imam of the mosque next to them and the followers praying behind him may be complicit in his killing? Maybe planned the whole thing, or at least gave the order to kill him that way? The Imam whom the dead man may have himself prayed behind many times?*

She remembered these kinds of zealots all too well. On the night they set fire to the Red Crescent Library, she saw them celebrating around the fire as if practising a ritual devoted to an ancient god of the forests. In London, during her research, she had seen them also recruiting people in the corridors of her university. And during the 80s, under the occupation, from the window of her clinic, she had even seen them, or their leaders, going in and out of the Israeli military headquarters. It was during that time that the occupation, and those who supported it, had become so disturbed by the growth of patriotic, nationalist and leftist forces, that they decided to initiate an alternative.

For those people, the battle was not with the occupation at the time; the call to religion was their priority, and this could not be achieved unless the other opponents were liquidated. So they made a pact. Or someone did.

She quietly turned on her bedside light and twisted round to contemplate her child's features who, by this point, had fallen into a deep sleep. She turned it off again, lay back down in one last attempt to sleep.

The silence was torn open by the sound of gunshots. This time it was close. So close in fact she thought she could feel it reverberating through every room of her flat

She rose from her bed, stumbled in the darkness and almost fell. As she reached towards her child instinctively, she heard heavy footsteps up the stairs of her building. She embraced her daughter who woke up in a fright.

'Relax habibti, we are used to this,' she whispered. 'Don't be scared.'

She heard the steps of the intruders stomping past the apartment door and listened as their heavy tread continued to higher floors. She put on some clothes and, warning Sondos not to follow her, advanced towards the flat's door ever so slowly. She nudged the door open a fraction and her heart leapt into her throat as she was greeted by the barrel of a gun. A raspy voice broke the spell:

'Get back inside! You can't leave!'

Not knowing where her own resistance came from, she answered: 'This is our home. What's going on? What do you want?'

'Get inside, doctor!' another equally hoarse voice shouted.

She took another step forward. One of them came closer and it was only then that she noticed they were all masked. From behind his balaclava, he said with a fake calmness: 'Please, madam. Return to your home.'

'I will not go in until I know what is going on.'

Her determination was renewed when she heard the cries of her neighbour and her children sound from the floor above. Before she knew it there was a commotion coming from the stairway, as a huddle of masked, armed men dragged her neighbour right past her, bound and blindfolded. She knew nothing about the man except that he was religious, worked as a taxi driver and had nothing to do with politics. He was being dragged down the stairs mercilessly kicking and screaming. Calmly she asked Sondos to come with her, and, taking her daughter's small hand and despite the armed men screaming at them both, she calmly picked her way between them and led the girl upstairs. The taxi driver's wife was sprawled across the floor with blood dripping from her mouth. Her six children crouched around her. One was screaming, another was sobbing quietly. They all seemed helpless. With the help of other neighbours, she tried to calm them down and helped them inside. Sondos followed them and watched quietly throughout. A few moments later, she found herself among the children, some of whom were her age, embracing the youngest and repeating her mother's words to stay calm.

Sondos and her mother stayed up there till the morning. During those hours, single shots could be heard reverberating from different directions around the city. With each crack, the woman's body flinched, making her rock back and forth, hugging herself and groaning: 'Allah have mercy, they have killed him! Allah have mercy!'

Dawn came with the sound of the national anthem playing on some radio stations, as the Holy Qur'an was recited on others... Every so often that damn music interrupted everything, followed by the voice of the presenter: 'In the last hour, a mutilated body has arrived at the Shifa hospital, having been found on Al-Shuhada Street. The body belongs to a well-known merchant.'

On the other side of the city, minarets were broadcasting

their calls to prayer, interspersed with statements of condemnations and threats of revenge.

'Mama, why did would they kill the taxi driver?' Sondos asked when they got back to their flat.

Her mother struggled to hide her own despair.

'I hope this bloody episode will be over soon, habibti,' she said, pausing for a moment, before going on: 'You should take a break from school today. We both need to rest.'

Sondos' mother had an urge to turn the TV news on instantly, but changed her mind. Both parties were broadcasting horrific images on their opposing channels, with each opposing leader using their media contacts to peddle carefully selected scenes of carnage. This was not spontaneous reporting, but the delicate art of managing savagery amid planned chaos. The battle was ongoing and it would not end until one of the parties settled it decisively in their favour; whoever won, the victory would achieve the same goals, goals planned by others, behind the scenes, long before this war started. When the oppressed, fighting for their freedom, turned into murderers and thugs in a dirty civil war, their 'return' could never be bet on; whoever kills with this savagery could never return.

Sondos interrupted her mother's thoughts: 'Mama, can't one of the parties intervene and stop this fighting?'

The question surprised her. She turned towards her with a sad, pale smile that she had struggled to summon. 'Your question is important, Sondos. Remember yesterday I told you that if you want to find the real answers, first you have to ask the right question? Well, the right question is: who benefits from us being where we are today? And how did they succeed in bringing all this about?'

'But, what's next, Mama?' Sondos asked. Her mother didn't reply, so she proceeded ever so slowly towards the western window overlooking the Peace Resort. Just as she reached the blinds, a volley of bullets rang out, marking not only the start of the morning's drill but also the exact time she should be leaving for school.

# Afterword: 'Our Guy'

## Iyad S. S. Abujaber
Sakarya University
Translated from the Arabic by Basma Ghalayini

ISLAMIC GROUPS IN THE Middle East have long occupied a large portion of the US foreign policy strategy in the context of what is referred to as 'preventive war'. The use of hard force, however, has not always been effective, especially given that there is no international consensus on the classification of Islamic groups – particularly moderate ones like the Muslim Brotherhood[1] and Hamas – as terrorist groups. The former, for example, adopts political diplomacy in its relations with ruling regimes across the Arab world, and has offices and followers in different parts of that world; while the latter combines political activity with what it sees as legitimate resistance against a foreign occupation (Israel's).

That is why, at the beginning of the new millennium, the American strategists adopted a softer approach with these groups by pushing them to engage in political processes. This is what was recommended by a study in 2003 conducted by RAND[2], entitled *Civil Democratic Islam*,[3] which called for support for secular and modernist movements in the fight against fundamentalism. Two years after this study, Mubarak's regime in Egypt allowed for the participation of the Muslim Brotherhood movement in its legislative elections; and for a while this conciliatory approach offered a positive example to the Hamas movement in Palestine, which had previously rejected the idea of participating in elections as they were seen to be part of the outcome of the Oslo Accords' compromise.[4] This, combined with the regional and international pressures placed on Hamas and the President of the Palestinian Authority (PA), Mahmoud Abbas, to encourage Hamas's participation in the legislative elections of 2006 opened a path, so Hamas believed, for its political normalisation.

It seemed the only space for political progress available to Hamas in 2006 was to be a partner in the PA system, even if it would be without any real influence; that is to say to be part of the Oslo Accords without playing any real role in executive decision-making, or in the relationship between the PA and Israel. After the death of President Yasser Arafat in November 2004 and the installation of Mahmoud Abbas, through the presidential elections in early 2005, the situation in the Palestinian territories was a source of optimism for the US administration, the region and even Israel. These transformations would be the driver for a new round of negotiations which had been stalled since the failure of the Camp David II negotiations back in 2000, that had in turn resulted in several security incidents in the West Bank and Gaza Strip.

The Palestinian elections of 2005 (presidential) and 2006 (legislative) were seen as a necessary evil for the PA and the Fatah movement in particular. The absence of local security and the ongoing instability throughout the Palestinian territories threatened to dismantle what little was left of the Oslo project; the elections were also a demand of the Israeli government, who wanted to restore order to *all* the Palestinian territories, seeing its own security as dependent on that order.

To rewind for a moment: it's important to remember the late Palestinian President Yasser Arafat had never approved of Mahmoud Abbas, and had purposefully removed him from the decision-making process within Fatah and the PA during the Second Intifada, which began in 2000 as a result of negotiations failure with Israel. On the other hand, Abbas was the most appropriate choice for Israel and the American administration;

thus, under the pretence of reforming the institutions of the PA, and introducing a radical change to its constitution, the position of prime minister was created (by Arafat under international pressure) and immediately filled by Mahmoud Abbas – thus creating a power struggle between a US and Israel-approved Abbas and the democratically elected President Arafat, with whom the US and Israel refused to deal. It was into this tension that Mohammad Dahlan – who had previously headed Fatah's Preventative Security Forces in Gaza (during which time he was accused of torturing Hamas detainees and diverting 40 per cent of all taxes levied at the Karni Crossing into his personal bank account) – found a new lease of political life, being appointed by Abbas as his Minister of Security Affairs.

However, this 'Abbas-Dahlan' government didn't last long in the face of President Yasser Arafat's interventions, with the latter succeeding in creating a competitive environment between Dahlan in Gaza and Jibril Rajoub[5] in the West Bank as a means of staying in control of the PA's institutions.

Dahlan and Arafat had been known to be close, and Dahlan had previously played an important role in the reconciliation between Arafat and Abbas. However, a rift between Arafat and Dahlan emerged in 2004, after the latter organised armed demonstrations in the Gaza Strip, during which members of the Al-Aqsa Brigades – a resistance movement affiliated with Fatah and run by Dahlan – attacked the security institutions of the PA. Among the most prominent of these attacks was the seizing of control of Palestinian police headquarters in the village of Zawaida and the city of Khan Younis, in July 2004, in the centre and south of the Strip respectively. During this unrest, some security figures were kidnapped, most notably Ghazi al-Jabali, the Palestinian police chief and Colonel Abu El-Ola in the southern Gaza Strip. A year later (and after the death of President Arafat in November 2004), these tensions were followed, in September 2005, by the assassination of the late President's cousin, Moussa Arafat, who was head of Military Intelligence. The assassination happened without any interference from local security services, who stood idly by as armed men stormed his house, located in a security compound only a few hundred metres from Mahmoud Abbas' own house.

This was all part of Dahlan's plan to eradicate the remaining supporters of Yasser Arafat's regime in Gaza and tighten his grip on the security services in the Strip.

Truth be told, Dahlan succeeded in presenting himself early on as a strong figure who was loyal to the security services of the PA and to the Fatah movement. This 'strong man' image also made him an attractive candidate for the American administration. Ironically Mahmoud Abbas' promise in the first few months of his presidency of the PA (in early 2005) – to get rid of the security chaos in Gaza and disarm resistance fighters in the West Bank – was in stark contrast to what his ally, Dahlan, was actually doing. It was Dahlan who was behind most of the armed activities in Gaza; the majority of military operations and training were organised by figures associated with Dahlan, including Mahmoud Nashabat, Nabil Tammous and Samih Al-Madhoun, who worked to form a militia-like security entity known simply as the 'Death Squad' with the sole aim of taking on Hamas, which had been entrenched in an almost permanent state of conflict with the Preventive Security Services, established by Dahlan when the PA first set up in Gaza under the 1993 Oslo Accords.

It is noteworthy that this conflict between the Preventive Security Services and Hamas goes back to 1996, when Dahlan's security apparatus claimed there was a secret agency run by Hamas to destabilise security in the PA territories, and as a result, hundreds of Hamas leaders were arrested and tortured within PA security headquarters.

The state of security chaos that preceded Abbas' arrival to the presidency and the unilateral withdrawal of Israeli armed forces from the Gaza Strip on 15 August 2005 coincided with Abbas' gradual transfer of the PA's decision-making centres from the Gaza Strip to Ramallah in the West Bank, fundamentally shifting the centre of political gravity that had been in Gaza since the mid-90s. This relocation changed everything; suddenly all official transactions between the government and its citizens had to be processed through PA ministries that had now moved to Ramallah; it also meant Abbas had effectively, partially withdrawn from Gaza leaving Dahlan to face Hamas on his own.

If Dahlan's efforts to confront the rise of Hamas during this period were guided or helped by the United States, one can only assume so were Abbas', who thanks to the US's General Keith Dayton, had succeeded in eliminating the armed resistance in the West Bank, opening the gates to a splurge of illegal Israeli settlements in the West Bank after 2005, as well as greater security coordination between Abbas and Israel.

There is no doubt that the US administration and regional players exerted great pressure on the PLO to hold the presidential and legislative elections and to involve Hamas. Qatar, for instance, played an important role in pushing Hamas to participate in the elections, but the same international pressure to re-empower the PA, through electoral legitimacy, was not prepared to cooperate with any Palestinian government led by Hamas. It's possible at this point to talk of a Plan B emerging in case the expected outcome – a Fatah victory at the polls – did not transpire. For when, in January 2006, the 'shock' result happened, and Hamas won a majority (74 of 132 seats) in Palestine's Legislative Council, Plan B quickly clicked into place.

It was clear the American response had been prepared in advance because the task of toppling the new Hamas government was not solely assigned to Dahlan. The PA President Abbas played a pivotal role when he asked the new Hamas government led by Ismail Haniyeh[6] to recognise the conditions set by the Diplomatic Quartet[7] and renounce armed resistance as well as recognise all previous agreements between the PLO and Israel. This move by Abbas was revealed as part of a *Vanity Fair* exposé by David Rose in March 2008, titled 'The Gaza Bombshell', in which documents were published, proving the American administration's involvement in an attempt to topple the Hamas government in Gaza by igniting a civil war between Fatah leader Dahlan and the Hamas government when Hamas refused to recognise Israel.

In order to put pressure on the Hamas government, America cut its financial aid to the PA, paralysing its ability to implement any political programme, especially as it was inheriting an empty treasury from the previous interim government, and making it unable to pay the salaries of public sector employees for about a year. Even the Hamas government's attempts to seek funding from allies and supporters abroad were bound to fail, as transferring money to Palestinian banks needs Israeli approval. And when it resorted to transferring funds in cash through the Rafah crossing with Egypt, the latter country prevented most of these funds from reaching Gaza.

According to the aforementioned exposé, Abbas met with US Secretary of State Condoleezza Rice in Ramallah at the beginning of October 2006, where she called for him to dissolve Ismail Haniyeh's government and hold early elections. The President agreed to do so but then asked for more time. He was clearly stalling. Instead, he leaked news about his intention to dissolve the elected Hamas government, through some of his advisers who were known for their loyalty to the US administration, news that he was forced to deny later.

President Abbas' inability to make the decision to dissolve Ismail Haniyeh's government subjected him to additional US pressure from the US Consul General in Jerusalem, Jack Wallace, who made a promise to Abbas to return US financial support to the PA in exchange for dissolving the Hamas government, which was already facing both political pressure from Abbas and military pressure from Dahlan's forces.

Thus Washington had placed the elected Hamas government (still largely based in Gaza) between a rock and a hard place, whether through Abbas' soft approach, or through Dahlan, who was now in charge of 70,000 security personnel affiliated with the PA in Gaza, as well as other security militias affiliated with Fatah. Dahlan confessed to *Vanity Fair* that he had agreed to confront the Hamas government and try to bring it down. This confession also appeared clearly in a leaked recording of him saying, 'I will make Hamas dance khamsa baladi.'[8] Indeed his closest associate at the time, Samir Al-Mashharawi didn't deny his role in attempting to topple the Hamas government, or in Fatah's refusal to recognise the results of the 2006 elections.

Faced with such financial, political and security pressures, and having seen many of its activists and leaders kidnapped and tortured throughout 2006 at the hands of Death Squad members, and the apparent inability of existing security services to implement the new Hamas government's policies, Hamas's Minister of Interior, Said Seyam, rushed to form an 'Executive Force' consisting of 12,000 soldiers, whose mission would be to control security in the Strip. Hamas faced a crisis. Its government was paralysed, even at a civil service level: Gaza's ministries transformed into almost entirely empty office blocks, where only the minister himself and a handful of employees ever turned up – the majority of staff refusing to come into work, understandably, given they were no longer being paid.

In light of these accelerating developments, the Hamas government signed a consensus agreement with Abbas, known as the Mecca Agreement, in February 2007, as a way out of the internal fighting and to end the financial crisis. The agreement, sponsored by Saudi Arabia, paved the way for a unity government, led by Hamas but with Fatah members taking key positions, with the Saudis underwriting PA employees' wages. What Hamas didn't know at the time was that its very presence in power was unacceptable to those really making the decisions: the US and Israel.

Frustrated by Abbas' refusal to dissolve the Hamas government, and apoplectic at this new unity government deal, the Bush administration focused all its attentions on Dahlan. He was seen as 'our guy', one Washington source told *Vanity Fair*: a can-do ally with the guile and the muscle to get results. General Dayton, it transpired, had been holding a series of secret meetings with Dahlan in Jerusalem and Ramallah since November 2006, with the aim of training and preparing armed forces under the guise of reforming the PA's security services.

The Dayton plan in the West Bank had its equivalent in Gaza, where Dahlan, who had now acquired the title of 'National Security Adviser' for the PA, received about $30 million from various Arab countries that had agreed to deliver the American plan after the Bush administration was unable to *directly* fulfil its promise to Dahlan (having failed to pass the bill through Congress) which would have given $1.27 billion, over five years, to train and arm tens of thousands in the West Bank as well as training and re-equipping 15,000 existing security personnel and recruiting 4,700 more in Gaza. Egypt and Jordan would also receive and train hundreds of military personnel from Palestine within the wider framework of this plan, being referred to by some as 'Iran-Contra 2'.

The entities affiliated with Dahlan, such as the Preventive Security Service, the Death Squad, and various armed groups, were not acting alone in the field. These latter groups were supported significantly by the newly-formed 'Presidential Guard', which had grown and seen thousands of new members join during the years 2006-2007, at the expense of other entities like the National Security Forces, whose role and power had dwindled.

It can be said then that Abbas was now developing and strengthening this apparatus as a direct result of his own, previous approval of Gaza Interior Minister Said Seyam's request for a 12,000-strong Executive Force. It was as if the President was trying to retake security superiority in the Strip, and thus thwart the democratically elected interior minister, Said Seyam, from exercising his security mandate.

Clearly the Ministry of Interior has the authority to provide security for institutions, borders and crossings, but what appeared at the beginning of 2007 was that the Presidential Guard that took its orders directly from President Abbas had effectively usurped the Ministry of Interior. So much so that the Presidential Guard, under Dahlan's command, felt confident enough by mid-May 2007 to storm the Islamic University in Gaza,[9] a well-known stronghold of Hamas support.

Under the pretext of confiscating missiles and arresting Iranian military personnel apparently holding up the university and manufacturing weapons, the raid, which set the university ablaze, caused an estimated $10 million in damages (according to Hamas). In reality, while this raid was taking place, *real* weapons were arriving into the hands of Dahlan's soldiers, as arranged in the US's 'Iran-Contra 2' plan, from four different Arab countries, through the Rafah crossing with Egypt, which was by now secured by the Presidential Guard and not by the Ministry of Interior of the Hamas government.[10]

Meanwhile, tensions increased and armed clashes began to take place between groups affiliated with Hamas and Dahlan's forces attempting to transport the cache of new weapons to the centre of the Gaza Strip.

There is no doubt that the core strength of Hamas did not lie in Seyam's recently formed Executive Force, but rather in its long-standing military wing, the al-Qassam Brigades, which had been in constant conflict with Dahlan's agencies throughout 2006 and 2007. This was the miscalculation that the US plan made when it bet all its chips on the forces run by Dahlan. Especially when we consider most of the generals leading these Fatah-affiliated forces secretly left the Strip months or weeks before all-out civil war broke out in mid-June 2007, some fleeing to Ramallah and others to Egypt. This is confirmed by the testimonies of many officers in the PA's intelligence and preventive security apparatus, who secretly left the Strip after Hamas took control of all governmental security headquarters and institutions.[11]

Five hundred new recruits to the Fatah National Security Forces (promised good wages by Dahlan himself) were received by Egypt where they underwent intensive training. They returned equipped with new, state-of-the-art weapons, vehicles, even black flak jackets that made them stand out from the usual scruffy soldiers. 'The idea was that we needed them to go in dressed well, equipped well, and that might create the impression of new authority,' Dahlan told *Vanity Fair*. They were indeed noticed, even by the 12-year old Sondos in Talal's story.

The appearance of these soldiers, as well as the leaked Dayton plan to the *Al Majd* newspaper, came as the final straw that forced Hamas's hand. To Hamas, the Dayton plan was a blueprint for a US-backed Fatah coup. They had no choice but to act. To quote David Wurmser, Dick Cheney's chief Middle East adviser, who resigned from his post a month after the attempted coup: 'What happened wasn't so much a coup by Hamas but an attempted coup by Fatah that was pre-empted before it could happen.'[12]

With the Hamas takeover of Gaza, Palestine entered a new era, one which it still occupies to this day: the country now exists across in two, diametrically opposed halves, with the Abbas Presidency and Fatah-dominated PA in the West Bank, and the elected Hamas government in Gaza. Hamas's early attempts to persuade Abbas to return to Gaza, to relocate his presidency there, and heal the rift fell on deaf ears. Instead, he issued a decree announcing the dismissal of Ismail Haniyeh's government, a government which he himself had legitimised in the Mecca Agreement. Abbas also held the local leadership of the PA and Fatah in Gaza responsible for the fall of Gaza into Hamas' hands.

Following the events of June 2007, Abbas' position on Dahlan turned profoundly hostile. Meanwhile, Dahlan (who is now based in the UAE) managed to turn a local conflict with Hamas into a regional one, fuelling the demonisation of the movement and bringing other Arab countries on board with the American and Israel narrative: that it is a terrorist organisation. And though Dahlan has left Palestine, he is not completely gone. Recently his relations with Hamas have taken a consensual turn, and he has sought to return to Gaza, first by providing humanitarian aid and, just this year, by organising a new political party, fielding candidates in the postponed 2021 legislative election. Palestine is not yet completely free, it seems, of Washington's 'guy'.

## Notes

1. The Muslim Brotherhood is a transnational Sunni Islamist organisation founded in Egypt by Islamic scholar and schoolteacher Hassan al-Banna in 1928. Al-Banna's teachings spread far beyond Egypt, influencing today various Islamist movements from charitable organisations to political parties.
2. RAND Corporation ('research and development') is a part-privately, part-publicly funded American non-profit global policy think tank created in 1948 by Douglas Aircraft Company to offer research and analysis to the US Armed Forces.
3. https://www.rand.org/pubs/monograph_reports/MR1716.html
4. The Oslo Accords are a pair of agreements between the government of Israel and the Palestine Liberation Organisation (PLO): the Oslo I Accord, signed in Washington, D.C., in 1993; and the Oslo II Accord, signed in Taba, Egypt, in 1995.
5. Jibril Mahmoud Muhammad Rajoub (born 14 May 1953), also known by his kunya Abu Rami, is a Palestinian political leader, legislator, and former militant. He was the head of the Preventive Security Force in the West Bank until being dismissed (along with the force's chief in Gaza, Ghazi Jabali) in 2002, was a member of the Fatah Revolutionary Council until 2009 and was elected to the Fatah Central Committee at the party's 2009 congress, serving as Deputy-Secretary until 2017, before being elected Secretary General of the Central Committee in 2017.
6. Ismail Haniyeh is the head of Hamas Political Bureau and formerly one of two disputed prime ministers of the Palestinian National Authority. Haniyeh became prime minister after Hamas won the Palestinian legislative elections of 2006.
7. Diplomatic Quartet, aka the Quartet on the Middle East is a group of nations and supranational entities involved in mediating the Israeli–Palestinian peace process, comprising of the UN, the US, the EU and Russia.
8. An expression referring to traditional Egyptian dancing, meaning he will drive them crazy.
9. The Islamic University is a university established by the Islamic Complex in Gaza in 1978.
10. '2000 Egyptian-made automatic rifles, 20,000 ammunition

clips, two million bullets' (David Rose, 'The Gaza Bombshell', *Vanity Fair*, 3 Mar 2008).

11. Based on conversations the author had with former PA security forces in Gaza.

12. David Rose, *ibid.*

# Grandma Saliha

## Najwa Bin Shatwan

Translated from the Arabic by Sawad Hussain

*Timespace: Benghazi, 19 March 2011*

'WHERE ARE YOU GOING?' her neighbour yelled out. 'Get inside, the soldiers are here.'

'What was that? I can't hear you.'

'I said, get inside, now. It's a war!'

'Have you seen my *shib-shib*? It's here in the bushes somewhere...'

'Like now is the time for flip-flops! Get yourself inside. There's a revolution going on! The Security Council is trying to keep us safe.'

'Wait, what revolution?'

'Get inside. Now. I'll explain later if we're still alive.'

Grandma Saliha should have died a costly death paid for by the state, with the very money they could have spent on giving her a good life instead. She would have died that way, if it were not for the unexpected lifeline gifted to her on the wings of French Rafale fighters that intervened, saving civilians from Gaddafi's latest attack.

Revolution or no revolution, Jedda Saliha wasn't concerned with anything other than survival in one of the city's poorest neighbourhoods, not thinking twice about the difference between a costly death or a valuable life; after all, she was used to existing in an area so wretched even soldiers hadn't bothered to descend upon it. Nonetheless, it's as if they had, what with everything lying in disarray – a place deserted by life itself: forever neglected, disregarded, forgotten.

Her second chance at life had cost NATO billions: arming themselves and preparing for intervention. Not much different, really, from Gaddafi's stockpiling of weapons that would have snuffed her out, again at a colossal price to the country's coffers.

For 42 years, the public treasury spent freely on arms, hoarding them, not caring about the fate of such weapons in Libya, who would pull the trigger, who would be the target. For poor souls like Jedda Saliha, a three-dollar pistol would have been enough to take her out; even a string of firecrackers would have done the trick, and been far more economical to boot.

On 19 March, she survived Gaddafi's weapons arsenal. She didn't cost her country a thing, not even the repair of her dentures whose wisdom teeth promptly cracked when they fell out of her mouth. Contrary to the expectations of the military operation, Jedda Saliha didn't die scared stiff of Gaddafi's battalions sinking their claws into her – battalions that would not have paid her old age any mind or given her existence a passing thought as they stormed in; battalions that would have destroyed her home, stolen her jewellery, knocked her son's photo from the damp wall it had been hanging on for a quarter century of grief; battalions that would not have respected all the possessions she had accumulated and toiled for like an ant – all for the sake of a simple marriage certificate back in 1933, when there had only been four witnesses and a one-eyed ram. She really would have died at the feet of the riff-raff ransacking her home, devastating everything in sight, even if she'd pleaded with them: 'I'm like your grandmother... Shame on you... Fear God!' Stomp on her is what they would have done – a locust to them, nothing more.

Jedda Saliha had faced death time and time again in different ways: life-threatening conditions such as high blood pressure and diabetes; sleeping on too low a bed, making her prime meat for a deadly bite; always forgetting to slather on kerosene to fend off scorpions. The gist of her existence had been escaping the clutches of death only to fall prey to it once more, and so on it went.

After confronting death during the military operation, she encountered it again in the form of stray celebratory bullets. A bullet case pierced the side of her head, leaving a scar two inches long – luckily it only damaged a small part of her brain, leaving her spirit – located as far away from her head as it was – perfectly intact. That's why the fake news of their liberation also failed to be the cause of her death. She had been watching the street festivities following the supposed fall of the dictator, but was empty inside. Maybe she was still alive because she'd never really ever been happy.

Breathless, Benghazi came back from the brink of Judgement Day. It happened in the early hours, just as Jedda Saliha was quietly relieving herself. Before she managed to finish, the Rafale planes swooped in cutting off the military convoy, dispersing it. With no water, electricity or even her spectacles, Jedda Saliha stood up, her hands unwashed, crashed into the toilet, and bounced off the bathtub. The city, whose inhabitants had been fleeing in every possible direction, was somehow protected by the pilots who had stayed up late into the night studying aviation, been subjected to harsh exams, and almost kicked the bucket during their harrowing training drills. Only God Himself could have orchestrated them being at the service of this illiterate old woman, who couldn't tell the difference between the letter alif and an electric pole; who thought the nasheed *Tala' al-Badru 'Alaynā*[1] was from the Quran; who was certain that the sacred Kaaba was somewhere in the furthest corners of the Libyan hinterlands, convinced that Libya was the world itself, with nothing else beyond its borders.

The news that Benghazi had been devastated all the same split her heart down the middle like a hollow almond shell. Rumours abounded, the Rafale jets hovered in the air, while lies roiled down below. Jets and lies, both hovering, both flying, both sacrificing one life for another, leaving Jedda

Saliha alive at times and dead at others.

Some days passed where death only threatened her a couple of times a day: sometimes armed, sometimes out in the street, sometimes next to her bed if she forgot to slather on kerosene, or at the government building where she went to collect her welfare payment. The only thing she met there was talk about the director having made a run for it, the empty public treasury and the delay in aid packages. The worst of it though was when she alighted from a jam-packed bus and toppled over, skinning her knee and bruising her forehead. A young man, the product of the current education system, jostled her: 'Why you even still here? Waste of space!'

She didn't die from her injured knee, or the greenish-yellow bruises between her eyes. Cuts and bruises wherever they were on her body wouldn't do in a woman whose entire life had been one long, drawn-out survival, a woman who was a month away from being a centenarian and turning into a relic that could only be treated under laws for the preservation of national treasures. How were a few nasty words or government incompetence going to be the end of her?

She wouldn't be felled as easily as a swallow in the sky when a man, electrified by the news, pointed his pistol out of the window. Without a shadow of doubt, Jedda Saliha knew that nine months of war had trained men, had trained their guns. Even the windows had learned to keep themselves open, and the wind to skip past the panes – let alone neighbours to not crane their necks out – when the bullets of such men were flying.

That day, one of Jedda Saliha's relatives died in a way unlike any other in Libya. One of the neighbourhood men shot bullets from his window right after some unconfirmed news: his head inside, following the bulletin, and his gun outside, popping away. Shortly after, another man followed suit. The channel he was watching was broadcasting news syndicated secondhand from other stations, hence his delay in grabbing something to fire out the window. God forgive his wife! She had used up all their ammunition on the midday news bulletin, only leaving him the choice of two grenades and a bomb.

Jedda Saliha didn't die from the bomb that man tossed onto the road in celebration of the good news. Not finding anyone on the road or the parallel streets, the bomb slipped through the nearby school gates, and lay in wait for the children to spill out. Who can forget the day when all that was left of that school were eleven toilets, and one classroom. A day when, once again, death failed to catch Jedda Saliha, one of the eyewitnesses. She considered that day with the same bitterness as the day her firstborn son left for the front. Her son said farewell and gave his own sixteen-year-old boy a gun to put his mother and sisters out of their misery should the battalions ever reach the outskirts of the city. But he ended up using it too early on them, promptly following in his father's footsteps.

One day, Jedda Saliha discovered a rat in her house: eating her food, chewing through her clothes and defecating in her coffee. For the longest time she had been blaming the lack of food on the djinn, holding the ifrit accountable for the holes in her pillows and clothes, and blaming the coffee sellers at the market for the new, peculiar taste. Before sleeping, she sought protection from them all: djinn, demons, and coffee sellers. Winding a towel round her head she hoped they wouldn't recognise her or hoodwink her. It's not as if it hadn't happened before with Abu Huraira during the reign of Umar Bin Al-Khattab, when the djinns were blamed for stealing wheat. Mosque sermons stated that djinns ate animal droppings and bones, but she didn't dare ask the imam why the djinns would steal something of no use to them. Why was it that, in the traditional biographies of the prophet, the djinns were cloaked in suspicion, while Abu Huraira was left with a clean slate?

Whatever happened, Jedda Saliha didn't die in those dark days, as if those days weren't good enough for anything to actually happen, even a death. Death wasn't occurring as naturally as it normally would in Benghazi or its outskirts. Death itself was finding it difficult to reap souls and take down a record of their deeds for the hereafter. The souls were too scattered, here and there, everything thrown into disarray – a very tricky situation indeed.

People were fleeing from death in any which way they could. Not satisfied with simply waiting for them at the battlefront, death would chase them into their bathrooms. With more casualties brought to the general hospital than there were people to carry them, moving corpses and digging graves grew quite impossible.

Despite the terribly inconvenient time for death, Jedda Saliha did, however, eventually manage to die a most unusual death, quietly joining the mass of otherwise young, strapping bodies, without anyone being the wiser. She really should have sought permission from the national artefacts department. Insulin levels soaring, freshly bathed and perfumed, she stuffed her jewellery into her pockets. Without the usual white discharge round her eyes, her hair and hands were henna-stained, size 36 shoes fastened on her feet, clad in a robe she had only worn on two previous occasions – occasions when she had cried so hard, her hot tears had left bleach-like streaks down the front of it.

Dying wasn't the problem, rather the issuance of her death certificate was. Her second son, once informed of her death, pressured the doctor in various ways to issue a certificate that said she had died of natural causes. Fed up with the son's insistent nagging whilst trying to sort out martyrs' limbs, the doctor snapped: 'It's like you can't wait to get rid of her! Have you forgotten that we're in Benghazi? What's the hurry to bury her? Can't you see that even the martyrs stuffed in our fridges and lining our hospital hallways don't have a hole yet? Like you or me, your mother will get her hole, eventually. Someone or other will carry her to the cemetery, toss dirt over her – all for free or for the next-to-nothing paid to walking-dead municipality labourers, shovels in hand.

Jedda Saliha's son realised that he could die in the most insignificant way, unlike his mother, and the dusty shovel-bearing labourers would still come chasing him. The doctor was warning him that his in-laws' cellar where he had hid, leaving his mother in the line of fire, wouldn't save him from the old-yet-new hand of death in Benghazi. When the time had come when Jedda Saliha's son was meant to die, he had twisted the truth about his whereabouts on the day the battalions stormed the city, deceiving others that he had been on the frontlines, confronting and slowing their advancement. But who can cheat death? It would hunt him down and kill him like a stray dog, his chance at an honourable death gone. Humiliation and shame washing over him, he felt his heart beat for the first time outside of the cellar, thinking of how his mother had died; how her heart exploded afterwards in the morgue; how her brain dissolved into a puddle while her body was washed; how two bloody clots oozed out into her shroud. God alone knows what awaited her until she could be buried.

Returning with some paperwork, Jedda Saliha's son thought maybe the doctor had been able to sort out the death certificate during his short absence. It was a financial transaction after all. But the doctor appeared more than just that, he could have been a geologist, a ground station engineer, someone who'd studied endlessly and whose knowledge of the human body's complex mechanisms knew no bounds. Akin to how a mechanic can diagnose a vehicle's problems, he would come across some telltale sign on Jedda Saliha's body that couldn't be faked. Every body tells a story, but how it's read is another matter.

Suddenly the doctor stood up, pulled open the fridge door and stole a look inside.

'How is she?' her son enquired.

'Still dead as ever. She'll probably find herself at the graveyard and wonder why she's there, among all those young men.'

'What to do now?'

'I can't forge a certificate, the hospital doesn't even have a director right now. You've got to wait till they appoint a new one.'

'When's that?'

'Maybe after the interim government is formed.'

'When's that?'

'Maybe after Libya is declared free.'

'When's that?'

'This whole thing with your mother is tied up with the last two cities being freed from Gaddafi's grip. Thank your God it's got nothing to do with the constitution because that's all linked to conducting a correct and valid census. You already know how since 1945, no one's ever counted the *real* residents here, and since 1969 it's been like a free-for-all, a building with no doorman.'

'Please, can't you do something? Anything?'

'I can't. The time when your 'own' death certificate could be delivered right to your doorstep into your still-living hands, is long gone. The benefits to having one – like tapping into a pension, escaping conscription, or getting access to the oil revenue handouts – don't apply in your mother's case, due to her advanced age. Even the causes of death that are eligible for these have changed, akhi; dying the way she did, she isn't an asset.'

The doctor caught himself as if he had forgotten something. 'Oh yes… yesterday, we found some whip scars on your mother's back. Did you know about them?'

'Oh, those old things? Nothing out of line with verse 34, surah Al-Nisa. You know, the old, *Strike them, but if they obey you, seek no means against them.*'

'I'm sorry, I really am, but I won't be able to help her.'

Fuming, Jedda Saliha's son leaned against the fridge door, thinking of how he wouldn't be able to capitalise on her death unless she was buried, and he wouldn't be able to bury her unless a death certificate was issued, and he wouldn't be able to get one issued unless it was done officially with a stamp and everything, and if he didn't do it quick enough, who's to say someone else wouldn't pounce on her body claiming her as a relative, magicking up a new identity card to claim compensation from the state, saying she was a victim of the NATO bombing or the American intervention.

He was afraid that denying her existence altogether might be easier than actually proving her real identity. Everything had become much more complicated for her in death.

## Note

1. Tala' al-Badru 'Alaynā is a traditional Islamic poem or nasheed that the Ansar – residents of Medina – sang for the Islamic prophet Muhammad upon his arrival into the city.

LIBYA, 2011

# Afterword: The Past, Present and Future of Violence

Matteo Capasso

> Ben Ali, Mubarak and Gaddafi are standing in the desert, and each one of them is asked to divide their country's money between themselves and their own people. Ben Ali starts. He draws a line in the sand, he takes the money and says, 'I will throw the money in the air, what ends up on the right side of the line goes to the people, what falls on the left side goes to me.' Then it's the turn of Mubarak, and he draws a circle in the sand, saying 'I will throw the money in the air and what falls in the circle goes to the people, what stays outside of it goes to me.' Then, Gaddafi goes. He draws a line in the air and says, 'What falls goes to me, what remains in the air goes to the people.'

There is no question that, in the years leading up to 2011, a large part of the Libyan population had grown profoundly frustrated towards a government that appeared increasingly repressive and domestically illegitimate. Jokes, such as the one quoted, were indicative of the wider popular discontent that had been boiling in society for some time, and then exploded in February 2011. This shared discontent, coupled with the widely held desire to improve the people's socio-economic conditions, were, however, not enough to explain how Libya, its people and places descended into yet another Arab-world war zone. Or at least they didn't seem enough to me, conducting my doctoral research on the developments a few years after. Like Iraq, Syria and Yemen, Libya had spiralled into a conflict, where foreign actors support multiple armed gangs that, in turn, operate with impunity. How did this happen?

The most common explanation provided by mainstream accounts seemed to be that the long legacy of Gaddafi's rule was the culprit. Suddenly stripped of its sole ruler for the previous forty-two years, the country was suffering from a chronic lack of democratic institutions, and of the rule of law; on top of that an economy that was profoundly oil-dependent (some might say 'oil-cursed'), left it unable to adapt. Implicit in this narrative is that war and chaos are transitional, and somehow entirely natural states of affairs for a country of the Global South to go through before arriving at and being welcomed into the land of democracy and globalisation. Mainstream accounts regurgitate this story endlessly, of course, in order to distract from and omit the historical role Western states and US-led imperialism have played in influencing and shaping the formation of the Libyan post-colonial state from 1969 onwards. Such interpretations not only identify 2011 as the chronological start of the war, but – most importantly – position this conflict as one between the regime and the people. The omission of history and the lack of reflection on the role that structural, geopolitical context played in igniting this war leads to the removal of *ongoing* violence from this narrative, that key element in the prevailing world order: namely the US-led domination over the Global South.

After the 1969 al-Fath revolution that overthrew King Idris I, the Libyan government pursued a revolutionary project of national independence, while also advocating for a radical change in the power relations of the international order. For the Libyan revolutionaries, the process of national liberation required a wider restructuring of the unequal exchange and power hierarchies that allowed the US-led world order to dominate the Global South. If we acknowledge the influence of anti-imperialist and socialist ideas on the practices of the Libyan government since the early years of the 1969 revolution, it becomes easier to understand how crucial the struggle was to imagine alternative paths to development and regional cooperation, a struggle which was ultimately for the right to shape one's own economy, culture and society. Daring to reclaim its sovereignty over national resources, which materialised with the nationalisation of the oil industry and the shutdown of numerous Western military bases (Dietrich, 2021), the revolutionary government pursued a model of political and economic development that challenged the idea of a state-centric and market-oriented world political system. Post-colonial resistance did not mean abandoning the idea of the nation; rather nationalism became an inherent part of a revolutionary project that also required a radical change in the relations of domination in the international order (Getachew, 2019). The Libyan revolutionary regime launched redistributive programmes and infrastructural development at a national level, while pursuing projects of political, economic and monetary integration at a regional one.

Their belief lay firmly in the necessity of overcoming the international hierarchy that facilitated the domination of the Global South (Capasso, 2020a). These political and economic strategies, including the military support for numerous independence movements (including the Palestinians), were conceived of as integral to securing any true independence. Inevitably, the US and its allies did not sit back, and the confrontation escalated soon after the revolution. Their responses gradually developed into a set of policies aimed at disciplining the Libyan government, thus destabilising and containing its political ambitions which clearly imperilled Western influence on the region. This tension evolved into a full-scale military confrontation that materialised in a variety of forms; most notably, at first, through the Chadian civil war (1978-1987), which Libya entered into in support of anti-French group, Front de Libération Nationale du Tchad (FROLINAT), at which point it quickly turned into a perfect arena for an international 'proxy war' between Libya and its allies, and the imperialists (US and France) and their allies: Egypt, Israel, Saudi Arabia and Sudan; other examples of this confrontation included the US bombing of Tripoli in 1986, and UN's international sanctions (1992-2003).

Under the constant threat of war, the cost of defeats and attacks, and the weight of international sanctions, the revolutionary, Pan-Arab and egalitarian ambitions initially adopted by the Libyan government slowly began to fade. Economic pressures, starting with military defeat in Chad and deepened by sanctions, triggered a slow reconfiguring of the class structure of Libya's state-elites, gradually transforming them (Capasso, 2020a). Ultimately, the changing geopolitical conditions represented a major ideological defeat for the Libyan regime, one ironic consequence of which was that the ruling class actually became *more* integrated with international financial capital, meaning Libya lost its autonomy over economic policies. Consequently, the progressive social and economic gains made in the previous decades were, by the late eighties, being reversed. The result, inevitably, was the emergence of much greater socio-economic inequalities, the increasing use of corruption and political repression (such as the 1996 Abu Salim prison massacre), declining job opportunities and the revival of tribal affiliations as both tools of control and as societal 'safety valves', releasing pressure whenever necessary (Capasso, 2020b).

These changes are important to understand for two reasons. First, the role of US-led imperialism in shaping the political trajectory of the country was fundamental. The use of bombings, sanctions and gunboat diplomacy did not just play a marginal role in the transformation of the country's policies, they represented an essential coercion. Secondly, the threat of war and the reality of sanctions set in motion a substantive transformation of the regime's policies, and an increase in socio-economic inequalities in a country that was rich in natural resources. These grievances, which had begun to appear in the late 1980s, only worsened and solidified at the start of the twentieth century. Throughout the 1990s, the government launched a second wave of liberalisation and privatisation and, by the 2000s, all Gaddafi's offspring occupied critical government positions in financial, political and military roles, which in turn translated into lucrative contracts and their progressive accumulation of wealth and political capital. Gaddafi's eldest son, for instance, Muhammad Mu'ammar, was the head of the Libyan Olympic Committee and three national telecommunication companies (Almadar, Telecom, and General Post). Hannibal was the head of the General National Maritime Transport company, specialising in oil exports; Khamis controlled one of the most powerful military brigades in the country, the 'Khamis Brigade'; and Mutassim and Saif al-Islam were considered to be possible heirs to the throne and were heavily involved in the country's political dynamics, setting up all sorts of organisations, from non-profit organisations to armed battalions (Chorin, 2012). The Panama Papers further revealed that other regime insiders embezzled large sums of public funds, originally allocated to build hospitals and public infrastructure, in order to buy luxury properties in England and Scotland (Garside, Pegg, and Mahmood, 2016).

Understanding these developments from 1990 onwards allows us to answer the question of how the 2011 uprising led, on the one hand, to a large mass movement of Libyans who angrily protested in the streets and, on the other hand, to the speedy mobilisation of the military power of NATO to direct the course of events. These two processes were not mutually exclusive but rather the dual, logical outcome of the long war of economic and political attrition unleashed on Libya since the late 1970s. In the context of this popular discontent and revolutionary defeat, the NATO-led military intervention should not be seen as the humanitarian intervention it was sold to us as, but rather as part of a long continuum of war and violence between Libya and US-led imperialism, which was inevitable as soon as the 1969 Libyan government came into power.

After the brutal televised capture and killing of Mu'ammar Gaddafi in October 2011 (which included him being sodomised with a bayonet knife), the US Secretary of State, Hillary Rodham Clinton, summarised the success of the NATO-led regime-change operation with the phrase 'We came, we saw, he died' (CBS News, 2011). By 'protecting and saving' the lives of the Libyan people, the humanitarian intervention promised to pave the way for them to build a democratic government. Yet since 2011, Libya has only descended into deeper and deeper chaos and internecine violence. After the 2012 elections, those Western-armed groups – also known as militias – that had contributed to the fall of the regime did not acknowledge the results of the elections and began fighting against each other. To this day, Western powers and their allies – mainly Turkey and the Wahabi-led Gulf monarchies – have been attempting to consolidate and formalise their gains made over the past years. However, when key divergences broke out and military-financial support was provided to different factions, the country remained convulsed by violence and war.

A major change in the balance of forces took place in 2014, which witnessed the emergence of two distinct political groups across the east-west divide. In May 2014, former General Khalifa Haftar announced the formation of the Libyan National Army (LNA) and launched 'Operation Dignity,' the aim of which was to restore security in the east of the country, particularly Benghazi, targeting so-called 'terrorist groups' – a term the LNA applied to a wide range of Islamist groups. A month later, a new national election took place aiming to create a Council of Deputies, which was supposed to take over from the General National Congress (GNC). The Islamist party (Justice and Construction Party) rejected the victory of the liberal alliance (National Forces Alliance) and broke away from the GNC, forcing the newly elected House of Representatives (HoR) to flee from Tripoli and move to the east in Tobruk, thus allying with the LNA. As a consequence, the HoR in the east attempted to gain control over state finances by creating its own branches of the National Oil Company and the Central Bank of Libya. At the same time, in the west of the country, the conflict escalated when Tripoli's Islamists and Misrata militias launched 'Operation Libya Dawn' to seize Tripoli International Airport, capturing it from the Zintan militia, which had decided to ally with General Khalifa Haftar.

More recently, a UN-led initiative brought about the installation of an interim government, the Government of National Accord (GNA), in Tripoli in March 2016. Despite previously supporting it, the Libyan HoR in the east later withdrew its recognition of the GNA. To this day, the GNA technically remains the only legitimate government recognised by the UN, yet the LNA continues to maintain a stable presence on the ground, being backed by regional powers (Egypt, the UAE and Saudi Arabia in primis) as well as EU member states, such as France. Therefore, while new elections are scheduled to take place this coming December 2021, the kernel of this war remains, as ever, of a geopolitical and economic nature, considering how militarism – and its technological and financial spinoffs – provide a secure revenue of profit in the midst of ongoing Libyan suffering.

Profit is generated through the increasing securitisation and international arms' sales to the region (a founding stone of any empire is its ability to export and sell its own products out to the people it has colonised). As the Forum of Arms Sales notes, US arms' sales to the MENA in 2019 increased 118% compared to 2018, reaching a sum of $25.5 billion. In the past five years (2014-2019) there has been a dramatic increase in the sale and flow of weapons from European countries to the MENA region, and many of these weapons eventually are diverted to their local proxies in Libya, Syria or Yemen. Italy, for instance, has managed to sell a total of €1,334 billion worth of armaments to countries in the Middle East and Africa (Capasso, 2020b). What is most striking is how the war industry profits from both sides of the tragedy: First, by fuelling conflict in the region (selling arms, military hardware and security services to the country at war); and second, by selling infrastructure and technology to stop refugees from coming to Europe as a result of said war (Akkerman, 2016). In Europe, the top arms sellers to war-torn countries and oppressive regimes – Finmeccanica, Thales and Airbus – are also beneficiaries of EU-provided border security contracts. In the case of the ongoing Libyan war, we should consider this windfall for the war industry in the context of other initiatives: the border wall construction along the Libya-Tunisian border, undertaken jointly by Germany and the US; French military operations in the Sahel (e.g. Operation Barkhan, 2014-present); AFRICOM (United States Africa Command) military bases; and 'ISMariS', the new EU digital surveillance installation along the coast of Tunisia, (Capasso, 2020a).

These events, and the profiteering behind them, have ultimately turned Libya into yet another Arab-world war-scape; and the divisions they have engendered seem intractable and irreparable. To ask even the simplest question about the conflict – was 2011 a revolution or a civil war? – is to divide the population down the middle. To frame it as 'revolution' is seen by one half as condoning the suffering and sacrifices of countless Libyans, and ignoring how the country had been forced into a corner for over three decades. To frame it as a 'civil war', while acknowledging the constellation of historical assaults against Libya, for many Libyans, equates to wholeheartedly supporting the authority of Gaddafi, and negating Libyans' long-standing grievances under his increasingly repressive and domestically illegitimate government.

Another way of considering this division is to consider the word used by each camp to stigmatise the other: the *ṭaḥālib* (algae) and the *jurdhān* (rats). *Taḥālib* (algae) is how the anti-Gaddafi faction describes those who supported him and his regime, clinging to old beliefs, slimily like algae – the green also denoting the all-green national flag Gaddafi's supporters waved alongside *The Green Book* (Gaddafi's political manifesto) they carried; *jurdhān* (rats) is how supporters of Gaddafi and his *al-Jamāhīrīyah* government describe those who allegedly aimed to overthrow the regime and destabilise Libya under NATO's clout (field notes, Italy, 2015).

The answer, of course, is lost somewhere in between. The ongoing violence that has engulfed the country since 2011 has not provided sufficient space to reflect on the wider historical, national and geopolitical developments. Today, much more than before, Western violence has become a historical continuity in the everyday reality for Libyans. While the ways in which it is justified have changed throughout history, Libyans – and many more countries of the Global South at large – continue to be the ones paying for it.

## Bibliography

Akkerman, Mark. 2016. 'Border Wars: The Arms Dealers Profiting from Europe's Refugee Tragedy.' Amsterdam: Transnational Institute. https://www.tni.org/en/publication/border-wars.

Capasso, Matteo. 2020a. 'The War and the Economy: The Gradual Destruction of Libya.' Review of African Political Economy, August. https://www.tandfonline.com/doi/pdf/10.1080/03056244.2020.1801405?needAccess=true&.

Capasso, Matteo. 2020b. 'Wars, Capital and the MENA Region.' *Project on Middle East Political Science,* no. 42 (October): 35–41.

CBS News. 2011. 'Clinton on Gaddafi: We Came, We Saw, He Died.' YouTube. 2011. https://www.youtube.com/watch?v=mlz3-OzcExI.

Chorin, Ethan. 2012. *Exit Gaddafi: The Hidden History of the Libyan Revolution*. London: Saqi Books.

Dietrich, Christopher R. W. 2021. 'Strategies of Decolonization: Economic Sovereignty and National Security in Libyan–US Relations, 1949–1971.' *Journal of Global History,* no. First View: 1–20. https://doi.org/10.1017/S1740022821000140.

Garside, Juliette, David Pegg, and Mona Mahmood. 2016. 'Gaddafi Insider Accused of Using State Cash to Buy Luxury Scottish Hotels.' *The Guardian*, 2016. https://www.theguardian.com/news/2016/may/16/gaddafi-insider-accused-of-using-state-cash-to-buy-luxury-scottish-hotels.

Getachew, Adom. 2019. *Worldmaking after Empire: The Rise and Fall of Self-Determination*. Princeton: Princeton University Press.

PAKISTAN

# A Bird with One Wing

## Bina Shah

WHEN THE WEDDING WAS over, Zarghuna climbed aboard the bus, leaving the evening's cool breeze for the pungent, stuffy air of the women's section. All in all, there were about forty of them – men, women and children – returning home from the celebrations in a neighbouring village. The women sat at the front, swathed in burqas hiding wedding finery underneath, their faces made up in carefully hoarded foundation, bright red lipstick, eyes rimmed with kajal. Earrings and necklaces clinked as they laughed and talked and gossiped, while children lay bundled up around them, tired and sleepy in the dark. Further back, their husbands sat together in the men's section, rubbing stomachs full from the six rice dishes served at the feast.

It had been Zarghuna's cousin's daughter's wedding; the other women had teased her cousin, asking if she was ready to become a grandmother. She was only thirty-five.

'May you be the grandmother of seven grandsons,' they called out to her raucously making her laugh and the bride cover her face in embarrassment, clearly smiling through her hennaed fingers. Everyone knew you needed sons for inheritance, for land, and for feuding. That is to say, for war. Each house had its own graveyard, at the front of which the bodies of recent casualties were buried, each grave marked only by a small, modest stone. The more stones, the more honour for the family.

As she reached the top of steps, Zarghuna wondered to her husband which seat was a better bet in case of a crash. Her husband conveyed this question to the bus driver, who said a crash would be very inconvenient for his schedule, and both men laughed while Zarghuna chewed on the end of her burqa, embarrassed. The bus driver was her father's cousin's son, a boy she'd known since she was small. He exchanged a few pleasantries with her husband, a little friendly greeting – *May you not get tired* – and the response – *May you never know poverty* – falling easily from their lips, with smiles and enquiries about aged parents and young children. It was improper to address another man's wife directly even if she was standing in front of you, so her cousin did not speak to her, showing her husband the respect he deserved. But he gestured silently behind him to a pair of seats in a better condition than the rest.

As she sat down, her husband moved on to the back, entrusting her to her cousin's silent care. The young man had already pushed the rear-view mirror up to face the ceiling so that his glance would not fall on any woman's face. The woman next to her, Shugla, smiled and offered her a piece of mithai from the wedding feast.

'Sit next to the window,' Shugla said. 'I know you get carsick.' She got up and offered Zarghuna the window seat; Zarghuna accepted both the seat and the sweet, popping the coconut barfi into her mouth and chewing it slowly so that it lasted a long time.

It was only a two-hour drive from the neighbouring village to their hamlet, in a small enclave of North Waziristan not far from Shewa. There had been some discussion about which route to take: whether the old, winding, single-lane mountain road or the Shewa-Miranshah paved road would get them to the wedding faster. The mountain road was treacherous, the scene of many accidents, but the paved road had more checkpoints, and nobody wanted to shepherd their women on and off the bus to be glared at by the Pakistani soldiers. The decision was made: to take the back road. They would take the same road now, on the return journey, at three in the morning, and would be home hopefully before dawn.

As a girl, she'd dreamed of being married to a soldier. Zarghuna and her sisters used to watch them from a distance, spinning around in their army trucks, tall and authoritative in their uniforms. But there was no question of marriage with a man from the army. They were the occupiers, and she could only ever be married to a relative, or at best a kinsman.

At fourteen, Zarghuna married the cousin she was promised to when she had been ten. She'd accepted her fate as she'd accepted most of the realities of her life: the many children she was expected to bear, the hard scrabble of living on the mountain, taking care of the house and goats, cooking and cleaning, serving her in-laws. Her husband was better than most; he'd finished high school, and he didn't hit her, even though her sisters whispered to her that a man who hit you was better than a man who didn't care.

And life had its bright spots, like the wedding parties they attended several times a year. This was the first time Zarghuna had traveled so far outside the village since giving birth to her son. But it was a special occasion, the first wedding since the truce had been declared between the two warring sides of the family, who had each sworn allegiance to a different warlord in the fighting that was going on around them, here and across that invisible line the Pakistani Army called a border. The presence of the womenfolk was a parley, a promise that trust, like a toppled tree, could take root again and grow in a different direction. The men had still worn their rifles and kept their guns in their pockets, but the bullets were stored separately, as a gesture of goodwill. It had all gone well, and when the bride had been carried in her palanquin to her husband's home, everyone allowed themselves to relax and enjoy the rest of the night.

The bus chugged on, climbing steadily towards home. Zarghuna whispered a prayer as they rounded a hairpin curve; the steep mountain bends made her feel nauseous. Her husband had instructed her not to look down, but to focus on a point far away, out the window. It was not yet dawn, but Zarghuna sought out the white thread at the horizon that indicated the end of the long night. She wanted to see her son, who was back in the village, spending the evening with her mother, who had stayed home to look after him.

They made it past the turn and were on a straight stretch of road now. She could see Sahar Sthoray,[1] the morning star, glittering in the night sky. Zaghuna cheered up when she spotted it, forgetting her queasiness. She recited to herself, *Which of the favours of your Lord will you deny?* Then a humming sound caught Zarghuna's attention. She didn't have time to register whether it was a military helicopter or just the wings of a giant bird. Just as she turned her head to search for it, there was a loud noise: *dum dum*. And then a flash, and the entire bus shook and everything turned brilliant white to signal the end of Zarghuna's world.

At first, there was nothing. Then slowly sound came back. Zarghuna was standing in the women's public call office and the telephone bell was ringing above her head. She shook her chin from side to side; the clamour didn't stop.

It wasn't dark any more; the weak light of the winter sun, an hour after dawn, pressed painfully against her eyelids. When they finally opened, she saw that she was still in her seat, a bar from the seat next to hers pressing into her waist, right above the scar from her C-section. Then she remembered: the wedding, the bus, the winding road. The heat, the light, the impact. She opened her mouth to scream but summoned no one with her cries.

*A drone,* she thought to herself suddenly. The word, sharp and pointed, quivering with significance, an odd intrusion into the dullness of her brain. *A drone,* she thought again, and wondered if she'd gotten it right. Why was it so important that she had?

Zarghuna checked her own arms and legs to see if they were still there, and her fingers moved of their own volition to push the bar away from her stomach. Something hurt inside her belly, but not enough to keep her from trying to wobble to her feet. As soon as she was upright, vertigo hit her with the strength of a hammer, and she reeled, left to right, bobbing up and down helplessly. Spinning and ringing, ringing and spinning. She held the seat in front of her to steady herself.

Her fingers touched her hair, and then stickiness. The bus driver, her kinsman, didn't move when Zarghuna prodded his shoulder. Now her hand was on her cousin's forehead, and his skin was still warm. But he was gone, already far away from where she was, moving in a different direction. Her hand, when she removed it from his forehead, was red with his blood, mingling with the floral designs painted on her palms. What about his wife and children, sitting just behind her in the women's section? Had he left them behind or were they travelling to the next world with him?

She looked around but could make no sense of the twisted metal, the shards of glass, and the charred bodies slumped in their seats. Nothing moved; there was only the ticking sound of metal cooling down and the hiss of acrid smoke curling into her nostrils. She would suffocate if she didn't find her way outside quickly.

Zarghuna couldn't tell whether the bus was lying straight or lopsided; only that it was roughly the right side up. She looked for the front door of the bus, but it was welded shut from the heat of the explosion. A cold wind was knifing in through the shattered front windows; too much jagged metal blocking the frames for her to try and hoist herself through. The side windows were nothing more than small squares, lined with iron bars. Zarghuna decided to head backwards, into the bowels of the bus, with the vague thought of finding one of the men of her family still alive. The men would tell her what to do, whether it was safe to go and wait at the side of the road for help from the very military men they'd been trying to avoid.

Clawing, stumbling, her hands pulled her body in the right direction. She held onto burst seat backs for balance, their plastic and stuffing melted into clumps. It was difficult to see the floor with so much debris blocking the way: bags fallen from the overhead rack, shawls, shoes, a Quran. And more women's bodies, or the fragments of them; whatever was left after the drone had found its target, and released its rockets.

Zarghuna passed all the men, dead in their seats, or thrown onto the floor. Broken glass crunched under her feet as she walked by the remains of her husband, her brother-in-law, her cousins. Some were intact, lolling backwards, others were taken apart, like butchered goats. There were empty seats, too, which meant that some had been thrown clear of the bus, a gaping hole in its ceiling. That's where the rocket had struck, blowing out the top of the bus. But it was as if the dead were the living, and Zarghuna, the ghost moving amongst them.

And then the image of her child came to her, the infant who had emerged from her body a wriggling, struggling lump, all elbows and knees and large hands and feet and head. She had been lucky to be taken to the THQ hospital in Shewa for his birth; her husband had wanted his firstborn son to be perfect, and for Zarghuna, his young wife, to survive the birth. She had been attended by a midwife – an unheard of luxury for the women from the more remote villages, most of whom laboured and gave birth in their homes, sometimes dying there in the process.

The moment her son had emerged from the slit in her stomach, everything was wrong and right at the same time. Zarghuna had known it before they'd even told her. Her husband had taken another wife after the child had been born, wanting healthy children that Zarghuna would obviously never be able to give him. She remembered just then that Shugla, her co-wife, was sitting at the front of the bus with her head and limbs blown off. If they had not exchanged seats at the beginning of the journey, Zarghuna would be dead.

Zarghuna's son had been afflicted with mild Down's Syndrome, a diagnosis she had not understood when they told her, and only understood it a little better now. They watched her carefully for weeks after the birth, worried that the news of her afflicted child and the second wife would make her suicidal. They had misunderstood her completely. She had been terrified her child would spend his life crawling on the floor, unable to sit up by himself, talk, or feed himself. The child she got instead was sweet and pliable, sharply intelligent, humorous and loving. He couldn't speak clearly and walked with difficulty, but she loved him all the same, perhaps more, in place of her unreliable husband. Her son was her bird with one wing; she whispered the endearment as she bathed him, rocked him to sleep, nursed him. *Fabi ayyi ala i rabbikuma tukazzibaan…*[2]

It was for her son that she forced herself to take step after painful step, pushing herself along the bus's blasted insides. This was how he felt when he walked. She could do the same for him.

She was breathing hard, sweating with effort. The sickening odour of smoldering steel, chemicals, gasoline and electrical wiring assaulted her senses. And other, worse smells: charred flesh, burnt hair. But there seemed to be no immediate danger of fire; what flames had burned the bus were already dead. Still, another explosion could come at any moment; drones would often circle back and strike again at the same target. She had to keep going. Onwards she pressed, until she reached the end of the bus. Her husband and his brother had taken the seats at the back, wanting to laugh over silly WhatsApp videos on each other's phones, away from prying eyes.

She could see as soon as she reached them that they were both dead. Her husband's legs were blown off; his brother was leaning forward with his forehead torn open. To the side, the gaping hole in the ceiling reached all the way down to include their window. Cold air whistled in, invigorating her. All she had to do was climb up on top of them, push herself out through the hole, and she would be free.

But she hesitated. Maybe she should stay here until someone came to get her out. Surely it was the safest thing to do. The drone might be lurking around, waiting for signs of life, to strike again – to finish the job. Suddenly she realised that it wasn't inevitable she would get out alive.

For a moment, she considered huddling in the corner of the bus, or crawling under the bodies of her husband and his brother and staying there until death came for her too. The relief that such a decision offered her for those few moments was more powerful than any sedative. The struggle would be over: all the striving and back-breaking housework, the scrimping and saving, the endless need to be cheerful for everyone else's sake. What a pointless charade, just for others to look at – her life with her husband, his second wife and her disabled child – and still feel superior about. For sure, they would continue to whine about the imperfections and frustrations of their everyday lives, but secretly they were all grateful for their better fortune. If she gave up now, she could stop being everyone else's cautionary tale.

But just as Zarghuna was about to sink down, she heard a second explosion in the distance – the drone had found its true target: maybe a house in which a militant lived. There were a few in their village, though none belonged to Zarghuna's family or kin.

She stood stock-still. The voices came to her gradually, at first as a wall of sound, then slowly as individual strands of words.

'Ya Allah! God have mercy!'

'Another one! God curse America!'

'Is anyone still alive?'

Zarghuna wanted to call out to them, but fear put its hand over her mouth. Fear of those birds that brought death, that kept them hiding in their houses, that stopped their children from playing outside. Her family had thought it safe to go to the wedding, since it had been a long while since the last drone strike. That calculation had been their last mistake. And now forty of them had met God, but not her. And not her son, her bird with one wing.

Soon there would be the growl of the military cars coming to check on the strike and eventually the wailing ambulances arriving from Shewa Hospital. All that fuss for only one survivor.

Zarghuna whispered to herself: *Which of the favours of your Lord will you deny?*

She put one unsteady foot into her husband's seat, where his legs had once been, then the other, balancing herself against the skeleton of the bombed-out bus. She glanced down to check the steadiness of her position: her toes were blue and cold in her wedding sandals, her nails painted pink a million years ago for the occasion. She climbed carefully out through the window, pushing her head and shoulders out of the broken pane of glass.

The villagers on the road, milling around the bus, spotted her and began to shout encouragement. 'Subhanallah! A survivor, praise God!'

'Khoray,[3] that's right, come on, you can do it!'

'We'll take revenge, Khoray, if it takes a hundred years!'

She knew their vows served no purpose. They could not stop the drones from coming. All they could do, after it was over, was sort through the bodies, and protest with raised fists against the killer in the skies.

The villagers kept cheering her onwards. Strong arms reached for her, to help her climb down. The black burqa flapped around her as she emerged, like the wings of a butterfly emerging from a chrysalis. She tried to keep it wrapped around her head and mouth, conscious of her honour. If she died, they would tell her son that she'd behaved like a proper Pashtun woman even in the face of death.

When she felt her feet touch the icy ground, she collapsed, trembling, onto her side. Dust filled her nostrils, and she coughed hard, her lungs seared with the heat and smoke from the burning trees that had caught fire from the explosion. The ambulances and fire tenders were already there, rescue workers and policemen swarming all over the road. Zarghuna closed her eyes and waited for one of them to notice her. Now her job was done, and it would be up to all the others to bring her back to life.

If she listened very carefully, the voices of the shouting villagers started to blur into the sound of a muted trumpet – Jibrael's on the day of Qiyamat. Tomorrow the mourning would start, and perhaps in a hundred years there would be revenge. But Qiyamat was a long way off, and her son was waiting for her to return. She closed her burning eyelids and saw her son's face, his smile, and she stretched her arms and legs out, to swim like a dolphin in the epicanthic folds of his eyes.

## Notes

1. The Pashto name for Venus.
2. Arabic, from the Quran, Surah Rahman: *Which of the favors of your Lord will you deny?*
3. The Pashto word for 'sister'.

# Afterword: The Forever War

## Dr Ian Shaw

University of Leeds

DRONE WARFARE HAS COME to define a new way of war. In shadow and silence, death is delivered by robots in the sky. The architects of this remote conflict were the CIA – the US intelligence agency that has long committed terror from the darkness, forever stained by its involvement in brutal assassinations and coups in the Cold War. In Pakistan, a country that the US never declared war against, drone strikes numbered 430 between 2004 and 2020, according to the *Bureau of Investigative Journalism*.[1] Most of these strikes took place in the tribal areas, a territory shaped by the colonial era, and still governed by archaic British legislation. Given the secretive nature of the strikes, it is difficult to accurately track who has died during this period. Perhaps as many as 4,000 people in total, with up to 969 civilians. But these categories are slippery. After all, who decides the boundary between civilian and combatant? Who lives and who dies? What is lawful and unlawful? Those seeking answers usually find only doublespeak and military jargon. When you kill from the shadows the lines of accountability and responsibility fade to black.

Globally, there have been *at least* 14,040 confirmed US drone strikes across the world between 2010 and 2020, with as many as 16,901 people killed.[2] Drone strikes collapse into a wider campaign of aerial bombardment by the US and its allies. In Iraq and Syria, there have been 34,000 air and artillery strikes targeting Islamic State, commencing in 2014. The crosshairs of the covert Predator drone first focused on the tribal areas of Pakistan in the early years of the US-led war on terror in 2004. The region – so the CIA's logic went – was harbouring terrorists of all stripes. Many of these groups had been supported by the CIA with arms and training in the 1980s during the Afghan mujahideen resistance to Soviet intervention. Other intelligence services across the globe, including Pakistan's own Inter-Services Intelligence, also funded Islamic extremists to contain the Soviets and imprint their geopolitical strategies onto the region. Yet in a matter of decades, allies would be enemies. Blowback: the unintended consequences of covert intervention. US foreign policy is defined by blowback piled upon blowback.

After a handful of strikes under the Bush administration, President Obama accelerated the CIA's drone programme in 2008. This was accompanied by a change in targeting rules of engagement. Human targets no longer had to be individually identified on a kill list. Instead, what became known as 'signature strikes' targeted suspect 'patterns of life.' This required the widespread surveillance of peoples' everyday movements and communications, creating an oppressive atmosphere for civilians. Signature strikes became a controversial cornerstone of the drone hunt under Obama's CIA. Drone warfare appeared to offer a miracle solution: a liberal and 'humane' way of killing without putting a single boot on the ground, which meant no American bodies returning in coffins. The robots would win the war on terror: surgical, precise, and with no oversight required from Congress or pesky questions from human rights lawyers. By shifting the kill chain from the US military to the CIA, the US government bypassed the more transparent Congressional checks-and-balances of traditional armed conflict. But the drones failed to create anything but more problems. The legacy of US drone strikes in Pakistan is one of a deep injustice that will fester for generations.

The mainstream media have typically failed to challenge the narratives of US officials when covering drone strikes. Civilian casualties are hard to verify, and the rhetoric about drone strikes being surgical, precise, and risk-free, have been unreflexively repeated by journalists (with important exceptions). Moreover, unlike large-scale conflicts, such as Operation Enduring Freedom – the official name used by the US government for the Global War on Terror – drone strikes produce an amorphous conflict that is hard to conceptualise, let alone accurately report. Beginnings, ends, limits, borders, enemies, civilians, all bleed into each other. Killing by robots is rapidly becoming (or has already become) something like a 'forever war.' With no clear objectives or timelines, drone warfare slips into the background of the news cycle and our collective unconscious. *The news report followed by the weather report followed by the drone report.* Each as empty as the other. The mainstream media's failure to actively challenge the drone era has permitted a creeping normalisation of extrajudicial assassination.

Killing cannot bring peace and justice to the world. It only brings more death and misery. A drone is utterly incapable of creating anything – only destroying. Wrecking lives, communities, even weddings. One aspect of drone warfare that is crucial to understand is how these aerial invaders dominate the intimate spaces of everyday life. Because of their unparalleled ability to hover in the skies, drones can be ghostly companions during breakfast, lunch, dinner, and while you sleep. The constant noise. Little wonder that Pakistanis in drone country referred to them as 'mosquitos'. The idea that there is a single 'battlefield' that contains drones is simply false. Instead, the war on terror – and the CIA's drone strikes in particular – blanketed the planet in amorphous and shape-shifting spaces of killing. Homes became legitimate surveillance targets. This 'civilianisation' of the kill chain introduces families and the private domestic spaces into the drones' crosshairs. Regardless of guilt or innocence. The deathly whir of the drone can be heard continuously in areas under high levels of surveillance. A technological god that passes between clouds, the drone is simultaneously remote and intimate. In the sky but also in your ears. A thousand feet up but also jangling deep down in your nervous system.

Eating and sleeping with the drone takes its toll. Rates of post-traumatic stress disorder (PTSD) in lives watched and wrecked by the drone are high. At the height of drone strikes in Pakistan, a 2012 report by Stanford University's International Human Rights and Conflict Resolution Clinic, and New York University School of Law's Global Justice Clinic, detailed how civilians suffer from a constant 'anticipatory anxiety,' as well as nightmares, insomnia, and a range of other medical maladies.[3] The psychological impact of living with the drone is difficult to measure, but in places – such as Pakistan and Palestine – many communities carry this entrenched trauma. The fear of extrajudicial killing is pervasive. Too many young people have grown up under the gaze of Predators and Reapers watching them from above. In turn, this constant low-level anxiety affects their development, social mobility, and life opportunities. The idea that drone strikes are *precise* is therefore false. Neither in time nor space, can the impact of a drone strike be contained to a 'kill box' – the military jargon word for the area of attack.[4] Consequences cascade. The imperial logic of targets, accuracy, and efficiency are oblivious to the complex life-worlds of innocent people caught in the crosshairs of the manhunt. This collision between humanity and technology is a defining feature of life in drone country. But even by the military's own logic, drone warfare does very little to win the long-term support of anybody other than war hawks that benefit from the forever war. Dropping Hellfire missiles is a tactic masquerading as a strategy, and while strikes may be able to 'pacify' an area, how can they possibly bring peace to a region? How can they offer hope to civilians trapped between extremists and the drone?

Drone warfare has been decades in the making. The Vietnam War was a laboratory for automating US conflict and testing drones.[5] The common denominator between these battlespaces is the endless drumroll of corporations that feed on death.

Predator and Reaper drones – as novel as they appear – both spawn from the US military-industrial complex, which has profited from war for generations. A single Hellfire missile (which Predator and Reaper drones are both equipped with) costs around $100,000. That single metallic explosive tube is worth much more than the annual salary of a public-school teacher or nurse. Death is extremely profitable for the military-industrial complex. A handful of drone strikes can run up a bill of millions of dollars, diverting resources from American communities blighted by poverty. Even if there is absolutely zero gain from drone strikes, capital keeps on circulating. Military failure can mean big bucks for these vampiric arms companies. There is no incentive to succeed – and this is the real logic of the military-industrial complex. The US Department of Defense has an annual budget of around £705 billion, with President Biden proposing a 2022 budget of $715 billion.[6] The figure is staggering, and the logic is crystal clear for empire: forever war. Everything else be damned. The innocent victims of drone warfare in Pakistan are simply part of a profit and loss account. Collateral in every sense of the word.

More broadly, the drone is at the centre of a robot-oriented mode of killing that militaries across the globe are replicating. By 2021, 19 states were operating their own armed drone programmes.[7] What might be the future of this globalising drone warfare? Spiralling out from Pakistan, Afghanistan, Yemen, Somalia, Iraq, Syria – from wedding convoys bombed, children killed, lives destroyed, to communities ruined – the drone spreads its wings and stalks the planet. What began as a way of war, monopolised by the US and Israel, has spread to multiple nations across the Earth. The same remoteness, the same trauma, endlessly repeated. The US has set a terrible precedent for other countries to follow around the world: extrajudicial killings conducted in the shadows. President Obama streamlined and institutionalised a liberal way of killing that was palatable to a domestic audience and disseminated by an acquiescent media. But this was always a conceit. The drone is not a distant, disembodied technology. It lives intimately with the communities it stalks. And it creates blowback that will be felt for decades to come by civilians of all flags. The military drone is a weapon system stripped of its humanity but still a destroyer of humanity. The abdication of ethics, thought, and decisions to drones and the algorithms that enchant them is a growing danger to a peaceful world.

The forever war must be understood as a conflict like no other. The large-scale mobilisation of human soldiers, government agencies, public, and news agencies – as with the Vietnam War or the War on Terror – is an outdated mode of state security and warfare. Instead, this endless conflict is much more like a global policing operation. Less of a once-in-a-generation spectacle, and more of an amorphous background condition, which cannot even compete with the celebrity-obsessed and event-oriented US and UK media. The Reapers reap, and everyday life continues, unperturbed by far-away trauma. This normalisation of robotic killing is not located in some future horizon, it is already here. And it is driven by a tragic form of nihilism, that is to say, the belief that life is devoid of meaning. The emptying of the world of intrinsic value and purpose. How clearly the drone performs this metaphysical war against life! People become targets. The Earth is translated into a grid of kill boxes. And suffering is reduced to an algorithmic calculation. This technological nihilism, perfected by Reapers and their Hellfire, has been decades in the making. But this is a future still being written. The wings of the drone may have spread far and wide – but there is always a saving grace in the power of listening. Of listening to the stories of the watched, the surveilled, and the hurt, so that they may teach us the perils of life beneath the drone's unblinking eye.

## Notes

1. https://www.thebureauinvestigates.com/projects/drone-war
2. *ibid*.
3. https://www.thebureauinvestigates.com/stories/2012-09-25/drones-causing-mass-trauma-among-civilians-major-study-finds
4. As defined in the US's Department of Defense Dictionary, a Kill Box is 'a three-dimensional area reference that enables timely, effective coordination and control and facilitates rapid attacks.' https://publicintelligence.net/fm-3-09-34-kill-box-tactics-and-multiservice-procedures/
5. https://www.upress.umn.edu/book-division/books/predator-empire
6. https://www.cnbc.com/2021/05/28/pentagon-asks-for-715-billion-in-2022-defense-budget.html
7. https://dronewars.net/who-has-armed-drones/

# About the Authors

**Wilfredo Mármol Amaya** was born in El Savador in 1959. He works at the Supreme Court of Justice of El Salvador, and was previously an advisor to the Secretary of Culture in San Salvador (2015-2018), whilst Nayib Bukele was city mayor. He is a writer and poet, and his works include *Equinoccio de un Crisol* (2011) and *Cuentos y Relatos Viroleños* (2019).

**Gabriel Ángel** is the literary and political pseudonym of Germán Gómez Camacho. Born in Bogotá in 1958, Ángel was an active member of the FARC guerrilla movement for 30 years, until the signing of Colombia's peace accord in 2016. He has since returned to his former profession as a lawyer, and is part of the national leadership of FARC's new political party, Communes. He is a journalist and author of two novels, *A Quemarropa* and *Algún día será*, and one collection of short stories: *La luna del forense.*

**Gioconda Belli** is a Nicaraguan poet, writer and political activist. She was involved in the Nicaraguan Revolution from a very young age and occupied important positions in the Sandinista Party and in the revolutionary government. She won the Biblioteca Breve award for *Infinity in the Palm of her Hand* and the Casa de las Americas Prize in 1978 for her poetry book *Line of Fire*. Her memoir, *The Country Under my Skin,* was a finalist for the *Los Angeles Times* Book Prize in 2001 and she was awarded the 2018 Hermann Kesten Prize by PEN Germany. She is President of PEN International, Nicaragua, a member of the Spanish Royal Academy of Letters and Chevalier des les Arts et Lettres of France.

**Gianfranco Bettin** is an Italian sociologist, writer and long-time leader of the Greens in Veneto. During his long political career, he was a member of the Italian Parliament (1992–1994), deputy mayor of Venice for Mestre (1995–2005) and member of the

Regional Council of Veneto (2000–2010). He is the author of eighteen books, including *Cracking* (Mondadori, 2019) and *Qualcosa che brucia* (Something Burning, Garzanti, 1989), a novel exploring working-class Venice.

**Hassan Blasim** is an Iraqi-born film director and writer. Blasim settled in Finland in 2004 after years of travelling through Europe as a refugee. His debut collection *The Madman of Freedom Square* was published by Comma in 2009 (translated by Jonathan Wright) and was longlisted for the Independent Foreign Fiction Prize in 2010. His second collection, *The Iraqi Christ*, won the 2014 Independent Foreign Fiction Prize, the first Arabic title and the first short story collection ever to win the award. His first novel, *God 99*, was published by Comma Press in 2020.

**Paige Cooper** is a freelance copywriter and the author of the short story collection *Zolitude*, which was nominated for several prizes, including the Giller and the Governor General's Award. She grew up in the Canadian Rockies, went to the University of British Columbia, and received a Masters in Library and Information Studies at Dalhousie. Her stories have appeared in *West Branch, Canadian Notes & Queries, Michigan Quarterly Review,* and *The Fiddlehead,* and elsewhere. She is the editor of *Best Canadian Stories 2020.*

**Hüseyin Karabey** is a Kurdish-Turkish film director, screenwriter and producer. He attended the Fine Art Faculty of Marmara University and was also a member of the Mesopotamian Cinema Collective at the Mesopotamia Cultural Center (MKM) in Istanbul. His first feature film, *Gitmek: My Marlon and Brando*, was selected for the 37th Rotterdam International Film Festival and the New York Tribeca International Film (Best Director Award). His other works include the award-winning *Come to My Voice* (2014) and *Insiders* (2018).

**Lidudumalingani** (full name Lidudumalingani Mqombothi) was born in the village of Zikhovane in the Eastern Cape, and is a

South African writer, filmmaker and photographer. His short story 'Memories We Lost' won the 2016 Caine Prize. In 2016 he was also the recipient of a Miles Morland Scholarship.

**Lina Meruane** is an award-winning Chilean writer and scholar. She has published two collections of short stories and five novels. Translated by Megan McDowell into English are her latest: *Seeing Red* (Atlantic) and *Nervous System* (Atlantic). Meruane has written several non-fiction books, among which is her essay on the impact and representation of the AIDS epidemic in Latin American literature, *Viral Voyages* (Palgrave MacMillan). She has received, among others, the prestigious Sor Juana Inés de la Cruz Novel Prize (Mexico, 2012), the Anna Seghers Prize (Germany, 2011) grants from the Guggenheim Foundation, the National Endowment for the Arts, and a DAAD Writer in Residence in Berlin. She currently teaches Global Cultures and Creative Writing at New York University.

**Fiston Mwanza Mujila** was born in Lubumbashi, Democratic Republic of the Congo, in 1981, and writes poetry, prose, and theatre. He currently lives in Graz, where he teaches African literature at Universität Graz and works with musicians in Austria on various projects. His first novel, *Tram 83*, was longlisted for the Man Booker International Prize and the Prix du Monde, and was awarded the Etisalat Prize for Literature and the Internationaler Literaturpreis from Der Haus der Kulturen der Welt.

Born in 1969, **Payam Nasser** is an author and screenplay writer. His debut collection of short stories, *Consternation* (2012), was a finalist for the Golshiri prize, as well as the Haft-Eghlim Literary Award for the best short story collection of the year. It also featured the story, 'Wake it Up', which received the 2014 Houshang Golshiri Literary Award. He is the author of one novel, *The Trifles Thief*, as well as numerous screenplays, including the film *One Long Day,* which was awarded the Special Jury Prize at the International Orthodox Film Festival in Russia in 2015.

**Fariba Nawa** is an Afghan-American freelance journalist based in Istanbul. She was born and raised in Afghanistan until she was nine, then fled the Soviet invasion with her family to the US in the 1980s. She authored *Afghanistan Inc.* (CorpWatch), an oft-cited resource in international debates on the effectiveness of reconstruction efforts in Afghanistan. She is also author of *Opium Nation* (Harper Perennial, 2011), a personal account of the drug trade in Afghanistan and its impact on women. She is the host and chief editor of *On Spec* podcast. This is her first piece of published fiction.

**Ahmel Echevarría Peré** was born in Havana, Cuba, in 1974. One of Cuba's most acclaimed younger writers, he was a student at the Jorge Onelio Cardoso Centre for Literary Formation, where he now works as the editor of its website. He is also editor of the website *Vercuba*, and writes a column in the literary magazine *Cuba Contemporánea*. His books include: *Inventario* (Unión, 2007, Cuba); the short novel *Esquirlas* (Letras Cubanas, 2006, Cuba); *Búfalos camino al matadero* (Oriente, 2013, Cuba); and *La noria* (Unión, 2013, Cuba). He was awarded the David Unión Prize in 2004 for his book *Inventario* and the 2011 Franz Kafka Novelas de Gaveta Prize in the Czech Republic for his book *Dias de entrenamiento*, which was also awarded the Italo Calvino Prize in 2012. His book *La Noria* was awarded the Critic Prize 2013.

**Jacob Ross** is a novelist, short story writer, editor and creative writing tutor. His crime fiction novel, *The Bone Readers*, won the inaugural Jhalak Prize in 2017. His literary novel, *Pynter Bender*, was published to critical literary acclaim and was shortlisted for the 2009 Commonwealth Writers Regional Prize. His latest book is *Tell No-One About This*, a collection of stories written over a span of forty years. He is Associate Fiction Editor at Peepal Tree Press, and the editor of *Closure, Contemporary Black British Short Stories.*

**Bina Shah** is a Karachi-based author of two collections of short stories and five novels, most recently *Before She Sleeps* (Delphinium). A regular contributor to *The New York Times, Al Jazeera, The*

*Huffington Post,* and a frequent guest on the BBC, she has contributed essays and op-eds to *Granta, The Independent*, and *The Guardian*, and writes a regular op-ed column for *Dawn*, Pakistan's biggest English-language newspaper. She works on issues of women's rights and female empowerment in Pakistan and across Muslim countries. In 2020, she was awarded the rank of Chevalier in the Ordre des arts et des lettres by the French Ministry of Culture.

**Najwa Bin Shatwan** is a Libyan academic and novelist, the first Libyan to ever be shortlisted for the International Prize of Arabic Fiction (in 2017). She has written three novels: *Waber Al Ahssina* (The Horses' Hair), *Madmum Burtuqali* (Orange Content), and *Zareeb Al-Abeed* (The Slave Yards), in addition to several collections of short stories and plays. She was chosen as one of the thirty-nine best Arab authors under the age of forty by Hay Festival's *Beirut 39* project (2009). In 2018, she received a Banipal Writing Fellowship Residency at the University of Durham and in 2020 was chosen to co-lead a series of creative writing workshops in Sharjah for Arab writers.

**Talal Abu Shawish** is Assistant Director of the Boys Preparatory School for Refugees in Gaza. He has published three short story collections – *The Rest are Not For Sale, The Assassination of a Painting* (2010) and *Goodbye, Dear Prophets* (2011) – as well as four novels: *We Deserve a Better Death* (2012), *Middle Eastern Nightmares* (2013), *Seasons of Love and Blood* (2014), and *Urban House* (2018). His work has won three awards (the Ministry of Youth and Sports' Short Story Competition in 1996 and 1997, and the Italian Sea That Connects Award, 1998).

**Kim Thúy** was born in Vietnam in 1968. At the age of ten she left Vietnam along with a wave of refugees commonly referred to in the media as 'the boat people' and settled with her family in Quebec, Canada. A graduate in translation and law, she has worked as a seamstress, interpreter, lawyer and chef-restaurant owner. She lives in Montreal and devotes her life to writing. Her awards include the Governor General's Literary Award in 2010, and she was one of the top four finalists of the Alternative Nobel Prize in 2018. Her books have sold more than 850,000 copies around the world and have been translated into 29 languages and distributed across 40 countries and territories.

**Ahmet Halûk Ünal** is a screenwriter and director. After studying economics at Hacettepe University, he worked as an author and project designer from 2000 to 2004, and then as a manager and scriptwriter at various workshops and universities. In addition to two feature films, he was part of the directing collective that made the documentary film *Little Black Fish* in 2014 about childhood in Turkish Kurdistan in the 90s. With the film *Jiyan's Story*, he participated in the War on Peace history festival at the Maxim Gorki Theatre in 2018.

**Carol Zardetto** is a Guatemalan writer, lawyer and diplomat. She writes novels, short stories and essays, as well as plays and scripts for documentaries, including *La Flor del Café*, which was nominated for a best documentary award at the Ícaro International Film Festival in 2010. Her first novel, *Con Pasión Absoluta,* won the 2004 Mario Monteforte Toledo Central American Novel Award. Her other works include *Cuando los Rolling Stones llegaron a la Habana* and *La ciudad de los minotauros*. Since 2007, she has also worked as a political columnist for Guatemalan newspaper, *El Periódico*.

# About the Consultants

**Iyad S. S. Abujaber** is a political analyst and writer, specialising in Palestine. He has contributed to various publications exploring the Palestinian issue and is currently a PhD candidate at the Middle East Institute at Sakarya University, Turkey.

**Julio Barrios Zardetto** is a Guatemalan-born social researcher, political scientist, travel writer and translator. He is currently writing a book of literary journalism called *Banana Republics*.

**Raymond Bonner** practiced law for a decade and taught at the University of California, Davis, School of Law. He later became an investigative reporter and foreign correspondent for the *New York Times*, where he was a member of a Pulitzer Prize-winning team in 1999, and a staff writer at *The New Yorker.* He has also written for *The Economist* and *The New York Review of Books*, and blogs at the *Daily Beast* and theatlantic.com. He is the author of *Weakness and Deceit: US Policy and El Salvador*, which received the Robert F. Kennedy Book Award; *Waltzing with a Dictator: The Marcoses and the Making of American Policy,* which received the Cornelius Ryan Award from the Overseas Press Club and the Hillman Prize for Book Journalism; *At the Hand of Man: Peril and Hope for Africa's Wildlife;* and *Anatomy of Injustice.* He lives in London.

**Matteo Capasso** is a Max Weber Fellow at the European University Institute and specialises on the role of US imperialism in the Global South. He completed his PhD in 2018 at Durham University and, from 2022, he will start working as Marie Curie Fellow between Venice University and Columbia NY University. Since 2014, he has been working as Associate Editor of *Middle East Critique*.

**Victor Figueroa Clark** wrote his doctoral thesis on the Sandinista Revolution in the context of the Cold War. During his research he interviewed many Sandinistas, including Edén Pastora and other founders of the FSLN, along with many veterans of the Contra War from both sides. Uniquely, he was also given access to the Sandinista archive in Managua. He is also the author of *Salvador Allende: Revolutionary Democrat* (Pluto, 2013), and a contributing editor at *Alborada* magazine and has written on Latin American issues in *Red Pepper, The Morning Star* and *Tribune*.

**Maurizio Dianese** is an Italian investigative journalist, specialising in organised crime. He has written numerous articles and books about the Mala del Brenta, also known as the Mafia veneta, and has also acted as a consultant on films and programmes exploring the world of crime in the the Veneto region. With Gianfranco Bettin, he has carried out investigations and written extensively on members of the Ordine Nuovo.

**Francisco Dominguez** is head of the Research Group on Latin America at Middlesex University. He is also the national secretary of the Venezuela Solidarity Campaign and co-author of *Right-Wing Politics in the New Latin America* (Zed, 2011).

**David Harper** is Professor of Clinical Psychology at the University of East London where he is also Programme Director (Academic) of the Professional Doctorate in Clinical Psychology. In addition to writing on mental health and qualitative research, he has a long-standing interest in the history of psychological research into, and involvement in, national security interrogations.

**Chris Hedges** is a Pulitzer Prize-winning journalist who was a foreign correspondent for fifteen years for *The New York Times,* where he served as the Middle East Bureau Chief and Balkan Bureau Chief. He previously worked overseas for *The Dallas Morning News*, *The Christian Science Monitor*, and NPR. He writes a weekly column for the online magazine *Truthdig* out of Los Angeles and is host of the Emmy Award-winning RT America show *On Contact.* Hedges, who holds a Master of Divinity from Harvard University, is the author of the bestsellers *American Fascists, Days of Destruction, Days of Revolt,* and was a National Book Critics Circle finalist for *War is a Force That Gives us Meaning*. He has taught at Columbia University, New York University, Princeton University, and the University of Toronto.

**Neil Faulkner** is an archaeologist, historian, and political activist. He works as a writer, journalist, lecturer, and field director. His books include *A Radical History of the World* (Pluto), *Creeping Fascism: what it is and how to fight it* (Public Reading Rooms), and *System Crash: an activist guide to making revolution* (Resistance Books).

**Emmanuel Gerard** is Emeritus Professor of History at KU Leuven–University of Leuven. He was Chair of the Political Science Department (1993-2000), Dean of the Faculty of Social Sciences (2003-2010), General Director of HIVA Research Institute for Work and Society (2013 until 2017), and president of KADOC Documentation and Research Center on Religion, Culture and Society (2007-2017). He is Curator of the Flemish Parliament Visitor's Centre and holder of the Gülen Chair for Intercultural Studies. His works include *Death in the Congo: Murdering Patrice Lumumba* (Harvard University Press, 2015).

**Daniel Kovalik** teaches International Human Rights at the University of Pittsburgh School of Law. He has represented plaintiffs in ATS cases arising out of egregious human rights abuses in Colombia. He received the David W. Mills Mentoring Fellowship from Stanford Law School, has written extensively for the *Huffington Post* and *Counterpunch*, and has lectured throughout the world. He is the author of numerous books, including *The Plot to Overthrow Venezuela: How the US is Orchestrating a Coup for Oil*.

**Olmo Gölz** is a lecturer in Islamic and Iranian Studies and a primary investigator within the Collaborative Research Centre 'Heroes–Heroizations–Heroisms' at the University of Freiburg, Germany. He received his PhD with a thesis on rackets and racketeers in Pahlavi Iran, 1941–1963, published by the University of Freiburg. His research and teaching focus on the history and culture of modern Iran, and the sociology of revolution, violence, gender, heroism and martyrdom in the Middle East. His publications include both theoretical and historical studies on the Coup d'état of 1953.

**Meral Çiçek** was born in 1983 to a Kurdish guest-worker family in Germany. She started political and women's activism at the age of sixteen within the Kurdish Women's Peace Office in Dusseldorf. While studying Political Science, Sociology and History at the Goethe-University in Frankfurt she began working as reporter and editor for the only daily Kurdish newspaper in Europe, *Yeni Ozgur Politika,* for which she still writes a weekly column. In 2014, she co-founded the Kurdish Women's Relations Office (REPAK) in Southern Kurdistan (Northern Iraq). She is also editorial board member of the *Jineoloji* journal.

**Ertuğrul Kürkçü** is a Turkish politician, socialist activist and the current Honorary President of the Peoples' Democratic Party (HDP) and Honorary Associate of the Parliamentary Assembly of the Council of Europe (PACE). In 1972, he joined the armed resistance against the military takeover and spent fourteen years in prison after taking part in an operation designed to bargain for the release of Deniz Gezmiş and other activists who were condemned to death under the 1971 Turkish military memorandum. Kürkçü is also known for his political journalism and has previously edited various publications, including the *Encyclopedia of Socialism and Social Struggles* and the *Political Gazette.*

**Félix Julio Alfonso Lopez** has a PhD in Historical Sciences, MA in Interdisciplinary Studies – Latin America, Caribbean and Cuba, degree in history, and diplomas in Social Anthropology and Public Administration. He's professor and Associate Dean of SAN Geronimo University. He has published more than 50 articles on Cuban history, culture and baseball.

**Brian Meeks** is Professor and Chair of Africana Studies at Brown University. He previously served as Professor of Social and Political Change and Director of the Sir Arthur Lewis Institute of Social and Economic Studies at the University of the West Indies, Mona, Jamaica. He has also taught at Michigan State University, Florida International University and Anton de Kom University of Suriname and served as Visiting Scholar at Cambridge University, Stanford

University and Brown University. He has published twelve books and edited various collections, including *Critical Interventions in Caribbean Politics and Theory, Caribbean Revolutions and Revolutionary Theory* and *Narratives of Resistance: Jamaica, Trinidad, the Caribbean* and *Envisioning Caribbean Futures: Jamaican Perspectives.* His novel *Paint the Town Red* was published in 2003 and his volume of poems *The Coup Clock Clicks* was published in 2018.

**Xuân Phượng** was born near Hue, Vietnam, in 1929. She is the owner and Director of the Lotus Art Gallery in Ho Chi Minh City, and was previously a chemist, physician, journalist and filmmaker. In 2004, she published her memoir, *Ao Dai: My War, My Country, My Vietnam.*

**James Sanders** is a journalist, researcher and academic. He has written extensively about South Africa, in such books as *South Africa and the International Media: 1972-1979* (Routledge, 1999) and *Apartheid's Friends: The Rise and Fall of South Africa's Secret Service* (John Murray, 2006), and has lectured at the School of Oriental and African Studies. He worked as researcher on Anthony Sampson's *Mandela,* J.D.F. Jones's life of Laurens van der Post, *Storyteller,* and on John Irvin's film *Mandela's Gun.*

**Ian Shaw** is Associate Professor of Global Security Challenges at the University of Leeds. He studies political violence in its many forms: from global capitalism and ecological injustice, to warfare and conflict. He is the author of 2019's *Wageless Life: A Manifesto for a Future Beyond Capitalism* and his research into drone warfare, military strategy, and domestic policing, culminated in the 2016 book *Predator Empire: Drone Warfare and Full Spectrum Dominance* (University of Minnesota Press).

# About the Translators

**Orsola Casagrande** is a journalist and filmmaker based variously between Venice, the Basque Country and Havana. As a journalist, she worked for 25 years for the Italian daily newspaper *Il manifesto*, and is currently co-editor of the web magazine *Global Rights*. She writes regularly for Spanish, Catalan and Basque newspapers. While living in Cuba, she covered the Colombia peace process. She has translated numerous books, including *The Second Prison* by Ronan Bennett (Gamberetti, 2004) and *The Fountain at the Centre of the World* by Robert Newman (Giunti, 2008) as well as written her own books: *Tower Colliery* (Odradek, 2004) and *Berxwedan* (Punto Rosso 2008). She is the editor and co-translator of Comma's *The Book of Havana* and *The Book of Venice*, and co-editor of *Kurdistan + 100* (with Mustafa Gündoğdu), forthcoming from Comma.

**Adam Feinstein** is an acclaimed author, translator, journalist and Hispanist. His biography *Pablo Neruda: a passion for life* was published by Bloomsbury in 2004 and reissued in an updated edition in 2013. Feinstein's translations from Neruda, Lorca, Benedetti and others have appeared in many publications, including *Modern Poetry in Translation* and *Agenda*. His book of translations from Neruda's *Canto General* was published by Pratt Contemporary in 2013. Feinstein has written for *The Guardian*, *The TLS* and *New Statesman*, and has broadcast for the BBC on Neruda and autism.

**Basma Ghalayini** has previously translated short fiction from the Arabic for the KFW Stifflung series, *Beirut Short Stories*, published on addastories.org, and Comma projects, such as *Banthology* and *The Book of Cairo* (edited by Raph Cormack). She is also the editor of *Palestine + 100*.

**Nicholas Glastonbury** is a translator of Turkish and Kurdish literature. He is a doctoral candidate in cultural anthropology at the Graduate Center of the City University of New York, and a co-editor of the e-zine *Jadaliyya*. His translation of Sema Kaygusuz's novel *Every Fire You Tend* received a PEN Translates award and was the winner of the 2020 TA First Translation Prize from the Society of Authors.

**Mustafa Gündoğdu** has worked as a coordinator for various human rights and conflict resolution NGOs for over twenty years, where his roles included in-house translator. He has since worked as a freelance editor and second reader on a number of Kurdish translations, including *Sara: My Whole Life Was a Struggle* by Sakine Cansiz, translated by Janet Biehl (Pluto) and *Uprising, Suppression, Retribution* by Ahmet Kahraman, translated by Andrew Penny (Taderon). He is the founder and former coordinator of the London Kurdish Film Festival, and has organised Kurdish film festivals and screenings in London, New York, Dublin, Glasgow, Istanbul, and Busan. He has published numerous articles on Kurdish cinema in Kurdish, Turkish, English and Korean.

**Sawad Hussain** is an Arabic translator and contributor to journals such as *ArabLit* and *Asymptote*, and was co-editor of the Arabic-English portion of the award-winning *Oxford Arabic Dictionary* (2014). Her translations have been recognised by English PEN, the Anglo-Omani Society and the Palestine Book Awards, among others. Her recent translations include *Passage to the Plaza* by Sahar Khalifeh and *A Bed for the King's Daughter* by Shahla Ujayli. She holds an MA in Modern Arabic Literature from SOAS.

**Sara Khalili** is an editor and translator of contemporary Iranian literature. Her translations include *Moon Brow* and *Censoring an Iranian Love Story* by Shahriar Mandanipour, *The Pomegranate Lady and Her Sons* by Goli Taraghi, *The Book of Fate* by Parinoush Saniee, *Kissing the Sword* by Shahrnush Parsipur, as well as several volumes of poetry. Her short story translations have appeared in *AGNI, The Kenyon Review, The Virginia Quarterly Review, EPOCH, Granta* and *The Book of Tehran* among others.

**Diep Lien Nguyen** graduated from Ho Chi Minh City University of Economics and Technology (Vietnam) in 2010. She has worked as an assistant at the of the Lotus Art Gallsery in Ho Chi Minh City since 2016.

**J. Bret Maney** is a translator and writer based in New York City, where he is an assistant professor of English at The City University of New York. A book of his translations of Fiston Mwanza Mujila's poetry, *The River in the Belly and Other Poems,* will be published by Deep Vellum in 2021.

**Megan McDowell** has translated many of the most important Latin American writers working today, including Samanta Schweblin, Alejandro Zambra, Mariana Enriquez, and Lina Meruane. Her translations have won the English PEN award and the Premio Valle-Inclán, and been nominated four times for the International Booker Prize. Her short story translations have been featured in *The New Yorker, The Paris Review, Tin House, McSweeney's* and *Granta*, among others. In 2020 she won an Award in Literature from the American Academy of Arts and Letters. She is from Richmond, KY and lives in Santiago, Chile.

**Jonathan Wright** is a literary translator and former journalist. He studied Arabic at St John's College, Oxford, and worked in the Middle East as a correspondent for *Reuters* for many years, living in Egypt, Sudan, Lebanon, Tunisia and the Gulf. He turned to literary translation in 2008 and has since translated about fifteen books, including two works of fiction shortlisted for the Man Booker International Prize. He has translated three titles for Comma: Hassan Blasim's *God 99* (2020), *The Iraqi Christ* (2013), which was awarded the Independent Foreign Fiction Prize in 2014, and *The Madman of Freedom Square* (2009).

# Special Thanks

The editors would like to thank Natasha Hickman, Trudi Shaw, Mark Danner, Seumas Milne, Darren Newbury, Jan-Bart Gewald, Maite Martinez and Rasso Enzenbach.